Praise for USA TODAY bestselling author
Debra Webb

"A hot hand with action, suspense and, last but not least, a steamy relationship."
—*New York Times* bestselling author Linda Howard

"A steamy, provocative novel with deep, deadly secrets guaranteed to be worthy of your time."
—*Fresh Fiction* on *Traceless*

"Flawlessly combines action, adventure, mystery and romance."
—*RT Book Reviews* on *Colby Roundup*, Top Pick

"Interspersed with fine-tuned suspense...the cliffhanger conclusion will leave readers eagerly anticipating future installments."
—*Publishers Weekly* on *Obsession*

"Webb reaches into our deepest nightmares and pulls out a horrifying scenario. She delivers the ultimate villain."
—*RT Book Reviews* on *Dying to Play*

Debra Webb is the award-winning *USA TODAY* bestselling author of more than one hundred novels, including those in reader-favorite series Faces of Evil, the Colby Agency and the Shades of Death. With more than four million books sold in numerous languages and countries, Debra's love of storytelling goes back to her childhood on a farm in Alabama. Visit Debra at www.debrawebb.com.

Visit the Author Profile page
at Harlequin.com for more titles.

USA TODAY BESTSELLING AUTHOR

DEBRA WEBB

Cries in the Night
&
Person of Interest

<H> **HARLEQUIN**® INTRIGUE CLASSICS

ISBN-13: 978-1-335-15998-4

Cries in the Night & Person of Interest

Copyright © 2018 by Harlequin Books S.A.

The publisher acknowledges the copyright holder
of the individual works as follows:

Cries in the Night
Copyright © 2004 by Debra Webb

Person of Interest
Copyright © 2006 by Debra Webb

Recycling programs
for this product may
not exist in your area.

Printed in U.S.A.

www.Harlequin.com

CONTENTS

CRIES IN THE NIGHT

This book is dedicated to a very dear friend of mine, Melany Gardner. She is everything that a good teacher should be. Her love of children, of people in general, is something to behold in this day and time. Huntland School is very fortunate to have on their staff not only a phenomenal teacher, but also one of the finest people I have ever had the privilege of knowing. This one's for you, Mel.

PROLOGUE

SHE DREAMED OF the cemetery again.

A cold, steady drizzle fell in the dark October night. The full hunter's moon seeped through the thick gray clouds, casting an eerie glow over the deserted graveyard. Acres of headstones protruded from the lush green grass like ugly yard ornaments.

Positioned around the newest of the graves were a dozen wreaths of varying sizes and shapes, forming a sort of temporary barrier from the harsh reality that lay beyond it. The carnations of one heart-shaped arrangement drooped with the weight of the rain and the passage of seven days since their cutting.

Melany pushed between the wreaths and dropped to her knees before the freshly turned soil. Her icy fingers tightened around the wooden handle of the shovel she held. Droplets of the unseasonably cold rain trickled down her cheeks. Her clothes were soaked through, but she no longer cared.

Nothing mattered to her anymore.

She squeezed her eyes shut and tried to silence the cries inside her head. Uncertainty shuddered through her, making her hesitate. The sound of her child crying echoed in the deepest recesses of her soul. Melany's eyes opened abruptly and she jerked with renewed determination.

"I'm coming, baby," she murmured. Her heart thudded in her chest. "Mommy's coming."

She plunged the shovel into the loose, damp soil with a vengeance. The sound of the metal sliding into the soggy earth made her flinch. Gritting her teeth, she flung the scoopful of soil to the side, then sank her shovel into the ground once more. She prayed for God's forgiveness as she worked harder, faster.

She had to do *this*.

She had to know.

The shovel struck something solid. Melany sat back on her heels, the shallow, muddy walls of the grave on either side of her. A frown etched her forehead, rivulets of water slipping down the worrisome creases. This wasn't right. How could this be right?

It couldn't be.

She tossed the shovel aside, a new surge of hot tears blurring her vision as she summoned her waning resolve. A dozen questions flitted briefly through her mind despite her newly gathered determination. Why was the grave so shallow? Why was there no vault?

Melany almost laughed at the absurdity of it. This was just a dream, she reminded herself. She would wake up at any moment to the agony of not knowing for sure.

"No," she said aloud, as if saying it out loud would make it so. "This has to be real." She lifted her face to the rain for one fleeting instant and realized that she couldn't stop now, even if it was only a dream.

She had to know.

Melany dug furiously with her hands then, pushing aside the shallow, remaining layer of earth. Her breath caught. The small, white casket felt smooth beneath her palms. All of her questions instantly flew from her mind. There was only the reality that she would soon know. A wounded moan tore from her throat as she leaned forward and pressed her cheek to the cold, slick surface. A wave of pain so overpowering she couldn't breathe for a long moment washed over her.

"Oh, baby, baby, please forgive Mommy," she mumbled between sobs. The haunting cries grew stronger inside her head, urging her on. She pushed herself up and scrubbed her face with the wet, muddy sleeve of her sweatshirt. Now, she told herself again. She had to know now.

She quickly shoved away more of the concealing mud. Her hands trembling, she released the tiny latches and lifted the small viewing lid with ease. Rain and mud splattered the pristine pink satin and lace interior during the five or so seconds it took Melany's brain to assimilate what her heart already knew.

Her daughter's coffin was empty.

Melany sat bolt upright in bed. She gulped in air, filling her starved lungs. "No!" she cried, then buried her face in her hands and forced away the last lingering remnants of the horrifying dream.

Her hair felt damp with sweat…or was it the rain? It was a dream…only a dream. Her baby was gone. A sob rose in her throat, then ripped out of her on a tide of anguish.

Her baby couldn't be dead. There had to be a mistake. The dreams…the voices…it just couldn't be.

She plowed her fingers through her sweat-dampened hair. She was losing her mind. She'd lost her baby and now she was losing her mind.

But what if she was right? She'd tried to tell them

that her baby couldn't be dead. It just wasn't possible…
she could feel her.

Melany blinked in the darkness of her room. Everything stilled inside her.

What if she was right?

Melany struggled from the tangled sheets and fumbled for the clothes she'd discarded a few hours ago. All
she needed was a flashlight and a shovel and she would
end this misery now.

Five minutes later, and armed with the necessary
implements, Melany stepped out into the cold night air.
She lifted her face to the steady drizzle of rain. Just like
in the dream, she thought. But this was real. She took a
deep, harsh breath and started toward her car.

"I'm coming, baby," she murmured. "Mommy's coming."

CHAPTER ONE

"WE HAVEN'T FOUND the body yet." Supervisory Special Agent Bill Collins cleared his throat. "But, legally speaking, the child is dead."

Ryan Braxton absorbed the impact of those words as he studied the woman seated at the scarred table on the other side of the two-way mirror. A Memphis police detective stepped into the interrogation room and offered her a cup of coffee. She declined.

"But she doesn't believe it," Ryan suggested without looking at the man standing beside him in the tiny viewing room.

"No," Bill said on a heavy sigh. "She doesn't believe her daughter is dead or that her body is simply missing."

"I need more facts." Ryan looked at his old friend then. Bill's shoulders sagged in defeat. His suit was travel-rumpled and he looked far older than his fifty years. This case had gotten to him already. Ryan had thought nothing would ever shock him again, but, considering the woman involved, even he found this one unnerving. *This* was the very reason he'd left the Bureau and started a new career with the Colby Agency. He didn't want to do these kinds of cases anymore.

"The accident was eight days ago," Bill began. "Melany was in a coma for forty-eight hours." He shrugged, a weary gesture. "There was some sort of mix-up with her CT scan. She was diagnosed with an inoperable brain stem injury. Death was considered imminent."

Ryan gritted his teeth to prevent any outward reaction. He was a professional, he wasn't supposed to let his personal feelings show. Hell, he wasn't even supposed to be having any personal feelings. He kept his gaze carefully focused on the scene beyond the two-way mirror as Bill continued.

"While Mel was in a coma, her daughter died. A friend—" Bill reached into his jacket pocket and removed a small notebook. He flipped through it until he found the right page, then studied it a moment. "A Rita Grider," he went on, "made arrangements for the child to be buried in a local cemetery since there was no point in waiting for Mel's recovery. Hell, she even made tentative arrangements for Mel's burial right next to her daughter. Then, the next morning, to everyone's great surprise, Melany woke up." Bill stared through the glass at the woman seated on the other side. "As you can imagine, she was devastated."

"You have a copy of the death certificate?" Ryan asked, his voice carefully controlled.

Bill reached into his pocket again and produced a folded document. Ryan took it, opened it and reviewed the appropriate block of information. *Immediate cause resulting in death: Cardiac arrest attributed to internal hemorrhaging.* He refolded the document and slipped it into his coat pocket. He didn't look at the child's age or the father's name. He didn't want to know how soon after Melany had left him that she'd found someone new. And he sure as hell didn't want to know the other man's name.

"Any word on the guy who bumbled the interment?" He focused on the case rather than the woman who'd ripped open his chest and torn out his heart two years ago. Standing here looking at her now felt too surreal.

Bill flipped through a couple more pages in his trusty notebook. "According to the funeral director," he said as he reviewed his notes. "Garland Hanes has a reputation for heavy drinking and not showing up for work. And he's apparently dropped off the face of the earth since burying that empty coffin." Bill sighed. "Hell, no one would have been the wiser if Mel hadn't tried to dig up the thing."

The image Ryan's mind conjured of Melany digging into that shallow grave would torment him for the rest of his life. Though he hadn't witnessed firsthand her desperate act, he had seen the kind of pain and desperation it took to push a person that far over the edge too many times. Just another anguish-filled picture to add to his hard-earned collection. Only this one was different. He knew this woman. Knew her better than he knew himself. Had made love to her. Had told her his deepest secrets…had loved her.

This was a mistake. He shouldn't even be here. He, of all people, knew better than to get involved in a case where he had a personal connection. And this was definitely personal. Bill should never have called him in on one that hit this close to home.

He was not the man for this case. "I'm not sure I should—"

"Look," Bill cut him off. "I know I shouldn't have asked you to come down here, but she's one of ours—"

"*Was* one of *yours*. Need I remind you that neither of us are in the Bureau anymore?" Ryan corrected as he turned his attention back to the woman in question. He set his jaw firmly, restraining the old anger that tinged his tone even now. Melany Jackson had walked out on her career with the Bureau the same day she walked out on him. And she hadn't looked back on either even once. Apparently, she'd been too busy.

"Braxton, you're a cold-hearted son of a bitch, do you know that?"

Ryan again shifted his intense scrutiny from the scene in the interrogation room to his old friend. "That's what they tell me. But, when I was called in on a case in my Bureau days it was generally to help find a missing child, not one that's already been pronounced dead and then buried."

Ire lit in Bill's eyes. "We can't be sure the child is dead," he ground out.

Ryan bit back the first response that shot to the tip of his tongue. His history with Bill was almost as complicated as the one he had with Melany. He suppressed the emotions that instantly tightened his chest at the mere thought of her. Dammit. Where was his control? A muscle jumped in his tense jaw. He would not allow personal feelings to interfere with his professional analysis of the situation. And, he was here. He might as well say what he was thinking.

"There's a death certificate signed by the attending physician," he offered quietly, knowing Bill didn't want to think rationally at the moment. Ryan wasn't the only one battling with personal feelings. "I'd say that's pretty cut-and-dried evidence."

Bill squared his shoulders into that stubborn set that Ryan recognized from years of working on the same team. "Damn, man," Bill all but snarled, "give Mel a little credit. We've worked enough of these cases to know that once in a great while the connection between mother and child is so strong that they can sense each other's needs. Mel could be right on this."

That much was true to a degree, but more often than not it was mere wishful thinking. Ryan looked away. He didn't want to see the worried determination in his old friend's eyes, and he sure didn't want to look at the anguish in Melany's. He had seen that look far too many times in too many faces. When people lost a child, it left them empty. And they were never the same again. Ryan forced away the endless stream of memories that attempted to haunt his every waking moment. He shouldn't be here. But what could he do? This was Mel. She needed him. Could he take the easy way out? Just walk away?

"All right," he conceded, knowing he'd have to speak to Victoria Colby about the time off. Since he wasn't currently assigned to a case he doubted it would be a problem.

This was a mistake. He knew it. Bill knew it, too. Ryan's gaze moved back to Melany. But he couldn't just walk away. He owed her that much. If he let himself admit the truth, he owed her a lot more than that. He'd taken all she had to give for three years, all the time knowing he would never give her the one thing she wanted with all her heart. He forced those thoughts from his mind. This wasn't about him. She'd obviously forgotten him and moved on.

The idea of Melany with another man sat like a stone in his gut. But he couldn't ignore the facts. She'd had a child with someone since he'd last seen her.

"So all we have at the moment," Ryan deduced aloud

with as much objectivity as he could marshal, "is Mel's word against everyone else's that her daughter is, in fact, alive."

Bill closed his notebook and tucked it back into his pocket. He didn't look at Ryan this time, his full attention remained on the woman they both cared for far too much. "That's about the size of it," he said, resigned.

"Well, then." Ryan loosened his tie. "Let's start with what we've got."

He watched Melany for a few more seconds before leaving the viewing room. The one thing that made the whole damned situation different was Melany. She was a mother suffering through the kind of agony all mothers prayed they would never know, that much was true. But Melany Jackson was not like other mothers. She had received the same training as Ryan. She had seen many of the same cases and haunting faces as he had. And Ryan knew in his gut that no matter how far over the edge circumstances pushed her, at some point that deeply entrenched instinct kicked in.

If Melany believed her child was alive, he would damn well do everything in his power to help her find the truth.

Whatever that truth might prove to be.

MELANY SAT LIKE a statue, her full attention focused on keeping thoughts and images of the past two days away. Despite her best efforts, snippets of her tense conversations with Bill kept echoing in her head. Sounds from the psych ward at Memphis General. The endless pacing and murmuring in the corridor…doors slamming. The distinctive click of locks turning…patients moaning. And the smell. God, the smell. She swallowed hard.

Medicinal, yet somehow menacing. She never wanted to go back there.

She knew what they thought. All of them. They believed she had lost it. Her baby was dead, they thought, and she'd gone over the edge.

But it wasn't true. Well maybe she had slipped over that precipice temporarily. She squeezed her eyes shut and blocked the instant replay of those frantic minutes in the cemetery. She had lost it for a little while…that much was accurate. When she'd tried to explain what she knew in her heart, no one would listen. She was nuts, they'd murmured.

But she knew the truth.

Bill believed her.

She opened her eyes and stared intently at the scarred table before her, tracing the lines of age and abuse wrought by belligerent suspects and frustrated detectives. Anything to prevent those horrifying images from filling her mind. But it was no use. The dizzying emotions bombarded her, leaving her defenseless.

The tiny grave surrounded by wreaths of withering flowers. The cold rain plastering her clothes to her skin. The sodden earth oozing between her icy fingers. Needing desperately to find her baby. Lights shining in her face. Two policemen dragging her away from her daughter's grave. And then struggling with the hospital orderlies.

A pathetic sound intended as a rueful laugh but falling well short of the definition erupted from her throat. They hadn't even bothered running her downtown, she'd been taken straight to the hospital. No one would listen to her explanations of why she was at the cemetery or her concerns about her daughter. A nurse had, and with the help of an orderly, stripped her, forced her into a shower, then strapped her into a bed and sedated her. Twenty-four hours later, after she'd been questioned and analyzed by the shrink on duty, they had allowed her a telephone call.

Who else could she have called? She had no family. Melany rubbed her eyes, then dried her cheeks with the backs of her hands. She hadn't wanted to call Bill, but she hadn't known what else to do. She knew she could trust him and if anyone on earth would listen to her, it would be him.

He had listened. Despite her lack of hard evidence, he'd ordered the exhumation. She shuddered as those memories tumbled one over the other into her head. It was just like in her dream. No vault…just that tiny white coffin with its pink satin interior.

And just as she knew it would be, it had been empty.

She closed her eyes and struggled with the emotions twisting inside her. Where was her little girl? Why had they lied to her at the hospital? How had they fooled her friend?

She knew with every fiber of her being that Katlin was alive. But how would she ever prove it? The doctor had signed the death certificate. The funeral home attendant had signed for the body. Her good friend, Rita, had identified Katlin from a photograph. A new surge of pain constricted her throat.

How could all of them be wrong? But how could they be right? She wouldn't let them be right.

Another shudder quaked through her. She had to be strong. Her baby was out there somewhere and Melany had to be strong for her. She stiffened her spine and blinked back the tears welling in her eyes once more. Bill would help her find Katlin. She could trust Bill. He'd been her mentor at the Bureau. Her mentor and her friend. She'd known him for eight years. He wouldn't let her down.

The door opened behind her and someone stepped inside. Melany smiled weakly. She knew it was Bill even before he walked around to the other side of the table and took the seat opposite her. He smelled vaguely of Old Spice and the cigarette he'd no doubt just sneaked a few puffs from in the closest men's room.

Bill looked tired. Hell, they were both tired. They'd been up the better part of the past forty-eight hours. His suit was a little wrinkled, but still presentable. Lines of fatigue had scrawled themselves into his familiar face. He was like family and she was so glad he was here.

"How're you holding up, Mel?" he asked gently.

She forced a little more feeling into her smile. "I'm okay." It was a flat-out lie, but he understood. Her child was missing. How could she be okay? Her head still ached a little but most of the soreness was gone. None of that mattered right now. She had only one thing on her mind, finding her daughter.

"Have they found the employee from the cemetery who…" Her words trailed off. She couldn't say the rest. God, would this nightmare never end? She just wanted her baby back.

Bill shook his head. "Not yet. But don't worry, we'll find him soon."

She wasn't really worried on that score. Not anymore. Not with Bill here. He would see that this investigation was handled properly. He wouldn't be swayed by the local authorities who considered her just another distraught mother who wouldn't face reality. To them, this whole thing was nothing more than a misplaced body. The body would show up, they'd assured her. She might as well come to terms with the loss now.

But she couldn't do that. Wouldn't do that.

Bill leaned forward, propped his arms on the table and peered at her with those steady gray eyes. "We're going to need help on this one, Mel. I'm good, but not good enough. We need the best on our side."

Melany stilled. A new kind of emotion stirred inside her. A mixture of fear and a kind of anticipation she didn't want to feel. No. Not him. She shook her head. "I don't want you to call him. I trust you. You know how to do this."

"This is too important," Bill countered firmly, his voice carefully gentled. "You know it better than anyone. We need the best. *He* is the best."

She started to argue but he stopped her with an uplifted palm. "I've already called him. He's here. He wants to see you."

Dammit, she did not want to see Ryan Braxton. She twisted her hands together in her lap to keep them from shaking. "He's here? Now?"

Bill nodded. "He wants to help you, Mel. Let him. He's the best there is and you know it. We need him."

Bill was right. Ryan Braxton had been the best man at Quantico when it came to finding missing children and their predators. His instincts were uncanny. His skills unparalleled. He never failed. Katlin deserved the best. Melany needed him, even if she didn't want to admit it. But hadn't he left the Bureau?

As if reading her mind, Bill said, "He's with a private agency now, but he's willing to take the case if you want him."

If she wanted him? She almost laughed, but couldn't

manage the energy required. With monumental effort she pushed the past aside and focused on one thing, her daughter.

"All right," she agreed, her voice so stilted she hardly recognized it as her own. "Whatever it takes to find my little girl."

As if on cue, the door behind her opened once more. He'd been listening, she realized. He knew she didn't want him here, but then that wouldn't surprise him, she imagined.

That damned anticipation spiked again, sending adrenaline rushing through her veins. She moistened her lips, summoned her resolve, and looked up to greet the man she'd walked away from two years ago. The man she'd loved with her entire being. The same one who'd chosen his career over a life with her. And Bill was right, she suddenly realized. She needed Ryan Braxton. It would take his kind of relentlessness to look beyond the obvious and find Katlin.

When her gaze met his she wasn't at all prepared for the impact of those deep blue eyes. Her resolve crumbled immediately, leaving her as defenseless as she'd been two years ago, all over again. His dark hair was still short. There was a peppering of gray at the temples. Her gaze lingered there. That was definitely new. She would never have believed anything, not even age, could touch Ryan. He was far too invincible, too unreachable. But there it was. Did he look older, otherwise? She resisted the urge to shake her head. No, he looked exactly the same.

Tall and lean with broad, broad shoulders. His Armani suit looking as if he'd just put it on. The navy a perfect match for those dark eyes. His too-handsome face clean-shaven, the set of his square jaw all business.

"Hello, Mel."

He didn't sit down. She'd known he wouldn't. It was an indication of power. She'd seen him in action countless times. He was in charge now and the sooner she realized that, the better it would be.

"Ryan," she returned. Fierce emotions warred inside her. The need to drink him in with her eyes, the need to touch him…and at the same time the urge to run like hell. How could she talk to this man, tell him about her daughter, and not tell him everything? She considered the sculpted angles of his face again, the shallow cleft in his chin, the mouth she'd kissed so many times, and then she looked fully into those all-seeing eyes. Her heart lurched at what she saw there. Something more than the sympathy he wanted her to see. And then it was gone, but not quite quickly enough.

He still cared for her and, damn it, that only made bad matters worse.

"I want you to start at the beginning," he said in that deep, husky voice that made her shiver. His words were calm, quiet, as if they hadn't lived together for three years…as if they hadn't made love night after night all that time.

"Tell me everything," he added, then reached into his inside coat pocket and removed a document. When he'd unfolded it and laid it on the table, he pushed it in her direction. "Make me believe that this is a mistake."

Melany dragged her gaze from his to stare at the document. Shelby County Health Department. Certificate of Death. Katlin Jackson.

"Give me one shred of evidence that this is a mistake, Mel," he told her, "and I swear I'll move heaven and earth to find your daughter."

CHAPTER TWO

BY 7:45 P.M. Ryan and Bill had commandeered a fair-sized office with two incoming lines and a fax machine. Memphis P.D. was happy to help, and to turn the case they definitely did not want over to the Feds. Bill inconspicuously passed Ryan off as an agent, as well. The usual jurisdiction battle lines went undrawn. No one wanted to touch this case. Even the press had played it soft. Minimal coverage in the papers. None of the local television channels had spent more than a perfunctory thirty seconds on Melany's grave-digging escapade.

It was just as well, she decided. Any hype in the media could work against them. The last thing they needed were calls from people who thought they knew something when they really didn't. She wasn't ready for false Katlin sightings from strangers just yet. She'd worked in the investigation business long enough to know that most of the input generated by the media was useless. There were times when the media could actually be a very efficient tool, but those occasions were few and far between.

At least the local cops were no longer looking at Mel as if she was crazy. She almost smiled. Those accusations now rested firmly atop Bill's and Ryan's shoulders. The boys in blue merely looked at her with sympathy at this point. No doubt the possibility that the Feds were only dragging out the inevitable had been discussed by all on duty.

Mel didn't care what they thought. All that mattered was that she finally had help. Expert help. If anyone could find Katlin, it was Ryan. Her gaze drifted in his direction. They had to find her. Soon. Mel wasn't sure how much longer she could take the not knowing.

They had exchanged cell phone numbers for convenience and Ryan had already started a time line on a wall-mounted whiteboard. Sitting stiffly at the equipment console-turned-conference-table, Mel stared at the time line now, her abdominal muscles clenched in a familiar knot of anticipation. She knew this routine, somehow found it comforting. This was the first step and her relief was almost palpable. Bill was on the telephone getting a court order for copies of all the hospital reports related to Mel and Katlin, his voice a low, but gruff murmur. Any minute now he would snag one of the locals and make him his personal gopher.

"What can I do?" Mel's voice sounded stark in contrast to Ryan's silence and Bill's quiet cadence.

Ryan stopped labeling and dating incidents and turned to her. "What?"

The trance. A familiar pang of jealousy speared through her. The Braxton trance. Whenever he took on a case he immersed himself so completely that he was barely aware of anything else around him. He blinked now, focusing on her, waiting for a response, attempting to assimilate her comment. Their relationship had never stood a chance against his work. It consumed him...defined him. Nothing or no one else mattered. If only she could tune out all else as he could, maybe the next few days wouldn't be so bad.

"Would you like me to set up witness interviews?" she offered. She cringed at the old hurt weighting her tone. The flicker of surprise in his eyes told her he'd heard it, too. But she couldn't just sit here…she had to do something, to help in some way. "Additional interviews," she clarified when he only stared at her. "That's the next logical step, right?" She stood to punctuate the question.

He scrubbed a hand over the five o'clock shadow darkening his chin as if considering her offer. "Look, Mel. You know the drill. The fact that you're even in this room is a breach of protocol. You really—"

"Don't even think about it, Braxton." The hurt was gone from her tone, anger and an icy warning vibrated in its place. Bill looked up from the notes he was making, his end of the telephone conversation stumbling to a halt.

"This is my daughter." Mel pointed to the pictures taped to the wall and stepped closer to the man she refused to be intimidated by. Glared up into those cool blue eyes without flinching, which was a pretty amazing feat considering her heart was pounding like a drum. "She's not just some statistic in a case. She's my flesh and blood. And you're damned right that makes me personally involved. But the bottom line is, I don't give a damn what it makes me. You will not shut me out. Either I help you with this investigation or I start one of my own. It's your choice."

He hesitated, damn him, just long enough to make her sweat.

"Start with the paramedics and any witnesses at the scene," he ordered coolly. "I want a copy of the police report and I want to see the vehicle first thing tomorrow morning." He didn't miss a beat at her sharply in-drawn breath. "I want to know who else was on duty in the pediatric ward when the child coded. I want to know," he pressed, his voice harsh, demanding, "every little thing—no matter how insignificant—they did to revive her and their conclusions about what went wrong. I also want to know the name of anyone who so much as looked at her from the moment she was wheeled through the E.R. doors. Any questions?"

He wanted to scare her off. But it wouldn't work. Mel fought to control the trembling that had started in her legs and was working its way up her rigid body. "None."

"Good."

He gave her his back, turning his attention once more to the time line he was so meticulously constructing. She forced herself to take two unsteady steps back to the table that served as their workstation.

"Yeah, yeah, I'm still here. That's right," Bill said into the receiver as he watched her ease down into the seat across from him. "I'll send someone over for it, ASAP."

Melany picked up a couple of freshly sharpened number twos and dragged a yellow legal pad in her di-rection. She wet her lips and forced her attention to the task of list-making.

"You okay?" Bill asked quietly.

She nodded, still uncertain of her voice, then blinked back the fresh tears brimming. By God, she would not cry. Not now and give Braxton the satisfaction of think-ing he'd accomplished his goal.

Bill punched in another string of numbers and mum-bled something that sounded vaguely like self-righteous ass. Mel felt her lips curl upward in spite of the damned tears now spilling past her lashes.

"Ayers?" Bill barked. "What's the name of that rookie you said we could borrow?" He listened. "Well, send him down here. I have a job for him."

Bill hung up. No goodbye, no thank-you, just hung up. That was Bill. Mel covertly swiped her eyes, then quickly scribbled a couple of names she remembered onto her pad. He was the perfect contrast to Ryan. Bill was all grumpy bark and no bite. Ryan was the one to be wary of. Polished, silent and lethal. There was a kind of dangerous elegance about him. And why wouldn't there be? He spent ninety percent of his time dealing with the lowest of the lowlife. People who committed crimes against children.

The work had hardened him to the point that most who knew him well called him heartless. But Mel had been around during that other ten percent of his time. His lovemaking and sense of possessiveness were every bit as intense as his dedication to duty. He'd loved her the only way he'd known how, no question there. But he always held back part of himself. Never let go completely. He was the most guarded man she'd ever known. And no matter how much she'd loved him, she could never get past that wall he'd erected around his heart.

She recognized that it was a self-preservation instinct, pure and simple. But it didn't make it any easier to accept. So she'd left. And now, here they were, thrown together again by fate. God, how she wished she could go back and change what had happened. She closed her eyes and replayed her last hours with Katlin. They'd been in a hurry to get to the post office before it closed. She'd suddenly realized she'd forgotten her purse and had to turn around.

The light was green, but the other car didn't yield. She was halfway through the intersection before she realized he wasn't going to stop…then it was too late. She remembered reaching back to brace Katlin. Though the baby was strapped into her car seat, the move had been instinctive. She recalled vividly the sound of squealing tires. The horrible impact and groan of crumpling metal.

Then nothing.

"This is Greg Carter," Bill announced.

Startled, Mel looked up. A young man had entered the office without her realizing it. The gopher. Blond hair, brown eyes, and most likely still as green as he'd been the day they issued him the stiffly starched uniform he so proudly wore.

Mel stood, offered her hand and dredged up a thin smile. "Hey, Greg, good to have you on board."

He grinned and gave her hand an enthusiastic pump. "Thanks, ma'am. This is my first time working on a joint task force."

Translation: playing errand boy to the Feds and company. "I'm sure you'll be a big help." Though she wasn't at all sure the four of them actually fulfilled the definition of a task force, why burst the rookie's bubble?

"And this is Ryan Braxton," Bill said, gesturing in his direction. "He's the lead investigator in this case."

Ryan's wide hand engulfed the kid's and squeezed briefly. "We have two rules, Carter," Ryan said bluntly. "What's said between the members of this team goes no further without authorization from either Bill or me, and you never deviate from orders. You do it when, where and how we say, no exceptions."

Greg bobbed his head. "I understand, sir. You can count on me."

Braxton's rules. Though he had always been highly sought after for his awesome profiling abilities, he wasn't exactly team player material. His former Bureau superiors had long ago given up on making him play by their rules. Ryan Braxton was a rule unto himself. He did his job and nobody asked questions, because he was just too damned good. No one would risk losing his expertise. She was sure the Colby Agency felt the same way about him now that they had him on their team. Mel was no different. She would play by his don't-question-anything-I-say rules and she would do whatever he told her…to an extent, choosing her battles carefully.

Whatever it took to find Katlin. She swallowed back the ache that climbed into her throat each time she thought of her daughter. Focus on the steps of the investigation, she reminded herself as she directed her attention back to the newest member of their little group.

Bill gave Carter a detailed list of what he expected him to pick up at the hospital then said, "Pick up the court order first. And when you get to the hospital, I want you to watch the clerk pull the records and make the copies. Don't let those files out of your sight until you have a *complete* copy. With this kind of case you can't trust anyone. Got it?"

"Yes, sir."

Mel wouldn't have been surprised if the guy had snapped off a salute before hustling out the door. Talk about eager.

She studied Bill for a moment. It didn't matter to him that the records clerks were probably gone home by now. He wanted what he wanted *now*. In that respect he was very much like Ryan. But no one she had ever met in the Bureau could hold a candle where Ryan's single-minded determination was concerned. He had spent most of his Bureau time on the road for that very reason. He was relentless. He never gave up until he'd accomplished what he set out to do. She'd never been more grateful for that characteristic than she was now.

Following Bill's lead, Mel returned to her assigned task. She grimaced as her stiff muscles reminded her that she wasn't back to her old self yet. And, God, she was so tired. She massaged her neck, wishing the steady throb in her head would take a break. She really needed some sleep. But sleep was out of the question. Every time she closed her eyes…the voices came. She just couldn't go through another night of the dreams and cries.

She shouldn't be in here. Ryan rubbed his eyes and pinched the bridge of his nose. She looked like hell, definitely needed some rest. His brow furrowed into a frown. He wondered if she'd even eaten today. He forced his attention back to his time line. She was a grown woman. She could take care of herself, he reasoned. It was none of his business whether she'd slept or eaten. They were working a case together. Nothing more. And, had it been up to him, she wouldn't even be doing that.

He tried to recall the months they'd worked together before…before they'd become lovers. What was the point? Even then he'd been mesmerized by every little thing about her. The way she smiled…her laugh, the way her mouth quirked when she wanted to laugh and knew she shouldn't. Everything about her made him want her. The curve of her cheek, the taste of her lips, the heat of her sweet body as he sank deeply inside her. His lips tightened into a thin line of self-deprecation. How could he still think that way?

She wasn't his anymore. As soon as he solved the mystery surrounding her daughter's disappearance they wouldn't see each other again.

He'd go back to Chicago and she'd go back to…to whomever she'd turned to since she'd walked away from him. His frown deepened. Where the hell was the child's father now when Mel needed him most? Ryan snapped the cap onto the black marker he'd been using with enough force to crack it. Why did he even wonder? Somehow he had to get past this ridiculous feeling of possessiveness. He'd even caught himself studying the child's photograph to see if he could find any resemblance to himself. Of course there was none. The child was a carbon copy of her mother. Why had he done that?

He'd spent the entire afternoon, he glanced at his watch, and a good part of the evening closed up in this office with her. The subtle scent of her perfume was driving him crazy. It was the same fragrance she'd always worn. Sweet, light, natural. He wanted desperately to thread his fingers into all that silky blond hair. To taste those pink lips while he stared into those eager green eyes.

He massaged the back of his neck, the muscles tight and knotted there. He had to get out of here before he did or said something he'd regret. "I'm calling it a night." He turned to face Bill and Mel. "We could all use some rest." He sent a pointed look in her direction. She merely lifted her chin and glared back at him.

Bill closed his notebook. "I was just thinking the same thing." He glanced at his watch. "We've probably got time to have dinner before Carter gets back. I want to look at those files tonight."

Ryan resisted the impulse to shake him. Didn't Bill get it? He'd had all the Melany exposure he could take today. "Fine." Ryan headed toward the door. "I'll see the two of you in the morning."

"I thought we could take Mel to dinner and see her safely home," Bill put in quickly, stopping Ryan dead in his tracks.

They were going to have to have a talk. But not right now. Not in front of Mel. The last thing Ryan wanted was for her to know that she still affected him...on any level.

Ryan pinned Bill with a look. One he hoped relayed the depth of his irritation. "I'm sure you two can manage without me. I have things to do. Calls to make." He turned to Mel. "You have my number. Call me if you need me."

She nodded, her expression unreadable.

He didn't want to wonder what she was thinking, but he did. He walked out anyway, paused in the corridor and took a long, deep breath. He had to stay focused on the case...not Melany. He had to keep the face of the child before him...not the mother. It was the child who needed him. Whether she was dead or alive, he had to find her. That was his job. Holding Mel's hand was not part of the deal. Bill would just have to see to that task himself.

Ryan exited the building and unlocked his rental car.

He opened the door, but hesitated before getting inside. He cursed himself for the hesitation. Mel was strong, she could handle this, he assured that irritating little voice in his head. She didn't need him, anyway. Hadn't she been the one to walk out? Besides, if she wanted a shoulder to cry on or a hand to hold, why didn't she just call up the father of her child?

He gritted his teeth at that thought. Damn. He didn't want to feel this. He just wanted to do the job and get the hell out of here.

"Ryan, wait!"

Mel.

He turned in the direction of her voice. She was hurrying toward him, her face pale, her eyes suspiciously bright. Something he couldn't—or wouldn't—name shifted in his chest. He stood there, staring at her, until she'd reached him and caught her breath.

"Was there something else?" he growled.

She shook her head. "No, it's just that…" She paused and grappled for composure. "I didn't get a chance to thank you for agreeing to help me."

His fingers tightened on the door. Why hadn't he already gotten in and driven away? His own emotions were too raw and close to the surface to deal with this. "There's no need to thank me," he told her flatly. "I'm only doing my job."

She pushed a handful of silky hair behind her ear. She'd always worn it up around the office. Seeing her with it down like this reminded him of the time they'd spent together. Alone. Intimately.

"I know you didn't want to take this case." She looked away, but couldn't hide the tortured expression that had claimed her features. "You probably think I'm crazy just like everybody else, but I know my daughter's alive."

He flinched at the tormented sound of her voice, then grabbed back control. This was business, he had to make sure it stayed that way. "I don't think anything at this point," he said with more clinical detachment than he'd thought possible. "And, if I remember correctly, you were the one who didn't want me on this case."

Color rose in her pale cheeks as she looked up at him once more. "I was wrong." She shrugged one slender shoulder. "I didn't know how I would handle seeing you again."

An eyebrow shot up his forehead. "Why would you worry?" he demanded sharply. "We have been over for two years."

She looked away again, and he could have kicked himself. Where the hell was his control?

"I know." The words were hardly more than a sigh. "But I was worried anyway. We were—"

"*Were* being the operative word," he interjected roughly. This was going nowhere. Neither of them needed this right now. "Your appreciation is duly noted. Get some rest, Mel, you'll need it."

He got into the car, closed the door and drove away. There was nothing else to say about the past and one of them had to be big enough to admit it.

He just hadn't expected it to be him.

CHAPTER THREE

MELANY SAT IN Katlin's room that night.

She'd taken a long hot soak in the tub to ease her stiff muscles. Now, she just sat there, trying not to think. Or feel. She rolled her head, stretching her neck. It didn't help. Her head still ached, not like before, but just enough to be annoying.

The minute hand on the Little Mermaid clock sidled one notch closer to the hour. Twelve minutes before 1:00 a.m. She really should go to bed. She was exhausted. She needed to sleep. But why bother? If she slept, she would dream. If she dreamed she would have to remember.

She didn't want to remember. She wanted to focus on tomorrow and the day after that. Focus on finding Katlin. Bringing her home. She moistened her lips and clasped her trembling hands in her lap. She would bring her home. Maybe not tomorrow, but soon. And then she would sit and watch her baby sleep like so many other nights....

Nights she'd taken for granted. How could this happen? She pressed her lips together as the hot tears rolled down her cheeks. She'd seen it happen to other people. But, like the rest of the world, she'd never imagined it would happen to her. When she'd been at the Bureau she'd worked cases so unthinkable, so heinous that she'd carefully locked away the images in some rarely visited recess of her mind. She was a professor of law now. Had put her Bureau days behind her. She couldn't even remember the names of the victims anymore.

It was one of the most important tools an agent could possess. The ability to separate the facts from the emotions. Don't look at them as people…they're cases. Just cases. Ryan had taught her that. But now it was her name…her case file.

Her child missing…presumed dead.

A breath shuddered out. Her gaze settled on the frilly yellow coverlet in her daughter's crib. She'd sat in this rocker and watched her baby girl sleep the night before…*the accident.*

What she would give to be able to do that now.

Mel stood, wiped the tears from her eyes and stiffened her spine. She had to do something constructive. Make plans. Clean house. Something. Her gaze rested on the crib once more. She should have taken down the crib months ago. Katlin had climbed out a dozen times already. She was too old for a crib. There were youth beds available for that in-between age when a toddler was too old for a crib, but not quite old enough for a regular twin-size bed. The local superstore had them, she recalled.

She went in search of the sale catalog she'd gotten in the mail the other day. She may as well pick one out right now. She could have it ready and waiting when Katlin came home.

She flipped on the living room light and rummaged through the basket that held her magazines and catalogs. Katlin would love a pretty pink bed. Mel was relatively certain she'd seen a sort of storybook or princess style youth bed in here somewhere. Her little girl would be so excited when she came home and found it in her own room.

Melany paused, catalog in hand. *If* she came home. That damned trembling started again. Katlin was coming home. She was alive. Melany knew it. She felt it as strongly as she felt her own heart beating beneath her breast.

She sat down on the sofa and flipped through the pages. Other people just didn't understand. She and Katlin had a special connection. She sighed, thinking of the baby-sweet scent and pale silky hair of her child. Well, maybe all mothers and daughters had a special connection, but theirs was different. Mel always, always knew when Katlin needed her or when something wasn't quite right where her child was concerned. She could sense it, no matter how many miles stood between them.

If Katlin was…dead, surely that feeling wouldn't be so strong. Melany could feel the pull even now. Her daughter needed her. Every time she closed her eyes she could hear her cries. She shook her head. She didn't care if people thought she was crazy. She knew what she felt. All she'd needed was for Bill to believe her, and he had.

Ryan was another story. He was far too analytical to simply believe any old thing he was told. He would require evidence, solid proof that there had been some sort of foul play involved in the case.

And Melany had none. Just her intuition and an empty coffin. The authorities, including Ryan, had to admit that at least one law had been broken. A body was missing and that was a felony in itself. She'd been charged for a vault and a proper interment, which she hadn't received—that was also a criminal offense. Even if the funeral director claimed the body was merely misplaced, he still had the latter charge to explain. He'd taken the easy way out and blamed an employee, Garland Hanes. An employee who was suddenly missing and known for his bouts of alcohol abuse.

Melany shivered. Had that man touched her child? She closed her eyes and banished that thought. She would not allow herself to believe Katlin had been harmed in any way until someone proved it to her beyond a shadow of a doubt. She just couldn't bear the thought of it. She would search until she found the truth. Her child was out there somewhere and needed her. She would do whatever she had to in order to keep Ryan Braxton on the case.

Anything—except tell him the truth.

She couldn't do that. Couldn't take the chance. Bill wasn't going to like it when he found out. *If* he found out. He was one of those people who was honest to a fault. *Tell it like it is,* was his motto. But Melany couldn't do that this time, for more reasons than one.

She would face the consequences when the time came, if Ryan somehow discovered the truth—and he most likely would. When he'd had a chance to really look at the facts, he'd do the math and then he'd ask her. If he asked, she'd never be able to lie to him…not straight-faced, anyway. Katlin was his child. She could only pray that he wouldn't discover he was Katlin's father anytime soon. She needed that ruthless detachment for which he was known. The truth would only muddy the waters.

Melany set the catalog aside and drew her knees up to her chest and hugged her arms around them. She had to sort through all these leftover feelings where Ryan was concerned. She couldn't work with him day in and day out without getting her head on straight first.

He read her too easily. She had to get her emotions in check. She rested her chin atop her knees. If she focused, she could deal with it. She was tougher than she looked, always had been. Her mother had been a single parent, and only sixteen when Mel was born. Sixteen and an alcoholic. She didn't even know who Mel's father was.

Mel had sworn she would never do that to a child. And here she was hiding the truth, giving her child her own name, just like her mother had done to her.

But this was different. She laughed, a dry, grating sound. Yeah, right. This was different, all right. She hadn't had the guts to tell him the truth two years ago, how would she ever muster up the courage, now?

Enough, Jackson, she chastised. She had to have some sleep. Mel dropped her feet to the floor and stood. The kind of sleep where dreams didn't come. She glanced longingly at the catalog. She'd pick out the new bed tomorrow. It was late. Ryan would expect her to be on her toes come morning. He didn't like slackers and had absolutely no patience for excuses. She wasn't about to give him any reason to say she couldn't pull her weight.

She padded into the kitchen and turned on the light over the sink. The worst was behind her now. The investigation was under way, and she actually had people on her side. She could relax just a little. Exhaling a weary breath, she searched for the prescription Dr. Wilcox had given her. After checking the label, she opened the bottle and removed two of the little pills. She popped them into her mouth, then held her hair out of the way while she washed them down with a drink of water straight from the tap. Wiping her mouth with the back of her hand, she flipped off the light. Twenty minutes tops and she'd be asleep.

Though she hated drugs, for the time being they were a necessary evil. A first for Mel. If her mother were around she'd get a good laugh out of that one. She'd accused Mel of being too uptight for her own good. *You'll see one of these days,* her mother had taunted. *You'll need help sometime. Just like me,* she added as she popped another Valium. Hitting thirty had been tough on Carla Jackson and her chosen profession. She'd taken up popping the pills along with her booze to ease the pain and block the image of her last steady John.

Mel pushed away those unpleasant memories. She hadn't thought of her mother in years. She supposed that if she really wanted to, that in some twisted way she could blame her mother for the accident. After all, if Carla hadn't made Mel want so badly to be the exact opposite of her, she probably would never have lent her SUV to a friend. God knew her mother had certainly never helped her own daughter, much less a friend. If Mel hadn't lent Rita the SUV, then she and Katlin wouldn't have been in a tiny compact vehicle when the accident occurred. Then maybe none of this would—

"Stop it," she ordered. She pressed the heels of her hands against her forehead and forced the tormenting thoughts away. Rest, she needed rest.

All she had to do, she reasoned as she made her way to her room, was find something unrelated to the accident to focus on for the next fifteen or so minutes. She climbed into her bed and pulled the covers up around her. The feel of Ryan's full lips pressed firmly against hers instantly invaded her mind. She almost pushed the vivid memories away, but didn't. Reliving nights with Ryan—before—was better than allowing the reality of this waking nightmare to slip to the forefront of her thoughts.

She had to keep the hurt at bay.

She had to be strong.

Her baby was counting on her.

RYAN BRACED HIS hands on the window frame and stared into the darkness. It was raining again. A streak of lightning temporarily brightened the hotel parking lot. The weather matched his mood, he decided, dark and stormy.

He blew out a disgusted breath and jerked the curtains closed. A quick glance at the digital clock on the bedside table confirmed his suspicions that it was well past time he'd gone to bed. He stripped off his shirt and tossed it onto the nearest chair.

But then, what would be the point? He definitely wouldn't be able to sleep. He couldn't get Mel out of his head long enough to concentrate on anything else. He needed files, interview reports, case studies. Anything to keep his thoughts from wandering back to her. If he were back at the office in Chicago, there would be plenty to keep him occupied.

But he wasn't in Chicago.

He was here…where she was.

He tunneled his fingers through his hair and slumped down onto the bed. She still held that same old power over him. She was the only woman who'd ever wielded that much. He could never resist her. The first year without her had been pure hell. He'd worked 365 days. Hadn't wanted a day off. Still rarely took one.

When she'd left the Bureau—left him—he'd thought

he would never be able to go on without her. But he'd managed, just barely—and only by leaving the Bureau himself and finding a fresh start.

What the hell was he doing in Memphis working a case that involved her child? A child she'd had with another man? He frowned trying to recall the child's age. Something over a year. He glanced at his briefcase. The death certificate was there. But he had no intention of getting up and looking at it. It made no difference how little time it had taken her to get over him. For that matter, she could have left him for another man, though he doubted it. But, who knew? Maybe she met someone who gave her the kind of attention she wanted…deserved.

Someone who didn't study cases about dead and missing children as a career. Someone who could bear to give her the child she wanted so desperately.

Anyone but him.

He'd seen too much. Knew too much about the evil men could do. His jaw clenched automatically and the images receded, a practiced response. He would never bring a helpless life into this world. Not after all he'd seen. He just couldn't do it. He'd wanted their relationship to be enough.

But it hadn't been. She'd wanted more and he couldn't give it to her. *Wouldn't* give it to her. So she'd taken the Pill their entire relationship to keep him happy.

Ryan leaned back onto the stack of pillows. No matter how he'd tried to forget her, he couldn't. No other woman made him feel anything even close to what he and Mel had shared. Oh, he'd tried to erase her memory. But he'd failed miserably.

Now he worked. He'd almost gotten used to going

home to an empty house on the rare occasions he bothered to go home. That diversion had come with its own costs. The plants had all died. He'd had to give his dog to a neighbor. But otherwise he'd managed. Had even reached the point where he seldom thought of her more than once or twice a day.

And now this.

What had Bill been thinking when he'd called him?

He hadn't been thinking. That much was clear. Bill loved Mel like a daughter and he intended to help her, whatever the facts indicated.

The facts all pointed to the child's death. There was absolutely nothing to corroborate Mel's theory.

Deep inside, in that place he kept all those messy emotions hidden away, he hoped like hell the facts were wrong. No matter who had fathered the child, he didn't want Mel to know this kind of loss. He didn't want her to live with this level of hurt for the rest of her life.

Close your eyes, Braxton, he ordered. *Get some sleep. You're going to need it.*

The instant his lids lowered, the image of Melany filled his mind. She smiled up at him, love shining in her green eyes. She was wearing that little black dress he'd liked so much. His fingers knotted in the rumpled sheet beneath him but he allowed the memories to come. Kissing the smooth skin of her shoulder. Lowering the zipper, then the silky dress. Following the path of the sensual fabric with his mouth. They'd made love over and over that night, then the light of day had brought reality back with a vengeance.

He'd asked her to marry him. She'd hesitated, begging him to change his mind about having children.

He'd said no. She'd tried a dozen different ways to sway him. He hadn't listened.

She'd cried.

He'd stood firm.

She'd packed.

He'd pretended not to notice.

Then she'd left.

He'd been certain she would come back. But she hadn't. The months went by and she didn't call. He'd almost lost his mind. Then the months had turned into a year and he'd faced facts. She wasn't coming back.

He started to call once or twice…but then a new case would come up and he'd be too busy. If she'd wanted to talk to him she would have called, he'd rationalized. It was over and he'd had to come to terms with that.

It hadn't been easy but he'd done it. At least he thought he had until he saw her again. Not one thing about her had changed. She still looked twenty-five, despite being thirty-four. She wore her hair the same…the way he liked it. The long silky strands of gold made him ache to tangle his fingers there. Having a child hadn't changed her slender figure much, either. If anything she looked more womanly.

Had bearing that child given her that extra touch of softness, those ever so slightly fuller curves? Did the man who'd made love to her last appreciate the subtle differences? He clenched his jaw until it ached.

Ryan pushed up from the bed and paced the suddenly too-small room. He needed a long, hard run to regain his perspective. He'd been to Memphis before, three or four years ago, had stayed in this very hotel. It was a safe enough area for a late night run. At this point he didn't really care. He had to work off these crazy mixed-up emotions and all the adrenaline surging through his body.

He pulled a pair of sweats and his running shoes from his duffel and sat them aside. Ninety seconds later, he was ready to go. He glanced at the clock—2:00 a.m. He functioned on less than two hours' sleep most of the time. A couple of nights without any at all wouldn't kill him.

He reached for the door. A loud knock rattled the hinges a split second before his fingers curled around the knob. Ryan tensed. He glanced at the clock again, then eased closer to the door as another knock sounded.

"It's Bill. Get the hell up, Braxton. I've got something for you."

Ryan removed the chain and jerked the door open. "What've you got?" he asked without preamble.

"A body." Bill looked smug. "And it isn't the kid's."

Ryan pulled him inside and shut the door. "Whose body?"

"Garland Hanes," Bill told him.

A new surge of adrenaline pumped through Ryan's veins. "The funeral home attendant?"

Bill nodded. "The guy who buried the empty coffin." Bill pulled out his trusty notebook. "Apparently gave himself a third eye and a one-way ticket to hell." He grinned. "And guess what Memphis's finest found in the wallet he left behind?"

Ryan's tension moved to the next level. "Just tell me what they found."

Bill pulled a plastic evidence bag from his inside jacket pocket and waved it in front of Ryan. "A picture of a little girl. A very much alive little girl." His grin widened. "A little girl named Katlin Jackson."

CHAPTER FOUR

RYAN SAT ON the side of the bed and stared at the telephone, waiting for the minutes to tick off. Bill would call Mel this morning and explain the latest turn of events. Ryan had asked him not to mention the picture until after he had interviewed Rita Grider, the friend who identified the child's body. He didn't want to raise additional hope that might not pan out.

Mel would be mad as hell when she found out he'd hidden any aspect of the case from her, but it was necessary. Not only would it prevent further hurt if things didn't turn out the right way, but it would avoid any additional distraction. Keeping her focused was difficult enough without adding another layer of false hope.

He watched as the digital clock on the bedside table next to the telephone clicked off one more minute, 7:29 a.m. He'd been up all night, hadn't been able to sleep at all. Staying put until this morning had been almost more than he could manage. He'd wanted to view the body of the funeral home attendant, Garland Hanes. He'd wanted to scour every square inch of the scene where he'd been found. But somebody had screwed up and gone through the steps at the scene, including moving the body, before realizing the victim was tied to this case. Bill hadn't gotten the call until after the body was already at the morgue. Taking all that into consideration going directly to the scene in the dark and rain hadn't made much sense.

It hadn't, however, kept Ryan from taking that run he'd decided upon before Bill's visit. He'd run until he'd exhausted himself, thrown his damp clothes to the bathroom floor and stood under a long, hot shower. Despite the depletion of adrenaline he still hadn't been able to sleep.

Now he only waited to make the one call necessary to his continued participation in this case. Afterward, he had one stop to make before rendezvousing with Bill at the scene where Hanes's body had been discovered by two teenagers. The clock's digital read-out blinked to 7:30.

Victoria Colby was almost always in her office by 7:30, he hoped today would prove no different. He punched in the proper series of numbers and waited through the first ring.

"The Colby Agency."

Mildred. "Good morning, Mildred, this is Ryan Braxton." Victoria's loyal secretary was the first to arrive and the last to leave every day that the agency doors opened.

"Ryan, how are things in Memphis? You know I've always wanted to visit Graceland."

He would never have taken Mildred for an Elvis fan, but, hey, she could fool the best CIA interrogator if she so chose. "Things are *complicated*," he offered. "This case looks like it might take a while and…" He hesitated, knowing this was the point of no return. "I've decided to stay on and see it through."

"I understand," she said knowingly. "I'll put you through to Victoria."

There were no secrets kept from Mildred. She had a handle on everyone and everything that involved the agency.

"Ryan, it's good to hear from you. Have you learned anything new?"

The sound of Victoria's voice proved oddly calming. He couldn't say for sure precisely what it was, maybe the fact that she had believed in him when he'd felt certain total burnout loomed just around the corner. Or perhaps it was merely because she somehow seemed to sympathize with what had made him have to walk away from his past. Whatever the case, Victoria *understood*.

"The funeral home attendant's body was found last night." Ryan scrubbed a hand over his face, only then realizing that he hadn't shaved. He frowned, wondering how he could forget something he'd done every day since his junior year in high school. "There was a photograph of—the child—which would indicate she was alive at the time it was taken."

Victoria paused, then said, "Can you verify that assumption?"

"We're gonna try."

Another pause. "I see." The sound of leather shifting crinkled across the line as she apparently reclined fully into her high-back executive's chair. Ryan had watched her do that dozens of times as she'd considered the ramifications of whatever she'd just been told. "You've decided to participate in the case, then?"

He drew in a heavy breath and released it slowly before responding. She had to know how difficult a decision this was for him. "It's the only thing I can do. I can't just walk away...she needs me."

"You're doing the right thing. We can get by without

you for a while. Research will certainly miss your eye for detail, but we'll manage." She didn't have to say, but he knew she understood that the *she* he used referred to Mel as much as it did the missing child.

When he'd initially applied to the agency, Victoria had offered him the position of investigator, but he'd declined. The idea of dealing with real people no longer appealed to him. He much preferred working with facts and hypothesized scenarios. He'd had enough of investigative work for two lifetimes. But he had to do this one last thing…he had to do it for Mel. And the kid.

"I'll keep you up to speed on my progress if you'd like, though this isn't an official Colby Agency case." He wasn't sure of proper protocol under the circumstances. He would be working under the Bureau's umbrella.

"I'd like that very much," she said without hesitation. This time there was something different in her voice, something besides the usual confidence and determination.

Another frown inched its way across Ryan's brow. He had the distinct feeling that Victoria was holding something back. Before he could pursue the thought, she spoke again.

"What are the chances you'll find this child… alive?"

There was a definite quality of uncertainty in her tone now. He considered her question. It was the same one he'd been asked a thousand times before in his old life at the Bureau. His answer was always the same. "Slim to none." The statement was blunt and cold, as he'd intended it. The worst thing a man in his position could do was engender false hope. He'd seen others do it, only to watch the families of victims fall apart later when things turned out badly. He never went that route.

"How is Miss Jackson holding up?"

It wasn't until that moment when he heard Victoria say *Miss* Jackson that two things struck Ryan. Why was Mel still single? And why did her child carry her surname? Why not the father's? Mel was too careful to, without due consideration, get involved with a guy on that level. She never acted before she analyzed the situation. That's why she hadn't become Mrs. Ryan Braxton two years ago. She'd considered what he offered, assessed the data and concluded that it wasn't enough. How had she managed to end up a single parent?

"As well as can be expected," he said in answer to Victoria's question. "This is the worst thing that can happen to any parent. There's no way to accurately describe the sheer torment she'll endure." He closed his eyes and wished for one long moment that he could make it go away. No matter that she'd obviously run into another man's arms when she left him, she was still Mel. The woman he'd loved…the woman he'd lost.

"Don't hesitate to call if this agency can do anything at all to help."

Again he heard the vulnerability in the usually strong woman. "I'll do that. Thank you."

When the call ended, Ryan was sure of one thing. Victoria Colby *understood* this situation a little too well. He didn't know how or why, but in one capacity or another she had been in this very situation. The Colby Agency had worked a number of cases involving missing children…or maybe it was more personal. Maybe he'd look into that theory.

Then again, if she wanted him to know her personal

business she would tell him. The best thing he could do was keep his mind on the matter at hand.

His own entirely too-personal business.

VICTORIA COLBY SAT very still and prayed the horrifying sensations would pass.

The past had been catching up with her for a while now. No matter how she tried to push the memories away, they somehow managed to surface. She found it especially difficult anytime a case involved a missing or endangered child. Her mind went automatically to Trevor Sloan. She remembered well what he'd gone through losing his son. But his story had had a happy ending that included finding his son as well as saving Rachel Larson's son. They all lived happily ever after as a family down in Mexico. She recalled Nick and Laura Foster. Their child had been missing. Again, fortunately for all involved, they'd found the boy unharmed. Most recently, Pierce Maxwell had discovered he was to be a father. He'd had to race against time to save his child from those who would have used that innocent life to further their own goals.

But there wasn't always a happy ending.

Despite everything she could do tears welled in her eyes, emotion clogged her throat. Some children were lost forever. No clues…no bodies were ever found to give closure to their cases. To allow the families left behind to move on.

Victoria knew exactly how that felt. Her son's body had never been found. For eighteen long years she had harbored hope. In the beginning, she and James had exhausted every means to find him. But seven-year-old Jimmy was nowhere to be found. He'd simply van-ished, not leaving a trace.

Only three years after he'd disappeared, James had been murdered. Victoria closed her eyes to hold back the tears. She surely would not have survived that blow had it not been for Lucas. Once she'd buried her hus-band, she'd turned back to the one thing she could cling to: this agency. She had worked hard to make it what it was today and along the way she'd never given up on finding Jimmy...at least for the first dozen or so years.

It had been easy to maintain that sprout of hope then. She'd been fully engrossed in building the agency, so she never had time to allow reality to sink in. Then she'd had to face the facts. After nearly two decades, Jimmy wasn't going to be found, dead or alive. He wasn't com-ing back. Again, Lucas had gotten her through that black time.

And still, here she was once more, reliving the past. Allowing hope to glimmer...wondering what her son might be doing now and if he looked as much like his father now as he had at seven. It was foolish...a waste of time.

James Colby was dead. James Colby, Jr., was dead, as well.

But she was alive.

Victoria pushed to her feet and squared her shoul-ders. She would not dwell on the past for another mo-ment. She could not change history. God knew that if she could, she would. She would give her life for her son's this minute...this very second if it would bring him back.

But nothing was bringing him back. He was gone. Forever.

Her heart thundering in her chest, she skirted the desk and walked out to Mildred's desk. "I think I'll step out," she said, her chin tilted at an angle that dared her secretary to question her reasons.

Mildred looked taken aback or maybe she was just surprised since Victoria rarely left the office for anything once she arrived. "If you're waiting for an argument," Mildred offered sagely, "you'll get none from me. The weather is beautiful." She waved a hand toward the bank of elevators in invitation. "Have a nice walk."

Victoria's palms were sweating and that foolish heart of hers just kept beating harder and harder. She felt flushed and chilled to the bone at the same time. This was ridiculous. She couldn't remember the last time she'd suffered from a panic attack, and, yet, this felt exactly like the onslaught of one.

"When Ian arrives let him know that I'll be back in an hour or so." Her throat had gone bone dry and the room tilted just a little.

Victoria railed at herself for showing weakness. She was made of stronger stuff than this. She found it hard to believe that the Melany Jackson case had undone her so thoroughly. Where was that steel armor she generally wore? That hard-earned determination?

Vivid flashes of memory cut through her thoughts as she waited for the elevator car to arrive. She squeezed her eyes shut to block the visions but she just couldn't stop the images. Her little boy running, the sun glinting against his dark hair. His toys scattered haphazardly around his room. And then that moment—that soul shattering moment—when she'd realized he was gone.

She'd only looked away for mere seconds. The telephone had rung and she'd hurried to answer it. But when she'd looked through the kitchen window to see that Jimmy hadn't wandered from the kid-size fort he and his father had built in the backyard he'd been gone. It hadn't taken her more than thirty or forty seconds to step from the yard to the kitchen to grab the telephone. She'd stretched the long cord until she could watch him through the window while she talked.

But he was already gone.

Despite every security measure they'd taken.

In the blink of an eye.

Gone forever.

The room spun wildly and Victoria clutched at the wall to no avail. She marveled briefly at the glittering colors that exploded before her eyes and then the lights went out.

VICTORIA DIDN'T DARE move when her mind turned itself back on. She tried to think but couldn't. Where was she? What happened? And then she remembered. She opened her eyes very slowly, hoping to diminish the spinning in her head.

"Ah, there you are," a kindly male voice said softly.

She concentrated on focusing her vision for a few seconds before it actually worked. Her brain had obviously kicked back into gear since she recognized the voice. Kyle. Dr. Kyle Pendelton. What was he doing here?

She tried to sit up but he held her still. "Not just yet, Victoria," he said with uncharacteristic sternness.

"What happened?" She looked around the room to get her bearings. The office lounge. She was lying on the sofa in the lounge. Kyle sat in a chair that had been pulled close. He peered down at her now, concern marring his attractive features.

"That's what I'd like to know," he responded with clear accusation in his tone. "The last time we spoke I was under the impression that you intended to take a vacation. That you were going to start working fewer hours."

Oh, God, Mildred had been running off at the mouth again. Victoria would have rolled her eyes had she possessed the necessary strength. But, as it was, she felt too weak to breathe, much less argue the point.

"She never leaves the office before six," a voice piped up.

Victoria did manage a scowl this time. The voice belonged to a loose-lipped traitor. "Mildred, we'll discuss this later," she said with as much intimidation as she could muster.

Mildred harrumphed. "I'm shaking in my boots."

Victoria felt the blood pressure cuff tighten on her arm, the squeezing sensation accompanied by the wheeze of the pump. "Your numbers are still a little higher than I'd like," Kyle interjected. "Arguing isn't going to help lower them."

"I'll just get back to my desk," Mildred said petulantly, but paused at the door. "Talk some sense into her, Doc. God knows we've all tried."

As the door opened and then closed Victoria caught a glimpse of Ian Michaels and Trent Tucker, two of her investigators, holding vigil outside. What a fool she was. All this worry and excitement because of her stupidity.

"I'm sorry they called you in, Kyle," she said wearily. "I'm fine, really."

He arched a speculative brow. "I can see that." He

settled his stethoscope into place and listened to her heart, encouraging her to breathe deeply from time to time and effectively putting a halt to further conversation for a bit.

When he'd removed the instrument and laid it aside, she told him the truth. "I let this new case get to me. That's all. I'll be fine in a little while. There's nothing weak about me. I'm as strong as an ox. I'll bounce back from this just like I always do." Kyle was one she'd left off her list of those who understood what it was like to lose everything. He'd lost his wife and child to a vicious animal who still rotted in prison. Of all people, he would understand how she felt.

He took her hand in his. "Victoria, I know how strong you are and stubborn as the proverbial mule. But I also know what you go through every single day of your life." He leveled those solemn brown eyes on hers. "I do exactly the same thing. Work, sleep, eat. You and I do all those things that are expected of us. And, if we're lucky, the monotony will distract from the reality of the gaping hole in our hearts."

Victoria blinked furiously. Dammit, she would not cry. She couldn't do this…not now with Kyle watching. She'd made a big enough fool of herself already this morning.

"Nothing is ever going to change what we've lost. We can forge onward or bury our heads in the sand, either way it's still there." Moisture glistened in his eyes and Victoria railed at herself once more for putting him as well as herself through this. What had she been thinking letting the past catch up to her?

"Kyle, I know you're right." She shrugged helplessly.

"This case down in Memphis just brought back those old memories, that's all."

"Do yourself a favor, Victoria. You have a highly competent staff here. Take a vacation. Get your life back. This agency is wonderful, but it's not everything. You've spent years making it the best in the business. Now it's time you got on with who *you* are. You'll be fifty your next birthday. Still plenty young. You need a *life*." He looked at her pointedly. "A love life, too."

She'd heard it all before. And maybe her upcoming birthday was part of the problem. For all those long years she'd grieved the loss of her son. She'd only been thirty-five at the time James had died, even younger when Jimmy had been taken from her. She'd hidden from any kind of personal life ever since. Moving on had meant leaving them behind. She hadn't been ready to give them up…still wasn't, actually. But Kyle was right.

The time had come.

"All right, Doc," she said, a smile surprising her lips. "I'm going to follow your advice to the letter. Give me two weeks to get things in order here and I'll take that long awaited vacation." A hint of wickedness laced her tone when she continued, "And I'll invite a friend along."

"A male friend?" he pressed.

Her smile widened as she thought of Lucas. "Definitely male."

The blood pressure cuff puffed around her arm again. "That's much better." He removed the cuff, folded it and tucked it into his bag. "Since those high numbers appear to be an isolated event, we won't talk medication."

She rolled her eyes successfully this time. "I don't

need any medication." She could pull it together. She'd done it before. She was Victoria Colby, after all. She had a reputation to maintain.

"So," he began as he packed away his stethoscope, "where do you plan to go for this mandatory three-week vacation?"

Three weeks? Oh, he wasn't going to let it go until he had her nailed down to a destination as well as a length of stay.

"An island would be nice," she considered out loud. Her stomach roiled a little when she thought of the scary hours she'd spent on that island off the coast of Georgia just a few months ago. Maybe an island wasn't such a good idea. The whole concept brought back other disturbing memories. Leberman, the man responsible for her husband's death, and possibly for her son's, was still at large. He didn't intend to stop until he'd finished destroying everyone that he considered having had part in his own loss. She and Lucas were on that short list.

"That sounds perfect," Kyle rambled on as he readied to go. "The more exotic, the better."

Admittedly, the thought did intrigue her. Perhaps Lucas could find them a nice, thinly populated exotic location where Leberman wouldn't think to look.

"Exotic is good," she agreed.

Kyle helped her to a sitting position. "You'll need to sit for a while before you try standing. Let your equilibrium get back on an even keel one level at a time."

She snagged his hand before he stood. "What about you, Kyle? Are you getting on with your life?"

His smile was slow in coming, but when it arrived, Kyle Pendelton became the handsome young doctor he'd once been…before tragedy had struck and taken everything away from him. "Yes. As a matter of fact there is someone."

Victoria hadn't realized until then that she'd been holding her breath, hoping. "Good." She squeezed his hand. "You'll be my inspiration, then."

Kyle looked sheepish for a moment before turning solemn once more. "We don't want to lose you, Victoria. The people who come to this agency for help count on you. But you can't help anyone if you don't help yourself first."

He was right.

Today, she decided then and there, would be a new beginning. Today would be the first day in the rest of her life.

With that settled she paused to say a quick prayer for Ryan Braxton and Melany Jackson. Maybe their situation would have a happy ever after.

If there was any hope at all, she had a feeling that Ryan would make it happen.

CHAPTER FIVE

THE RAIN DRIZZLED down his collar as Ryan waited for Rita Grider to answer her door. Why was it that when he had a case like this, it always rained. He surveyed the overcast sky. Tears from heaven, he supposed.

Heaving a sigh, mostly at his ridiculous sentimentality this morning, he rapped on the door again.

He glanced at his watch, eight-fifteen. According to Bill, Ms. Grider didn't report to work at the rec center downtown until 10:00 a.m. Surely she hadn't left already.

Shrugging his lightweight trench coat up around his neck, he scanned the parking slots in front of the town house. He couldn't be sure what she'd be driving since Mel had totaled her tiny compact. He shuddered—from the rain, he told himself—as the idea that she could have been killed whipped through his mind. According to Bill, she was lucky to be alive. The passenger side of the car had sustained the most damage. The child had been buckled into a safety carrier in the middle section of the rear seat. That was another thing Ryan wanted to see, the vehicle. He sighed again when he thought of all the interviews that needed to be conducted *today*. The sooner the better.

When he raised his fist to knock again, the door opened. Rita Grider looked far younger than her twenty-six years. She had the athletic figure that went with her position as an aerobics instructor. Her dark hair was braided and looked to be about shoulder length. This morning her brown eyes carried bags and dark circles beneath them. This tragedy had weighed heavily upon her since she'd borrowed Mel's bigger, much safer vehicle for that fateful weekend.

"Ms. Grider, I'm Ryan Braxton." He flashed his Colby Agency ID. "I'm working with the FBI to try and find out what happened to Katlin Jackson."

She didn't invite him to step inside out of the rain. What she did do was inspect him thoroughly from head to toe. "You're Mel's Ryan," she said with something like accusation or suspicion in her tone.

Surprise raised an eyebrow. "That's right," he admitted, though discovering Mel had talked about him to this woman startled him to some degree.

She jerked her head toward the living room and stepped back from the door. "Come on in."

Ryan stepped across the threshold, immediately taking stock of the woman's small home. Tidy, sparsely furnished. No pictures on the walls yet. But then, she'd just moved in.

"Have a seat," she offered.

He pushed a routine smile into place. "No, thanks." He glanced down at the small tiled area where he stood. "I'm making a puddle already." The carpet beyond this three-by-three section of foyer looked pristine. He wasn't about to be the one to soil it.

She shrugged. "What can I do for you?"

Ryan asked casually, "How long have you known Mel?" He told himself the question had nothing to do with the past…only the case. The information was pertinent to the case, though he imagined Bill had already asked this and more.

"Two years." The fabric of the running suit she wore rasped as she folded her arms over her chest. "I was a student in one of her classes a while back. We hit it off right away."

Ryan considered for a moment what Mel could have in common with this woman. Eight year age difference, student versus teacher, considerable standard-of-living gap. Nothing that was immediately apparent. He reached into his jacket pocket and withdrew the photograph that had been found on Hanes. The Polaroid had been cut down to a size that would fit into a man's wallet. It looked smudged, likely with dirty fingerprints. The crime scene techs had already done their magic and stored the photo in a plastic evidence bag before turning it over to Bill. It was amazing how much more sinister a simple photograph looked once stored in that harmless plastic container.

"Take a look at this and tell me if you've ever seen it before."

Slowly, as if she feared what she might see, she accepted the bag, gripping it by one corner between her thumb and forefinger.

"It's Katlin," she murmured. Her breath caught and her eyes brightened with tears. "It's…" She frowned, then stared at the photo more closely. "Is this a Polaroid?" She looked to Ryan for the answer. He nodded. She turned her attention back to the picture. "It's like the one they showed me when I identified…the body." Her gaze shot back to Ryan's. "But her eyes were closed. They told me she was dead."

The child in this photograph clearly was not dead.

Her eyes were not only open but the picture had caught her arms in motion as if she'd reached for something or someone.

"You're sure this is similar to the one you saw at the hospital's morgue. Look carefully. I need you to be absolutely certain."

She studied the hacked off Polaroid for a long while. "Well, the gown she's wearing is the same." She shook her head. "I won't ever forget that. It's one of those hospital gowns they use in the pediatric ward." She inclined her head and regarded the photo again. "The stainless steel table looks the same too, but I can't be sure about that since so much of the background has been cut away." She handed back the evidence bag and stared up at him with a haunted look. "Where did this picture come from? How could she be alive in this one and dead in one almost exactly like it? I don't understand."

"Ms. Grider," Ryan said carefully, "I can't give you any answers right now. I would appreciate it if you would call me if you remember anything at all that has happened relevant to this case since you arrived back in Memphis." He handed her his card. "My cell number's on there. Call me anytime, day or night."

"Momma!"

Ryan's attention snapped toward the doorway on the other side of the room that led into the interior of the home. A toddler, perhaps a year or so old, came stumbling into the living room, her arms outstretched.

Beaming a smile, Rita Grider reached for the child. "Mommy's here," she cooed.

"This is your child," Ryan said, startled for the second time today. Bill hadn't mentioned the friend having a child about the same age as Melany's. But it made sense, he supposed, since Mel hadn't had any I.D. with her when the accident occurred, the cops had run the vehicle's plates and assumed she was the owner, Rita Grider, who, as it were, had a daughter.

Rita nodded. "Yes. Her name's Chloe. Say hi to Mr. Braxton, Chloe." The child snuggled against her mother's neck, attempting to hide her face from the stranger. "She's the reason I recognize the hospital gown. Chloe was a patient there when she was just an infant."

He filed the information away for later analysis, then glanced at her left hand. Before he could ask, she said, "No, I'm not married. I'm a single parent, just like Mel." Her pleasant expression turned grim. "And Chloe's father couldn't be counted on, either, just like Katlin's."

"Well." Ryan swallowed at the hard lump forming in his throat. "Thank you for your assistance, Ms. Grider. I'm sure we'll have more questions." He blinked once, twice. There were other, personal questions he wanted to ask. But she was Melany's friend. She likely wouldn't answer them. And if he were smart, he wouldn't ask. He'd simply go.

"Mr. Braxton." She stopped him as he opened the door.

He met that deep brown gaze again, noting the haunted look had returned. "Yes?"

"Is there any chance that Katlin's still alive?" Tears glimmered on her lashes. "Did I do something wrong? I was devastated... I wasn't thinking straight, but they told me she was dead." She shook her head as the emotion she could not restrain slid down her cheeks. "They said that Mel was going to die, too. I thought I was doing the right thing."

Ryan squeezed his fingers into fists to prevent himself from reaching out to her and giving her a reassuring pat. He had to keep his distance. It was the only way. He couldn't focus on missing and dead children and get close to the people involved. He simply couldn't. "You didn't do anything wrong, Rita." He used her first name, offering at least that small reassurance. "You did exactly what Mel would have done had the circumstances been reversed."

She nodded and swiped at her tears with the back of her hand. "I keep telling myself that." Her baby made a distressed sound. Her mother's anxiety frightened her. "But then I think about what I could have done differently. I should have insisted on seeing the body...on touching her."

He couldn't hold out any longer. He reached out, squeezed her arm. "We'll figure this thing out. Remember to call me if you think of anything."

She nodded and he left.

He barely noticed the unrelenting rain as he crossed the street and climbed into his rental. Dropping behind the wheel, he turned the ignition and scrubbed the dampness from his face.

He stared at his reflection in the rearview mirror. Rain. It was only the rain.

Ryan Braxton hadn't cried since he was a kid and his beloved dog had been hit by a car. He'd witnessed too much as an adult. He wasn't capable of that kind of emotion any longer.

Just another reason Mel had left him.

THE RAIN HAD finally stopped.

Melany pushed open the car door and climbed out of

Bill's rental. She kept her gaze carefully directed away from the cemetery. Don't look, a voice whispered. Her stomach clenched violently. *Don't look.*

Bill waited a few feet away, determined not to allow her to enter the crime scene without his being right next to her. She appreciated that more than he could possibly know.

She'd managed scarcely four hours of sleep last night even with the sleeping pill. The only thing, she decided, the medication had done was leave her with a hangover and a bad case of the shakes.

"You're sure you want to do this?" Bill asked again. Concern telegraphed from every grim line of his face.

He didn't want her here. If it were up to him, she'd be at home in bed, under heavy sedation, until this case was solved. But she couldn't do that. She had to be a part of the investigation. Had to see that every single clue…every possibility was considered to the fullest extent.

"You know the answer to that," she said patiently, knowing he wouldn't give up. The man was just as stubborn as she was. The FBI hammered that trait into those who weren't so genetically inclined. Persistence Pays Off was the Bureau's guiding principle.

Bill shrugged half-heartedly. "Let's do this, then."

He led the way across the lawn that bordered the parking area behind the massive funeral home and separated it from the encroaching forest that looked wholly out of place this close to the city. Mel couldn't help wondering why Garland Hanes would have chosen such a place to die. Why not at home or some place less eerie? She supposed it took a certain breed to work with the dead on this level. It wasn't about hope or justice or even vengeance. It was about taking care of final, necessary details. She shivered again.

At the edge of the woods Bill hesitated once more. He indicated the battalion of trees that stood at attention along the edge of the meticulously cared for landscape. "About a hundred yards this way. A couple teenagers found him just before dusk last evening. They'd stolen some beer from their fathers and decided to hide it in the woods for the weekend." He made a sound that could have been a laugh. "Damn fool kids, tracked all over the scene before they rushed back home to call the cops. They'd left the beer on the ground, otherwise their parents might never have known what they were up to."

Mel nodded. "Lead the way." She knew he was stalling. And she didn't understand the big deal. The body had already been removed from the scene. Besides, it wasn't like she hadn't seen more than her share of corpses. Something was up. He was hiding something from her.

A sudden blast of chilled wind slapped her in the face, taking her to a higher state of attention, adding an edge to her sleep-deprived thoughts. Hugging her double-breasted wool jacket a little closer around her, she entered the shadowy wooded area that flanked the funeral home's property to the right and the rear, setting it apart from the middle-class homes that lay beyond. The cemetery where she'd been taken into custody sprawled on the left of the property. A tall, decorative wrought-iron fence surrounded it, kept intruders out after dark. Unless they were determined like she had been. She'd simply climbed over.

Forcing those memories away, she focused on moving forward, through the damp foliage. The air was heavy with the clean scent of rain and a dank woodsy smell. Decaying leaves smushed under her feet. Straight ahead she could see the yellow tape that cordoned off the scene.

Mel stilled for a moment, her mind whirling with emotion, memories, images—some real, some imagined. She didn't want to think of her daughter in these woods. What had Hanes been doing out here? Bill hadn't given her many details regarding the scene or what the police suspected. He'd assured her that Ryan didn't suspect any sort of child predator in Katlin's case. He leaned more toward the malpractice scenario, which meant her child was most likely dead, in his opinion. But Mel would not think that way.

Bill had moved several yards ahead when he realized she wasn't following him anymore. "You okay?" he called back to her.

She nodded and pushed forward, praying for the numbness she'd felt for days. But it was suddenly missing, replaced by so many conflicting emotions her mind couldn't settle on just one. She wanted to burrow into this case, to find the truth. But the victimized side of her, the part of her that was woman, mother, could scarcely keep those more fragile emotions at bay. Where was her baby?

When she reached the designated crime scene perimeter Bill lifted the tape slightly so that she could join him on the other side. "Watch your step," he warned unnecessarily.

"Stop treating me like a civilian," she chastised without taking her gaze from the evidence markers.

"You are a civilian," he countered.

She glanced at him, noting that he, too, was review-

ing the markers. "I'll never be a real civilian again."
Their gazes met briefly and she saw the understanding
in his eyes. There was no way a mere human who'd seen
what she'd seen in her former line of work could ever go
back to the true innocence of civilian life. Not possible.

Bill popped a piece of chewable Nicorette into his
mouth and pointed to a large maple tree in the center
of the cordoned off area. "He was in a sitting position
there. The gun was in his right hand, a bottle of bourbon in the left." He chewed, then explained, "I'm trying to quit."

She nodded, knowing he was only trying to distract
her with the mundane.

He cleared his throat. "Let's take a closer look."

Feeling a little like a participant in an out-of-body
experience, Mel took those final few steps, then eased
into a crouch and surveyed the base of the tree as well as
the leaf- and twig-ridden ground around it. Bill tapped
her shoulder and she glanced up to see a pair of latex
gloves in his hand.

"Thanks." Though she hadn't actually planned to
touch anything, she tugged on the protective wear just
in case. The techs had no doubt already scoured the
place…any evidence already discovered and bagged.
But then, one never knew what another set of eyes
would find. That's why hard-assed investigators never
took the chance, always took a second look and came
prepared.

"Look here." Bill pointed with one gloved finger.
Mel shifted slightly to peer at the area he indicated.
"Someone stood over here—less than five feet away—
and surveyed his handiwork."

The partial impression of a shoe imprint in a small

muddy spot of earth where the leaves had blown away or otherwise shifted had already been plastered for evidence. The gray, crumbly residue the tech had left behind looked stark against the rust and browns of the forest floor.

Mel turned back to the tree. "Where's the blood?" The brain matter, she didn't add. If the victim had shot himself in the head, trace evidence would have sprayed for some distance beyond his position.

"No blood, no nothing, except what was on the vic's clothing."

She pushed to her feet, her investigator's sense jolting hard. "Then he didn't die here."

"Bingo." Bill rocked back on his heels. "He was posed. Our guy stood back and took one last look before leaving the scene. Probably never realized he'd stepped backward into the one patch of bare, muddy ground for a dozen yards in either direction."

Inspecting the shoe print more closely, she noted, "It's only a partial. Doesn't look like sneaker tread. Any chance it'll help?"

Bill shrugged. "You never know. Any sort of indentation or irregularity could be significant. I doubt if it's enough to speculate on height and weight."

Cases had hinged on less.

Moving cautiously so as not to disturb anything unnecessarily, Mel slowly covered the entire scene. The forensics techs had marked the position of the body and the shoe print. Those were the only two evidence markers. "No sign of the slug or was it still in the vic's brain?" She turned back to Bill. "Did you take a look at the guy?" A shudder quaked through her as she thought of the man who had touched her daughter. Her lips clamped together to hold back the moan of agony welling in her throat. She was glad he was dead. The thought came out of nowhere and she immediately felt guilty for having thought it. That wasn't fair…she couldn't be sure what part he'd played. Shaking off the distraction, she forced her attention to Bill.

"Yeah, I took a look. The bullet went clean through, but they won't find it here. The shirt he wore was splattered but there was no blood trail on the fabric. My guess would be that he died in a reclining position, flat on his back or face-down, maybe. Not upright. I don't need an M.E. to tell me that."

He was right about one thing. No way the man had died here. She couldn't help scanning the area once more for some sign that her child had been here. Her stomach twisted with the anguish that, even when she tried to focus on the task of analyzing a crime scene, wouldn't completely be ignored.

What did you do with my child? she wanted to scream.

But no one would answer. Garland Hanes was dead. He was the man who'd signed for Katlin at the hospital. Had taken her away in the funeral home's hearse. Had buried an empty coffin in a shallow grave without a vault.

She closed her eyes and tried to block the gruesome pictures. *Please, God,* she prayed, *don't let him have hurt my baby.*

"I think it's going to rain again."

Mel's eyes snapped open at the sound of Ryan's voice. Their gazes locked across the short distance that spanned between them. How had he sneaked up on her like that? He was like a damned cat, soundless. Only not the domestic kind…the untamed, predatory sort who could pounce on you in an instant.

Bill looked up at the patch of blue-black sky that peeked between the towering trees. He made an agreeable sound. "I believe you're right, Braxton."

"I'd like to stop by the E.R. this morning," Ryan said to Mel. "I checked and Dr. Wilcox is on duty."

Before she could answer, Bill said, "I need to get back to the morgue and see if they have a prelim report on Hanes. The medical examiner said he'd put a rush on it."

For a moment, Mel wasn't sure what to do. She didn't want to be alone with Ryan, but she also didn't want to miss anything he might discover while interviewing Dr. Wilcox. "You should go with us," she said pointedly to Bill. The one time she had talked to Wilcox since her release from the hospital he'd been sympathetic but skeptical of her sanity. The tranquilizers he'd prescribed had helped, she had to admit, but his closed attitude had not.

"You know the drill, Mel." This from Ryan. That blue gaze narrowed on hers when she turned back to him. "We can accomplish more by going in different directions. If you'd prefer to go with Bill, that's fine by me."

No contest there. Someone at that hospital had to know what really happened. "I want to be in on the interviews at the hospital," she told him flatly. "So let's not waste any more time discussing it."

"I'll check in with you two later." Bill didn't bother waiting for a response from either one of them. He, better than anyone else, knew the tension would only escalate, if anything. He headed back in the direction of the parking lot.

Mel didn't see the point in waiting for a response, either, but when she would have moved past Ryan, he stopped her with a hand on her arm. She waited for him to say whatever was on his mind, but she kept her gaze trained front and forward, childishly refusing to look at him.

"There are questions I'm going to need to ask that you may not want to hear the answers to."

His voice was soft. The deep timbre echoed through her, making her shiver with something other than cold or dread. How could he still do that to her? Mel dragged in a deep breath and summoned her anti-Braxton resolve. "Like you said, Braxton, I know the drill." She looked at him then, with all the ferocity she could marshal. "Now let's stop wasting time. You're not my protector, you're an investigator on this case. This isn't personal, don't try to make it that way."

For a mini-eternity he simply looked into her eyes, that relentless stare never wavering. "This isn't personal. I'd say the same thing to any family member of a victim. This isn't about you and me and the past. It's about here and now and a missing child. The fact that the child is yours isn't my concern."

If he hadn't been touching her she could have believed him without reservation. That Braxton stare…the chill he knew how to turn on in his voice. It was all there: cool, objective, to the point. But those long fingers had tightened around her arm, generating an undeniable heat all the way to her bones. That subtle move, however unconscious, gave away what those eyes, that face, would not.

This was definitely personal.

For her.

And for him.

CHAPTER SIX

EVERY MUSCLE RIGID, Melany stood next to the nurse's desk in Memphis General's E.R. She tired to block the smell of pain and fear...the sounds of worry and anguish. She closed her eyes against it, but with the loss of visual stimuli, her other senses only clutched harder at the environment.

Investigator mode kicked in and immediately conjured the sights, sounds and smells from that night just over one week ago. Though she'd been unconscious when she arrived at the E.R., she could easily imagine how it would have been.

The paramedics would have wheeled her into a trauma room...the doctor and nurses slipped quickly into their well-choreographed dance of life and death.

Somewhere, in another room, Katlin would have lain, the same rapid-fire observations and decisions being made to determine her condition...to evaluate the urgency.

But someone had made a mistake—no, two mistakes. Mel's life had never been in grave danger. But Katlin...

"Melany."

Mel snapped her eyes open and jerked toward the sound of Ryan's voice. He watched her closely, as if he feared she might evaporate before his eyes.

"Yes?" she said, the word scarcely a whisper.

"Dr. Wilcox can give us a few minutes now." Ryan kept his tone even, quiet. But worry etched itself across the masculine terrain of those lines and angles.

"Good." She stiffened her spine and lifted her chin in defiance of her own weakness. "I'm ready."

She wasn't ready. Not in the most remote sense of the word. Ryan wanted to shake her and demand that she go home and lie down. She looked ready to drop. He'd never seen her so vulnerable…so fragile.

But she wasn't about to back off and nothing he could say or do would change her mind. He marveled at how a person, man or woman, could love a child so much… could risk this very kind of hurt. He couldn't see it, couldn't give that much. Wouldn't give that much.

Ryan led the way to the doctor's lounge where Wilcox had agreed to take a brief break and spare them a few moments of his precious time. Already Ryan did not like the man. He was arrogant and indifferent—two things Ryan despised in medical professionals. Maybe because those traits reminded him too much of his own self-protective faults. The E.R. was crowded, but he'd seen at least one other doctor on duty and there didn't appear to be any true emergencies. Not life-threatening ones, anyway.

Five minutes wasn't going to kill anyone.

Inside the lounge, Wilcox paced impatiently. He drew deeply on a cigarette then quickly plopped it into an abandoned, half-empty foam coffee cup on the closest table. "We're not supposed to smoke in here, but everybody does it," he offered unapologetically.

Ryan resisted the urge to take a seat in hopes that Mel would follow suit, but he needed to be on the same level with Wilcox as he questioned him. Needed the man to understand the significance of the questions.

"No problem," Ryan said in regard to his comment as he reached into an interior pocket and retrieved his notepad and pen. Unlike Bill, Ryan never bothered with notes, but in this instance, it was a deliberate tactic. He wanted Wilcox to know that whatever he said was on the record. "You remember Ms. Jackson," he said casually.

Wilcox's beady eyes darted between Ryan and Mel. He swallowed hard, the nervous movement visible along his long, skinny neck. "Of course." He blinked and reached a hand up to smooth back his short reddish hair. He was fairly tall, but rail thin. Small brown eyes. Long, narrow nose. Birdlike features, Ryan decided. And a cocky attitude. A rooster. He gritted his teeth for a second to hold back a grin, then he asked, "You were on duty the morning Melany Jackson and her daughter were brought to the E.R.?"

He nodded, stealing another glance at Mel. "Yes. I've already given my statement to the police."

"You said—" Ryan flipped through a few pages as if he were referring to something he'd written previously "—that Ms. Jackson appeared to be in a coma. In fact, a CT scan identified an inoperable brain stem injury."

Wilcox stretched his neck to one side, then the other. "Dr. Reddi made that diagnosis. He was the radiologist on call. A neurosurgeon later confirmed that assessment and determined that our hands were tied."

"But," Ryan pressed, with his gaze as well as his tone, "in reality, she was simply in a trauma-induced coma from the severity of her concussion, is that correct?"

He cleared his throat. "That's correct." Another quick cut of his eyes toward Melany.

"So, it's safe to say that someone made a mistake."

"We're only human," he insisted humbly, the tone clearly feigned. "Mistakes are made at times. We do the best we can. There was every indication that her condition was fatal. She was completely unresponsive."

Ryan scribbled meaningless letters. "It's possible then—" he lifted his gaze to the doctor's "—that another mistake was made that day."

Wilcox's posture grew rigid. "If you're referring to the child, Katlin. There was no mistake."

From the corner of his eye Ryan saw Mel stiffen. Damn, how he wanted to shield her from this. "How can you be so certain? The child was under another doctor's care when she coded."

"Dr. Letson," Wilcox provided, since Ryan didn't bother checking his nonexistent notes this time. "He and Nurse Helen Peterson."

"But you weren't there. You didn't see her expire," Ryan persisted. He didn't have to look this time, he felt Mel's discomfort span the three or four feet that stood between them. "You didn't view the body at any time after she left the E.R. Is that correct?" Ryan knew that even if a doctor questioned his peer in a matter such as this, it wasn't something he would willingly discuss. But then, the body was missing, there was no denying that glaring fact.

Wilcox nodded. A slight flush had crept up his neck and face and he worked hard at not looking Ryan directly in the eye.

"Yet, you're certain there was no mistake." Ryan tucked his notepad and pen away. "I'm sorry, Doc, but, as you say, you guys are just human. Dr. Letson could have made a mistake."

The flush deepened to a crimson red. His long, slim fingers balled into fists. "Dr. Letson pronounced. She was transferred to the morgue where she was *refrigerated* until she was identified the next morning, then the funeral home attendant signed for her body that afternoon. I hardly see how there could be any doubt."

Melany did an abrupt about-face and bolted from the room. Ryan had to physically restrain the need to go after her. He had to finish this…couldn't show any sign of weakness to this man.

"But the medical examiner never saw the body," Ryan suggested.

Wilcox looked startled.

Ryan was fishing. An assistant medical examiner had signed the death certificate, but he'd bet his right arm that the guy had simply gone along with Letson's call.

"Why would you say that?" Wilcox said, doing a little fishing of his own.

"Because the M.E.'s office is closed on Sunday and that's the day the funeral home attendant signed for the body."

The color drained from the good doctor's face. "I'm sure he must have. Dr. Letson likely called him in on Saturday night."

Maybe. The assistant M.E. was just someone else he intended to interview—if the guy ever got back into town. He'd had a family emergency that took him back to Iowa, his home state. How convenient.

"Thank you for your time, Dr. Wilcox." Ryan offered his hand. "I'm sure I'll have more questions before we're finished here."

Wilcox shook his hand briefly. "You know where

to find me." He reached for his breast pocket and the cigarettes there and Ryan took that as his cue to leave.

When he stepped back into the long white corridor outside the lounge, Ryan steeled himself before facing Mel. She'd leaned against the wall, looking pretty much like that was all that kept her vertical. The urge to take her into his arms was almost overwhelming.

He'd already made one mistake this morning. He'd touched her—wrapped his fingers around her arm—and even through the layers of clothing the effect had rattled him. Going down that road would be a catastrophe. One he intended to avoid.

"Look," he said tautly, "this isn't going to get any easier. Are you sure you're up to this?"

As weary as she looked with those dark circles under her eyes and her lips thinned into a grim line, she still managed to come to life with fury. "Don't be stupid, Braxton," she snarled. "Of course I'm not up to this. It's hell." Her voice quaked and she blinked furiously. "But it has to be done." She pushed off from the wall and squared her slender shoulders like the good little soldier she was. "What's next?"

For one fraction of a second he considered manacling her by the arm and dragging her out of there. He could take her home and force her to eat a decent meal and get a few hours' sleep. But then reality slammed back into his brain and he pushed aside that option. Mel had had the same training as him. When assigned a case like this, going without the usual creature comforts, even the more basic ones, was the norm. Standard operating procedure.

"We pay a visit to Nurse Helen Peterson," he said

offhandedly. "Dr. Letson isn't on duty today, which is good since I want to talk to her alone."

"You mean," Mel corrected, "since we want to talk to her."

"Yeah." Ryan felt his lips quirk. Sleep deprived or not, she was still on her toes. "Right."

The pediatric wing occupied the fourth floor at Memphis General. Brightly painted cartoon characters danced on the walls. The nurses' smocks were equally colorful. Mothers sat in chairs in the rooms they passed, the televisions alive with their ill or injured child's favorite program. Mel ordered her tense muscles to relax, but that wasn't happening. She kept thinking that this was the last place her little girl had been…the last things she had seen before…

She'd fallen behind. Ryan stood watching her closely, waiting for her to catch up. If he asked her one more time if she were all right, Mel felt certain she would scream. Of course she wasn't all right! Her child was missing…presumed dead. A shudder rocked through her. She wouldn't be all right again until they found her.

And for that very reason she had to be strong. She swallowed back the rock climbing into her throat and forced determination into her step.

Seeming to read her mind, he chose not to comment, but simply continued toward the nurses' station. He displayed his credentials for the first nurse who looked up.

"Ryan Braxton, special advisor to the FBI. I'd like to speak with Helen Peterson."

Stuffed animals and plants for delivery littered the counter. The nurse peered over her glasses and beyond the clutter to glance from Ryan to Mel and back. "She's doing inventory right now. She just got started, she's going to be a while." The uncertainty in her voice was impossible to miss.

Surely the police had been here before, these ladies should know the situation by now, and yet this nurse—McCormick, according to her name tag—appeared oddly startled. Then Mel remembered that Ryan had said FBI. That, to most people's way of thinking, especially with all the talk of terrorism in the news, was cause for alarm.

"I'll only take a few moments of her time," Ryan assured the woman as he slipped his credentials case back into his pocket. "If you'll just point me in the right direction."

Nurse McCormick moistened her lips, then pointed down the corridor behind the station. "First door on the left."

"Thank you, Ms. McCormick."

She blinked but didn't respond.

A frown of irritation working its way across her brow, Mel followed Ryan to the door marked pharmaceuticals. No matter the excuse, somehow she got the feeling that cooperation was not in the hospital employee training program.

Without knocking, Ryan turned the knob and pushed open the door. Mel assumed the door would usually be locked but was open now because there was already someone inside doing inventory.

Helen Peterson looked up from the logbook in her hand. "I'm sorry, sir, but only authorized personnel are allowed—"

"Ryan Braxton," he interrupted smoothly. "I'm working with the Bureau on the Katlin Jackson case."

That same expression of dread mixed with a measure of fright that had claimed the other nurse's face crept across Helen Peterson's. "I don't understand," she said, only then noting Mel's presence. Her eyes widened briefly before she composed herself. "I've already told the police everything I know."

Ryan moved the three steps required until he stood directly in front of the woman who'd gone on the offensive. "As I said, I'm working with the FBI. This case is now under Federal jurisdiction. I'll need to ask you a few questions."

She painstakingly placed her pad and pen on the stainless steel cart she'd been using to facilitate her inventory, then closed and locked the one open cabinet door. She glanced about the room ensuring that all else was secure. Row after row of locked glass and steel cabinets lined three of the walls in the small room. Two beige file cabinets, also locked, sat against the wall next to the door. Satisfied that all was as it should be, she clasped her hands in front of her. "I don't know what else I can tell you," she said with finality, "but ask away."

Ryan watched the woman drop a firm mask in place, concealing the whirling emotions he'd seen only moments before. Her voice was too stiff, too formal. Mentioning the Bureau generally had that effect on civilians. Like the nurse at the desk. She'd been nervous, uncertain what the federal authorities could possibly want with a co-worker. But this woman, Helen Peterson, displayed a different kind of anxiety. She posed herself, made a show of checking the security of the room before she gave him her full attention. He knew the tactic for what it was, buying time. Then she clasped her hands to ensure she didn't fidget.

When a person was merely nervous, it showed despite their best efforts. Being nervous didn't send off warning bells, but deliberate efforts to conceal emotions, to put on a show of normalcy, control, now that set him on edge.

"You were with Dr. Letson when Katlin Jackson coded?"

She nodded once. "Yes. It was about 12:35 p.m. She'd been brought up to pediatrics approximately thirty minutes prior and appeared to be in stable condition. She presented absolutely no symptoms prior to going into cardiac arrest."

Twelve thirty-five, not twelve-thirty. Too precise. Planned, not recalled. "You remember the specific time because..." Ryan suggested, allowing his amaze- ment at her detailed answer to show.

She blinked, but that was the extent of her reaction. "It was past time for me to take a lunch break. I remember thinking that I should have left earlier." She flicked another glance at Mel. "I pride myself in maintaining a steady routine."

"Do you usually go to lunch around 12:35 when you're on duty?" he prodded. She didn't look like the type who put food before all else. Helen Peterson was medium height and impossibly thin. Gaunt, almost. The smock hung on her slight shoulders as if it were a size or two too large. In fact, she looked exactly like the type who more often forgot to eat than not. Like Wilcox.

"At noon," she insisted. "I always go at noon. We work as a team here. If one of us gets off schedule, it throws everyone off."

Ryan nodded. "What warned you that the child had gone into distress?"

Annoyance furrowed her brow. "The monitor. She flat-lined." Another surreptitious look beyond him.

"So, she was stable but being monitored. Is that routine procedure? Cardio monitoring, I mean."

Her eyes flared briefly. "Well, for…for MVA patients we take extra precautions."

"You're saying then that whenever a patient has been involved in a motor vehicle accident, you pull out all the stops even if they appear stable enough that they would otherwise go home?" He pulled out his notebook and flipped through a few pages. "According to Dr. Wilcox, the only reason the child was kept for observation was to allow time for family to be contacted."

Another of those slow blinks. "You'll have to ask Dr. Letson about that. I only followed his orders."

"You assisted when he attempted extreme measures to resuscitate the patient?" He didn't have to spell it out. She would know what he meant. Saying the words out loud would only add insult to injury with Mel so close by.

She nodded. "Yes."

"Did you, personally, take her down to the morgue later?"

"No." She looked from him to Mel and back. "A morgue attendant came for her."

Ryan resisted the urge to look back at Mel just to be sure she was holding up all right, but he couldn't risk breaking the tension he'd built. Her pain was reflected well in the nurse's expression. Each time she glanced at Mel she seemed to lose a bit more control of that staunch composure.

"How long does it generally take you to do the inventory in here?" he asked casually, doing a hundred-and-eighty degree turn in his line of questioning.

Surprise flashed in her eyes. "About two hours. Sometimes a little longer. If I'm not interrupted."

"You usually work straight through this task without stopping?"

Annoyance replaced the surprise. "That's right. This isn't the kind of task you can come back to. Once you've started you have to finish, otherwise someone will need something that changes your figures and throws off your inventory."

"Nurse McCormick said you just got started," Ryan plugged away.

"That's right." She reached for her pad and pen. "If you don't have any more questions I'd like to get back to it. It's imperative that I finish before we prep for afternoon meds."

Ryan looked at his watch—10:40 a.m. "You'll be late taking your lunch break again today," he noted.

"It certainly looks that way," she returned shortly.

"Well, thank you for your time, Ms. Peterson."

When he would have turned away he hesitated. "Just one more thing."

Her impatience abraded the air with a sigh.

"Did you know that Katlin's mother wasn't expected to survive?"

Helen Peterson focused on the inventory log in her hands. "Yes. We'd all heard. It was terrible. Just terrible."

"Had someone already attempted to contact next of kin?" Ryan knew the answer to that one. Wilcox had insisted that steps were taken in the E.R. to contact family the moment the severity of Melany's situation was known.

"There was no next of kin." She cleared her throat. "At least that's what we were told. We were operating under the assumption she was Rita Grider, single parent. No next of kin."

Ryan waited until she was forced to meet his gaze once more. "I imagine that you'd considered that if the child had survived she'd be alone…with no family left to take care of her."

"That's what Child Services is for," she said tightly. "They take care of the children when there's no one else." She cast another glance in Mel's direction. "If there'd been any hope at all we…we would have reacted differently." There was a plea in her tone this time… one directed at Mel.

"In what way, Nurse Peterson," Ryan pressed. There was something here…something important.

She jerked her gaze back to Ryan's. "We…we would have kept her longer…waited for the mother to recover before…"

"Before you took an irreversible step?"

She looked away. "I have to get back to work now."

Ryan turned to leave. This time his hesitation had nothing to do with the nurse and everything to do with Mel. The look of pain on her face was so stark, so vivid, it sliced right through his chest.

Knowing it would be a mistake but unable to stop himself, he touched her…ushered her from the room, pulled the door closed behind them, more to give them privacy than for Helen Peterson's benefit.

In the corridor she stalled, whispered harshly,

"What's she hiding?" She looked up at Ryan. "She is hiding something, isn't she? It's not my imagination."

He held her gaze for a few seconds before allowing her the answer, knowing it would shore up the fledgling hope that her child was alive. "Yes. She is hiding something, but it may not be what you need it to be."

Fury whipped across her face, chasing away some of the devastation that had taken occupancy there. "That's your damned perspective, Braxton. We're all entitled to our own conclusions."

Another of those near irresistible urges to touch her broadsided him. He clenched his fists at his sides and fought the need. "I know what you want to believe, Mel. I'd be remiss in my duty if I didn't remind you that, in all likelihood, we're looking at a missing body here, not a missing child. I don't want you getting your hopes up about finding her alive."

The devastation clouded her features again, but this time it remained laced with fury. "Thank you for the reminder, Braxton. We all know just how much duty means to you. I would be the last person to consider you remiss."

She stormed away without looking back.

Ryan let her go ahead of him. They needed the distance. Every moment he spent with her muddied the waters a little more. He couldn't stop thinking about the past…about her. All she remembered was how he'd let her down. She was right about that. No one could ever accuse him of being remiss in his professional duties.

Ryan Braxton didn't let go…not until the job was done.

It was in his personal life that he fell apart. He'd let her down in a big way. She'd loved him. He didn't have to wonder, she'd told him. But he hadn't been able to give her the child she'd wanted so desperately. So she'd found that completion in another man's arms.

If he'd just given in…just once. Would the child she'd lost have been his? Would she have stayed in D.C. with him? Then this life-shattering accident would never have happened.

A wave of agony so profound washed over him that he grabbed for the wall.

That was one question he'd never know the answer to.

He'd lost her…lost any chance of a future with her. She'd lost the child she'd longed for, had brushed so close to death herself…and, somehow, it all felt like it was entirely his fault.

CHAPTER SEVEN

JUST WHEN MEL thought her tension could escalate no further, they passed through *the intersection*.

She gripped the car's armrests. Held her breath. Memories of the sound of brakes squealing…the crunch of metal all zoomed into her awareness. Desperate emotions grabbed her by the throat. She remembered her baby crying…horns blowing. Someone screaming.

Mel jerked from the trance. Released the air in her lungs in one long puff. She'd never remembered that last part before. She must have heard those sounds as she slipped into unconsciousness.

The cry had been of fear…not pain.

A mother knew the sound of her child's cries. Katlin had been afraid. How could it be possible that she'd appeared fine and, yet, had sustained such massive internal injuries? It didn't make sense. But then she wasn't a doctor…but she knew what she sensed on the most basic levels.

Katlin was alive. No matter what anyone said—she glared at Ryan—or thought.

"Is that it?"

She snapped her attention to the deli half a block ahead. The EMTs had agreed to meet with them on their lunch break. Ryan wanted to hear their account of what they'd found at the scene. Mel wanted to hear it, too. Though she had to admit that she'd almost lost it this morning. *Refrigerated* kept echoing inside her head. Dr. Wilcox had seemed so nice when she'd first left the hospital almost a week ago. He'd felt so sorry for her. Had told her over and over how he wished things had turned out differently. Even the nurse had been kind the one time Mel had seen her the day she was to be released from the hospital. It had been obvious that she'd felt immensely sympathetic.

"Mel?"

Forcing her attention back to the present, she muttered, "Yeah. That's the place." She didn't look at Ryan. She knew what he was thinking, she didn't need to see it in his eyes. And he was looking at her. She could feel his gaze on her.

Instead of dwelling on his assessment, she considered the concept that things were very different now. Dr. Wilcox and Nurse Peterson were no longer sympathetic to her plight. Due, in part, to the investigation. No one liked being suspected of wrongdoing whether they were guilty or not. But deep down she knew it was more than that. Both of them were hiding something. She'd felt it so strongly it had almost overwhelmed all other emotion.

As soon as Ryan had parked she unfastened her seat belt and scrambled out of the car. She didn't intend to give him the opportunity to go through the "Are you all right?" ritual again. She wasn't all right, but that wouldn't stop her.

Inside the neighborhood deli most of the tables were already taken this close to noon. Smack in the middle of the throng, the blue uniforms of the EMTs stood out amid the Monday lunch crowd. Ryan went directly to their table.

He showed his I.D. "Ryan Braxton. One of you is Lonnie Keller?"

The older of the two waved a hand. "That's me. This is my partner, Reg Carson."

"Melany Jackson," she offered when Ryan didn't. She extended her hand, first in Keller's direction, then toward Carson.

"Ms. Jackson," he said, pushing to his feet. "Glad to see you're doing all right." He clasped her hand and shook it enthusiastically. His partner did the same.

"We sure thought you were a goner," Carson added.

Keller elbowed him. "I hated to hear the news about your little girl."

Mel saw the sympathy flash in both men's eyes. She hated this part. "Thank you," she murmured.

"Have a seat," Keller put in, suddenly realizing they were all standing. "How can we help you?"

When they'd settled at the small table for four, Ryan wasted no time getting to the point of the visit.

"According to your report you arrived at the scene six minutes after the initial 911 call."

"That's about right. It wasn't that far from our post. We'd just rolled in from another MVA. We jumped back in the truck and headed out."

"Is that typical protocol?" Ryan wanted to know. "There wasn't another unit standing by?"

Carson shook his head. "Most times that's the way it works, the units rotate calls, but that day we were a little busier than usual."

Ryan nodded. Mel simply watched the proceedings waiting for the more crucial questions. She wanted—

no, she needed to hear about that morning. To know what they'd found at the scene.

"I'd like you to tell me what you saw when you arrived on the scene."

Keller exhaled a considering breath and thought about the answer for a moment. Mel imagined he was gathering his thoughts from that hectic morning.

"Memphis P.D. was there. One cop was directing traffic and the other was checking out the victims. As we unloaded he said the guy in the delivery truck was okay, just shaken. He was still sitting behind the wheel of his truck, his head down."

Ice slid through Mel's veins. She remembered that split second when she'd known that he was going to hit her. She couldn't recall what he looked like, maybe there hadn't been enough time for her eyes to analyze the details. But she remembered vividly knowing what was going to happen...reaching for her child.

Keller angled his head toward his partner. "Reg checked him out just to be sure while I went to the car." His gaze flitted to Mel for a half a second. "The baby was crying at the top of her lungs. No blood. She looked okay, vitals were good, so I went for the driver." He swallowed hard, the muscles of his throat constricting with the effort. "She was still restrained by a seat belt but she was slumped forward. There was no visible blood. A large, mushy mass on the left side of her head. Her respiration was weak, her blood pressure thready."

"I left the truck driver—" Carson picked up the conversation from there "—since he was conscious and checked out okay. Vitals were strong, a little elevated from the trauma, but fine other than that. I took charge of the kid—the little girl. She checked out fine, too." He shrugged. "I just can't believe I missed anything. She was mobile, flailing her arms and legs, trying to get to her mom. Her cries were strong, angry and scared, not pained. I just don't get it."

Mel grasped the edges of her chair to keep herself seated. She wanted to move…to do something. His words evoked heart-wrenching pictures in her head. The idea that her little girl had been so hysterical and she hadn't been able to help her.

"On the way to the E.R. your vitals dropped really low," Keller commented as he stared at the uneaten sandwich on his plate. "I was sure we were going to lose you."

Ryan shifted in his seat, drawing Keller's attention back to him. "Does this happen often? This complete reversal of situations? Mel recovered completely and the child, apparently, didn't."

Keller shook his head. "Not often, no. But it's not unheard of. Ms. Jackson," he said to Mel, "that car you were driving took a hell of a beating from that truck. An E.R. doc explained to me once that sometimes the body is so shocked—so traumatized by the impact of an accident—that it tries to shut down. Respiration and BP drop, all functions go into survival mode in an attempt to allow the body to recover from the shock. It's not uncommon for a coma to result, even flat-lining. You were pretty banged up."

The soreness was pretty much gone now, but he was right about that. Those first few days after she'd awakened she'd wondered if her body would ever feel the same again. She'd felt a little like one big bruise, throbbing and aching.

"The kid's situation is a lot less typical," Carson

spoke up. "It's still hard for me to believe that she was hurt that badly."

"Did you mention this to Dr. Wilcox?" Ryan wanted to know.

Carson nodded. "I was so shocked when one of the nurses told me what happened the next day that I tracked Wilcox down and asked him what the hell—pardon my French, ma'am—happened."

"And how did he explain the sudden turn of events?"

"He didn't, not really. He said we'd screwed up, missed the obvious. 'Course, he admitted that he'd missed it, as well. By the time Dr. Letson noted problems it was too late."

"He didn't describe the internal injuries to you?" Ryan asked. Carson shook his head.

This was the part that bothered Ryan the most. What kind of internal injuries? He hadn't wanted to bring up the matter with Wilcox since ultimately it had been Letson's call and he sure as hell didn't want Letson to get any warning. When Ryan asked that question he wanted the man off guard, not prepared with a pat answer from a classic textbook case. In the state of Tennessee, autopsies were only required when the manner of death appeared to be questionable. To Ryan's way of thinking, this was certainly one of those situations. When a patient came into a hospital in stable condition and got carried out in a body bag, questions needed to be asked. The reports claimed that everything had happened too fast to even attempt emergency surgery, but it was all a little too pat.

Ryan kept a close eye on Melany as they exited the deli. However strong she wanted to appear, he could see the utter exhaustion in her every move, every breath.

He suddenly wondered when she'd eaten last. He'd been so absorbed in the details of the case he hadn't thought to ask if she wanted to order something for lunch. It was almost 1:00 p.m. now. She had to be hungry. Then again, he hadn't had the first hunger pain until they'd started to leave. Only then had the rich, pungent aromas gotten past his preoccupation with the answers he'd gotten from the EMTs.

"We should take time to eat," he commented when they reached the car. He opened Mel's door and looked to her for some sort of response.

"You go ahead. I'll wait in the car."

"Look." He detained her when she would have gotten in. Instantly the feel of her arm in his hand sent his every sensory perception on high alert. "I know this is difficult, but you're not going to be of any help to anyone if you don't take care of the essentials. You have to eat. Maybe not here, but somewhere. We can go back to your place if you'd be more comfortable there. I need to touch base with Bill anyway and analyze what we have so far."

"We have nothing," she said bluntly.

He took a moment to come up with a plausible explanation that wouldn't depress her further. "We're hardly twenty-four hours into the investigation, it would be unlikely that we'd have anything just yet. Or have you forgotten how this goes?"

She wouldn't look at him, kept her gaze glued to some place beyond his shoulder. "I haven't forgotten *anything*."

He wondered at that but didn't push it. "Let me take you home. You can eat and get some rest. We'll let you know when we've reached any significant conclusions."

"All right, Braxton," she relented, finally allowing her eyes to meet his. He knew she used his last name for distance. And that was good.

"We'll eat," she went on, "but some place neutral."

There it was. She didn't want him in her home. The home she'd made after leaving him. She'd probably slept with the other guy in that house…in the bed she slept in even now. She'd nurtured her child—the other man's child—there.

He looked away before muttering, "Whatever you want." He released her and skirted the hood. Ryan had never been a glutton for punishment. Why the hell was he putting himself through the punches now?

"Where are we going?" He slid behind the wheel and turned the ignition.

Mel closed her eyes and exhaled the anger that had mushroomed only moments ago. Why did they have to do this?

"There's a diner by the river. The food's good and it's quiet."

When she'd given him the directions he eased out onto the street. For the next fifteen minutes they didn't speak. Not a word. Mel appreciated the silence. She closed her eyes and surrendered to the images and voices. She'd been fighting it all day, but no longer had the strength.

Maybe Ryan was right. Maybe she did need to eat something, anything, and get some rest. She couldn't help Katlin if she didn't keep her energy level up. She was no green recruit fresh off the Farm. This was old hat to her, it was past time she started acting like it. Katlin needed her to be strong.

The rain had started again, just a drizzle. Opening

her eyes wasn't necessary, a slow back and forth swish told her Ryan had turned on the wipers. She could hear Katlin crying out for her…one of those frantic screams for mommy, full of fear, full of desperation for the only thing she knew was safe with a complete certainty at seventeen months old—her mother.

The EMTs had said she'd been wailing at the top of her lungs. It took strength to do that. *She's stable… wait…the woman's going to crash….*

A frown creased her forehead as the voices faded. Did she remember that or was she simply creating the memory based on the EMT's story? But it sounded so real. Was it possible to recall things during an unconscious state? Her body had been shutting down…that was the overall consensus. Too much trauma…too many things going haywire, overreacting. Closing down her body, her senses, had been a survival instinct. Shut down the unnecessary and focus on the essential. Made sense. But could things slip through? Sounds, voices, slices of time? That was the question to which she desperately needed an answer.

The car slowed and Mel opened her eyes. The rain had let up again. The wipers slid down one last time. Ryan parked at the curb only a couple of car lengths from the diner's entrance. It looked overflowing with the lunch crowd but she'd been here a couple of times and had noticed that the tables in the back were scattered far enough apart to give some amount of privacy even with a full house. On the other hand she hadn't been here enough to be readily recognized. She didn't want anyone to ask—anything. She didn't want to hear or see their offerings of sympathy.

By the time she'd unbuckled, Ryan was already at

her door. He waited patiently as she climbed out. Quiet and fully prepared for her to fall apart. Well, she wasn't going to do that. Finding her daughter was too important.

Keeping up the silent vigil, he followed her inside. Mel surveyed the tables in the front, a couple were empty but she asked the waitress to give them something in the back.

"It's smoking, do you mind?" she asked, retrieving her pencil from behind her ear.

"It doesn't matter."

Clad in a freshly starched beige uniform and matching baseball-style cap, the waitress led the way. Only one table was occupied in the farthest reaches of the diner. She now knew the reason for the distance from the rest of the tables. Smoking section. Apparently smoking had grown even less popular of late. Or maybe it was just the first time Mel had noticed. She always asked for non-smoking when she went into a restaurant. For Katlin.

"What can I get you folks to drink?"

"Water," Mel said automatically.

"The same," Ryan echoed. "And two coffees. We can both use some caffeine," he said to Mel.

"Cream? Sugar?" The waitress gave Mel a cursory glance and she shook her head.

Ryan held up a hand. "None for me," he said in that deep, husky voice that sounded a little scratchier than usual. He hadn't slept, either.

Hypocrite, Mel thought dryly. He would rant at her for doing the very same thing he did. But that was Ryan. Do as he said not as he did.

"What do you recommend?" he asked casually as he scanned the menu.

"That you treat me like an equal," she said flatly. When his gaze collided with hers she added, "I know it's difficult for you since you're smarter and stronger than the rest of us, but try, would you?"

Ryan closed the menu and set it carefully aside. What did she want from him? He was here. He was looking into her child's disappearance when every instinct warned him that it would end badly. What else did she want?

"I don't know what you mean." He shouldered out of his coat and let it fall over the back of his chair.

She shook her head and heaved a breath of exasperation. "Of course you don't. You never have."

He reclined fully in his chair and braced his right arm on the back of the chair beside him. "I'm here. I've done everything you've asked, kept you informed and working on the case against my better judgment. What else do you want me to do?" Indignation and something that felt entirely too much like hurt knotted in his empty gut. Hell, he hadn't eaten since sometime yesterday himself. Not good.

Another shake of that pretty blond head. "Just forget it. You're never going to see it." She pushed her fingertips up the bridge of her nose and across her closed lids. "The…ah…" She opened her eyes and picked up the menu. "The burgers are good, cooked the old-fashioned way. I've had the ham and cheese before, it's good, too."

"Who is he?"

The question came out of nowhere. He hadn't meant to ask. She definitely hadn't expected him to judging by her startled expression.

"What?"

She pretended not to understand but, too late, he saw comprehension in her eyes. She knew exactly what he was asking. She knew and she didn't want to talk about it.

"Who did you run to after you left me?" Unbridled fury burst into flames inside him. He had to consciously refrain from slamming the fist his hand had instantly curled into against the table. He wanted the truth. He wanted to shake her…to kiss her and make her admit that it had never been as good with anyone else. He wanted to hear her say she'd made a monumental mistake.

With the blink of an eye she schooled that caught-in-the-web-of-deception expression into one of calm, cool indignation. "That's none of your business. Any more than who you've been involved with since we parted ways is any of mine."

"Oh, yeah," he said, his tone dripping sarcasm. "That's right. When it's over, you move on, right? No looking back." He laughed dryly, the sound scarcely a laugh at all. "I guess I missed that part somewhere along the line when I learned about relationships. I keep trying to figure out how we got to this point."

A haunted look abruptly replaced the indignation. "Don't do this, Ryan," she pleaded with such pain, with such desperation that he flinched. "Don't make this about us…."

He closed his eyes against the devastation in those familiar green eyes. He was an ass. A selfish fool and that had been a low blow. "Sorry," he muttered. "You're right. I—"

"What's it gonna be, folks?"

Saved by the waitress.

He'd almost said more than he intended…more than she needed to know.

Some things were better left buried.

MEL CLOSED AND locked the door before Ryan could ask to come in. He'd wanted to…she'd felt the anticipation in him, the curiosity. But she couldn't be with him right now, not on any level. And she couldn't share her home with him, she'd worked too hard to keep him—even thoughts of him—out of her life.

She sagged against the door and let the emotions overwhelm her. Something had changed at lunch. The tension had moved to a new place…one she feared she was reading wholly wrong.

She couldn't think about that. Pushing off from the door, she forced herself to go through her usual routine. Whenever she came home for the day, she picked up around the house while Katlin played with the toys she'd missed all day at nursery school. Mel glanced at the mound of stuffed animals and colorful shapes in the corner by the television set. She closed her eyes for a second, until she pulled it back together.

Housework had been the farthest concept from her mind these past few days. Rita had come by and done the biggest part of it, but Mel had needed so badly to be alone her friend had steered clear after the second visit. Now was as good a time as any to catch up. She had to do something to keep from going crazy. And she had to call her friend soon. It wasn't fair to Rita to leave her out like this. She'd suffered, too. Mel knew she felt guilty for having borrowed the SUV to move back to Memphis.

Mel shook her head. How did this happen? She and Rita were both smart women. How had they fallen for the wrong men? Rita had finally agreed to marry the man who fathered her child, had even given up her job and schooling here to move to Jackson with him. Only to discover that he was an abusive womanizer. How could she not have seen it before? Moving back had been a tough decision. An admission of failure.

Mel knew all about failure. Though Ryan would never in a million years be abusive or a womanizer, he had his own set of problems and Mel had screwed up just like Rita had.

She couldn't think about this anymore right now. The case. She had to focus on the case. They hadn't learned much today, but it was enough that she recognized elevated anticipation in Ryan in that regard. He wasn't convinced as she was just yet, but suspicions had been raised.

After loading the dishwasher, she ventured into the small laundry room off the kitchen and surveyed the piles of laundry. She sighed and began the task of sorting. Her fingers tangled in the soft fabric of one of Katlin's gowns. The one she'd slept in the night before...

Mel drew the small pink garment to her face and inhaled the sweet essence of her baby. Her eyes closed in a useless attempt to capture the tears that sprang instantly. They slid down her cheeks, leaving a hot, salty trail of helplessness.

How could this have happened? Why hadn't she been more careful? If she'd only seen the truck in time...

A sob hacked at her chest, twisted in her throat, finally erupting from her lips.

"God, please don't let it be true," she murmured. It

couldn't be. She felt her…knew she needed her mommy. It just couldn't be.

The telephone rang.

Clutching the gown to her chest with one hand, Mel scrubbed at her tears with the other. Dammit, she had to keep her emotions in check here. Ryan would be watching for her to slip…to become a liability.

The telephone rang again.

It could be him now…or Bill.

She stumbled past the piles of soiled laundry and hurried to the cordless handset hanging on the wall next to the breakfast bar.

"Hello." She heard the shakiness in her voice and cursed herself for the weakness. She didn't want Ryan or Bill to hear her vulnerability.

"Ms. Jackson?"

Female…hesitant.

"Yes." Mel struggled to place the voice. She'd heard it before.

"This is Helen Peterson."

The nurse.

Mel froze…afraid to move, to even think. "Yes."

"I need to see you…just you."

Her voice sounded strange…strained almost beyond recognition.

"Is this about my daughter?" Mel tried not to allow it, but her heart kicked into high gear as new hope soared.

"Yes."

The one word was like a gift straight from God. She clutched the phone in both hands. "Please." A sob choked out. She tried to hold it back…she tried so hard. "Just tell me where she is. I know she's alive. Do you hear me?" She swallowed at the choking sensation, tried to pull herself together, but now that the emotions had been unleashed, she simply couldn't. "I know she's alive."

"I… I can't talk now. But when I saw you today… I knew I couldn't keep this to myself any longer."

Mel tensed. "You have to tell me. Please!" Stay calm, she railed silently. Don't scare her off!

"Meet me tomorrow," she urged, her tone furtive. "At the River Walk. Around noon. I'll watch for you."

"Please, just tell me if she's all right," Mel cried, afraid she would hang up.

"I promise I'll tell you everything tomorrow." Silence. "I'm so sorry this happened, Ms. Jackson. It was a mistake. It went too far.…"

"I don't understand—"

A definitive *click* cut off the rest of her words, told her the nurse had hung up.

Mel stared at the telephone for three endless beats, her thoughts whirling with all the possibilities. Then a glimmer of rationale kicked in.

She had to find Ryan.

CHAPTER EIGHT

RYAN RIFLED THROUGH the statements once more. There had been four eyewitnesses to the accident. All four had said the same thing: the delivery truck failed to yield at the traffic signal.

He reached for the new file Bill had given him. Accident scene photos. He winced when he looked at the shots of the car Mel had been driving. But he'd needed to see. A small compact, foreign model, two door hatchback. If there had been a passenger in the front seat, he or she would not have walked away. The truck hit the front fender and passenger side door, caving in the entire area. He shuddered at the prospect of what could have happened.

Sorting through the rest of the pages he found Dr. Wilcox and Nurse Peterson's statements. Short, direct and to the point. The statements relayed the same information the two had conveyed to him today. Dr. Letson's statement read much the same way.

But Ryan knew that Wilcox and Peterson were hiding something. He could feel it in his gut. Subtle mannerisms gave them away. That was the reason he'd followed up on their initial statements to Bill. He'd needed to see their eyes, hear their voices…watch them closely. Bill had noted the same evasiveness, but Ryan had needed to see it for himself.

He shoved the mass of papers away and pushed up from the desk. It was time he got out of here. He surveyed the office M.P.D. had lent them. Bill had headed out already. He wanted to keep an eye on the funeral home director, Clyde Desmond, from Forest Lawn. Ryan supposed it was possible the man wasn't involved, but he doubted it. Bill was damn good at reading people.

The only question was, were they covering up some sort of medical wrongdoing or was the child still alive for some other purpose? The doctors and nurses at Memphis General would certainly want to conceal any negligence. Obviously there were staffing problems or mere human error if the case was isolated, considering Mel's misdiagnosis. The funeral home director could be in on it from that perspective. He may have destroyed the body for the hospital and decided not to waste money on a vault and proper burial. Garland Hanes was likely the scapegoat. Bill already had Memphis P.D. looking into the possibility of the funeral home director's involvement in Hanes's murder.

Ryan gathered his files and shoved them into a briefcase. The handgun he'd opted to bring along on this trip gave him pause. He hadn't carried a weapon since he left the Bureau. But, he'd decided to play it safe rather than sorry when he came to Memphis. He passed a hand over his face. He was tired and on the verge of actually being hungry. As was par for the course with him and investigations, he wasn't in the mood to mingle with the human race, so he would order room service tonight. Hell, he'd lived on the stuff half the time in his Bureau days.

Unbelievably, it had stopped raining yet again. It had done nothing but rain off and on since he'd arrived in the River City. The weather matched his mood. As he left the Downtown Precinct, he found himself wondering again if things could have been different between him and Melany. He told himself not to go there, but the voice of reason failed to stop him—as usual.

He tried distracting himself with the river view of the mighty Mississippi. He drove down Beale Street, the Bourbon Street of Memphis. There was always Graceland if he really wanted to push the envelope. He could pick up a post card for Mildred.

Braking for the traffic light that went from yellow to red before he could pass under it, his thoughts went back to Mel with scarcely a smidgen of resistance. He should call…just to see if she was all right. But she'd only resent his asking. Just like she'd gotten angry when he'd asked about the other guy. That, he had to admit, had been a damn fool thing to do.

She didn't owe him any explanations.

He eased off the brake and pressed down on the accelerator. He didn't know what difference it made. The guy was obviously out of the picture now, anyway. And what difference did that make? He wasn't here to pursue their old relationship. But some genetic defect in his DNA had allowed him to wonder if she would want him…if she were still attracted to him.

She wanted nothing to do with him. Hadn't even wanted his help on this case, not really. But she knew he'd find her an answer, so she'd given in. He hadn't actually expected her to go all starry eyed when she saw him again…he didn't know what he'd expected. Certainly she had her child on her mind…and not much else. But he couldn't help wondering. Then, maybe, he considered, she was still in love with the other guy.

Ryan cut the wheel a little too sharply, making the tires squeal as he barreled into the parking lot of his motel. Why the hell was he playing this game? This wasn't about them. Just like she said…it couldn't be about them. It had to be about the child.

He hesitated a moment before climbing out of his car. He dragged the picture from his jacket pocket and looked at it for the hundredth time. The little girl looked so much like her mother. Same silky blond hair and vibrant green eyes. A frown driven by empathy nagged his forehead. The horror Mel must have suffered the moment she awoke from that coma. The realization that her child wasn't safe in some room in the same hospital.

The horrible news that she was not only dead, but already buried. And then the dreams. Bill had told him about her dreams. She'd dreamed of the child, dreamed so vividly, claimed to have heard her voice, that she'd ended up in that cemetery attempting to find the truth on her own when no one else would listen.

He should have been there for her…she should never have had to go through that alone.

Here he sat, only a few miles away, selfishly holding back that part of himself just like before. He'd never given her everything there was to give. She'd needed more and he hadn't even offered it to her.

Ryan tugged out his cell phone and started to punch in Mel's number, but changed his mind. He swore. Maybe he'd call her from his room.

Ryan emerged from the car, retrieved his briefcase from the back seat and strode across the well-lit parking lot. His room was on the ground floor with a view of the pool.

He nodded to the front desk clerk as he passed

through the lobby on his way to the inner courtyard. Dammit. He'd forgotten his trench coat. It would be his luck it would be raining tomorrow morning. He exhaled a disgusted breath. Forget it. He wasn't going back for it.

Halfway across the meticulously landscaped courtyard he stalled, squinted to see in the low lighting who waited in front of his door.

Mel.

He jerked back into motion, quickening his pace. A half dozen scenarios explaining her presence ticked off in his head, from her belatedly realized need for the comfort of his arms to a break in the case. As soon as she looked up, her watery gaze connected with his and he had his answer. She'd learned something new…had remembered something relevant….

"Ryan, where the hell have you been?" she demanded in a rush when he got within range without her having to yell across the courtyard. "I've been trying to call you on your cell phone."

"I've been at the precinct. Service is hit or miss in there." He pulled out his keycard, but waited for her to fill him in before bothering to go inside. There was just as good a chance that they'd have to head back to the precinct or the hospital.

"She called me." Her hands knotted in front of her and her eyes wide, anxious, she stared helplessly up at him.

Ryan slipped the card into the lock and opened the door. "Come inside."

The hesitation lasted about two seconds.

"Who called you?" He tossed his briefcase onto the desk in the room and turned to face her.

Clearly grappling for calm she took a breath and pushed the door closed behind her. "Helen Peterson."

Now she had his attention. "The nurse called you?"

Mel nodded. "She wants to meet with me tomorrow. She says she'll explain everything then. When I couldn't reach you by phone I decided I couldn't wait until morning so I drove by her house."

Ryan didn't like this. "Mel, that was not a smart move. It could have been some sort of setup."

She held up both hands in defense of herself. "I know it wasn't but I had to know now…tonight."

He pocketed his hands and strode a couple of steps closer to her. "What did she tell you?"

Mel sighed wearily. "She wasn't home. The house was dark. I called the hospital and she's not scheduled for duty tonight. I waited for a while then I tried to call you again." She glanced around his room as if only now realizing where she was. "Then I came over."

"Have a seat." He indicated a chair near the window. "I was going to call room service."

She shook her head. "I'm not hungry. I want to go wait outside her house for her to come home."

"Mel, slow down." He moved to the other chair and settled into it. "Sit. I need to know exactly what she said to you."

Knowing she would get nowhere once he made up his mind, Mel sat down in the chair adjacent to Ryan. The small side table that separated them wasn't nearly enough of a barrier…but it would have to do. She needed him right now…had to take the risk.

"She said she had to talk to me…just me." Mel mentally recounted the conversation before continuing. "When I asked her if it was about my daughter, she said yes. I kind of lost it for a moment at that point, but she seemed to understand. She kept saying she was sorry. That it was a mistake and that she'd tell me everything tomorrow."

Ryan looked thoughtful for a moment. She watched the familiar contours of his handsome face tense. "Did she give you any indication that Katlin was alive?"

Mel wet her lips then chewed the lower one for courage. "I begged her to tell me if she was all right, but she wouldn't say. She just kept saying it was a mistake." She swiped at another confounded tear that escaped her fierce hold on her emotions.

"Why did she call?" Ryan scrubbed a hand over his stubbled chin. The sound sent an unexpected shiver through Mel. She shook off the sensation and told herself to focus. She was tired, that's all.

"She said that when she saw me today that she knew she couldn't keep it to herself any longer."

Sounded like the woman was ready to confess to whatever wrongdoing she had witnessed…or perhaps participated in. Ryan raked his fingers through his hair. Damn, he was suddenly completely exhausted. He settled his gaze on Mel, saw the hope, the desperation there. He did not want to play devil's advocate here. But he didn't have much choice. She had to consider both sides of this.

"Mel, she didn't actually give you any indication of the child's condition. This could be the break in the case we've hoped for, but it may not be the answer you want to hear."

She shot to her feet. "Dammit, Braxton, don't you get it?" She flung her arms outward and glared at him. "I know that. I'm not that dense. I'm fully aware that with the length of time my daughter has been missing, not to mention the fact that the entire medical staff at Memphis General considered her dead days ago, the odds are against me. But I have to know." Her bottom lip quivered and something inside him twisted painfully. "I have to know for sure. I can't just leave it like this."

He got up without taking his eyes off hers. "I'm not asking you to leave it like this, Mel. I'm warning you not to go into this with blinders on. You want your daughter back, there's a big chance that isn't going to happen. But there are discrepancies. Foul play of some sort and we're damn sure going to find out what the hell happened."

The quiver in her lip seemed to spread until her whole body shook with a fine tremor. "Come with me, Ryan. I need to talk to her the moment she comes home. Please... I can't wait until noon tomorrow."

He knew he shouldn't do this. It was likely a big mistake not to mention a colossal waste of time. But he had the time to waste if it made her happy. Who needed sleep?

"All right." He looked around his room as if trying to decide what to do next. "Grab a pillow," he told her. When she stared at him in confusion he said, "You're going to get some sleep."

Apparently too thankful for his cooperation to argue, she grabbed the pillow and hugged it to her chest. "Ready?"

He shrugged. What the hell? "Sure. We'll have to get some coffee on the way, though."

She thought about that and then tossed the pillow back on the bed. "In that case I'd better use your..." She pointed to the bathroom door. "Before I go."

"Good idea."

Mel closed the bathroom door and braced her forehead against it long enough to gather her wits. She thanked God again for the nurse's change of heart and, then, she thanked him for Ryan. She did need him... even if she hadn't wanted to admit it in the beginning. She needed him. He knew how to work this kind of case like no one else alive.

Summoning her resolve as well as her waning strength, she unbuttoned her slacks, shimmied them down and settled on the toilet seat. While nature took its course, she studied the toiletries that belonged to the man waiting in the other room. The same subtle aftershave he'd worn two years ago...the same brand of razor. She smiled. He'd forgotten to use it this morning. She couldn't remember him ever forgetting anything. He was always cool and suave, meticulously dressed. But not today. Today he'd been a little off his game.

She wondered about that. She rubbed her eyes and told herself it had nothing to do with her. Maybe he was just tired. Then again, she hadn't seen him in two years. A lot of things could have changed in two years.

When she'd finished, she flushed the toilet and washed her hands, and took some time to study her reflection in the mirror. She looked like hell, but didn't care. Nothing really mattered to her right now...except finding Katlin. She did wonder, foolishly so, what Ryan saw when he looked at her now? She laughed at herself and turned away. That was the least of her worries at the moment.

Shoving her hair behind her ear, she opened the door and faced the man she needed so very much right now.

The one she couldn't tell the whole truth…even when he'd asked, point-blank, today.

"I should do the same," he said and gestured to the room she'd just vacated.

She nodded and thought of all the coffee it would take to get them through the night. Thankfully she'd noted an all-night convenience store in the neighborhood less than two blocks from Helen Peterson's house. It might just come in handy if the woman was late coming home. Mel wondered again where she would be if not at work. Visiting friends or relatives, she supposed. Or with Katlin.

Mel closed her eyes, told herself not to do this…not to get her hopes so high. *Please, God, let this be good news,* she prayed. She just didn't think she could bear any more bad.

"Ready?"

She looked up and found Ryan watching her. She nodded quickly. He could always do that to her…sneak up on her like that. But then, she'd been lost in the tidal wave of agony attempting to wear down her defenses.

It took less than twenty minutes to make the trip back to Helen Peterson's house. Ryan insisted on taking his car, which was just as well. Someone involved in all this insanity might recognize her SUV. The pink angel hanging from the rearview mirror made her vehicle hard to forget. Becoming a mother had softened her that way. Forced her to consider what was really important.

He parked across the street. Since there were several other cars parked along the curb, it didn't seem necessary to fall back half a block. The dark sedan blended in well with the others. If Mel leaned to the right and squinted, she could see the lights of the convenience store down the street and just beyond the slight curve.

She sipped the coffee Ryan had picked up at an all night drive-thru. The bitter brew definitely kicked any thoughts of sleep right out of her head. She shuddered and took another. It was going to be a long night if Helen Peterson had decided to bunk somewhere else. And, if she was afraid for her own safety, she just might hide out.

Mel replayed the conversation over and over as the minutes ticked off, turned into an hour. Any way she played it, she had reason to hope. If Katlin were dead why would it matter to Helen whether Mel learned the truth or not? What would it accomplish?

Wishful thinking, Mel knew. She wanted to read the best in the scenario. What mother wouldn't? She'd worked these sorts of cases herself dozens of times in her Bureau days. No one ever wanted to believe the worst until there was no other alternative. The woman might simply want to relieve her conscience.

Mel set her foam cup in the holder and relaxed into the seat. She closed her eyes to prevent them from straying to the man sitting behind the wheel. That damnable scent that was uniquely his, a mixture of man and the remnants of aftershave, was driving her crazy.

He'd always smelled so good. Like pure heat and rock-solid strength. She remembered those powerful hands...capable of showing such tenderness....

Don't go there, girl.

It was a dead-end street. A one-way ticket to regret and heartache. No place she needed to go. Even to distract herself from the perpetual hurt of needing to hold her child. She folded her arms over her middle and hugged herself. All she wanted was her baby back. Despite her best efforts, her eyes opened and she stole a sidelong glance at Ryan.

He didn't suspect a thing.

Oh, she was sure he'd considered the idea, but he'd known she was on the Pill. Apparently he hadn't looked at Katlin's birth date. If he had, he would have known that she was his daughter.

The Pill had failed.

That had been the beginning of the end.

She'd been thrilled and at the same time scared to death. She'd known better than anyone how the unmovable Ryan Braxton had felt about children. He did not want any offspring, no exceptions.

Too late, she'd wanted to tell him.

Ironically he'd asked her to marry him that same week. She'd used that opportunity to push him about the issue. He'd given her an uncompromising no. Absolutely not. There would be no children in his future. He'd seen too much, wouldn't take the risk.

So she'd done the only thing she could, she'd walked away.

From him…from the Bureau. Everything.

She wanted this child. Wanted him, desperately. But she would not choose him over their child. If she'd told him that she was pregnant and he'd went off the deep end and asked her to terminate the pregnancy, she could never have forgiven him. If he truly was that heartless she didn't want to know. Not then, not now.

As much as she longed to tell him, to share the joy as well as the weight. She would not. Could not.

"You know, I was just thinking," he said suddenly, startling her with the deep, resonant sound of his voice after more than an hour of silence. "Some of your things are still…there. At my place."

She turned her head to look at him. "Really?" She couldn't remember leaving anything, but then she'd been more than a little upset when she'd left.

He nodded once then turned to look at her. "I opened one of the boxes a few weeks ago." He made a sound like a laugh only softer, more like a sigh. "I was looking for…" He shrugged. "I don't know what. But I opened that box and I smelled your perfume…*you*." He stared straight ahead then and lowered his voice to a whisper. "It took my breath away. Even after all this time."

He didn't say more and neither did she.

There was too much that needed to be said and neither of them had the courage to go there just now.

Maybe they never would.

CHAPTER NINE

She could hear her baby crying...calling for her...but she couldn't find her no matter how hard she looked. It was so dark. The air felt thick...too thick to breathe. She pushed through the darkness, feeling her way since she couldn't see. But the cries faded away into nothingness.

"No!" Melany cried. She couldn't find her in the dark without some sort of guide. "No! Please!"

Another voice echoed through the murky blackness... Ryan's voice. He was calling to her....

"Mel! Wake up. It's only a dream."

Her eyes flew open. She looked straight into the worried blue eyes of the only man she'd ever loved.

In the gray predawn light she could see the worry etched across the landscape of his face, could feel the tension in his strong fingers where they clamped around her arms.

"It's okay, baby, it's okay. It was just a dream," he murmured.

His face was so close to hers. He'd moved into the middle of the car seat, or maybe she had. Somehow he was holding her. Watching her.

"I...couldn't find her...." Katlin. She couldn't find her baby. And in a single fraction of an instant it all came rushing back to her. Every harrowing moment...

Her head fell against the seat and she let the tears

flow…didn't bother trying to stop them. Sweet Jesus…
where was her baby?

Ryan pulled her to his chest. Closed those warm,
powerful and comfortingly familiar arms around her.
Words weren't necessary. What could he say? What
could anyone say? Nothing. Her child was missing. The
whole world thought she was dead, the police, the doctors, the nurses…everyone but her.

And maybe Bill and Ryan.

…the nurse.

As good as it felt to be in his arms, she pushed him
away. "Did she come home?" God, how long had she
been asleep? Mel glanced at the clock on the dash—5:30
a.m. She'd slept practically the whole night through and
without a tranquilizer. She hadn't had this much unin-
terrupted sleep since this whole nightmare began. If the
dream hadn't intruded…how long would she have slept?

Better yet, how, without the aid of something to dull
her senses, had she managed it now?

Him. Her gaze tangled with the man still watching
her every move. It was because of him. She knew she
was safe with Ryan. He would take care of everything.
She scrutinized that handsome face more closely and
realized that, unlike her, he hadn't gotten any sleep at
all. He'd done that for her.

"Is she back?" she urged, needing desperately to
know.

A slight shake of his head gave her the answer she
didn't want.

"She never came home, but I'm not surprised." He
eased back behind the wheel, putting some distance
between them and leaving an emptiness that ached
through her. "She's running scared. If whoever she's

in this with suspects she plans to tell you what really happened, she could be in serious danger."

She thought about Garland Hanes. Someone involved in all this had certainly put an end to his life. Then again, his murder could have nothing to do with Katlin. But she didn't believe that for a second. This was all tied together, somehow. In a neat little package, only things were beginning to unravel one piece at a time.

The hope Helen Peterson's call had engendered in Mel might also have something to do with her good night's sleep, but she had a feeling that it was more likely the man at her side.

She glanced at Ryan again and wished she could read his mind. Wished she could risk telling him the truth. But the last thing she wanted was him involved in their lives out of obligation. Maybe she wasn't being fair to him, or to Katlin, but, right now, she simply wasn't willing to wager on it. His admission about opening a box of her things told her that he still felt something for her…but it would never be enough.

For now, she would keep her secret. The chance that the news would cause his attention to splinter was too great. He needed all of his focus right now. And so did she.

IF SHE LOOKED at him like that once more he'd be tempted to pull her back into his arms again. Ryan exhaled a heavy breath. He'd been closed up in this car all night with nothing but the sight of her—the scent of her—to keep him company. The coffee had kept him awake. That and a couple of brisk walks up and down the block. He felt immensely lucky that no one had awakened, seen a stranger on the street and called the cops.

He was even more thankful that his quick trip into the thick copse of trees at the end of the block hadn't garnered him an indecent exposure charge. He'd managed that feat without getting spotted by an insomniac resident or a neighborhood dog.

"Did you happen to ask if Nurse Peterson would be on duty today when you called the hospital?" he inquired, deciding a change of subject was definitely in order.

"She's not on duty again until three this afternoon," Mel told him wearily.

She'd slept well until the end. Ryan had kept a close eye on her the whole time. But the exhaustion she felt right now was an accumulation of a whole week's worth of sleeplessness and worry. Pepper that with disappointment that she would have to wait until noon to learn whatever the nurse had decided to tell her and weariness was the least one could expect.

"If she's not here by now, she's not coming. I should take you home. I'll need to get back to the hotel to shower and change." He rubbed a hand over his jaw. "And I definitely need a shave."

Mel's attention remained riveted to the house that had stayed dark all through the night. "I hadn't considered it until now," she said distractedly, "but she might hire out as a private nurse on the nights she's not on duty at the hospital. That could explain why she hasn't come home."

Ryan followed her gaze. "That's possible." It was also possible, he didn't add, that the nurse had gone into hiding…or that someone had shut her up already. Mel didn't need to hear that just now.

She sighed then. "You know, I'm fully aware it's

considered breaking and entering, but for a little bit I'd go in there and see what I could find."

"And render whatever you discovered inadmissible as evidence," he chastised. "Don't even think about it." He wouldn't mention that he'd thought about it himself a couple of times as he'd consumed three cups of coffee, alternately sat and walked his way through the night.

"It was just a thought."

Respect prompted a smile. How many women could sit here and be this strong after all that she'd been through? Only a very few.

"My car is at your hotel," she said thoughtfully.

"I'll drop you off at your place and come back for you in your SUV. That okay?" He started the engine and eased away from the curb.

"Sounds okay. I'm probably not safe behind the wheel right now, anyway."

She didn't have to spell it out. Her thoughts were fragmented, disjointed. How could she be expected to think under the circumstances?

They made the trip to Mel's house in a comfortable silence. He thought about last night's admission of how he'd opened that box and inhaled her essence. It had taken his breath, and still did, now. But he wouldn't tell her that part. He'd already admitted more than he'd intended to. The sweet fragrance that was mostly her and the vaguest hint of her perfume had tantalized him all night long. Even when he'd breathed in lungfuls of night air as he walked off the sensations she wrought in him. He had watched her sleep and thought about all those times before when he'd come home late and found her asleep on the sofa. He had watched her, amazed that such a wonderful woman could love him…in spite of his numerous faults.

But even a love that strong had worn thin.

Ryan put the brakes on his stroll down memory lane, as well as the car's forward motion, and pulled into her drive. He would walk her to the door and then get the hell out of here. He needed some real distance to clear his head. A time-out to pull it back together.

"You don't have to walk me in," she protested when he reached for the door handle.

He just looked at her and opened his door, anyway. She knew better than to suggest anything different.

At her door she gave him the keys to her SUV and said a hasty goodbye. He would pick her up at ten and they would rendezvous with Bill at the precinct.

He made a quick mental checklist of the things he wanted to accomplish today, including interviewing Dr. Letson. Running down a more detailed background profile on Wilcox and Letson was also at the top of the list. Whatever this thing was, it started with those two doctors.

If either of them had harmed Melany's child, there would be no place on earth safe they could hide from Ryan.

At ten o'clock Ryan picked up Mel at her home. Navy slacks and a paler blue sweater fit her trim figure like a glove, making his mouth water and his throat dry. Damn but she still looked good. To his irritation, she met him at the door and hurried outside, making sure there was no reason for him to come inside. It shouldn't, but it bothered him all the same. Were there pictures of the other guy placed strategically around that she didn't want him to see?

He blew out a disgusted breath and pushed the whole idea away. It didn't matter. A hot shower and a much-needed shave had given him a new perspective. Though he was going on fifty hours with no sleep at this point, he felt marginally human.

The Downtown Precinct buzzed with activity. Several detectives acknowledged his and Mel's journey into their sacred territory. Ryan was continually amazed at how little resentment he'd encountered. Then again, he imagined that they were so damn glad not to have this case that they wouldn't consider acting any other way.

Bill was already in the command center when they arrived. He'd added numerous details to the time line on the board, reflecting the activities of all involved from the time the accident occurred.

He growled a good morning. Mel smiled. "Same to you, bulldog." She'd always called him that when he started off the day snarling.

Bill chuckled and the whole scene reminded Ryan of days past. "Let's go over what we've got," Ryan suggested as he pulled out a chair.

Mel took a seat opposite him and Bill chose to stand so that he could point out milestones on the time line.

"The accident occurs," Bill began, "and the paramedics arrive on the scene." He pointed to the representative marks he'd scratched on the whiteboard. "They head to the hospital where Mel is treated as a code red and Katlin is pronounced stable and ushered off to the pediatric ward for observation until next of kin can be located. At that point—" Bill parked a hand on his hip and faced his captive audience "—the child is out of

Wilcox's hands and into Letson's. Who, by the way, called in sick today. He's not at home, either."

"Mel is run through the drill to see what can be done to save her," Ryan picked up where he'd left off. "Wilcox eventually turns her case over to a specialist."

"We know a number of things about the three doctors involved," Bill continued. "All are in good standing, professionally. In fact, both Wilcox and Letson are big supporters of community projects. Wilcox, in particular. He isn't married and has no family commitments so he spends all his spare time in a free clinic on the north side."

Mel nodded thoughtfully. "I think I remember one of the nurses telling someone that he'd have to catch Dr. Wilcox at the free clinic." But she couldn't see how his community service was relevant. Though she imagined that Bill would get to that. He liked to tell a story from the beginning, not leaving out any of the facts or jumping around too much.

"At this point I can't see how any of the three would have benefited from this scam—if it is one—" Ryan qualified. "It doesn't make sense. What was the point? Unless they're covering up some medical misstep by one or all three."

Bill tapped his chin and paced back and forth in front of the timeline. "I've reviewed the medical files our boy Carter picked up from the hospital and everything looks in order. Just like the death certificate."

Mel remembered that Officer Greg Carter was the rookie Bill had borrowed from M.P.D.

"I even faxed them up to Cuddahy at Quantico. You know he started out in med school before deciding he wanted to go into criminology."

Mel hadn't known that about Cuddahy. He was just another of the brainiac blue suits who worked in the bowels of Quantico. "What was his take on the reports?"

"All the *i's* dotted and the *t's* crossed. Logical reasoning for every step as well as documented tests and screenings. Nothing he could point to as being out of order."

"Yet something obviously is," Ryan countered. "Let's keep trying to track down Letson. Meanwhile what about the funeral home director?"

"Clyde Desmond is as clean as a whistle," Bill said with a smooth swipe of his hand through the air. "We don't have as much as a speck of fly shit on any of these guys' records."

"But the nurse is on the breaking point," Ryan reminded. He'd told Mel that he'd filled Bill in when they talked earlier.

Bill nodded. "She may be our only ace in the hole."

Mel said another quick prayer that Helen Peterson would verify that Katlin was alive. She had to be. Mel would not think otherwise.

"All right," Ryan said, drawing their attention to him. "In my experience when things look this clean, this cut-and-dried, it's time to look more closely at other possibilities. Maybe Letson and Wilcox are squeaky clean. Desmond, too, for that matter. But we need to find a connection between them. If we find the common link, we'll find the dirt. Individually these guys can't be touched, have no visible flaws. But are there other cases where their paths crossed, their professional conclusions coalesced into something questionable?"

"What are their finances like?" Mel piped in, her

senses humming with that old familiar anticipation. Ryan was on to something here. "Are any of the three living above their means?" They'd all pretty much ruled out the neurosurgeon's participation as nothing more than incompetence. He'd never been involved with Katlin's case. He hadn't even remembered Mel's name when he'd been questioned by Bill.

"Now we're cooking with gas," Bill said with a wide grin. "I'll get Cuddahy to delve into the financial aspect of our three primary suspects. He can reach out and touch that spot better than any of us. My last federal warrant got me on a first-name basis with the hospital administrator. I'm sure he'll be happy to give me a look at hospital records without the due process."

Mel smiled. Bill was one of a kind. Only he could put a spin on a situation like that. He had the smoke and mirrors act down to a science. Ryan on the other hand went straight for the jugular with no foreplay.

"Mel and I will look into Wilcox's extracurricular activities starting with that clinic on the north side."

Surprised that he had willingly paired them together again, Mel looked over at Ryan.

"Unless," he amended, "you have a problem with that."

She shrugged. "No problem." As long as she was involved with something constructive, she was game. She suppressed the little shiver that danced over her flesh when she thought of waking up with Ryan holding her...and then when he'd put his arms fully around her. She shook off the memories. This was not the time.

Their time had passed already. She had to remember that.

Ryan glanced at his watch. "We'll head to the River

Walk now and wait out our nurse. I need to scope out a position where I can watch without being seen." He rose and gathered his briefcase and the notes Bill had provided. "I'll give you a heads up after the meet," he told Bill.

Mel got to her feet and rounded the table to stand beside Ryan at the door. Her heart rate accelerated at the prospect of learning the truth. Whatever it was, it had to be better than not knowing.

THEY WAITED UNTIL almost two o'clock and Helen Peterson didn't show.

Ryan could feel the disappointment and anxiety welling inside Mel with each passing minute. Dammit, where the hell was the woman? His gut told him she wasn't coming. She'd either backed out or someone had taken her out. Either way, she wasn't coming. He'd joined Mel about twenty minutes ago, seeing no point in staying out of sight since the woman was a no-show.

"Mel, I think it's time to go."

She surveyed the thin crowd walking along the mock-up of the lower Mississippi River. It was a one-of-a-kind exhibit, probably fascinating. But they had other things on their minds.

"I guess so." Mel shook her head. "I don't understand. Maybe I scared her off." She shrugged listlessly. "I did get a little hysterical during the call."

"Maybe she'll call again," he offered, knowing full well that the odds were against it. Every instinct warned that she was out of the picture entirely.

"Maybe."

After swinging through a fast-food drive-thru, they

headed to the clinic where Dr. Wilcox volunteered a great deal of his free time.

Row after row of rundown housing and dilapidated shops flanked the narrow streets of the crime-infested neighborhood. Other than a few stray dogs, the littered North Memphis apartment complex they encountered next looked mostly deserted. Ryan found it hard to comprehend how the brick buildings, all suspended in varying stages of extreme disrepair, had escaped the wrecking ball. It was harder still to imagine people living in them.

He had no trouble assuming that the residents would be very thankful for the clinic's presence. He hadn't seen the first sign of any other medical facilities. He parked Mel's SUV at the curb in front of the fairly well-maintained building. The pink angel hanging from her rearview mirror swung side to side, drawing his attention in spite of his determination to ignore it. The Mel he used to know wouldn't have bothered with angels. She'd seen too many monsters just like he had to put much stock in winged creatures who supposedly watched over the innocent.

That had been before, he told himself. The faith she appeared to have now in a higher power reminded him that Mel had a daughter, one that was missing, one that connected her to another man.

Focus, he ordered himself, directing his attention back to the clinic. The parking lot was filled to capacity with a range of vehicles from the proverbial rattletraps to the higher-end sports cars and SUVs. Priorities, he ruminated. Some people cared about nothing else except image as they cruised down the block.

When they reached the lobby, it offered standing

room only. Ryan took a look around and decided that he would have better luck trying to get in alone.

"Why don't you wait here and let me see what I can find out," he suggested quietly. When she would have protested, he added, "If we approach the receptionist together she's going to figure we're either prospective patients or pissed-

off parents." He counted at least a dozen teenagers, all female, all clearly pregnant. Chances were that the rest, those who didn't look with child, were either here to try and find out if the period they'd missed meant bad news or to get something to prevent that very scenario. But then, he was a bit cynical.

"Okay," Mel relented.

Ryan gave her arm a little squeeze before moving away. If he wasn't careful, he was going to keep pushing the issue until he had no choice but to act on the impulses pounding away at his brain. He wanted to do more than touch her....

That line of thinking was off limits at the moment.

Probably forever.

He produced a wide smile for the harried receptionist. When she blinked and then returned his smile, he flashed his credentials. "I'm Ryan Braxton, special advisor to the FBI." He'd already tossed that deception around a time or two since starting this case, but then, Bill had given him carte blanche. "I'd like to see the person in charge."

The receptionist, Carol Ann Henley, looked startled but quickly recovered. "None of the doctors or nurses are on duty today," she said stiffly. "But the counselor is here." She looked relieved to have come up with that sacrificial offering.

Ryan surveyed the waiting room, taking note of Mel's position. Someone had vacated a chair and she'd taken up the space.

"These people are all here to see the counselor?" He let his disbelief show.

Carol Ann nodded. "They're required to submit to counseling as a condition of treatment."

"I'll need to see the counselor, then," he told her. He wasn't about to waste the trip. The counselor could be informative, as well.

Carol Ann stood, a strained smile plastered into place. "Let me see if she's about through with the patient she's seeing now."

Ryan was thankful that it appeared she intended to work him in between patients. Otherwise he might be here until midnight. He glanced across the room once more. Most of these girls looked high-school age. Where were their parents? he couldn't help wondering. A couple were accompanied by what appeared to be boyfriends. Poor kids just didn't know what they were getting into. His gaze sought out Melany at the thought. Had she known what she was getting into?

"Mr. Braxton, Dr. Rodale will see you now."

Ryan thanked the receptionist and headed in the direction she'd indicated. As he reached the first door in the long corridor that lay beyond the waiting room a young girl, fifteen maybe, stepped out.

He offered her a perfunctory smile but she hurried past as if embarrassed at being caught on the premises. She didn't look pregnant, but then, she could be only a few weeks.

"Mr. Braxton?"

A woman, forty maybe, waited in the open doorway

now. She managed a smile that was about as heartfelt as his own. "How can I help you?" she asked.

"I have some questions about the service you're providing here," he told her, not beating around the bush.

She nodded once. "Come into my office and I'll tell you what I can."

After she'd settled behind her inexpensive metal desk, Ryan dropped into one of the molded plastic chairs in front of it. There was nothing lavish about the lobby or this office, basic functionality. Nothing more. Cost-cutting measures, he assumed.

"So, tell me what you'd like to know. I'm not the person in charge by any means, but I've worked here for three years. I'm pretty informed."

Open, forthcoming. Good. She might not be in charge on paper, but she was confident in her position. Not afraid to speak to the authorities on sensitive issues. "I'm interested in Dr. Wilcox. I understand that he's a major contributor, timewise as well as financially."

She folded her hands on the desk. "That's true. Without generous souls like him we wouldn't be able to do what we do here. We provide a very important service to this neighborhood."

Ryan pulled out his trusty pad and pen and flipped to a page free of doodles. "What is it exactly that you do here?"

"We provide general medical care to female patients and we provide counseling for teens, especially in the area of teen pregnancy. As you must have noticed they start out pretty young. We offer birth control and adoption counseling. Of course, if the patient wants to keep the child and has some support network we prefer that route."

Adoption. An alarm went off in his brain. "You provide adoption services?" He looked around the room. If they did, it had to be for free, and that didn't quite mesh with the high demand versus the low supply of newborns. It was big business. But it wasn't outside the realm of possibility, he supposed, that *generous souls* might not be interested in the money. The idea merely surprised him. In Wilcox's case, it damn well shocked him.

"No, we don't actually provide the service," she clarified pointedly. "We simply offer counseling." She reclined in her chair and considered her words carefully before proceeding. "The idea is a bit frightening for most of the girls. We explain the steps and suggest a number of excellent agencies in the area."

His investigator's radar was on high alert. "So you don't actually see to the adoptions here. Dr. Wilcox would have nothing to do with the proceedings."

"Absolutely not," she said succinctly. "That's my territory."

And she'd said she wasn't in charge.

Ryan smiled. "Tell me more about *your* territory."

MELANY LOST COUNT of the times she'd looked at the clock. It had only been twenty minutes, but still she was antsy. She'd forwarded her home number to her cell phone and prayed Helen Peterson would call. She needed to hear from her. She could feel her fingers slipping, her grip on her emotions tenuous at best. She needed something to hang on to.

Something besides Ryan.

But what if Helen was gone or dead?

"You pregnant, too?"

Mel jerked from her troubling thoughts and managed a half hearted smile for the young girl sitting next to her. "No. But I do have a two-year-old daughter."

The girl's big brown eyes looked uncertain, a little worried. "My mom and dad just want me to get rid of her."

Her? "Your baby is a girl?" She glanced at the girl's protruding belly and smiled. Remembered her own pregnancy and her sweet, sweet baby girl. She swallowed back the paralyzing emotions. Had to keep it together. "That's great. Have you picked out a name yet?"

The girl looked away and Mel realized her mistake. She'd just said that her parents didn't want her to keep the child. Dear God. How old was *this* child? Fourteen? Fifteen?

"Ain't no use, I don't guess." She shrugged as if it didn't matter, but her face, her eyes told a different story. "Dr. Wilcox said he knows a real good family that's looking for a mixed baby." The girl shifted in her seat and looked at Mel then. "Black-Asian babies are hard to find. Dr. Wilcox said so. He knows people who wants them really bad. I can stay in school and even get my college paid for and a brand-new car if I let them have my baby."

Mel stilled. Her heart slowed to a near stop. "They're going to pay you?" she whispered…unable to manage more than that. This girl was clearly underage.

The girl glanced around the room and swore softly. "I don't think I was supposed to tell that part." She looked at Melany wistfully. "You won't tell him I said so, will you? Please, lady," she whispered harshly. "I want my baby to get a good family and if I get a decent education maybe I can make something out of my life."

Somehow Mel placed a hand on hers. She wasn't sure how the message got from her brain to her hand, but it did. "Don't worry. I won't say a word. It'll be our secret."

Relief replaced the terror in the girl's young face. "I just want to do the right thing," she murmured.

Mel closed her eyes and blocked the images. All these young girls. All those babies. Surely Dr. Wilcox wasn't…

Her train of thought abruptly derailed when Ryan breezed back into the lobby and hustled her outside before she could even say goodbye to the girl she'd been talking to. "We have to talk to Bill," he said. "There's something going on here."

"Tell me about it," Mel shot back. "I just learned that—"

Her cell phone rang. She snatched it from her belt clip and flipped it open. "Hello." She held her breath, praying it would be the nurse.

"Mel."

Bill. She swore softly. "Yeah, Bill, what's up?"

"I need to talk to him," Ryan reminded her.

She held up a hand for him to wait while she listened to what Bill had to say. The silence on the other end of the line made her frown. "Bill, are you there?"

In the seconds before he answered, dread flooded through her chest, pooling in her stomach. Her face must have paled for Ryan suddenly reached for her.

"Mel, they pulled Helen Peterson's body out of the river this morning. She's dead…murdered."

CHAPTER TEN

THE NUMBNESS HAD RETURNED. In some ways Melany was thankful. She sat now, perfectly still, in one of the chairs around the small conference table in the makeshift command center at the Downtown Precinct.

Helen Peterson was dead.

Shot twice in the chest.

Murdered.

Before she could tell Melany what she desperately needed to know.

Bill and Ryan were arguing. She wasn't sure about what since her brain had practically shut down an hour ago. Both had shed their jackets. They circled the room, growling at each other like male dogs marking their territory.

Bill mentioned the hospital administration, Lance Upton, and Mel's senses perked up a bit, though she wasn't sure it really mattered at this point. She could feel the depression, the desire to give up, bearing down on her. She didn't want to believe it was too late…over… finished. But holding on to hope had grown so hard. She tightened her fingers into fists in her lap and forced herself to focus on the conversation around her that grew more heated with each exchange.

"There have been five other cases in the past four months," Bill argued. "All low-income single parents who were fatally injured, and in each incident the child or children were killed, as well."

Ryan threw his hands up. "What the hell does that prove? That low wage-earning single parents drive carelessly? If the accident was bad enough, nobody would be expected to survive no matter their income or marital status. Surely you've got more than that," he snapped.

Bill glared at him for five full seconds. Mel recognized the strategy. He was cooling down, preparing for the next parley.

"This is personal, Ryan, I'll give you that," he said in a quiet yet lethal tone, "but I'm not going to make a mistake of this caliber even if it is personal." He reached for his shirt pocket and swore. "I need a smoke."

"You said you were quitting," Ryan grumbled.

Bill exhaled a disgusted breath. "Oh, yeah." He reached for a piece of the gum that was supposed to thwart his craving.

Mel shook her head to clear it. She'd missed the part about Bill taking this too personally or something similar. Apparently Ryan had accused him of falling down somewhere along the lines since this one was personal. She'd heard him toss that accusation at Bill a couple of times in the past two days. She hated the tension thickening in the room, between old friends. But what could she say to stop it?

"So what other relevant factors do you have?" Ryan's voice sounded a bit calmer, as well. "We need a connection between Letson and Wilcox."

Both men were on the edge. She couldn't say how much sleep Bill had had, but Ryan hadn't slept at all last night. She was pretty certain of that.

"I cross-referenced the MVA reports. What do you think I've had Carter doing? It was the same each time.

The children appeared to be fine, and suddenly took a turn for the worst *after* being transferred to the pediatric ward."

Mel snapped to full attention. "Dr. Letson is the one behind this, then," she said, anticipation pounding through her veins. Helen Peterson was a nurse in his department. "Do you think *he* killed Helen?"

Both men looked at her then. "I don't know. Maybe," Bill allowed. "But Wilcox has to be in on it, too. He screens the situations, lets Letson know which ones are candidates. There's the connection. According to my guy at Quantico, both men have unusually high incomes. If we look closer, I'll bet we'd find that the hospital doesn't lay out all that dough."

"That's it." Melany pushed to her feet, the legs of her chair scraping across the floor. It all came to her at once…why hadn't she thought of this sooner? "He thought I was Rita. Single parent, low income, no health insurance, no family. I wouldn't be missed and neither would my child."

"But you didn't die," Bill said, the same realization dawning on him. He swallowed hard, his gaze connecting fully with Mel's allowing her to see just how right she was. "Not only did you not die, you're former FBI. Can you imagine how Letson and Wilcox felt when they learned the truth?"

"It was a mistake." The motive, the opportunity, the means. They all came pouring into Mel's thoughts. "Helen said it was a mistake. It wasn't supposed to go that far." She looked to Ryan then, knowing he would hold out, be the skeptical one. "*I* was a mistake. I didn't meet the agreed upon criteria, only no one knew."

Ryan held up both hands. "Stop right there, both of

you." When he was satisfied that he had their attention, he went on, "This is a great scenario. You've even got a few raw, emphasis on the raw," he said to Bill, "statistics. But a case this does not make. All we've got here is speculation. Hell, we can't even get a warrant based on your theory. When I said we needed a connection, I meant a solid one."

"I didn't need one at the hospital," Bill countered. "Upton was glad to cooperate."

"The girl told me that Wilcox was taking care of everything," Mel reminded them of what the girl in the clinic had told her. "She would get paid in the form of a college education and a brand new car. If the counselor was right, that they only provided advice, what the hell kind of offer was Wilcox making?" She purposely left off the title of doctor since she'd come to the conclusion that he didn't deserve that much respect.

"Hearsay," Ryan threw at her. "Did you even get the girl's name?"

Mel plowed her fingers through her hair. "No, I didn't get her name. She looked about fourteen years old and she was scared. Why would she lie to me?"

Ryan shrugged. "Who said she lied? She's fourteen, perhaps she misunderstood Dr. Wilcox's intent. Then again, you said yourself she was scared. Most lies start out based in fear."

Bill swore like a landlocked sailor and started pacing again. "Well, throw this into the mix and see what you come up with," he growled at Ryan.

Ryan waited for him to go on. Not a single crack in his impervious objectivity.

"Memphis General has the highest infant mortality rate in the state. In nearly every case, Dr. Letson ordered an autopsy. Why not in Katlin's or the other five cases so similar to hers?"

"You really have been busy this morning," Ryan commented dryly.

"Can't take credit for that one," he mused. "One of the clerks told me there'd been talk of an investigation, but nothing has come of it so far. But I did cross-check the deaths and saw the orders Letson had written. I find it strange that there appears to be no rhyme or reason to his selection of who should have an autopsy. I even noted identical cases, one would get the order, one wouldn't. Is the man senile or simply stupid? We both know Tennessee's law on autopsies. Same doctor, same hospital, same kinds of cases and absolutely no continuity or apparent reasoning for who gets one and who doesn't."

Mel held her breath as Ryan weighed the additional information. She could feel the tension pulsing like a living, breathing thing in the room. This was it…the defining moment. Did they have reason to pursue these accusations?

"This could all be about malpractice," he countered, looking from Bill to Mel and back. "It might have nothing to do with the fact that Katlin's—" he caught himself "—is missing."

"But it could have something to do with Katlin," Bill persisted. "We've operated on less before."

"All right," Ryan conceded. "Call it in. We need warrants for both doctors' offices, their homes, and, hell, get one for the hospital just in case Upton changes his attitude." He thought for a second. "And that north side clinic, too. Something's going on there. It may be totally unrelated, but my hunch tells me it plays into all of this, somehow."

Bill hadn't needed Ryan's authorization or agreement. For that matter, Bill was the one in charge. But he knew that Ryan had an instinct for this sort of thing. If Ryan Braxton had a hunch, you'd better listen up.

The door opened and Greg Carter, the rookie gopher Bill had recruited, rushed into the room almost colliding with Mel "Ah...ma'am," he stuttered, "Dr. Upton, Memphis General's administrator, left a message for Mr. Collins."

Bill had asked that Carter catch any calls they might receive while they hashed out the meager facts they had so far.

"Yeah, Carter, what's the message?" Bill massaged his neck. He looked tired. They were all tired.

"He said you'd probably want to know that Dr. Wilcox didn't show up for his shift this afternoon. No one's been able to reach him at home." Carter looked from one to the other. "He thought that might be important."

"Yeah, thanks, Carter. I'll work on the warrants," Bill said, the stakes rising with this new information.

"We're going to Wilcox's house. And Peterson's," Ryan announced as he grabbed his coat.

"Grab some coffee or something on the way," Bill said as he punched in a number on the telephone. "Don't you dare go in until the paper's done."

"Don't keep us waiting." He turned to Mel. "Let's go."

Ryan pressed his hand to the small of her back and ushered her toward the door. As they left she heard Bill barking additional orders to Carter.

Her anxiety was spiraling out of control and she tried to slow it...tried to keep her thoughts organized, but she couldn't do it. It was all happening at once. Too much information, too many questions and possibilities. But no real answers.

All she wanted was her little girl.

PETERSON'S HOUSE HAD been their first stop. A homicide detective had allowed them entrance to the property. Bill had realized that crime-scene techs would have been there today already and the house would be part of the ongoing homicide case so he'd tracked down the detective in charge and sent him in their direction. The man hadn't lost his touch.

To Ryan's utter disappointment, Helen Peterson's house offered nothing. Small two-story cottage. Ordinary furnishings and decorating, no hidden secrets, no files, no nothing.

Two hours scouring over the place wasted.

Ryan hoped Wilcox had made at least one mistake. If he was gone and hadn't left behind a single scrap of evidence then this thing might just grind to a halt or drag out forever. He wasn't sure Mel could hang on that long. He could see her wilting with each dead end. She needed something to hang on to. She needed a single shred of hope.

He had to find it for her.

The Wilcox home turned out to be an extravagant town house in a gated community. It had taken an act of congress to get through the gate. Carter had had to rush over with the original warrant in hand in order for Ryan to get in. A phone call or fax would not suffice. To say Ryan was ticked would be putting it mildly.

One of the guards accompanied them to the home and unlocked the front door. Ryan thanked him, but the man didn't go. He took up a post in the front yard, determined to see that no liberties were taken.

Ignoring the man's persistence, Ryan escorted Mel inside.

"We can move faster if we split up," he suggested. "And since Wilcox is likely already on the run, we need to make this quick."

Mel nodded. "I'll start upstairs."

"I'll cover everything down here."

Before moving deeper into the house, he watched as she climbed the stairs that ascended from the entry hall to the second-story landing. The entry hall rolled out past a parlor on the left and a guest powder room on the right to merge with a great room that made up the dining room, kitchen and family room in one. The furnishings were upscale though the decorating was a little drab. Like the man, Ryan mused.

He surveyed the great room for a time. Checking drawers and cabinets. Bookcases and under sofa cushions. Nothing. He'd figured as much. He liked to eliminate the least likely places quickly so he could focus on the higher yield possibilities.

Moving on from the great room, the guest powder room held no surprises, either.

But the parlor might be another story. On one side of the room Wilcox had set up an office. The desk was locked and required some time, but Ryan managed.

But his efforts were for nil. Wilcox had been careful. There was no computer, thus no electronic trail to follow. His paper files were clean. His Rolodex was empty, didn't contain even the first telephone number or address. This was scarcely an office at all. Wherever he kept the details of his "extracurricular" activities, it wasn't here.

Ryan walked through the downstairs portion of the house once more, looking for anything out of place in the orderly environment. The walls looked clean, painted in recent months. The carpet and tile showed hardly any traces of wear, much less signs of soiling.

Ryan wondered vaguely if the man even lived here.

Melany was still upstairs.

Maybe her search had turned up something.

He climbed the steps slowly, surveying left to right, top to bottom as he had on the first floor and finding nothing he hadn't expected.

The first bedroom he passed was empty. No out-of-season items stored in the closet. Not even a single stick of furniture. Nothing. Bathroom turned up the same.

He moved down the short hall and entered the master suite. The first thing his gaze landed on was Mel sitting on the floor in the middle of the room. Fear jolted through him. He was kneeling beside her in three strides.

"What have you got there?"

She was frantically pressing buttons on her cell phone. "It's…" She shook her head and let out an exasperated breath. "I can't get the call log up."

He reached for the telephone and started to ask why she suddenly needed to view her call log but she answered the question before he could ask.

"I found it on the floor near the bed."

Right where she was sitting, he'd wager. It wasn't her phone. "You think it belongs to Wilcox."

She nodded, then shook her head. "I don't know, but it belongs to someone who's been here."

As Ryan put the menu through the steps, he asked, "You didn't find anything else?"

"Clothes in the closet and dressers, toiletries in the master bath, but nothing else. Not even a magazine." She glanced around the room. "It doesn't look like he even lived here. Not really. There aren't any pictures. No jewelry."

"There are several numbers listed," he said, showing her the display. The phone chirped a warning. He frowned. "Is the battery low?"

"I don't know, it was on menu when I came in. I guess I got nervous or excited and I kept screwing up every time I tried to access anything." She trembled as if to punctuate the claim.

"It's okay, I've got it," he told her, his own hands rock steady. Oddly enough, it was during the calm that Ryan usually met with his own demons. Whenever he was preoccupied like now, he was the eye of the storm. A cool, tranquil center to the mayhem. But when things slowed down and the case was over, that's when he lived out the tension that had been building inside him for however long it took to solve the case.

"He has a voice message." Ryan punched the necessary buttons and held the phone where they could listen together.

"Wilcox, you son of a bitch! I don't know what's going on over there, but you'd better give me some answers today or else. That last payment was shy a couple thou...don't make me play hardball."

The message ended and Ryan pressed the save button, then checked the number from the received call. He fished his cell phone from his pocket and tapped in Bill's number. When Bill answered Ryan quickly rattled off the number of the caller who'd left Wilcox what was basically a threat.

"He'll call us back." He pocketed his phone as well as the other one. "Maybe Wilcox's friend will call again."

Ryan helped Mel to her feet. She smoothed a hand over her slacks and scanned the room one last time. "Do you think he's dead?" She asked the question but the voice sounded alien to her own ears, too weary, too frightened. Nothing like the strong woman she usually was.

Right now she just wanted to go home. She wanted to be near her baby's things. She'd run into too many brick walls today. Whatever the answer to this crazy scheme they weren't going to find it here. Unless someone on the other end of one of those telephone numbers in Wilcox's call log could help them.

Mel was beginning to doubt everything at this point. She was so tired. Too tired to think straight.

"I'm going to take you home," Ryan said, reading her mind with the same adeptness he'd always possessed. Even after two years apart, he knew her like the back of his hand, maybe better.

She didn't argue with him. Defeat had finally found her. She needed someone to take care of her right now. Why fight the inevitable? Her daughter was missing, presumed dead. Yes, Melany Jackson could be vulnerable. No matter how much training she had received. No matter how many similar cases she had worked. This time was different. She was losing something far more precious than mere energy as she ferreted out truth and justice.

She was losing hope.

RYAN STOOD ON the stoop next to her as she fumbled for her house key. She'd separated it from her key chain when she'd given him the SUV key. Now it appeared hopelessly lost in the bottom of her bag.

"Here it is," she muttered. She shoved it into the slot, gave it a twist and opened the door.

Ryan braced for her rejection. She hadn't allowed him into her home. He wasn't going to force the issue if she sent him on his way now. Additional stress was the last thing she needed. Mel was teetering very close to the edge right now and he wasn't sure he could do anything about it. But he damn sure wouldn't make it worse.

"Would you like to come in?" she asked when he made no move to follow her inside.

His pulse rate kicking up a notch, he managed an appreciative smile. "I'd like that very much."

She closed and locked the door behind them. "I'll make some coffee."

He grunted an acknowledgement, too lost to taking in the details of her place to do more than that.

Her home wasn't that large, but it was comfortable-looking and it smelled welcoming. The sofa and chairs were slipcovered in a fashionably chic manner. The walls were cluttered with pictures of her child. Dozens upon dozens of snapshots and professional photographs. A small television set occupied a corner along with row after row of book-lined shelves. On the floor in that same corner was a pile of toys. Stuffed animals mostly. Soft, plush objects befitting a child so young as Katlin. In the opposite corner was a small desk and computer, the screen saver flashed smiley faces.

A gas fireplace served as the focal point of the room. A handcrafted afghan lay across one end of its hearth. He could imagine Mel sitting before the fire reading bedtime stories to her daughter, both wrapped in the warm afghan. He could see them laughing and cuddling, enjoying their simple life, free of crime-scene photos and urgent, middle-of-the-night calls.

The only thing he couldn't imagine was the man that went with the package...the child's father.

Another man.

Not him.

Shifting his attention to the hallway beyond the room, he drifted into that course. Mel was in the kitchen, in the opposite direction...but he wanted to see where she slept. The place where she felt safe at night while she dreamed.

The first door he passed opened into the nursery. Bold colors and lots of little girl favorites had been included in the room's decorating theme. His gaze rested briefly on the empty crib. Something heavy shifted in his chest. He didn't want it to end this way...he wanted to save Melany from that kind of agony. The kind that followed you to the grave.

The very kind he'd spent his entire adult life running from.

Oh, he'd been ready to commit to marriage. But even that had been a last-ditch effort to keep her from leaving. He'd known she was going...he'd felt it in her withdrawal those last few weeks they were together. He would have done most anything to make her stay.

Anything but this.

He surveyed the child's room once more before moving on.

Mel's room was like her, simple yet elegant. Understated beauty and sophistication. The wide, king-size bed looked inviting, made him ache to hold her again. Floor-to-ceiling windows lined the far wall and an antique dresser acted as a stage for the collage of toiletries that served more as decoration than anything. Mel didn't need cosmetics or fancy fragrances. She had a natural beauty and a sweet, womanly scent that had brought him to his knees more times than he cared to admit.

"I found this place the first time I came to the city," she said from behind him.

He turned to face her and she smiled sadly. "When I realized that we weren't going to work out I started considering job options. The university here had an opening that fit the bill perfectly, criminology professor. I came for an interview while you were off in Oregon on the Wallace case."

Ryan felt his knees go weak and he sat down on the edge of the bed before he humiliated himself by dropping like a rock. She'd never told him any of this before…they hadn't talked at all really. She'd asked him to change his mind, he hadn't, she'd left.

"One of the university deans told me about this house and I made an appointment that very day to see it. I made an immediate offer on it."

A cold, hard chunk of long-buried hurt settled in the pit of his stomach. "So you'd already made up your mind before I came back and proposed?" He hadn't believed anything about their past could still cause him pain, but somehow, that did.

She nodded. "I already knew what your answer about having children was going to be." She came over to the bed and sat down beside him. His entire body reacted to her nearness in such an intimate setting. "I knew you, Ryan. I didn't have to wait and see how things turned out. You weren't going to change your mind and neither was I."

He looked long and hard into those shimmering green eyes before he worked up the guts to ask, "You wanted a child that badly? Bad enough to forget all that we'd shared?"

"I wanted *this* child more than you can ever imagine. But nothing could ever make me forget."

A flicker of anger unfurled inside him. "Not even *he*

could make you forget?" He glared at her then, wanting to hurt her the way she'd hurt him. Wanting her to see the depth of the pain she'd caused him. It was childish he knew, but he just couldn't help it.

Rather than snarl back at him as he'd fully expected, she reached up and tenderly caressed his jaw. "I'm sorry I hurt you, Ryan. But I had to do this…."

She'd left him…found someone else…had a child. They were working on a case together. This wasn't supposed to be about the past…or them. But it was. It was all tangled together and there was no getting around it.

He did what he'd longed to do from the moment he'd laid eyes on her in that interrogation room when he first arrived in Memphis.

He kissed her.

Not the hard and fast, lust-driven kind of kiss. The slow, savoring kind that was fueled by regret…and the kind of desperation known only between old lovers.

She tasted just like he remembered, warm and soft. He slid his arms around her and pulled her close, burrowing his face in the curve of her neck when he could bear the touch of her lips no longer. Her sweet scent took his breath, made him want to hang on forever.

How could he have let her go?

She pushed against his shoulder, a signal that the moment had passed. "The coffee's ready," she murmured before rising from his embrace and leaving the room. The same way she'd left him two years ago…without looking back.

He'd foolishly let her go.

It was far too late to take it back now.

CHAPTER ELEVEN

MELANY STRETCHED HER neck side to side and stared at the computer screen. She recalled a couple years back some sort of scandal about autopsies or organ removal involving children. She remembered being appalled that it could go on for so long without anyone knowing.

She shuddered at the whole concept and glanced toward the sofa and Ryan. Her breath stalled in her lungs when her brain and heart assimilated what her eyes saw, he was asleep. He'd finally given up. She wondered if he'd had any sleep at all since he'd arrived in Memphis. Maybe a couple winks here and there. That was his style when burrowed deeply into a case.

The clock above the mantel chimed once for the hour. She should be asleep, as well. But she hadn't found what she was looking for just yet. For a time she was content to study Ryan…the side rarely seen by human eyes. The vulnerable side. His jaw was shadowed by a day's beard growth. His muscles completely relaxed with those long legs stretched out in front of him. He'd peeled off his jacket and tossed it to one end of the sofa and released a couple of buttons on his shirt. The V of dark hair revealed there made her heart skip a beat. The rolled up shirtsleeves bared muscled forearms, making her shiver with the memory of those arms around her. The reports and statements he'd been reviewing were scattered around him like the discarded squares of a tattered quilt.

She closed her eyes then and relived that moment when his lips had touched hers. Subconsciously she'd wanted him to kiss her, though she hadn't admitted as much until he did just that. He'd tasted of coffee and Ryan, mysterious, complicated Ryan. That simple kiss had made her want more…had made her regret the mistake she had made. She'd only realized in these past few days what a mistake it had been.

Not telling Ryan the truth had been wrong…a terrible, terrible mistake. He thought she'd run immediately into someone else's arms and that hurt him more than she would have imagined it possible. But worst of all, she had deprived him of the first two years of his daughter's life…perhaps the only two. Tears welled instantly and she pushed the idea away. She would not believe that.

If she had told him the truth two years ago, had given him the option, at least the decision would have been his. But she'd taken that away from him and that was going to hurt him even more. She shook her head in defeat. Yes, she'd thought she was protecting herself and him from a life of obligatory misery. But he had deserved better than that. She knew it now, but it was too late.

She turned her attention back to the computer screen. There was nothing she could do to change the past, but she could help in the search for her daughter. She had to focus on that. The other would simply have to take care of itself.

Typing furiously, she went to another search engine and started again. If she could only remember the name of the hospital or the city.

A long line of possible sites filled the screen.

Organs Illegally Stored at British Hospital.
A chill raced up her spine. This could be it.

She scanned the article, her heart pumping harder and harder with each word she read. Organs stolen from more than eight hundred fetuses and infants. Alder Hey, a British Hospital in Liverpool, admitted to taking organs from aborted fetuses as well as living children undergoing heart surgery. According to the article, the thymus glands, the primary organ taken, plays a vital role in the immune system by producing healthy cells to attack foreign substances around the body. These organs were given to a pharmaceutical firm in exchange for financial donations.

Reading faster and faster, her morbid fascination mounting, she came upon the next related article. Children's organs found in warehouse operated by British pathologist. This pathologist was also linked to Alder Hey in the scandal involving the removal of organs and tissue from dead children and aborted fetuses. More than eight hundred cases.

All those children…all those parents.

She quickly printed off the most relevant articles. Ryan had to see this. She was halfway across the room with the documents in hand when she realized she didn't have the heart to wake him. He needed the rest.

Instead, she placed the articles on top of a stack of reports next to his briefcase and retrieved the afghan from the hearth. Moving with all the stealth she'd learned from tiptoeing around a sleeping child the past year and a half, she spread the cover over him and smiled when he continued to sleep. He definitely needed this night.

She turned the lights down low but not completely off just in case he woke up and forgot where he was.

When she'd padded quietly to her bedroom, she stripped off her clothes and pulled on her favorite nightshirt. The covers felt heavenly around her as she climbed between the sheets and closed her eyes with a sigh. She was glad this day was over.

Maybe tomorrow they would find Katlin.

Before she drifted off to sleep Mel decided there was something she had to do first thing in the morning. Visit all the local funeral homes. She wanted to speak to the morticians who'd prepared the bodies of those autopsied children. She would get the list of names from Bill.

They were getting close…she could feel it.

This time when she slept she didn't dream of Katlin… she dreamed of all those dead children whose organs had been stolen. Only in the dream it wasn't at some British hospital…it was here in Memphis. And she was the only one who could hear them crying….

THE PHONE IN Ryan's hotel rang as he stepped into a clean pair of trousers. He fastened the closure and zipped the fly as he strode across the room. "Braxton," he barked when he'd snatched up the receiver.

"I've got that list of names and addresses from Wilcox's call log," Bill told him without preamble.

"Great." Ryan shouldered into the shirt he'd tossed onto the bed. "Give me two minutes to hook up my fax machine and send 'em over. I want to get started on that right away."

"Where's Mel?"

Cradling the receiver between his ear and shoulder, Ryan's fingers slowed in their work of slipping buttons into their closures. Was that suspicion he heard in

Bill's voice? "She's at home. I'm supposed to pick her up in half an hour."

"I called and there was no answer."

Ryan knew a moment's panic. "Maybe she's still in the shower. I think she was up pretty late and…"

"Weren't you there?"

Blatant accusation now. "What is this, an inquisition?" He didn't like where he figured his old friend was going with this.

"I'm just warning you that Mel has enough on her plate right now. She doesn't need any distractions that will only lead to trouble when this is over."

"You think I'd take advantage of her vulnerability?" Ryan wanted to be pissed off, but a part of him knew that if she hadn't stopped him he would have done that very thing last night. Damn, he was scum. He'd wanted her so much he hadn't stopped to think about her needs.

Bill heaved a sigh. "Hell, I think you'll take advantage of each other if you're not careful and then you'd both regret it."

Spoken like a true friend. One who likely knew them better than they knew themselves.

"I won't let that happen." Ryan meant every word. He'd gotten close last night, but he'd had some sleep and he was thinking a good deal clearer this morning.

"All right. I'll try to reach her again."

"I'll be on my way to Mel's in five." Ryan dropped the receiver back into its cradle and swiftly rolled on his socks and stepped into his shoes. He didn't like the idea that she hadn't answered her phone. He'd left her less than an hour ago…still, bad things could happen in a few seconds. With Helen Peterson and Garland Hanes's murders and Wilcox's disappearance, he wasn't taking anything for granted.

He grabbed his cell phone from its charger and picked up his briefcase. As he hustled out the door he thought of the articles Mel wanted him to read. Something about some British hospital called Alder Hey that she thought might be relevant to this case. He'd intended to take a look at them as soon as he was dressed, but that would have to wait.

Confirming her safety was priority one.

MEL STOOD AT her desk watching the printed page slowly discharge from the fax machine. It couldn't have been more than ten minutes ago that she'd asked Bill for the list of names. He already had the data organized and quickly faxed it to her.

She scanned the page, twenty-one names in all over the past two years. God, that seemed like so many. All under the age of three. Plucking at her still damp hair she set the page aside to pull on a light wool suit jacket. The red one, her favorite. She smiled as she smoothed a hand over the soft material. All week she hadn't cared whether she ate or slept much less how she looked. But renewed hope had given her optimism a boost. Besides, it was chilly out this morning. Her black slacks and the long-sleeved white blouse wouldn't be enough. She told herself that taking an extra moment to consider her wardrobe this morning had nothing to do with Ryan.

And it didn't.

She needed to look professional. If she pulled off attractive as well, that couldn't hurt since the funeral home directors she intended to question were all men.

The knock at her front door told her that Ryan had arrived. She folded the list of names and tucked it into her purse. Now the question was, would she be able to convince Ryan to let her go off on her own this morning?

She opened the door and just did manage to stifle a gasp. He looked fantastic. Freshly showered and shaved, those blue eyes clear after a good night's sleep. He had apologized profusely for falling asleep on her couch, but she had assured him it was okay. She was just glad he'd gotten some rest.

"Good morning," he said in that deep, husky voice that would put wicked ideas in any woman's head.

"Morning." She mustered up a smile and hoped he couldn't read her mind as well as it always seemed he could. She resisted the urge to shake her head. She had definitely veered way off course here.

"I've got the list of names and addresses from Wilcox's call log. I'd like to start with that this morning. Bill is going back to the hospital to interview more of the personnel there. He thinks he'll eventually find someone who knows something and will talk." He seemed to consider the idea before adding, "It'll take time, but it could pay off. Carter is getting an update on the Peterson and Hanes homicides and the search for Wilcox."

She shifted, in hopes that he wouldn't notice her preoccupation with his charcoal-gray suit and crisp, silver shirt. How could he still look this good after living through the hell of ten years on the Bureau's payroll as a profiler specializing in missing children? Everything about him screamed masculinity. From his tall, lean yet muscular frame, to the chiseled good looks of that square face. And the eyes, the deepest blue she'd ever seen.

Damn! Those perceptual eyes were searching her face...trying to read her expression.

"Did you read those articles?" she asked, redirecting her dangerous thoughts and needing desperately to get past this awkward moment. Her nerves were frazzled to the point of distraction. That's all this could be. Nerves...stress.

"No, but I will get to it this morning." He smiled and her heart lurched.

What the hell was wrong with her this morning? Had some crazy kind of hormone suddenly awakened? Had last night's uncomplicated kiss turned her ability to reason into something unreasonable and immensely complicated?

"I was thinking," she began, going for a professional focus once more. "You said that we could accomplish more if we worked on different aspects of the case. I'd like to follow this lead of mine while you and Bill move forward with yours." She needed to do this and she needed some distance.

He passed a hand over his smooth, chiseled jaw, but the move did nothing to clear away the lines of concern that surfaced with her proposition. "Mel, I'm not sure that's a good idea. I—"

"Look, I know what I'm doing. I'm fine now. I can do this. I *need* to do this." He was going to argue, she could see it in his eyes. "Ryan, I've had the same training you have. I know what to do."

He expelled a weary breath. "All right. But if you get into trouble or just feel like you need me, call."

She nodded, grateful. "Do you mind taking me by your hotel to pick up my car?"

"I mind because I'd rather you stick with me or Bill," he said truthfully, "but I'll do it, anyway."

Mel locked her front door and followed him to his

rental car. Surely with all the leads they had now, a break would come soon. It had to.

It just had to.

BY 10:30 A.M. Ryan had scratched off most of the names on the list. He had two more. One was the clinic, which he intended to visit again today but it wasn't top priority, and the other was an uptown law firm. The attorney had been the one who'd left the threatening message for Wilcox. He'd stopped at Rodney Mason's office earlier that morning but the hours of business indicated that the place didn't open until nine-

thirty. He might as well head back there now.

He'd checked on Melany about an hour ago. She had visited three of the funeral homes in town already and had come up empty-handed. He wasn't sure what she was looking for but he was certain she had an appropriate agenda. As she'd said, they'd had the same training. He knew she was capable. Letting her out of his sight had been the hard part. He didn't even want to think about when the time came for him to return to Chicago. Leaving was not going to be easy.

Mason's office was nothing to write home about, far from upscale but not the worst Ryan had seen. He parked in one of the half dozen slots reserved for clients and made his way to the door. He frowned when he discovered it still locked. Since the entry door was glass, he could clearly see the reception area. No lights were on and there definitely didn't appear to be anyone on the premises. The hall beyond the reception area looked as dark as midnight.

The hair on the back of Ryan's neck stood on end and his gut knotted with anticipation. He needed to get his hands on this guy. If Wilcox was running some sort of baby-selling scam using the north side clinic and perhaps other means, he would definitely need an attorney to work the deals, to draw up the contracts. Mason was the only connection of that type they had to Wilcox.

Before he ran down Mason's home address, Ryan decided to take a little stroll behind the building. But first, he retrieved his weapon from his briefcase. He didn't carry it much anymore, but at times like this he'd rather be safe than sorry. If the two homicides were connected to Mel's daughter, as he suspected, being armed was a good thing. He swore under his breath. Mel wouldn't be armed. Dammit, he should never have let her go off on her own. As long as she stuck to the agenda she'd mentioned she should be safe. There would be employees, possibly grieving families, at the funeral homes. She wouldn't be alone. Still, he didn't like it.

Ryan slipped through the alley between the law office and a manicure salon. The rear alley that stretched between the buildings offered parking for employees and shop owners as well as Dumpster storage for trash. Behind the law office sat one car, a fairly new Mercedes. It could be Mason's. Glancing from side to side to make sure no one was watching, Ryan eased into the wide rear thoroughfare and crossed to the back entrance of the building. To his amazement, the door opened without resistance when he turned the knob.

For a few seconds before opening the door, he listened for any movement inside. Silence. He eased the door inward and stepped inside. The back corridor leading toward the front of the building was dark as he'd noted earlier. After palming his weapon he flipped the closest switch and the overhead fluorescents flickered to life. Still no sound, no movement. Allowing the door to close behind him he stepped cautiously toward the front of the building, checking each door he passed. Bathroom. Supply closet. Mini conference room. And, finally, Mason's office.

The brass desk lamp was on, bathing the mahogany surface in a warm glow. But there was nothing warm about the dead man sprawled across the floor in front of it, an ugly hole right between his eyes.

Ryan scanned the area, then crouched next to the body and checked for a carotid pulse. The flesh was room temperature, the complexion gray. Definitely dead. A quick look in the guy's wallet identified him as the former Rodney Mason, attorney at law.

Leaving the wallet on top of the corpse, Ryan pushed to his feet and did a quick check of the rest of the small building to ensure the place was clear as he punched in Bill's cell number. "We've got another homicide," he told him without bothering with hello.

"The mouthpiece?"

"Yeah." Ryan checked the final room, the lobby, and found nothing that looked out of the ordinary. "Listen, can you hold off on reporting this for, say an hour? I'd like to take a walk through this guy's files and get out of here before it becomes an official crime scene." He didn't have time to deal with questions unless it was crucial to his investigation. They'd find his prints and Bill would explain.

"One hour," Bill agreed. "Have you heard from Mel?"

"About an hour ago. She seemed fine, but why don't you check on her again?" If he kept calling, she'd know he was checking up on her.

"I'll do that now."

Ryan closed his flip-top phone and dropped it back

into his pocket. He moved swiftly to the back door and locked it. Surprises were not a good thing when one was ensconced in an office with a dead man.

Forty-five minutes of the hour he'd requested had flown by before Ryan found what he was looking for. Like Wilcox, Mason had taken precautions. Taped under a drawer in his desk was a computer disk that contained his secret files.

Ryan shook his head as he scanned file after file of so-called private adoption proceedings. And this could only be scratching the surface. Most of the adoptions were fairly recent. Who knew how many other disks were hidden away or, perhaps, had already been destroyed.

He slowed his search when he came to a file created only three days after Melany's accident. A couple in Dallas, Texas, were set to adopt a little girl matching the description and approximate age of Katlin.

Adrenaline rushing through his veins, he sent the document to the printer, then continued viewing the remaining files. Where were they getting all these children? Most were newborns but every now and then there was a toddler like Katlin. And then it hit him.

The clinic.

He remembered all those pregnant teens at the clinic.

And then he thought of Mel and the assumption that she had been Rita Grider at the time of the accident. Single parent, no health insurance listed, no family other than her child…no ties. She fit the criteria of someone who wouldn't be missed.

Ryan stared at the screen, his mind racing with scenarios. Each file was coded with a string of four numbers. Somewhere hidden away, maybe in this office, was a disk or document with a list of names that matched the coded families to the children. He needed that list.

He punched in Bill's number again. "I'm gonna need some backup over here," he told his friend. "I want the best hacker you can get your hands on and a team of techs to tear this place apart."

"Mason's the key?"

"He's definitely the linchpin that facilitated at least part of the operation."

"I'll see what I can rustle up for you," Bill told him before ending the call.

"I'll be here."

Ryan went back to his car and dug a pair of latex gloves from his briefcase. He didn't intend to wait. He tamped down the urge to call Mel. She would want to know what he'd found and he wasn't ready to tell her just yet. Though he still had no concrete reason to believe Katlin wasn't dead, her body having been disposed of to cover up a medical screwup, he had a feeling that her name was here somewhere among all these other children's.

All he had to do was find it.

MEL PARKED HER SUV in the lot of the sixth funeral home on her list. There was only one more after this. The one where Katlin had been taken. She was saving that one for last. Wasn't even sure she could handle going in there, but she'd damn sure try.

The director at the last funeral home had behaved nervously from the moment she mentioned the autopsies. He'd assured her he'd seen nothing out of the ordinary, but she had the distinct impression that he was lying. But, of course, she had no proof and couldn't exactly push the issue. After all, she was a mere civilian. At least to a degree.

"May I help you?" The lady who greeted her in the entry hall of the lavish funeral home smiled, the surface convention genuine. She dressed in the same dark, reserved manner in which all the others had. But her smile was definitely nicer.

"Yes. I'd like to see Mr. Walton." Mel manufactured a smile for her though it wasn't easy. There was something about the smell in these places. Something artificial and overly sweet. A shudder quaked through her.

"Certainly. I'll show you to his office."

The lady with the nice smile led Mel through the lavishly appointed house of the dead. No matter how you dressed it up, she mused, it was still eerie.

The lady paused outside a suite of offices. "May I give Mr. Walton your name, ma'am?"

"Melany Jackson…with the FBI," she added. God, she'd gotten almost as good with that lie as Ryan.

The brief flare of surprise in the other woman's eyes was swiftly concealed. "Right this way, Ms. Jackson."

Zacharius Walton was no young man by any stretch of the definition. But he had a presence about him that made him seem decades younger. He deftly moved around his desk and offered his hand when his employee introduced Melany.

"Ms. Jackson, please have a seat and tell me what we can do for you."

The lady who'd showed her to the office discreetly vanished. "Thank you," Mel said to the director.

When they'd both taken a seat, she got right to the heart of the matter. She would ask him the same questions she'd asked the other directors. "Mr. Walton, I'd like you to tell me which of the following names you recognize." She then called off the remaining seven names on her list.

After she'd finished, he braced his arms on his desk and steepled his hands in front of him. "Why, Ms. Jackson, I believe all of those names are familiar. Of course I'd have to check dates of birth and the like to verify that we're talking about the same folks."

"These names all belonged to children," she said pointedly.

He tensed, just the slightest twitch. "Then I would have to say that they have all likely passed through our doors. If I may, can I ask what the nature of your investigation is?"

This was the sticky part. "What I'd like to know is if you or one of your employees noticed anything peculiar to these children." She didn't want to put words in his mouth so she didn't mention autopsy.

He leaned back in his chair then. "I have two morticians on staff, Ms. Jackson, both worked with two or more of these children." He leveled his gaze on hers. "Both noticed, shall we say, oddities in the manners in which the autopsies had been performed."

Her heart leaped against her sternum. "Can you be more specific, Mr. Walton?"

"I can be considerably more specific," he said flatly. "We took pictures and prepared a file."

His answer stunned her. "You did? What did the authorities have to say?"

"I never went to the authorities. I confronted the hospital and they explained that a new M.E. was being trained and that I should overlook the situation."

Mel frowned. That wasn't the answer she'd wanted to hear. "Did you believe that to be a reasonable explanation?"

He shook his head resolutely. "But I kept my mouth shut. Especially considering the number of deceased that I've been called to pick up at Memphis General has dwindled to nothing in the intervening time. I'm sorry if that offends you, but it's the nature of the beast. We cannot survive in a marketplace where our good name has been blackballed. Ultimately, the children were dead and forcing the issue would only have injured the surviving families. We chose to look the other way but we didn't have to like it."

Mel took a deep breath and lied, "I understand, sir. Can you tell me any further details about the abnormalities you noted?"

He looked away for a moment, then drew in a heavy breath of his own. "There appeared to be items missing."

"Items?" Her pulse raced.

"Organs." He shrugged. "We even opened a couple of them up just to see. We have documentation."

Mel jetted to her feet. She had to get this information to Ryan. "Mr. Walton, I appreciate your candor. You must realize, sir, that you and your employees may be called to testify to what you've just told me and that those photographs will be evidence."

Walton pushed up from his chair, matching her stance. "We have the files and photographs locked away safely. In fact, I have a second copy at my attorney's office. I knew that evidence would serve two purposes, to cover my butt and to bring to justice those vile hypocrites. But let me warn you, unless you bring down the hierarchy behind this evil, you won't stop this. I'll do my part, but it'll be up to you to stop them or we'll both lose."

"They're going down," Mel assured him before walking out.

ZACHARIUS WALTON WATCHED the lovely young woman in the red jacket hurry from his office and he silently cheered. By God, someone was finally going to get those bastards.

Reveling in the victory, he picked up the telephone and entered the number he would never forget if he lived a dozen lifetimes. When the bastard answered his cell phone Zacharius smiled. "Well, well, you've finally been caught."

The voice on the other end of the line demanded to know what he was talking about.

"I'm talking about the pretty young lady from the FBI who just dropped by my office. They're building a case against you bastards. And I have a feeling they're going to get you. I hope you burn in hell!" He slammed the phone down and took a deep, calming breath. God had finally answered his prayers.

WALTON'S WORDS ECHOED again and again in Mel's head as she drove away from the funeral home. She punched in Ryan's number but got his voice mail again. "Damn it," she muttered. "Ryan, I've found the proof we need. Meet me at Forest Lawn. Jesus, Ryan, it's just like Alder Hey."

Half an hour later, as she waited to see Clyde Desmond at Forest Lawn, she struggled with the images her mind kept conjuring. They'd brought her baby to this place. It smelled, just like all the others. Deathly sweet. That man, Garland Hanes, had signed for her. And that's where the trail ended. She looked at her list of names. They'd all been checked off. None of the autopsied children had been brought to this funeral home. That seemed odd. Why wouldn't Forest Lawn have gotten at least one?

Maybe because they provided another service for Wilcox. Maybe they took care of the live ones. Mel shuddered and hugged herself. She had to be on the right track.

Annoyed that she hadn't heard from Ryan, she pulled out her cell phone and checked the ringer volume. He should have called her back by now.

"Ms. Jackson?"

She got up and faced the man who'd called her crazy just a few days ago. "Mr. Desmond." She didn't even bother with a smile and certainly not a handshake.

"Is there something I can help you with? I believe I've already answered all the questions your friends at the Bureau had as thoroughly as I can."

"I'm not here to ask any questions," she said saccharinely. God, she was going to enjoy this. "I just wanted you to know that we know what you and *your* friends have been up to." She did smile then. "And we're going to stop you."

Crimson climbed up his throat and spread across his pudgy cheeks. "I realize you've been through an ordeal, but I will not tolerate your threats." He kept his voice low but the tone was deadly.

"It's not a threat, Mr. Desmond, it's a promise. Do yourself a favor and cooperate with us and maybe you'll get off with a slap on the hand." She looped her bag over her shoulder. "You have our number, give us a call before it's too late to save yourself."

With that said, she walked out.

A blast of wind kicked up, flapping her hair across her face as she hurried to her car. Since Ryan hadn't called, she'd try Bill. She had to reach one of them. They had to know what was going on.

She pulled out onto the street and headed back toward Memphis proper as she entered Bill's number. She got his voice mail, as well. Where the hell were those guys?

Forest Lawn was located on the edge of the city, in the suburbs, almost. Though she hated the place, she could understand why Rita had selected it. The cemetery was lovely—for a graveyard. The whole setting was picturesque, if one didn't know the people behind it. Garland Hanes had been nothing but a scapegoat. The real evil resided in Desmond. She wondered how many other empty coffins were buried in that cemetery.

She slowed for the upcoming curve and something in her rearview mirror caught her eye.

A vehicle, truck or SUV maybe, dark in color, roared up behind her. The driver wore dark glasses and a baseball cap. She jerked her attention forward and pressed harder on the accelerator.

"What's your hurry, jerk?" she muttered.

The vehicle stayed right on her bumper as she reached the section of highway that was bordered by the river on one side and trees on the other. He was way too close. So close he made her nervous. Then he swerved into the next lane to pass.

"Thank God," she breathed the words. All she needed was some—

He crossed the yellow center line.

Metal slammed against metal.

She screamed. Whipped the steering wheel to the left.

He came at her again.

CHAPTER TWELVE

RYAN STOOD BACK as Rodney Mason's body was removed from the office he would no longer need. The M.E. had estimated the time of death between 7:00 a.m. and 9:00 a.m. this morning.

If Ryan had only gotten here sooner.

But he hadn't.

So far, the search through the office had turned up nothing in the way of a list of names to connect with the disk he had found. The hard drive from his office computer as well as that of his secretary were being dismantled byte by byte by the resident hacker associated with the Bureau's Memphis field office. Unless he could find concealed information or a trail to some electronic site, they had reached a dead end.

"Our boy Wilcox has been a busy fellow," Bill said offhandedly as the M.E.'s office left with the body. He'd personally seen to it that the examiner in charge handled this case. No assistants since they couldn't be sure which ones were on the up and up just yet.

Ryan surveyed Mason's office once more, disappointment settling in. Dammit, he'd wanted to find more—something specific to Katlin. "Or he may be running from whoever the killer is." There was no proof yet that Wilcox was the shooter. Just one of the players.

Bill nodded. "That's a definite possibility. He doesn't

really fit the profile of a cold-blooded killer, but desperation can push a man beyond his normal capabilities."

That was also true. "I should call Mel," Ryan said, more to himself than to Bill. He'd been on the line for most of the last hour in an effort to track down Mason's secretary only to discover that she'd run off with some Internet boyfriend and her former boss had yet to hire anyone new. Since none of her friends and family knew where she was, Ryan hoped her office computer would reveal the Romeo with whom she'd disappeared. She might have information that could help, even if she didn't realize it was significant. Sometimes the benign was the most telling.

Bill scratched his head with his pen as he studied his notes. "I'm going to get Cuddahy up at Quantico on Mason's financial background and any criminal record he might have."

"Let me know what you find out," Ryan told him but doubted if he'd heard since he looked so deep in thought.

The abrupt roar of the vacuum drowned out all else as the crime-scene techs searched for trace evidence. Ryan took that as his cue to step outside. In the rear parking area, more forensics guys were going over the Mercedes before towing it in to Memphis P.D.'s evidence holding and analysis facility. More testing would be done there, but since any disturbance could contaminate evidence, as much as possible would be done at the scene.

Ryan surveyed the alley between the law office and the salon again as he made his way to the front of the building. Had the shooter come this way?

If the M.E. had the time of death right, someone next

door may have seen something. Memphis P.D. would be canvassing the area, interviewing anyone who might have noticed the arrival or departure of a vehicle at the law office.

Ryan frowned when Mel's phone went to her voice mail. He depressed the end button and almost didn't see the icon on the screen denoting that he had a voice message before he dropped the phone back into his pocket. He quickly accessed the message and listened as an excited Mel asked him to meet her at Forest Lawn Funeral Home.

A sensation of dread moved through him. He would have preferred she not go there alone. He liked even less that the message was nearly an hour old. He hissed a curse and loaded into his car. He'd let Bill know his destination en route.

Once he'd pulled out onto the street and taken a moment to get his bearings and plot the quickest route to the funeral home, he entered Bill's number. After four rings the call went to his voice mail. Ryan swore again when he considered that Mel had gotten that same option when she'd tried to call him. The call waiting had never worked properly on his phone. He wondered if that was Bill's excuse for not taking his call or if he was simply too absorbed in his present conversation to notice who was trying to get through. Either way, Ryan couldn't reach him.

If Mel had been in trouble when she tried to call…

He punched the accelerator and shoved away that line of thinking. She'd sounded excited not scared. She'd likely discovered something she wanted to share with him.

But…that had been almost an hour ago, he reminded himself. Why hadn't she tried to call again when he didn't show?

A lump of fear gelled in his gut.

Maybe she couldn't call.

He floored the gas pedal and the car rocketed forward.

During the tension-filled journey to the outskirts of Memphis on the opposite side of the city, Ryan attempted to call her a half dozen more times with no success.

By the time he reached the road that wound alongside the Mississippi River and would take him to Forest Lawn, hysteria had crowded into his throat.

The cold, calculated calm he was known for had flown out the window. He could do nothing but imagine all the horrible scenarios that could take Melany from him yet again.

Damn, what a fool he was. She didn't belong to him anymore. But, somehow, it felt like she did...that he was responsible for keeping her safe.

And he'd failed.

Just like he'd let her down the last time.

The cluster of cars in the distance had him braking hard. The throb of red and blue lights captured his attention first. The sight of the boxy white ambulances with the red and yellow lettering claimed his gaze next.

A patrolman directed traffic to the far right to avoid the tangle of official vehicles on the left.

A steel band tightened around Ryan's chest. He searched the vehicles...the people milling around at the site...and he prayed that this had nothing to do with Melany.

A loud banging jerked him back to attention. He hadn't even realized he'd stopped until the patrolman slammed his hand down on Ryan's hood.

"Come on, buddy, move it along!"

His foot still heavy on the brake pedal, he caught sight of one of the vehicles involved in the mishap.

Big…black… SUV…badly damaged on the driver's side.

But there were lots of black SUVs on the road.

Just because Mel had a similar…

The blood rushing through his veins rendered him all but deaf, doing nothing to lessen the clarity of what he saw next.

His gaze narrowed. The target he zeroed in on zoomed into vivid focus.

A pink angel hanging from the rearview mirror.

He was out of the car and moving toward the official throng before the reality fully assimilated in his brain. Vaguely he heard the patrolman ranting at him as he tried to stop the car Ryan had left running and in gear.

He pushed past the beat cop who attempted to block his entrance to the scene, not bothering with his I.D., his gaze never leaving the damned angel that drew him like a guidepost through the sea of pandemonium.

All thought except one ceased: she had to be all right. He refused to consider any other possibility.

"Ryan!"

The sound of her voice cleared the fog from his head. A thousand fragmented synapses fired at once. He spun around, his gaze seeking the sweet face that went with the voice. She burst from the back of the ambulance amid the protests of the paramedic. Two seconds later she was in his arms.

Ryan's eyes closed as he nuzzled against her hair. Thank God, thank God. He had refused to believe for even an instant that she might be hurt…or worse. But now that she was in his arms he imagined all the things that could have happened. And, just like before, he hadn't been there for her. Not even when she'd called.

"I'm sorry." He repeated the words over and over. He was sorry for so many things. There was so much he wanted to say. But he couldn't string together the right words...couldn't bring himself to let her go long enough to look her in the eyes and say what needed to be said.

Not for a moment had he ever stopped loving her.

"Ma'am, we really need to tape up that wound."

The paramedic's words filtered through the haze of relief and Ryan pulled away, holding her at arm's length to visually inspect her from head to toe.

He swore violently at the blood matted in her hair. A small gash on her forehead, at the edge of her hairline still leaked the red, life-giving liquid.

"You're okay?" He had to know, unable to determine with mere human eyes if there were other injuries not readily seen on the surface.

"I'm okay." Her lips trembled. He felt the quake go through her body.

The paramedic put a hand on Ryan's arm. "Sir, we need to get this done."

Ryan released her. "Of course."

The paramedic led Mel back to the ambulance with her looking back at Ryan every step. He wanted to go with her, but his more rational senses were finally kicking in. He needed to find out what happened.

While Mel got patched up, Ryan sought out the officer who appeared to be in charge. He flashed his I.D. "FBI Special Agent Bill Collins and I have been working on the Jackson case," he explained. "Can you tell me what happened here?" He took in several things at once. Mel's SUV was damaged on the front and rear ends as well as the driver's side. Another vehicle, a car, had sustained front-end damage and was currently being towed away. The guardrail, about twenty yards back, had been battered, as well.

Just then a cop surfaced from the depths of the murky water beyond the narrow shoulder of the road. Even before the officer standing next to him said there was a third vehicle in the water Ryan knew someone had gone over the guardrail.

"Did the driver and passengers escape?"

The officer shook his head as a second cop surfaced empty handed. "Looks like he's still inside."

"He?" Ryan resisted the urge to shuck his jacket and shoes and jump into the water himself and see if it was Wilcox in there. "Any I.D. yet?"

"Not yet." He looked at Ryan, as if only then realizing that he might be telling more than he should. "Did you say you were with the FBI?"

He nodded, keeping up the farce Bill had started.

"Then you'll want to question the woman, Ms. Jackson." The officer glanced toward the ambulance. "She says that the guy in the vehicle down there—" he gestured to the water "—tried to run her off the road but ended up there himself. We've got an APB out on any eighteen-wheelers heading north on this road. She says the driver of the eighteen-wheeler saved her. According to her, if he hadn't come along when he did, forcing the guy down there—" he nodded to the water again "—to swerve, she'd be the one in the river."

MEL WAS STILL shaking so hard her teeth chattered from time to time when Ryan drove her home. He took it slowly because she couldn't tolerate otherwise. Every car seemed to veer too close. The seat belt, the airbag, none of it was enough. She wasn't safe…and if she were injured or killed who would look for her baby?

She turned to the man driving and studied his profile. He'd been scared to death. For the first time since she'd met Ryan, she'd seen him vulnerable with his eyes open. Not once in all their time together had she seen him that scared. Ryan Braxton wasn't afraid of anything.

Pressing her fingers to her mouth, she considered what that meant. Could he still be in love with her? Even after she'd walked out? After she'd had a child— a child he thought another man had fathered?

That just didn't seem feasible. But it felt exactly that. He'd held her, intense emotion shining in those blue depths, murmuring the same words over and over. *I'm sorry. Thank God.*

Could she possibly still mean that much to him?

Mel chewed on her thumbnail and tried to think more rationally. Impossible, she decided. Closing her eyes, she leaned her head against the seat and tried to calm her frazzled nerves. She would be sore tomorrow. Like last time. Besides the cut on her head, the seat belt and airbag would leave their own reminders that once again she was lucky to be alive. Her hands and arms felt weak from wrestling with the steering wheel. She kept seeing that other vehicle coming at her, trying to force her over the guardrail. That huge eighteen-wheeler had suddenly been heading for them and the other vehicle accelerated and swerved hard to cut in front of her. If she hadn't hit her brake at that precise second, he would have clipped her front end, likely forcing her over the guardrail with him.

She had slammed on her brake with all her weight and the guy behind her had hit her, forcing her forward just enough to bump the rear end of the other vehicle before it hurdled over the guardrail. She hadn't even realized anyone was behind her until then. That's why the guy had cut in front of her, there was no time to drop far enough back to dart in behind her. The driver of the big rig hadn't even slowed. Probably lacked the time and initiative to be a material witness.

The cops were looking for him, though. Mel or the driver behind her hadn't been able to give much of a description, but an all points bulletin had been issued for any eighteen-wheelers traveling that road. She hoped they found him so she could thank the guy. He'd saved her life.

She shivered as she considered that she'd escaped near death twice in the last week and a half.

And still she hadn't found Katlin.

"You're sure you didn't get a look at the guy who tried to run you off the road?" Ryan asked, breaking his long minutes of silence.

"No. He had on dark glasses and a baseball cap. No facial hair, nothing distinguishing about his mouth and chin which is basically all I got a glimpse of. I was too busy trying to stay on the road."

After another lengthy silence, he said, "I shouldn't have missed your call. I shouldn't have let you do this alone."

The memory of this morning's discoveries piled one on top of the other inside her head in that instant. "Ryan, despite your belief otherwise, you couldn't have stopped me. I had to follow my lead. Too much time has wasted already. The only reason I called you was because I figured out part of what Wilcox and Letson have been up to."

She spent the next few minutes telling him all that she had learned, with an emphasis on Walton's statements. By the time she'd finished, Ryan had parked in front of her house.

"We should call Bill and pass this information on to him," Ryan suggested, his gaze settling on hers. "We're going to need the Memphis field office to get in on this now."

"Why can't we go straight to the command center? Is Bill there?"

Ryan shot her a firm look. "You're not going anywhere. You've been through enough, already."

To have argued with him would have been a waste of energy at this point. She'd already gotten past him once today, he wouldn't let it happen again. Instead she shoved the car door open and climbed out. "Just make sure you call him and get someone on this before Walton goes missing like all the rest of our information sources."

Ryan grabbed his briefcase and followed her inside. She checked her telephone for messages and disappeared into her bedroom. Her white blouse was stained with blood. She probably wanted to change. And to be alone...away from him.

He shrugged out of his jacket and draped it across one end of the sofa. His cell phone in hand, he headed to the kitchen to make her something warm. He doubted if she'd bothered with lunch, so he scanned her cabinets for soup as he put a call through to Bill.

By the time he'd relayed the gruesome details of Mel's discoveries to Bill and thrown in a few hypoth-

eses of his own, the soup was ready. Before ending the
call, he told Bill to track down Letson. He'd been con-
veniently out of pocket the last couple of days. Ryan
definitely wanted to talk to him. He wasn't going to
tolerate the man's evasiveness any longer.

He tossed his phone onto the counter and searched
for a tray. When he'd found what he was looking for, he
arranged a bowl of soup on a plate with some crackers
on the side. Then poured a glass of milk and a cup of
the coffee he'd brewed. With the meal and a napkin on
the tray he went in search of Mel.

He found her in her room sitting in the middle of the
bed holding a picture of her daughter. The adrenaline
had gone, leaving her weak and grieving once more. He
set the tray aside and eased down on the bed next to her.

"She's a beautiful little girl," he said softly.

Mel nodded and sniffed, then her gaze locked with
his. "What if they cut her up like that, Ryan?" Tears
crested on her lashes. "What if they did that to my
baby?"

He cleared his throat of the lump rising there and
reached into his shirt pocket. "Mel, there's something
you should see." He handed her the clipped Polaroid
they'd found in Garland Hanes's wallet. "Hanes had
this on him. Rita Grider confirmed that Katlin's wearing the same gown in this photograph that she was in
the one she was shown to identify the body. Clearly,
Katlin is alive in this one."

Mel's breath caught. She looked from the photo
to him. "Why didn't you show me this before?" She
blinked rapidly to hold back the tears but a few escaped
and slid down her porcelain smooth cheeks.

He had to look away a moment before he could an-

swer. He wanted so desperately to touch her. "We...
ah..." His eyes met hers once more. "We didn't want
to give you false hope until we knew more." He shook
his head and looked a second time. "I've seen it happen
too many times. I couldn't..." The rest was too difficult
to say without giving away too much. She already suspected his feelings went way beyond the professional
scope. He'd seen the realization in her eyes.

"Ryan."

He looked at her then, knowing his eyes revealed too
much, but unable to deny her. "Yeah."

"Promise me that no matter what happens...that no
matter what you discover, you won't stop looking for
my daughter until you've found her."

The request confused him, startled him, too. Why would
she think he'd do otherwise? "You know I won't stop."

She smiled weakly. "I'm counting on that."

He couldn't stop himself now either... God knows
he tried. But he had to kiss her.

Mel should have stopped him...she really should
have. But she needed this as much as he appeared to.
She lifted her mouth to his and closed her eyes. The
feel of his lips against hers wrenched a gasp from her.
He hesitated but only for a second and then his mouth
opened and came down fully on hers.

Sensation after sensation exploded along her nerve
endings. Heat stirred way down deep inside her, making her melt with anticipation. He kissed her long and
deep, allowing the heat to build before he thrust his
tongue inside.

She moaned loudly, uncaring now of how wanton
and desperate she sounded. Of their own accord, her
arms went up and around his neck. And suddenly the

wall of his wide, muscled chest was pressed against her breasts. One hand glided along her spine while the other delved into her hair, careful of her latest injury.

Instinct took over completely then, led by a desire so strong, a need so desperate that she could deny neither.

She fell back onto the pillows, drawing him down with her. His heavy male body moved over hers, aligning hard lines and contours with her soft feminine curves and mounds.

"Melany," he murmured between kisses, "I've missed you so much."

His words sent a new kind of thrill through her. Her fingers speared into his hair and she kissed him harder, pressed her hips to his, reveling in the feel of his desire for her.

The ring of the telephone shattered the momentum.

Ryan froze, his mouth mere centimeters from hers. "We should answer that."

A fierce ache of need arrowed through her. "You're right," she said on a frantic breath.

He shifted up and off her as she reached for the telephone on her bedside table just as the third ring rent the air.

"Hello."

"Mel? Are you okay?"

Rita.

"Rita. Yes. I'm fine." She scooted up to a sitting position and pushed the hair from her face. Guilt immediately tugged at her. She hadn't even called her friend lately. "Is everything okay with you?"

"Thank God you're all right. The hospital called and wanted to know if I was okay. Apparently they still had my number listed for you."

Mel stilled. Her gaze met Ryan's. Those blue eyes had cleared of their lust and were watching her intently.

"I don't understand," Mel said carefully. "Who at the hospital called you?"

"I don't know. He might have said who he was, but I kind of lost it when he asked if I was all right after my latest accident and then he called me Ms. Jackson and I figured…" She lapsed into silence for a moment. "God, Mel, if I hadn't borrowed your SUV none of this would have happened. Katlin…" She made a painful keening sound. "It's my fault," she sobbed.

"No, Rita," Mel said firmly, clutching the receiver with both hands as if she could reach through and touch her friend. "None of this is your fault. Do you hear me?"

"I hear you." Rita cried harder in spite of her acknowledgement.

"Listen," Mel ordered, "we have every reason to believe that Katlin is alive. So you just stop crying this instant." Her own tears welled. "We're going to find her. Do you hear me?"

"Yes." Rita took a breath. "I'm sorry. I didn't mean to fall apart on you."

Mel massaged her aching forehead. With all that had been going on she hadn't realized how badly her head hurt until now. Maybe the blessed numbness had saved her until…until Ryan had distracted her. "It's okay. Everything's going to be okay."

"You'll call me as soon as you know anything?" Rita urged.

Mel swiped at her damp cheeks. "Definitely. Take care."

She hung up the phone and looked straight into those analyzing blue eyes focused steadily on her. "A man from the hospital called Rita by mistake and asked if she was all right? He thought she was me. He already knew about the accident."

"Eat," Ryan ordered. "And then we're going to the command center. I'll call Bill."

MEL PACED THE floor of the office Memphis P.D. had lent them for a command center. She couldn't sit. She had to keep moving. Bill and Ryan were doing the same.

"Here's what we've got," Bill said, pausing to pop another piece of nicotine-laced gum. He'd already brought them up to speed on what he'd learned today, but rehashing the information they had so far was the best way to glean previously missed details. "The M.E. is certain the caliber of the bullet that ripped into Hanes's head is not consistent with the .38 we found in his right hand. But since there's no slug, we can't confirm that. The M.E., however, feels the damage is more consistent with the 9 mm that offed Peterson and Mason, which was the same weapon, by the way. Ballistics confirmed that a little while ago."

"So the shooter is likely the same person," Ryan suggested.

"Maybe the same guy who tried to run me off the road," Mel added to the mix. "Except, why didn't he just shoot me?"

Ryan winced. Bill said, "Good point."

"Our M.E. is working on his assistant now. The one who signed off on all those autopsy reports. His boss apparently dragged him back from his little emergency trip back home. The M.E. hopes to wrench a confession out of the guy before we put the cops on his office. Apparently he's taken some heat in the past and wants to try to do this discreetly."

"And someone from the local Bureau office is verifying Walton's statement now?" Ryan asked.

Bill nodded. "I've got 'em swarming all over the hospital's files, too." He grinned. "Upton and I are no longer on speaking terms."

Mel liked Bill's style. Reel 'em in with whatever works and then go for the jugular.

"Do we have anything on Mason yet?" Mel wanted to know. This was all good and fine, the hospital was likely going to pay dearly for their misconduct, even if they never found Wilcox. But that didn't put her closer to finding her daughter. "And what about Letson?"

Bill lifted a skeptical brow. "Letson is missing in action. Has been since late yesterday. Cuddahy's working on Mason's finances, while our friendly hacker-for-hire is tracing where he's been on the World Wide Web."

"So," Mel began thoughtfully, "basically we're at a standstill. We have a number of things going on, but no place to go relative to the search for my daughter."

Ryan fixed his relentless gaze on hers. "We've got someone watching Desmond and Forest Lawn night and day. Anyone who could possibly have seen or heard anything relative to the hospital, the accident, and Mason's office is being questioned. We're on the right track, Mel. We just have to play the game...take the steps. Wait it out. You know the drill."

Yes, she knew the routine all too well. The longer her daughter was missing the less likely they were to find her.

Ryan looked to Bill then. "Anything on that couple in Dallas?"

Bill stole a look at Mel before clearing his throat.

"What couple in Dallas?" They'd been hiding stuff from her again. "Tell me. What couple?"

"In Mason's office I found a disk. It contained files related to private adoptions. A couple in Dallas were set to adopt a little girl matching Katlin's description three days after your accident."

Her heart rocketed into her throat, making speech near impossible. "Get me on a plane to Dallas," she demanded. "I want to see if she's there. Now!"

Ryan took her by the arms, she tried to jerk away, but he held on tight. "Mel," he said quietly, "we've got the Dallas Bureau going to the house right now. They'll call us the moment they have confirmation."

Didn't he understand? Her daughter might be there. "I have to go and see for myself. They could lie. The feds in Dallas don't know Katlin." Hysteria made her voice shrill. She told herself to calm down but she couldn't.

"We've faxed them all the pertinent information including a picture," Bill reassured her, drawing her attention to him. "They know what they're doing, Mel."

"We need you here," Ryan urged. "Katlin could still be close by."

When she would have argued the door burst open and Carter rushed in. "They I.D.'d the guy who tried to run Ms. Jackson over," he said breathlessly.

A hush fell over the room as they waited for him to continue.

"It was a Dr. Curtis Letson, chief of pediatrics at Memphis General."

CHAPTER THIRTEEN

RYAN'S CELL PHONE rang in the tense silence that settled after Carter's announcement.

"I'll...ah...go see what else I can find out," Carter stuttered as he backed out of the room.

Ryan's gaze shifted to Mel. The look of helplessness, disbelief, something on that order on her face, in her posture, made him want to put his arms around her. Letson had tried to kill her. Even worse, to her way of thinking, one more connection to her missing child was gone forever.

His phone rang again, seemingly more insistent this time. Reluctantly he snapped it open. It could be important. "Braxton."

"Ryan, this is Trent Tucker."

Trent. From the Colby Agency. A frown tugged across Ryan's brow. "Yes, Trent. How's it going in Chicago?"

Since his case wasn't connected to the agency, Ryan hadn't considered calling in. Maybe he should have. Then he remembered that Victoria had asked him to. Damn, he'd completely forgotten her request.

"I hope I'm not calling at a bad time."

Ryan glanced around the room and decided to take the call outside. "No, not at all. How can I help you?"

"Victoria wanted an update on the case you're working. She...wondered if you'd found the missing child."

Trent's tone sounded stilted as if there was something more behind his question than mere interest in the case. "We haven't located the child yet, but we now have reason to believe she's alive as the mother suspected." He closed his eyes and shook his head at the words he used, *the mother*—as though he had no feelings for her. Yes, there was still something between them, but the *they* he and Mel had once been would never be again. He'd hurt her too badly...she'd hurt him and then there was Katlin. And, somewhere in the mix, another man.

"That's good news," Trent agreed, sounding genuinely glad to hear it.

"I should have kept Victoria posted, but things have been a little crazy here," Ryan admitted. Other than basic human compassion, he couldn't see the need to keep anyone at the agency informed. This wasn't their case.

"I understand crazy," Trent offered, then, "Look, Ryan, I know you haven't been with the agency long, but Victoria lost a child about eighteen years ago."

The news surprised him. Victoria Colby was so strong, he had a hard time imaging any sort of evil touching her. "I didn't know that."

"It's not something she talks about. But whenever a case like this one comes up, you can still see remnants of that old devastation. It always takes its toll on her. We'd appreciate it if you'd let us know how it goes down there."

"Sure. I'll do that."

"Also, let us know if we can provide any assistance."

Ryan thanked him and ended the call. As he tucked

the phone back into his pocket he wondered at the information he'd just learned. His instincts automatically went on point whenever he learned of a missing child. He wondered if, when he got back, there was anything he could do to help Victoria. The case would be stone-cold by now. But he would gladly look into her son's disappearance. Eighteen years ago they hadn't possessed the advanced technology they had now. Not to mention a lot of headway had been made in understanding and identifying child predators. He might just be able to find something that had been missed.

Before Ryan could step back into the command center Bill and Mel came rushing out.

"Just got a call from the detective working Helen Peterson's homicide. They've found Wilcox's body and it looks like he left a note confessing to everything."

HOWARD WILCOX LAY crossways on a rumpled bed in a seedy motel room. Any dignity he'd had had drained out on the cheap sheets from the supposedly self-inflicted head wound caused by the 9 mm in his hand.

Ryan would bet a sum matching the national deficit that the 9 mm was the weapon used in Hanes's, Mason's and Peterson's murders. He'd also wager that all three, this one making four, had been carried out by the same unknown subject. The one they needed to find before anyone else who might know Katlin Jackson's where-abouts turned up dead. But if the shooter had been Letson, all was lost.

He glanced around the room, a couple of crime-scene techs were standing by waiting for the M.E.'s office to come take the body away while others were busy doing what had to be done prior to the body's removal.

Mel had taken one look at the scene and opted to stay outside.

"Another neat little package," Bill said facetiously as he skimmed the confession note once more. The document had been bagged as evidence, the protective plastic allowing them to analyze the final words of the victim without contaminating any trace evidence or prints it might carry.

"Forgive me, I could not stop myself. The money... I needed the money. I killed Garland Hanes, Helen Peterson and my friend and attorney Rodney Mason in hopes of hiding what I had done. But I can no longer live with myself," Bill read, his tone revealing his lack of conviction. "It was my fault Katlin Jackson died. I wanted to cover up my mistakes but things just got out of control. Please forgive me. If it will help, please know that Letson and I acted alone. We are the guilty ones...now I'll answer to God. Letson can tell you everything." Bill made a disgusted sound. "How frigging convenient."

"Case closed," Ryan offered with a serving of his own sarcasm. It was convenient that the police hadn't been tipped off about the body until after Letson was out of the way.

Bill handed the letter back to one of the techs. "Damn, this throws up another brick wall. All our leads keep turning up dead."

Ryan was certain Melany would be coming to the same conclusion about now. "Let's get the hell out of here," he muttered. There was nothing else they could do here, anyway.

Bill nodded. "I'll meet you two back at the command center."

Ryan went in search of Mel. As he'd suspected, she looked ready to burst into tears.

"Is it true?" she asked. "Did he say he'd killed my daughter?"

Jesus, someone had a big mouth. "We can't put any stock in anything in that letter. We can't even say for sure that he wrote it."

She jerked away from him when he would have reached for her. "Tell me, Ryan! Did he say that he hurt Katlin?"

He took a deep breath and told her the truth. "He said it was his fault she was dead."

A wail like that of a wounded animal issued from her throat and she fell against him sobbing so forcefully he felt sure she couldn't possibly breathe.

"Mel, I'm certain the letter was composed to throw us off track, to make us give up." He held her tighter against his chest. "Don't give up on me, okay? We'll find her. I know we will."

Long minutes later when she'd composed herself as best she could, he led her to the car and they drove in silence to the Downtown Precinct. He wished a thousand times that there was more he could say or do… but there was nothing he could offer except the relentlessness on which he'd built a reputation in the Bureau.

Ryan Braxton never gave up.

He wouldn't now.

WHEN THEY ARRIVED at the command center, Bill waited at the door. He had that look…the one that said *What took you so long—I've got an update.* Mel prayed he didn't have more devastating news. She wasn't sure how much more she could handle. She felt cold inside, cold and empty. And so damned fragile. Any second now she might just shatter completely.

She hated like hell that she'd fallen apart back there. Sucking in a ragged breath, she told herself to be strong. Don't lose hope. Be strong. For Katlin.

"What now?" Ryan growled.

A wave of relief washed over her at his tone. It was comforting to know that she wasn't the only one on edge here.

Bill looked taken aback. "Don't bite my head off. I didn't kill Wilcox."

Mel had to laugh, the sound brittle and pained. The things Bill could think to say.

Bill grinned. "Now that's more like it."

Ryan looked ready to explode with frustration. "Get to the point."

"Let's take it inside," Bill suggested, since M.P.D.'s finest moved about the long corridor that extended a good twenty yards in either direction in front of their borrowed office.

When Bill had closed the door behind them, he indicated the table and chairs. "Sit." This he directed at Mel.

Dread pooled in her stomach, dragging her down into the closest chair. "Tell me straight-out, Bill. I don't need protecting." She hadn't forgotten how they'd hidden that picture they'd found on Hanes from her.

Ryan sat down as if, he too, could bear the weight of holding himself up no longer.

Bill took a seat at the head of the rectangular table and braced his arms in front of him. "First, the M.E. has estimated Wilcox's time of death well before Mason's. He couldn't have killed Mason. So we can safely

assume that the rest of the bullshit in the so-called confession letter is just that."

She released a grateful sigh. Thank God.

But Bill had more. He turned fiercely solemn. "Mel,
I don't want you to get your hopes up just yet."

She held her breath. Please, God, let this be good.

"I'm waiting for a fax or an e-mail attachment from
the Dallas office. They contacted the couple we found
in Mason's secret files. An adoption had been arranged.
The payoff is first thing in the morning and then they're
supposed to pick up the child at the Dallas/Fort Worth
airport immediately afterward."

Melany's heart rate climbed to the point of causing
her head to spin just a little. "Is it Katlin?" The voice
sounded alien to her ears. Flat…vulnerable. She was so
damned afraid to believe…to hope.

"We don't know yet, but the couple did receive a
photo of the child. The Bureau is getting a copy to send
to us as we speak. We should know soon."

Her pulse thumping in her brain, Mel fought back the
tears burning behind her eyes. "If…it's not her, what
then?"

"We keep looking." Ryan answered the question.
"Mason had a lot of files. All recent. There will be others somewhere. We'll find them."

Mel nodded stiffly. She braced herself for disappointment and at the same time she clung to the glimmer of hope that still survived despite every reason to
shrivel and die.

The door opened and Carter spilled into the office
with his usual abruptness. "Got it, Agent Collins." He
thrust a single page at Bill.

He reached for it, then hesitated. "Give it to Ms. Jackson."

Carter nodded uncertainly. He turned to Melany, his smile a little strained. "Here you go, ma'am."

The whole world seemed to slow to a stop as Mel reached out to take the sheet of paper from the eager young officer. Snippets of memories flashed one after the other through her mind. Seeing her baby for the first time…holding that precious bundle and wishing that Ryan were there to share the blessed event with her… kissing her sweet blond head that last night before… before evil invaded their lives.

Her fingers closed around the document and Mel drew it toward her knowing that whatever she found her life would never be the same again. If, by the grace of God, she got her baby back she would make up for the mistakes she'd made. She would never take another second for granted and she would make sure her daughter knew her father. And, if this was not her child, she would make it her life's work to find her…one way or another.

Mel trained her tear-blurred gaze on the photo and it took about three seconds for her brain to assimilate what her eyes saw. Every ounce of emotion she possessed drained out of her in one ragged breath.

"It's her."

She looked up at Ryan and then Bill, tears tumbling down her cheeks. "It's my baby."

For one beat the two men she cared most about in this world stared at her, too relieved or too shocked to speak or act. Or maybe the world was still at a standstill. She couldn't say for sure which.

Suddenly the entire room burst into motion.

"Get me a duplicate of that photo," Bill ordered Carter. "I'm heading to the hospital to put the push on Upton. I've been pondering the idea all afternoon that his chiefs of E.R. and pediatrics couldn't possibly have pulled this off without his help. You go after Desmond. He has to know more than he's telling."

Mel looked to Ryan who hadn't spoken yet. Lost in his own thoughts, it was as if he hadn't heard Bill at all.

"No," he said then. "Not Desmond. He's just a pawn. They used him to get rid of evidence or to cover for them. He's not a major player. It started somewhere else."

The answer hit Mel with all the force of a rocket blast. *Dr. Wilcox knows people who want them really bad.* "The clinic."

CAROL ANN HENLEY was just preparing to close up the clinic when Ryan and Mel barged in. She'd already put on her coat and gotten her purse from beneath her desk.

"Is there a doctor in today?" Ryan asked when she looked up with something less than enthusiasm.

"I'm sorry, Mr. Braxton," she said with a lackluster smile. "Everyone's gone for the day except me." She sighed and pushed her chair in. "Is there something I can help you with?" she asked grudgingly.

Ryan walked up to the desk, his steps purposeful, his expression fierce. He was going to approach her a different way this time.

"Ms. Henley, do you know the penalty for being an accessory to a federal crime such as kidnapping?"

She made a sound of disbelief. "Are you accusing me of something, sir?" Her uncertain gaze flitted to Melany.

"Are you aware, Ms. Henley," Ryan pressed as he leaned forward and flattened his palms on her desk, putting himself eye to eye with her, "that Dr. Wilcox and Dr. Letson are dead. So is one of the nurses they worked with as well as an attorney named Rodney Mason?" Her eyes grew wider with each word. "You may be next."

She wagged her head vigorously from side to side. "I don't know anything about their dealings with that lawyer. I didn't want to know! I just wanted to help these girls." She looked out over the lobby as if it were filled to capacity as it had been two days ago.

"Illegal adoptions are just as much a crime as kidnapping," he went on. "They've already killed one scapegoat, Garland Hanes. If you cooperate with us, we can protect you."

Her mouth worked frantically before any words came out. Her face had paled several shades and she looked on the verge of getting to know the floor better.

"I... I don't know anything. You can look in the files but I don't think they keep anything here."

Ryan leaned nearer to her. "With the others dead, who would take care of business? Tie up the final loose ends?" He looked straight into those frightened eyes. "Like killing you?"

She blinked once, twice. "That only leaves one person."

Ryan could feel Melany literally vibrating with anticipation behind him. Before she climbed over the desk and shook the answer out of the woman, he demanded, "Who?"

She jumped. "Dr. Rodale. She knew everything. I think she came up with the idea to sell the babies these girls didn't need."

"Where is Rodale?" Ryan kept his roar to a minimum but the woman jumped again all the same.

She eased back a step. "She's…she's gone for a long weekend at the cabin. She won't be back until Monday."

"Where is this cabin?" Ryan straightened, but kept his savage glare focused on the woman.

"I don't know. I—"

"Then who does?"

She shrugged awkwardly. "Maybe her boyfriend, Dr. Upton. He's the administrator at Memphis General. It's his cabin."

"Thank you, Ms. Henley."

A new kind of anticipation buzzing to life, Ryan did an about-face and headed for the door with Mel right beside him.

"Wait!" the receptionist cried. "What about my protection?"

Ryan paused at the exit and shot her a look of feigned concern. "Call 911, tell them Special Agent Bill Collins needs a unit to see you home."

She grabbed for the phone.

Ryan wasn't worried about her. She wasn't a player. Besides, Upton and Rodale didn't have time for clean-up detail at the moment. He had a feeling they had a delivery and a getaway to make.

Ryan opened the car door for Melany. "What now?" she asked before getting in.

"We're going to catch up with Bill at the hospital and beat some information out of Upton."

His cell phone rang and he answered it as he skirted the hood. It was Bill.

"Upton's made a run for it."

"Let me guess," Ryan cut in, "he's gone to spend the weekend at his cabin."

"No, I mean he's gone. Hasn't been here all afternoon. According to his secretary he had out-of-town business."

"Find out where his cabin retreat is. That's where Dr. Rodale, the clinic's counselor, supposedly went for the weekend. She and Upton are a couple."

Bill swore. "I'll call you right back."

Ryan pulled out onto the street and took a few minutes to steel himself for the fight he was going to get. "Mel, I'm taking you to the precinct and I want you to stay there until we…get this done."

"Don't kid yourself, Braxton," she retorted. "No way in hell are you going after my daughter without me."

"You know how it gets during hostage negotiations. You'll be nothing but a distraction."

Her next response was not only anatomically impossible, but less than flattering.

Before he could toss out another perfectly good reason she shouldn't be involved his cell phone rang again.

"Braxton," he snapped. This was going to get sticky and the last thing he needed was his mind on taking care of the kid and her mother.

"Mr. Braxton, this is Greg Carter."

"You have that address for me?" He sure as hell didn't have time for anything else.

"We're working on that, sir. Agent Collins called me from the hospital. Apparently no one on Dr. Upton's staff knows anything about his cabin."

Big surprise. "Tell me what you do have, Carter," he asked pointedly.

"Well, sir, I've got the county clerk on another line

and she's found two records of property owned by Dr. Upton. One is his residence here in Memphis. Hold on, sir."

Ryan could hear the rookie speaking to someone on another line. He took a long deep breath to counter the frustration mounting in his chest.

"Mr. Braxton, the second property is located a ways out of town. About seventy miles. She has to cross-reference with another county but the clerk's gonna give me driving directions and I'll pass 'em on to you. She can't guarantee this is the place you're looking for. It could be nothing but a plot of land."

"I understand. Carter, after you've given me the directions, call Agent Collins and give him the same. Then send some backup either from your department or the one closest to the location."

"Yes, sir."

Ryan handed the phone to Mel. "You give me the directions as he gives them to you so I can focus on driving."

She nodded and identified herself to Carter.

Ryan flexed his fingers, then tightened them on the steering wheel. If they didn't find Katlin tonight, they'd just have to set up a trap with the Dallas couple tomorrow.

If he had to drive all night long he wouldn't stop—wouldn't quit—until he personally placed that child back in Mel's arms.

IT WAS DARK by the time they reached the turnoff to Upton's cabin. They'd left the delta of Memphis behind and had reached the gently rolling hills of middle Tennessee. They'd followed an unpaved road for the past five miles and now they sat at the bottom of the drive that would take them to their final destination—Upton's property.

Mel waited as patiently as she could for Ryan to park the car on the side of the road about twenty yards from the turnoff. When they'd last had cellular service, he'd told Carter that he would leave the car where backup could locate it before going in.

He reached in back and took a gun from his brief-case. Mel hadn't realized he still carried a weapon. She was suddenly very grateful that he did. There was no way to know what they would run into up there.

Her eyes had adjusted to the dark by the time he'd readied for the next step. "Mel." He looked at her. Though she couldn't read his eyes in the sparse moon-light, she could see the determined set of his jaw. "Stay here until backup arrives. They'll need someone to fill them in on the route I've taken."

She shook her head resolutely. "No, Ryan. I'm com-ing with you. If my daughter is up there, I need to be there, too."

He sighed. "If you're determined to take the risk, then so be it."

She grabbed his arm before he could open his door. "Don't preach to me about risks, Ryan. I've never been afraid of a risk. Can you say the same?"

Mel immediately regretted the words. She'd taken the biggest risk of all, but she hadn't given him the chance to take it. She'd kept her secret…kept it still while he operated in the dark.

"Never mind," she muttered and climbed out of the car.

Careful of every step they took and staying in the edge of the trees that ran alongside the dirt road, they made their way toward what they hoped would be a cabin. She prayed that they hadn't come all this way for nothing.

When they'd cleared yet another bend in the narrow drive, Mel caught sight of lights in the distance. She yanked on Ryan's sleeve.

"I see it," he whispered.

There was something here. A house or cabin. Something.

Still remaining cautious but moving a bit faster now, they reached the small clearing where the cabin stood in no time flat.

She and Ryan both had already turned off their cell phones since there was no service. They had no way of knowing how close behind backup might be.

"I'm going to try and get a closer look to determine if both Upton and Rodale are in there. You stay put and I'll be back as soon as I've had a look."

Mel nodded. His clothing was dark and he had the gun. His suggested move was the only reasonable option.

She watched his shadowy form disappear into the landscape, staying close to the trees and larger bushes.

Sitting back on her heels, she closed her eyes in an attempt to slow the thoughts whirling inside her head. Katlin could be in that cabin. She could be this close.

The people holding her child would have guns. She didn't doubt it considering the body count thus far. She chewed her lower lip and fought the trembling that was wreaking havoc with her ability to remain still. She didn't want to get this close only to have her baby hurt in the final showdown.

She didn't want Ryan hurt, either.

And, God, she still hadn't told him the truth.

She cradled her face in her hands and tried to think what to do. How could she keep this from him now… when they were so close…when he could be killed?

Leaves rustled a few feet away and she stilled. Listened intently. Something moved. Her heart stuttered to a stop in the three seconds it took her to identify Ryan.

He moved in close to her and took one hand in his for a moment before he spoke. "She's in there."

Those three little words tightened Mel's throat until speech was impossible. She held back the sob that threatened to burst through the clench of emotions.

"She looks fine. She's sleeping."

Mel nodded so he'd know she understood. If she opened her mouth now, the sobs would unleash.

"I didn't see any sign of Upton, but Rodale is there. She's armed."

She had to take a breath. "Okay," she managed to say. "What do we do now?"

"You stay here and wait for our backup to arrive. I'm going in to try and reason with her."

That could be a mistake! "Wait!" She snagged him by the arm. "What if she hurts Katlin? What if she—"

"Mel." He placed his hand over hers where it gripped his arm. "I know what I'm doing. Rodale and I have talked before. I've got a pretty good handle on her personality type. If I go to the door alone, she won't feel as threatened. I'm going to offer her a deal. She's no fool. She might just take it. Now, you wait for Bill and the others."

"Wait," she said again. She rocked forward onto her knees and held on to his arm with a death grip. "There's something you have to know before you go in there."

This wasn't the time! a part of her ranted. It was the only time, another internal voice shouted. If she didn't tell him and something happened in there to him or to Katlin she'd never be able to live with herself. She'd let it happen once, she wasn't going to risk it again. She'd almost lost Katlin and Ryan would never have known her.

If only for a few seconds, she wanted him to know that that little girl was his.

"Ryan, I didn't run to another man when I left you."

"You don't have to do this," he cut in quickly. "You don't owe me any explanations. What happened was—"

"But I do owe you an explanation," she countered. "I haven't been with anyone else since I left you."

Even in the murky moonlight she could see him frowning.

"That little girl in there is *your* daughter. I didn't tell you because I knew you didn't want children. I just left."

She knew that if she could see his face more clearly, it would reflect the shock he must feel. Those deep blue eyes would look at her with disbelief and accusation.

"I know I should have told you when you showed up here to help, but I couldn't. I probably shouldn't now. But it's the truth and I can't hold it in any longer.

"Katlin is your daughter."

CHAPTER FOURTEEN

KATLIN IS YOUR DAUGHTER.

Ryan didn't move for a second that turned into ten. He stared through the darkness knowing he wouldn't be able to see Mel's eyes but needing to try all the same. One emotion after the other raged through him. Confusion, frustration, anger, resentment...how could she not tell him something like this?

Before he could form the words to accurately describe the questions and emotions whirling inside him a twig snapped about ten yards behind their location.

"Don't move," he said under his breath.

Thankfully, she didn't argue.

Moving soundlessly, Ryan eased in the direction of the noise that had interrupted the engulfing silence. He assumed it would be Bill and the backup he'd requested, but without communications he couldn't be sure.

"Braxton."

The rusty, hushed voice belonged to Bill.

Ryan eased closer. "You whisper like my grandmother. This way." He touched Bill's shoulder and signaled toward Mel's location.

When they'd moved back into position, forcing away the new emotions clawing at him, Ryan asked, "What kind of team do we have?"

Bill patted Mel's arm. A gesture of reassurance since

they couldn't make eye contact in the dark. "We've got a two-man unit down by the road just in case Upton shows up, but I don't think he's going to. I believe he's decided to cut his losses and make a run for it or else he's already in Dallas setting up the final trade. M.P.D.'s checking out the mass transit options. And I've got four men with me."

Ryan surveyed the darkness behind them, before he could ask, Bill went on, "They've fanned out around the cabin."

Mel drew in a sharp breath. "They know not to make a move, right?"

The urgency in her voice tugged at Ryan…but too many other alien and unsettling feelings kept him from reaching out to her. A pang of guilt stabbed him but he suffered just enough resentment to ignore it. They all had to stay focused.

"They won't move without my command." Bill patted what appeared to be a radio clipped to his shoulder. Ryan's eyes had adjusted sufficiently to make out the familiar bulge.

"I need to go in alone," Ryan said, getting to the point. "I've met this woman before. She's not the type who'll react well to an invasion. She needs control. I'm going to let her think I'm here alone and that she's in charge."

"I don't know, Ryan," Mel said, worry weighting her tone.

Bill grunted. "You that sure about your impression of the woman after only one brief meeting, Braxton?"

"I'm sure," he said to Bill. He couldn't bring himself to respond directly to Mel right now. His equilibrium was still reeling with too many unfamiliar emotions related to her confession. *Katlin was his daughter.* "If we barge in…the child might pay the price."

One beat, then another, of tense silence passed.

"All right." Bill pulled something from the belt at his waist and fingered the controls before offering what appeared to be a second radio to Ryan. "Clip this to your waist. I've got it on transmit. I'll be able to hear what's going in there."

Ryan fixed the radio in place and tucked his weapon in his waistband at the small of his back. "I need to go in now before some fluctuation in the too-quiet ecosystem here warns her that she's got company."

"Something to consider," Bill warned, waylaying him for a moment. "If she knows we're on to them, she may react very differently from the last time you met."

"I'm going in under the assumption that she doesn't know."

"It's your call."

When he would have moved forward, Mel stopped him with a hand on his arm. His chest constricted with a new onslaught of emotions. "Be careful."

Part of him wanted to say something reassuring… but he still couldn't find the right words. Time was slipping away. He had to go now. He stood. Bill quietly conveyed his intentions to the team. Then, without looking back, Ryan strode toward the deck that spanned the front of the cabin.

The child inside was his daughter. For reasons he could not fully comprehend she was all that mattered at the moment.

When Ryan reached the deck he took special care of each wooden step leading up from the ground. Just one creak could startle the woman inside, sending her into defensive mode.

Once at the door, he stood to the side in case she fired first and answered later. He took a breath and knocked firmly.

Dead silence echoed from the other side.

He knocked again.

The door suddenly swung inward. The barrel of a small handgun landed in his face.

Though her frame was backlit from the interior glow, her surprise evidenced itself clearly on her face. "What're you doing here?" She glanced furtively beyond him.

"We need to talk."

"I don't know why you came all the way out here or how you found out I was even here," she said, suspicion rising in her tone, "but I can't imagine that we have anything to talk about." She covertly surveyed the yard again before meeting his eyes.

She was trying to decide if he was alone.

"Can I come inside?" he asked, determined to get a foot through the door before her suspicion mounted any higher.

"Fine," she snapped as she backed up a couple of steps. "Come on in."

Ryan advanced the two steps she had retreated.

"Close the door," she ordered, the weapon still trained expertly on his face.

"I wouldn't have taken you for the type who likes to play with guns," he said casually as he closed the door behind him.

She laughed. "I imagine there are a lot of things you don't know about me."

"I know a few things. Like the fact that your lover has run out on you?" he suggested pointedly.

Something resembling confusion cluttered her expression briefly. "He's on his way here." She glanced at the clock on the far wall. "Another twenty minutes and he'll be here. Unfortunately, I won't be able to protect you then. Coming here was a mistake."

Ryan shook his head slowly from side to side. "He's not coming, Dr. Rodale, and you know it. He's long gone. Probably left you to take the fall."

She cocked the weapon, the resounding click echoed deafeningly in the room. "Well, since we're being honest, I know you have friends out there. I'm no fool. Did you think you could come in here and talk me into surrendering?" She made a disgusted sound. "No way. I know what I'd be facing. You think you can convince me that cooperating will save my ass?" She laughed long and loud. "I'm a psychologist, Mr. Braxton, I know all the head games you people play."

Ryan moved a step in her direction. "We only want—"

"Stop right there!" She tightened her fingers around the grip of her weapon. "Take off your jacket and turn all the way around."

Careful not to make any sudden moves he did as she said, dropping his jacket to the floor. She jerked the weapon from his waistband and tucked it into her own. The radio was next. She tossed it onto the nearest chair.

"Dr. Rodale, we know how a man like Upton can use people," he offered quietly, hoping to get her thinking about the possibility of escaping punishment. "He used Wilcox and Letson. And Hanes. We're certain he used you. Help us straighten this mess out and your cooperation will be rewarded."

Another of those dry, sinister laughs. "Please. You think Lance used me?" She pressed her free hand to her chest as if the idea were simply ludicrous. "That idiot couldn't organize his own personal life much less a complicated operation like this."

"But Helen Peterson led us to believe that he was the man in charge," Ryan lied, hoping to push the right button.

"That stupid bitch lied!" She rolled her eyes emphatically. "I'm—" Rodale thumped her chest "—the man in charge. Lance didn't have the guts to do what had to be done when things started falling apart. You should have seen the look on his face when I told him how Letson and I had taken care of Hanes."

Ryan shrugged, hoping her loud voice didn't wake the child sleeping in the next room. He'd seen Rodale put the child in bed when he'd peeked around the edge of the blinds. Cheap, ready-made blinds rarely fit the windows exactly right, allowing for a narrow view inside. Lucky for him, whoever decorated this place hadn't known that or didn't care.

"He took care of the others for you, what else did you want him to do?" he prodded nonchalantly, hoping to get a clearer picture of who had done what. Even if he didn't make it out of here, Bill would hear everything.

Her posture stiffened, her chin lifted arrogantly. Oh yes, Dr. Rodale liked being in control…in charge. Her ego would stand for no less.

"That wimp didn't have the guts for it," she snarled. "I always had to see that the dirty work was done."

Ryan pulled a sympathetic face. "I suppose you did get used, after all."

Fury streaked across her features. "It wasn't his idea for me to tidy up his mess! It was mine. Just like all the other brilliant plans. I'm the one who came up with the idea to sell the unwanted children those little whores at the clinic mass produce." She shook her head in disgust. "He was the one who went on and on about how wasteful it was to put the child of a single parent into the foster-care system after tragedy struck. But I was the one who masterminded how to do something about it. Everything would have been perfect if that idiot, Wilcox, hadn't made a mistake."

"You were right," Ryan said, pumping up her ego. "The plan was solid, but Katlin Jackson was a mistake."

"Wilcox was supposed to screen the patients properly. Fool!" she roared. "He's the one who got us into this mess." She smirked. "But he paid dearly for that mistake."

Ryan ran a hand through his hair. She started as if she'd feared he'd somehow hidden a weapon there. "You know, what I don't understand is how you expected to get away with all those bungled autopsies. It was only a matter of time before someone figured out organs were missing from those dead children."

She scoffed venomously. "That was one of *his* bad ideas. Lance was doing that long before we met. He wanted to capitalize on the donations research companies were happy to make if he offered certain donations of his own. He knew the risk. I had nothing to do with it."

Ryan shrugged. "Who was going to miss them? The kids were dead, what did they need the organs for?"

She smiled. "Men. You all think alike. One should never reap a harvest without replenishing the fields as a proper reward. You see, at the clinic, those girls all got something for their trouble. Hell, we had repeat clients. You take a little something, you give a little something back. That keeps everybody happy and then you don't run into trouble."

"The barter system," Ryan offered. She was slick. No doubt about that.

"Something like that. I prefer to think of it as business. Supply and demand." She widened her stance and tightened her hold on her weapon. "Now, it's been fun reminiscing with you, Mr. Braxton, but it's time to get down to business. You tell your friends out there that you're taking me out of here. Play your cards right and maybe I'll let you go when I'm on a plane to some exotic place far from here." She smiled flirtatiously. "Or maybe you'll decide to go with me. I have enough money for both of us. That's something else I was better at than Lance. But he won't need it anyway since I'm quite certain he's too stupid to get away without being caught. Is that what this is about? Did *he* tell you I was here?"

"He said you were holding the Jackson child here until time to make the transfer in Dallas tomorrow around noon."

Shock widened her eyes. Until that moment she had still been fairly confident that her lover was off waiting for her as planned, which he probably was, but she didn't know that for sure.

"That son of a bitch," she hissed. "I'll kill him."

Ryan laughed dryly, echoing her previous hate-filled noise. "You'll have to find him first."

"He was supposed to wait in Dallas at the Cattle-men's Hotel. But I know he's not there, you have him, don't you? That's how you knew I was here."

"Yes, we do," Ryan lied. He'd know she was lying when she said Upton was on his way here. "If you'll leave the child behind for my *friends*, I'll drive you out of here just like you suggested. You can turn me loose whenever you feel safe."

Her eyes narrowed. "How do you know I have the child with me already? I didn't tell Lance when I was going to pick her up."

Ryan bit back a curse. A strategic error. "You're right, he didn't say, but I've seen the kid's photo. That's her behind you, isn't it?"

MEL'S HEART STALLED in her chest as the words crack-led over Bill's radio. Katlin was in the room… Rodale had a gun. Mel lunged to her feet. She had to protect her daughter.

In a flash Bill's hand snaked out and manacled her wrist. "Sit. He knows what he's doing."

"Bill, I have to—"

A gun blast echoed, splintering the silence of the night.

"Move in!" The order came from Bill.

Suddenly the woods were alive with the tromping of boots. Brush and twigs crackled. Bill released her and rushed forward. Mel couldn't move. Fear paralyzed her.

Her baby was in there.

Gunshot.

Her feet were suddenly moving. She was running to-ward the cabin. Tears blurred her vision but she didn't slow down.

"Mel! Wait!"

Somehow Bill's voice was behind her now.

She burst through the cabin's front door and skidded to a halt, momentarily blinded by the interior light.

Blood. There was blood.

A wail rent the air. Mel knew it came from her though she didn't remember issuing the sound.

The woman, Rodale, was on the floor. Dead or unconscious. There was blood. Ryan. He pushed to his feet. The bright, crimson red stained his shirtsleeve. Ran down the fingertips of that same hand. He was hit.

Mel's breath rushed out of her in one long whoosh as her gaze swept the room. Where was Katlin?

"In there." Ryan nodded toward another door.

Before Mel could order her feet into forward motion she heard the whimpering.

Her baby!

She was across the room and through the door when she heard Bill and the others swarm in. What had felt like an eternity had only been mere seconds.

The room was dark. Mel flipped on the overhead light. Katlin sat in the middle of the bed rubbing her eyes against the sudden brightness or the tears or maybe both.

A sob burst out of Mel as she ran to her child. She thanked God over and over as she hugged her baby to her chest. She lost count of the times she told Katlin she loved her. Then, when she'd calmed a bit, she inspected her for any sign of injury.

Katlin cried at the injustice of it all. She never had liked being awakened before she was ready. Mel cried with her, held her close.

"Mel."

She looked up to find Bill in the doorway. "We need to go. Ryan's going to need a doctor."

The blood.

His arm.

Fear closed around her heart. She'd seen the injury but hadn't fully absorbed the ramifications. All she'd had on her mind was her child's safety.

She sprang to her feet, Katlin in her arms, and rushed into the other room. The moment her gaze fell upon Ryan she gasped. There was so much blood. The entire shirtsleeve appeared soaked.

"It's no big deal," he said. "It looks worse than it is." And then he fell silent, those deep blue eyes settling on Katlin.

"It may be nothing, but we're taking you to the nearest hospital. Now," Bill barked, sending the team he'd brought with him into double time.

Rodale had been handcuffed and was currently being dragged out the door. She was still unconscious.

Ryan hadn't taken his eyes off Katlin. Mel summoned her courage and walked over to where he stood and offered her child to him. "This is Katlin," she said softly as he curled his good arm around the protesting child. "Your daughter."

He didn't have to say anything in response. The kaleidoscope of emotions on his face and in his eyes spoke for him. He didn't even seem to mind the baby's fretful cries.

"Save the reunion for when he isn't bleeding all over the place," Bill growled, looking wholly confused by what he'd just seen and heard.

Mel relieved Ryan of a squirming Katlin. "I'll explain it to you later," she said to Bill.

Ryan looked from Mel to Katlin and back, but Bill ushered him out the door before he could say anything.

Mel followed. All the uncertainties of the past came rushing back. Ryan had not wanted children. That had made her sure she was doing the right thing. But now, it seemed so wrong. She'd lied to him. Kept his child from him.

What kind of future could they possibly have?

Where did Katlin fit into their damaged relationship?

SOME TIME THAT night or maybe it was the next morning, Ryan sat in Mel's bedroom watching her and her daughter sleep.

The gunshot had only been a flesh wound, just a nasty gash through soft tissue. Lots of blood but no real damage. He'd tried to tell Bill it wasn't so bad but the man had acted like he'd been on the verge of death. Ryan decided then and there that Bill was going soft.

But then maybe he was, too.

He'd taken a chance that if Rodale thought the child had come into the room that she'd look, and Ryan had gotten the upper hand. Rodale had been booked and the Dallas P.D. had collared Upton at the hotel Rodale told them about. Forest Lawn's director as well as the assistant medical examiner had been taken into custody. They had learned that Walton had made a call to Upton to dash the investigation in his face, unknowingly putting Mel in grave danger. Upton had sent Letson to stop her. Finally all the loose ends had been covered.

Now there was nothing to do but wait. See where this day would really end.

Mel had waited at the hospital for him while he got patched up. Katlin had gone back to sleep after letting the world know she hadn't appreciated being awakened in the middle of the night. Ryan could find no words to explain what he'd felt when he'd held his child. But it was seeing her with Mel even now that truly amazed him.

That was the most incredible part. The bond between mother and child. All this time Mel had known her child was alive. No matter what anyone told her, she'd known in her heart that Katlin still needed her. How extraordinary that must feel, he decided. To be that connected to another human being. He'd watched them together on the long journey back to Memphis and after they'd arrived at Mel's house. She'd insisted that he stay...that they needed to talk. But then she'd fallen asleep while trying to get her daughter to do the same. He hadn't had the heart to wake her.

He'd been angry at first when she told him that Katlin was his daughter. How else was he supposed to react? Then things had gotten a little crazy and there'd been no time to dwell on it. After he'd had a chance to think about it he realized that the deception was no one's fault but his own. Now he knew why she'd made him promise that he'd keep looking for her child no matter what he discovered. But what he had really discovered was the depth of his own faults.

Fear had prevented him from allowing this very kind of connection to anyone...even to Melany. He wouldn't risk losing someone who meant that much to him. He'd seen too much. His mind simply hadn't been able to wrap around the concept of taking that kind of chance. But he'd lost Mel anyway and he'd definitely loved her.

Still did.

He'd left her with no choice. He'd been so adamant

about not wanting children that she'd felt she had no other alternative. The Pill had failed. That much she'd told him sometime during this night. The pregnancy was a surprise and complication to her at the time, but, unlike him, she had welcomed the risk…the possibilities. With good reason she had felt that he wouldn't respond the same way. So she'd let him off the hook. She'd left without saying a word about the child she carried.

His child.

How could he blame her for what she'd done?

He couldn't.

Somehow he had to make the past up to her. If she would allow him to.

His weary gaze roamed the beautiful features of her face. The bandage near her hairline made his heart twist with remembered horror. The bedside lamp cast a soft glow over her and the child nestled against her chest. The little girl—his little girl—was so beautiful. Just like her mother.

He'd wanted to hold her again but she'd had enough trauma in her life the past few days. He could hold her more later, when she'd gotten used to him. But he yearned to now. Though he hadn't known of her existence until a few days ago and hadn't known she was his until a few hours ago, the urgency to touch her… to protect her was overpowering. The sweet relief in Mel's voice when she'd called her friend Rita to relay the news had undone him even further.

Coffee. He needed coffee.

He didn't want to sleep until Mel was rested and awake. It was that whole protection thing he knew. He wasn't about to risk letting down his guard and losing the child he'd only just found. Or the woman who would own his heart until eternity.

In the kitchen, he poured water into the coffee-maker and dumped fresh grounds into the drip basket. He punched the appropriate buttons and the machine went to work.

"Ryan."

He turned at the sound of Mel's voice. The smile that stretched across his face was automatic. He'd seen her like this so many times before...when they were together. Standing in a nightshirt looking at him with her hair tousled and her skin flushed from sleep.

God, she was so damned beautiful.

"I didn't mean to wake you." He should have stayed out of her room and let them sleep, but he'd needed to be close to them and drink in the wonder of it all.

She shook her head and folded her arms over her middle. "You didn't. A dream woke me."

He frowned. "A dream?"

She moved over to the counter near the sink and leaned against it. She nodded. "I was dreaming of a big old house with lots of children running around in it."

Her voice remained soft and just a little thick with sleep, but her eyes glittered with something else.

Desire, he realized with a jolt.

"Where was this house?" He moved toward her, the step more instinct that conscious action.

She shrugged and the nightshirt slipped off her shoulder, bearing a creamy expanse of delicate flesh he yearned to touch. "I don't know. But it felt like home."

"Lots of children?" he encouraged as he took yet another step.

She nodded. "At least four."

The final step he took put him toe-to-toe with her. "But we only have one and we don't have a big house."

She looked up at him, uncertainty in those green eyes now. "But we could have a big house," she offered cautiously. "We could be a family…if we can get beyond the past."

His gaze locked on those lush lips and he had to dampen his own. "The past is gone…over. All we have is now." His eyes lifted to meet hers. "And forever. If—" he hesitated as he searched those emerald depths that had filled with such hope "—you can forgive me for being a fool."

"I've already forgiven you." She reached up and touched his face. Just a simple caress but her touch set him on fire. "Can you forgive me for doubting the man I knew in my heart you were all along?"

"Never happened," he murmured.

"Then I'd say we have an agreement," she whispered back.

He smiled and rested his forehead against hers. "I'm kind of new at this stuff," he said softly. "Is there any chance our daughter will sleep for a little while?"

"I put her in her crib and closed the door," she said silkily. "We can take this negotiation to the bedroom, if you'd like."

"Eventually," he murmured thickly. "But at the moment I have plans for an appetizer that starts right here." He nibbled that silky shoulder. "Right now."

He kissed her lips.

Mel melted against his chest, desperate for his touch. How she had missed this man. Those firm lips and that bold tongue teased her mouth playfully. She buried her fingers in his hair and pulled him more firmly against her.

Using his good arm he helped her up onto the edge of the countertop and burrowed between her thighs, spreading them until his hips rested firmly against her mound. Instinctively she pressed against him. He groaned a savage response. A sigh echoed in her throat, allowing him to feel as well as to hear her approval.

He stopped kissing her long enough to tug her nightshirt up and off, revealing her unrestrained breasts. For a while he simply looked at her, seemingly content to study the curve and shape of those aching mounds. She wanted him to touch her…to take her into his mouth.

As if he'd read her mind, that hot, wicked mouth closed over one taut nipple. He suckled and nibbled while she writhed uncontrollably. He took his sweet time, then justly pleasured the other breast. She wondered vaguely how she would ever last…she wanted him so desperately. It felt so good to have his mouth on her breasts…his hands sliding over her skin. Her body threatened to erupt into climax even now.

Unable to stand anymore she reached for the closure of his trousers. The belt and button out of her way, she slowly lowered the fly over his hardened flesh. A tingle shimmered through her at the thought of having him inside her. She remembered well what a good lover he was.

He lifted her slightly from the counter and dragged her panties to her thighs. Her bare bottom settled back onto the cool surface as he slid her lacy underwear all the way down to her ankles and then off. He tossed them aside and, while she watched intently, unbuttoned his shirt so slowly she wanted to scream with frustration.

The shirt drifted to the floor, leaving that broad, muscled chest naked. He kicked off his shoes and shoved the trousers she'd unfastened to his feet, then kicked them aside, as well. She looked pointedly at his briefs and he shucked those next.

It was her turn to revel in the sight of pure male beauty. He was big and hard…for her. His body was as perfectly lean and sculpted as it had been two years ago. Her gaze bumped into the bandage on his arm and she winced.

"Does it hurt?" she asked softly.

"I don't know," he said bluntly. "The only thing I know right now is how much I want you."

She opened her thighs wider in blatant invitation and he moved toward her. She had always loved the way he moved. So sleek and fluid. So incredibly sexy.

At over six feet, his height was perfect for what came next. He wrapped her legs around his waist and nudged her intimately. She gasped at the contrast of cool counter beneath her bottom and hot, hard steel parting her desire-swollen channel. He groaned a primal response.

"I've never stopped loving you, Melany," he murmured, his breath ragged with the effort of holding back the instinct to thrust.

She looked into those blue eyes and smiled. "Show me."

He eased into her an inch or so. Her eyes closed and her head fell back to rest against the cabinet as she savored the ecstasy of the sweet, stretching sensation. It had been so long…two years. She hadn't been able to bring herself to allow another man to touch her.

"You're so tight," he whispered, surprised.

She opened her eyes and smiled at him. "There hasn't been anyone since you, Ryan. I never wanted anyone else."

He eased his hips forward another fraction. Her breath caught. Fire erupted low in her belly and she knew instantly that she would come before he was fully inside her.

"Hurry, Ryan," she urged, her fingers digging into his shoulders. She wanted him deep inside her when the explosion started.

With one powerful flex he filled her. Her concentration fragmented as wave after wave of sensation washed over her, centering on her innermost core.

He grunted savagely, holding still while her feminine muscles stretched and throbbed around him, rhythmically squeezing his thick sex, accommodating his grand size.

"Tell me," he growled, the sound guttural and breathless.

Ryan wanted desperately to know that she felt the same way he did. He needed to hear the words. His entire being stood on the precipice of tumbling headlong into orgasm when he'd scarcely gotten inside her and, yet, his heart wouldn't stop aching for the words. Had he not been ready to scream with release he would have laughed. The ruthless, determined and overconfident Ryan Braxton had his Achilles heel.

Melany.

And the child they had created together.

Those lovely green eyes opened to him, still glazed with the thrill of release. Her lips curled ever so slightly and she whispered the words he wanted to hear so badly.

"I love you, Ryan. I won't ever stop."

Before he plunged to his own climax, he kissed her. Not a gesture to make up for the past…a kiss filled with promise for the future.

Their future.

As a family.

EPILOGUE

VICTORIA FLIPPED THROUGH her schedule for the day. It was light. Too light. She preferred to keep busy. She glanced at the stack of messages left over from the day before. Lucas had called. But she hadn't called him back.

She seemed to be having more and more difficulty recently getting through the days, connecting with those who knew her best. It didn't make sense. But, deep down, she actually knew it did. Leberman had gotten close…too close. He'd almost taken Lucas's life. Could have, in fact. That didn't make sense, either. Why would he go to such lengths to develop such an elaborate set up only to walk away without killing her or Lucas? The very people he loved to hate.

He'd already killed her husband…and her son, she was certain. That old hurt welled inside her. No matter that eighteen years had passed, it still pained her to think of the loss. This case with Melany Jackson down in Memphis had reminded her, oh so sharply, how vulnerable she still was to the hurt.

Lucas had his people tracking Leberman, or at least trying to. No one knew exactly where he was. No one would until he was ready to make his presence known. Leberman had had the same training as Lucas…the same as James Colby. He knew how to lure his prey. How to go in for the kill. He was playing a game. Had been for all these years. He'd taken her husband and her son. What else did he want?

The agency, she felt confident. But there was more. He had plans. Plans that had been nearly two decades in the making. He hadn't passed on the opportunity to kill Lucas on that island a few months ago for no reason. However, they would not know his plans until he chose to reveal them.

Victoria slammed her fist down on her desk. She was sick to death of living with the threat of that devil. She was sick of living in the shadow of the past *period*.

What had she done to deserve this pain and suffering?

It was past time she rose from the ashes of her past and forged ahead with a future. One that included Lucas. They had a right to be together. She'd mourned James and little Jimmy long enough.

She swiped viciously at a lone tear that escaped her tight rein on her emotions. She was not looking back any longer.

A light tap on her door dragged her back to the here and now. "Yes?" She smoothed a hand over her hair and squared her shoulders. It was past time she proved her mettle.

Simon stepped into her office. "Good morning, Victoria."

"Good morning, Simon." She indicated one of the chairs in front of her desk. "You have an update for me this morning?"

"Yes." He settled into one of the upholstered chairs. "Ryan called. They found the child last night. She's fine."

Thank God. Victoria produced a tremulous smile. "That's wonderful news. Will Ryan be staying in Memphis for a while?"

She knew that he'd had a past relationship with the woman in the case.

"Yes," Simon confirmed.

That was good as well. Ryan Braxton was a fine man, he deserved to be happy. Didn't everyone?

"Excellent." Victoria sat up a little straighter. "Would you like to begin the morning briefing a little early?" Since Ian was on vacation with his wife and children, Simon was her second in command.

"Actually I wanted to discuss a personal matter with you."

"Certainly." He looked so serious. Surely all was well with Jolie. She'd moved to Chicago last month so that she and Simon could start a family.

"Ryan Braxton built a reputation in the Bureau for finding missing children. He was the best at one time. Considering the situation in Memphis, I'd say he likely still is."

A finger of dread nudged Victoria, elevating her senses to a higher state of alert.

"He has offered to look into your case," Simon went on, bringing to fruition her worst fears. "He may find something others missed. Trent Tucker has asked to be involved, as well."

Victoria went stiff with an emotion she could not name. It took several seconds for her to regain the ability to speak. "I appreciate Trent's and Ryan's kind offer, but it's been eighteen years. I don't see the point. My son isn't coming back." When Simon would have argued, she raised a hand to stop him. "I don't want to discuss it further, Simon. I'm putting the past behind me." She leveled her gaze on his. "Starting now."

Later, after the daily briefing, Simon left Victoria's

office, concern mounting inside him. It wasn't like Victoria Colby to give up on anything, even an eighteen-year-old case. He'd noticed her odd behavior of late, as if her attention were divided, splintered. And then, the other day she'd fainted. The doctor had recommended an extended vacation. Simon was pretty sure she'd made no plans to take his advice thus far.

It was time to call Lucas.

Simon strode straight to his office and put the call through. Victoria wouldn't like it, but he would just have to risk it. When he heard Lucas's familiar growl on the other end of the line, Simon didn't mince words. "Lucas, I think Victoria is in trouble."

"More than you know," was Lucas's startling response.

His tension climbing another notch, Simon waited for the man to explain.

"We've confirmed that Leberman has come up for air. We can't pinpoint his location. He moves too often and too quickly. But he's back. I don't know what he's got up his sleeve, but you can rest assured it involves Victoria."

"And you," Simon interjected.

"And me. I don't know why the bastard let me live the last time, but the one thing I can say without doubt is that it could only have been because he had a grand finale coming."

"You think he may be readying to unfold that finale?" Simon definitely did not like the sound of this. He would be putting through a call to Ian immediately after this one. He hated to interrupt the man's vacation, but this was far too pressing to wait.

"Who knows with that sick bastard?" Lucas admitted. "There doesn't seem to be any rhyme or reason to what he does. But I'm not willing to sit back and pretend he's no real threat. He has an agenda and he has a time line. We just don't know what either is."

"What do you want me to do?" Simon readied to take down any necessary notes.

"Keep a close eye on her. I already have two of my men assigned to maintain surveillance, but the more the merrier. I've got to have additional intel before I put together a team and a strategy. But there's one step that is crucial before we can go forward."

"What's that?"

"I have to convince Victoria that she should go away with me. I want her hidden where Leberman can't find her. I'm not willing to take the risk that this time might be *the* time in that psycho's perverted plan."

"I have just the leverage you can use," Simon said knowingly. "The order came from Victoria's personal physician."

"I'm all ears, Mr. Ruhl."

"The prescription is simple—Victoria Colby needs to take an extended vacation."

"And I know just the place," Lucas said with finality. "Now I just have to convince her to go."

Simon knew Lucas Camp was a bit of a legend, he just hoped the man possessed the power to move mountains. Moving Mt. Everest would likely be easier than persuading Victoria Colby to do something that wasn't on her agenda.

All Simon could do was wait…and watch every move she made.

* * * * *

PERSON OF INTEREST

There are people in our lives we encounter who make their marks. Those who leave some indelible influence on who and what we will become. But if we're really lucky, there are those whose presence in our lives makes a difference that goes so much more than skin-deep that our life would not have been what it was destined to be without them. This book is dedicated to one such person, with whom I have had the pleasure of love and laughter and the overwhelming sorrow of loss and grief. To my baby brother, John Brashier. You are my soul's twin. Never forget how very much I love you.

CHAPTER ONE

FINISHED.

With a satisfied sigh, Dr. Elizabeth Cameron surveyed the careful sutures and the prepatterned blocks of tissue she had harvested from inconspicuous donor sites. For this patient the best sites available had been her forearms and thighs which had miraculously escaped injury.

The tailored blocks of harvested tissue, comprised of skin, fat and blood vessels, were tediously inset into the face like pieces of a puzzle and circulation to the area immediately restored by delicate attachment to the facial artery.

Lastly, the newly defined tissue was sculpted to look, feel and behave like normal facial skin, with scars hidden in the facial planes. In a few weeks this patient would resume normal activities and no one outside her immediate family and friends would ever have to know that she had scarcely survived a fiery car crash that had literally melted a good portion of her youthful Miss Massachusetts face.

She would reach her twenty-first birthday next month with a face that looked identical to the one that had won her numerous accolades and trophies. More important, the young woman who had slipped into severe clinical

depression and who had feared her life was over would
now have a second chance.

"She's perfect, Doctor."

Elizabeth acknowledged her colleague's praise with
a quick nod and stepped back from the operating table.
With one final glance she took stock of the situation.
The patient was stable. All was as it should be. "Finish up for me, Dr. Jeffrey," she told her senior surgical resident.

Pride welled in her chest as she watched a moment
while her team completed the final preparations for
transporting the patient to recovery. Yes, she had performed the surgery, but the whole team had been involved from day one beginning with the complete,
computerized facial analysis. This victory had been
achieved by the entire team, not just one person. A team
Elizabeth had handpicked over the past three years.

In the scrub room she stripped off her bloody gloves,
surgical gown and mask, then cleaned her eyeglasses.
She'd tried adjusting to contacts, but just couldn't manage the transition. Sticking to the old reliables hadn't
failed her yet. She was probably the only doctor in the
hospital who still preferred to do a number of things
the old-fashioned way. Like working with a certain
team day in and day out. She'd worked with Jeffrey
long enough now that they could anticipate each other's
moves and needs ahead of time. It worked. She liked
sticking with what worked.

Exhaustion clawed at her. The muscles of her shoulders quivered with fatigue, the good kind. This one
had been a long, arduous journey for both patient and
surgical team. Weeks ago the initial preparations had
begun, including forming a mold from a sibling's right

ear to use in building a replacement for the one the patient had lost in the accident. The size and symmetry had worked out beautifully.

No matter how painstakingly Elizabeth and her team prepared, she wasn't fully satisfied until she saw the completed work…until the patient was rolled to recovery. The time required to heal varied, three to six weeks generally with this sort of tissue transplanting. The swelling would lessen, the red lines would fade. And the new face would bloom like a rose in the sun's light, as close to nature's work as man could come.

As Elizabeth started for the exit, intent on going straight home and crashing for a couple of hours, the rest of the team poured into the scrub room, high-fives and cheers of elation rumbling through the group. Elizabeth smiled. She had herself a hell of a team here. They were the best, each topping his or her field of expertise, and they were good folks, lacking the usual "ego" that often haunted the specialized medical profession.

"Excellent work, boys and girls," she called to the highly trained professionals who were quickly regressing to more adolescent behavior as the adrenaline high peaked and then drained away. "See you in two weeks."

Elizabeth pushed through the doors and into the long, white sterile corridor, still smiling as the ruckus followed her into the strictly enforced quiet zone. She inhaled deeply of the medicinal smells, the familiar scents comforting, relaxing. This place was her real home. She spent far more time here than inside the four walls of the little brownstone on which she made a monthly mortgage payment. Not really a good thing, she had begun to see. She didn't like the slightly cynical, fiercely focused person she was turning into.

A change was definitely in order.

Two weeks.

She hadn't taken that much time off since—

She banished the memory before it latched on to her thoughts. No way was she going to dredge up that painful past. Two months had elapsed. She clenched her jaw and paused at the bank of elevators. Giving the call button a quick stab, she waited, her impatience mounting with each passing second. She loved her work, was fully devoted to it. But she desperately needed this time to get away, to put the past behind her once and for all. She had to move on. Regain her perspective…her balance.

The elevator doors slid open and Elizabeth produced a smile for the nurses who exited. Almost three o'clock in the afternoon, shift change. The nurses and residents on duty would brief those arriving for second shift on the status of their patients. Orders would be reviewed and the flow of patient care would continue without interruption.

Dr. Jeffrey would stay with her patient for a time and issue the final orders. There was nothing for Elizabeth to worry about. She boarded the elevator and relaxed against the far wall. Her eyes closed as she considered the cruise she'd booked just last week. A snap decision, something she never, ever did. Her secretary had insisted she could not spend her time off at home or loitering around her office. Which, in retrospect, Elizabeth had to admit was an excellent idea. Hanging around the house or office, organizing books and files or personal items that were already in perfect order, would not be in her best interest. The last thing she needed in her life was more order.

Making a quick stop at the second-floor staff lounge

to pick up her sweater and purse, more goodbyes were exchanged with coworkers who couldn't believe she was actually going to take a vacation. Elizabeth shook her head in self-deprecation. She really had lost any sense of balance. Work was all she had, it seemed, and everyone had taken notice. One way or another she intended to change that sad fact.

Hurrying through Georgetown University Medical Center's expansive lobby, she made her way to the exit that led to the employee parking garage. She could already see herself driving across the District, escaping everything. As much as she loved D.C., she needed to get away, to mingle with the opposite sex. To start something new and fresh. To put *him* out of her mind forever. He was gone. Dead. He'd died in some foreign country, location unspecified, of unnatural causes probably, the manner unspecified. His body had not been recovered, at least, as far as she knew. He was simply gone. He wouldn't be showing up at her door in the middle of the night with an unexpected forty-eight-hour furlough he wanted to spend only with her.

Stolen moments. That was all she and Special Agent David Maddox had really ever shared. But then, that was what happened when one fell in love with a CIA agent. Covert operations, classified missions, need-to-know. All familiar terms.

Too familiar, she realized as she hesitated midstride on the lower level of the parking garage, her gaze landing on her white Lexus—or more specifically on the two well-dressed men waiting next to the classy automobile.

One man she recognized instantly as Craig Dawson, her CIA handler. All valuable CIA assets had handlers. It was some sort of rule. He'd replaced David when their relationship had gotten personal. There were times when Elizabeth wondered if that change in the dynamics of the interaction between them had ultimately caused David's death. His work had seemed so much safer when he'd been her handler.

Stop it, she ordered. Thinking about the past was destructive. She knew it. The counselor the Agency had insisted she see after David's death had said the same. Face forward, focus on the future.

Her new motto.

Time to move on.

If only her past would stop interfering.

What did Agent Dawson want today of all days? Annoyance lined her brow. Whenever he showed up like this it could only mean a ripple in her agenda. She couldn't change her current plans. It had taken too long for her to work up the courage and enthusiasm to make them.

Her irritation mounting unreasonably, her attention shifted slightly. To the man standing next to Dawson. Another secret agent, no doubt. The guy could have been a carbon copy of Dawson from the neck down, great suit, navy in color, spit and polished black leather shoes. The only characteristics that differentiated the two were age and hair color.

Well, okay, that was an exaggeration, the two looked nothing alike. Dawson was fifty or so, distinguished-looking, with a sparkling personality. He'd never performed field duty for the CIA, was more the "office" type. The other guy looked younger, late-thirties maybe, handsome in a rugged sort of way, and his expression resembled that of a slick gangster. At least what she could see of it with him wearing those dark shades. The five o'clock shadow on his lean jaw didn't help. Her gaze lingered there a moment longer. Something about his profile...his mouth seemed familiar.

She rarely forgot a face, and this one made her nervous. She looked away, settling her gaze back on Dawson and the kind of familiarity she could trust. Maybe she had run into the other man before. But that didn't seem likely since her dealings with the CIA had always come through David or Agent Dawson, discounting her rare command performance with the director himself. A frown nagged at her brow. It was doubtful that she knew the other man, yet something about him seriously intimidated her. Not a good thing in a CIA agent, to her way of thinking.

But then, what did she know? She was only a part-time volunteer agent whose existence was strictly off any official records. And she hadn't even been subjected to the training program. Calling herself an agent was a stretch. She actually had no dealings whatsoever with the CIA other than performing the occasional profes-sional service for which she refused to accept pay. To date, she had provided new faces for more than a dozen deep-cover operatives. It was the least she could do for her country—why would she allow payment for services rendered? Elizabeth saw it as her patriotic duty. The covert sideline was her one secret...her one departure from the dull routine of being Dr. Elizabeth Cameron.

"Dr. Cameron," Dawson said when she made no move to come closer, "the director would like to see you."

Elizabeth hiked her purse strap a little farther up her shoulder and crossed her arms over her chest. "I'm going on vacation, Agent Dawson," she said firmly as she ordered her feet to move toward her car. It was her car, after all, he couldn't keep her from getting in it and driving away. At least she didn't think he could.

"The meeting will only take a few minutes, ma'am," Dawson assured quietly while his cohort stood by, ominously silent, doing the *intimidation* thing.

She considered asking Craig if he was training a new recruit or if he'd worried that he might need backup for bringing her in. But she doubted he'd get the joke. She wouldn't have gotten it either until about a week ago. That's when she'd made her decision. The decision to put some spontaneity into her life. She was sick of being plain old quiet, reserved Elizabeth who never varied her routine. Who stuck with what worked and avoided personal risk at all cost. She got out of bed at the same time every morning, showered, readied for work and ate a vitamin-enhanced meal bar on the way to the office. After ten or twelve hours at the office and/or hospital, she worked out at the fitness center and went home, took a relaxing hot bath and fell into bed utterly exhausted.

Same thing, day in and day out.

She couldn't even remember the last time she'd gone to a movie much less had a simple dinner date.

But no more.

Still, she had an obligation to the CIA. She'd promised to help out when they needed her. Right now might be inconvenient but it was her duty to at least listen to what they needed. Growing up a military brat had taught her two things if nothing else: always guard your feelings and never, ever forget those who risk their lives for your freedom. Guarding her feelings was a hard-learned skill, the knowledge gained from moving every two to three years and having to fit in someplace new.

The other—well, patriotism was simply something every good American should practice.

"All right," she relented to Mr. Dawson's obvious relief. "I'll see him, for a few minutes only." She held up a hand when Dawson would have moved toward the dark sedan parked next to her car. "Anything else he needs will have to wait until I get back from my cruise," she said just to be sure he fully grasped the situation. "Even doctors take vacations."

"I understand, ma'am," Dawson confirmed with a pleasant smile. But something about the smirk on the other man's face gave her pause. Did he know her? She just couldn't shake that vague sense of recognition. Maybe he was privy to what the director wanted and already knew she was in for a battle if she wanted this vacation to happen.

She was still a private citizen. She accepted no money for her work and she had never refused the Agency's requests. But this time she just might.

Elizabeth settled into the back seat of the dark sedan and Dawson closed her door before sliding behind the steering wheel. The other man took the front passenger seat, snapped the safety belt into place and stared straight ahead. Elizabeth was glad he hadn't opted to sit in back with her. She didn't like the guy. He made her feel threatened on some level. A frown inched its way across her forehead. She had to admit that he was the first Agency staff member she'd met who actually looked like one of the guys depicted in the movies. Thick, dark hair slicked back. Concealing eyewear, flinty profile. She shivered, then pushed the silly notion away.

She wanted spontaneity in her life, not trouble. This guy had trouble written all over what she could see of that too handsome face. Upon further consideration, she decided it was his mouth that disturbed her the most. There was a kind of insolence about it…a smugness that shouted *I could kiss you right now and make you like it.*

Another shudder quaked through her and she reminded herself of what falling for a spy had cost her already.

CIA agents did not make for reliable companions. She knew better than most. A pang of old hurt knifed through her. She'd made a mistake, veered too close to the flame and she'd gotten burned.

Never again.

If she fell in love a second time, which was highly doubtful considering her current track record, it would be with someone safe, someone predictable.

Safe.

At one time she'd considered David safe.

But she'd been wrong.

He'd felt safe and comfortable, but it had been nothing but an illusion.

David Maddox had been every bit as dangerous— as much of an adrenaline junkie—as all the rest in his line of work. CIA agents were like cops; they thrived in high-tension situations, on the thrill of the hunt. No matter how quiet and reserved David had pretended to be, he'd been just like the rest of them.

Just like Craig Dawson and his companion.

Men willing to risk it all for their country, who broke hearts and left shattered lives.

She didn't want that kind of man.

Never again.

Elizabeth focused on the passing landscape, refused to dwell on the subject. The skyscrapers and bumper-to-bumper traffic of the D.C. area eventually gave way to trees and only the occasional passing motorist. It seemed odd to Elizabeth that the CIA's headquarters would be nestled away in the woods, seemingly in the middle of nowhere, like a harmless, sprawling farm. But there was nothing harmless about the vast property. Security fences topped with concertina wire and cameras. Warnings about entering the premises with electronic devices. Armed guards. Definitely not harmless in any sense of the word.

Dawson braked to a stop and flashed his ID for the guard waiting at the entrance gate while another guard circled the sedan with a dog trained to sniff out explosives and the like. Even now she imagined that high-tech gadgets were monitoring any conversation that might take place inside the vehicle. Every word, every nuance in tone scrutinized for possible threat.

The recruits here were trained to infiltrate, interrogate, analyze data and to kill if necessary. Their existence and proper training were essential to national security, she understood that. Respected those who sacrificed so very much. But she couldn't bring herself to feel comfortable here. It took a special kind of human being to fit into this world. Her gaze flitted to the man in the front passenger seat. A man like him. Dark, quiet, enigmatic. A man fully prepared to die…to kill…for what he believed in.

A dangerous man.

But not dangerous to her…never again. No more dangerous men in her life, she promised herself as she did her level best to ignore the premonition of dread welling in her chest. Safe. Occasionally spontaneous maybe, but safe. She had her new life all mapped out and the dead last thing it included was danger.

CHAPTER TWO

THE MAIN LOBBY of the CIA headquarters always took Elizabeth's breath away. The granite wall with its stars honoring fallen agents. The flags and statues… the grandeur that represented the solemn undertaking of all those who risked their lives to make the world a safer place. The shadow warriors.

Elizabeth looked away from that honorary wall, knowing that one of those stars represented David. Though she would never know which one since his name would not be listed. *Anonymous even in death.*

For the first time since his death she wondered if she'd known him at all. Was his name even David Maddox?

Her heart squeezed instantly at the thought. This was precisely why she had promised herself she would not think about the past. Not today, not any day.

She had to get on with the present, move into the future.

Like David, the past was over. She was thirty-seven for Christ's sake. Her fantasy of some day having a family was swiftly slipping away. Never before had she been so keenly aware of just how much time she had wasted. Though she loved her work, she didn't regret for a moment the sacrifices she had made to become the respected surgeon she was; it was time to have a personal life as well.

The rubber soles of her running shoes whispered against the gleaming granite floor where the CIA's emblem sprawled proudly, welcoming all who entered. The guards and the metal detectors beyond that proved a little less welcoming, reminding Elizabeth of the threat that loomed wherever government offices could be found. Even in her lifetime the world had changed so much. Maybe part of her sudden impatience to move forward was somehow related to current events as well as the recent past. Whatever the case, it was the right thing to do.

Dawson led her to the bank of elevators and depressed the down button. Uneasiness stirred inside her again. Somehow she doubted that the director's office had been moved to the basement. Before she could question his selection the doors slid open and the three of them boarded the waiting car.

When he selected a lower level, she felt compelled to ask, "Aren't we going to the director's office?"

Agent Dawson smiled kindly. He'd always had a nice smile, a calming demeanor. She was glad for that. "We're meeting in a special conference room this time. The director is there now waiting for your arrival."

Elizabeth managed a curt nod, still feeling a bit uneasy with the situation despite her handler's assurances. The fine hairs on the back of her neck stood on end the way they did whenever she sensed a deviation in the status quo of a patient's condition. She could always predict when things were about to go wrong. This felt wrong. For the first time since she'd agreed to support the CIA from time to time, she felt seriously uncomfortable with the arrangement. That premonition of dread just wouldn't go away though it refused to clarify itself fully.

The other agent, the one whose presence added to her discomfort and who hadn't been introduced to her as of yet, shifted slightly, drawing her attention in his direction.

He still wore those confounding sunglasses. Elizabeth found the continued behavior to be rude and purposely intimidating. Fury fueling an uncharacteristic boldness she opened her mouth to say just that and he looked at her. Turned his head toward her, tilting it slightly downward and looked straight at her as if he'd sensed her intent. She didn't have to see his eyes. She could feel him watching her. Something fierce surged through her. Fear, she told herself. But it didn't feel quite like fear.

Who the hell was this man?

She swung her attention back to Agent Dawson, intent on demanding the identity of the other man, but the elevator bumped to a halt. The doors yawned open and Dawson motioned for her to precede him. Pushing her irrational annoyance with the other man to the back burner, she stepped out of the car and moved in the direction Dawson indicated. She would likely never see this stranger again after today, what was the point in making a scene?

ON SOME LEVEL she recognized him. Special Agent Joe Hennessey couldn't jeopardize this mission by allowing her to recognize him before the decision was made. He'd kept the concealing eyewear in place to throw her off, but he had a feeling she wouldn't be fooled for long. He'd been careful not to speak and not to get too close.

But there was no denying the chemistry that still sizzled between them…it was there in full force. He could only hope that she was disconcerted with the unexpected trip to Langley and was off balance enough to give a commitment before the full ramifications of the situation became crystal clear.

The long corridor stretched out before them, the occasional door on one side or the other interrupting the monotonous white walls. Tile polished to a high sheen flowed like an endless sea of glass. Surface mounted fluorescent lights provided ample lighting if not an elegant atmosphere. He could feel her uneasiness growing with each step. She didn't like this deviation from the usual routine.

Hennessey knew this was her first trip to the bowels of the Agency and she probably hoped it would be the last. The adrenaline no doubt pumping through her veins would make the air feel heavier, thicker. It didn't take a psychic to know she was seriously antsy in the situation. Didn't like it one damned bit.

Dawson stayed to her right, a step ahead, leading the way. Hennessey stayed to her left, kept his movements perfectly aligned with hers, not moving ahead, never falling behind. If the overhead lights were to suddenly go out and the generators were to fail, he would still know she was there. He could *feel* her next to him. For someone who loved clinging to a routine, her energy was strong…her presence nearly overwhelming. With every fiber of his being he knew she was even now scrolling through her memory banks searching for what it was that felt familiar about him.

Thankfully they reached their destination. Dawson stopped at the next door on the left. "The director is waiting for you inside, Dr. Cameron." He reached for the door and opened it.

Elizabeth looked from him to Hennessey and back. "Aren't you coming in, Agent Dawson?"

She didn't like this at all. Hennessey could feel the tension vibrating inside her mounting.

"Not this time, ma'am."

SHE DIDN'T LIKE THIS. Her frown deepening, Elizabeth pushed her glasses up the bridge of her nose and moved through the open door. She had been briefed long ago about the various levels of security clearances within the CIA. Some were so secret that even the designation was classified. In most cases, the rule that every agent lived by was the "need-to-know" rule. One knew what one needed to know and nothing more.

Clearly Agent Dawson and his friend didn't need to know whatever the director was about to discuss with her. The door closed behind her with a resolute thud and she shivered. The sound echoed through her, shaking loose a memory from months ago. It had been dark…she'd scarcely seen his face, but she had known his reputation. The man who'd been sent to protect her that night had held her there like a prisoner in the darkness for hours insisting that it was for her own safety. He'd been rude and arrogant, had overwhelmed her with his brute strength…his absolute maleness. And then he'd been gone.

He'd almost taken advantage of her—she'd almost let him—and then he'd disappeared. Like a shadow in the night…as if he'd never been there at all. She'd known what he'd done. He'd reveled in pushing her buttons, in making her weak. But she'd resisted, just barely. If she hadn't, he would have taken full advantage, even knowing that she belonged to David. She wondered if David had ever suspected that the friend he'd sent to protect her from a threat the nature of which she hadn't been authorized clearance for had almost succeeded in seducing her with his devastating charm. Some friend.

But then that was Special Agent Joe Hennessey. He might be a superspy of legendary proportions, but she knew him for what he was: ruthless and with an allegiance only to himself. The guy waiting with Dawson in the corridor reminded her of Hennessey.

"Elizabeth, thank you for coming."

Elizabeth shoved the distracting thoughts away as Director George Calder rounded the end of the long conference table and made his way to her. A second gentleman she didn't recognize rose from his chair but didn't move toward her.

Present and future, forget the past, she reminded her too forgetful self. Like David, Joe Hennessey was a part of her past that was gone forever. Face forward. Focus on the here and now...on the future. Director Calder took her hand in his and shook it firmly.

"I hope you'll forgive my intrusion into your vacation schedule," he offered, his expression displaying sincere regret.

George Calder was a tall, broad-shouldered man, not unlike the two agents waiting outside the door. Nearly sixty, his hair had long ago silvered and lines drawn by the execution of enormous power marred his distinguished face. He'd presented himself as nothing less than gracious and sensitive each time he'd requested

Elizabeth's presence. But there was more this time. Something else simmered behind those intelligent hazel eyes. The sixth sense that usually centered on her patients was humming now, urging her to act.

"Technically," Elizabeth said succinctly, ignoring her foolish urge for fight or flight, "my vacation doesn't start until tomorrow so you're still safe for now."

George laughed, but the sound was forced. "Let me introduce you to our director of operations." He turned to the other man in the room. This one was slightly shorter and thinner, but looked every bit as formidable as Director Calder.

"Kurt Allen, meet our talented Dr. Elizabeth Cameron."

His fashionable gray pinstripe suit setting him apart from the requisite navy or black, Allen rushed to shake her hand, his smile wide and seeming genuine. "It's an honor to finally meet you, Dr. Cameron. Your work is amazing. I can't tell you how many of my best men you've spared."

Elizabeth realized then that Director Allen was in charge of the field agents who most often needed her services.

"I'm glad I can help, Director Allen," she told him in all sincerity. It felt odd now that she'd never met him before. Need-to-know, she reminded herself.

There was an awkward moment of tense silence before Calder said, "Elizabeth, please have a seat and we'll talk."

The director ushered her to the chair next to the one he'd vacated when she'd entered the room. Allen seated himself directly across the table from her.

The air suddenly thickened with the uneasy feel of

a setup. This was not going to be the typical briefing. There was no folder marked *classified* that held the case facts of the agent who needed a new face. There was nothing but the high sheen of the mahogany conference table and the steady stares of the two men who obviously did not look forward to the discussion to come.

To get her mind off the intensity radiating around her, Elizabeth took a moment to survey the room. Richly paneled walls similar to that of the director's office several floors overhead gave the room a feeling of warmth. Royal blue commercial-grade carpet covered the floor. The array of flags surrounding the CIA emblem on the rear wall and the numerous plaques that lined the other three lent an air of importance to the environment. This was a place where discussions of national significance took place. She should feel honored to be here. Whatever she could do for the CIA was the least she could do for her country, she reminded herself.

Elizabeth clasped her hands atop the conference table, squared her shoulders and produced a smile for Director Calder. "Why did you need to see me, Director?" Someone had to break the ice. Neither of the gentlemen appeared prepared to dive in. Another oddity. What could either of these men, who possessed the power to start wars, fear from her?

Calder glanced at Allen then manufactured a smile of his own. "Elizabeth, I think you understand how important the Operations Directorate is here at the CIA."

She nodded. Though she actually knew little about the Operations Directorate, she did comprehend that the field operatives who risked their lives in positions deep undercover and generally in foreign countries came from that division.

"The men and women who make up the ranks of our field operatives are the very tip of the spear this agency represents," he went on, verifying her assumption. "They are the forerunners. The ones who provide us with the data that averts disaster. They risk more than anyone else."

Again she nodded her understanding. The knot in her stomach twisted as she considered why he felt the need to tediously prepare her for whatever it was he really wanted to say. Every instinct warned that things were not as they should be.

"During the past two and a half years we've counted on you more than a dozen times to provide a means of escape for our operatives. Your skill at creating new faces has allowed these men and women to avoid the enemy's vengeance while maintaining their careers. Without your help, a number of those operatives would certainly have lost their lives."

"There are other surgeons in your field," Allen interjected with a show of his palms for emphasis. "But not one in this country is as skilled as you."

Elizabeth blushed. She hated that she did that but there was no stopping it. She'd never taken compliments well. Though she worked hard and recognized that she deserved some amount of praise, it was simply a physical reaction over which she had no control. Her professional life was the one place where she suffered no doubts in regards to her competence. If only she could harness some of that confidence for her personal life.

"I appreciate your saying so, Director Allen," she offered, "but I can't take full credit. My ability with the scalpel is a gift from God." She meant those words with all that made her who she was. A God complex was something she'd never had to wrestle with as so many of her colleagues did. She made it a point to remind her residents of that all important fact as well. Confidence was a good thing, arrogance was not.

Director Calder braced his hands on the table in front of him and drew her attention back to him, "That's part of the attitude that we hope will allow you to see the need for what we're about to ask of you, Elizabeth."

She didn't doubt her ability to handle whatever he asked of her. In that vein, she dismissed the uneasiness and lifted her chin in defiance of her own lingering uncertainty. There was only one way to cut to the chase here—be direct. "What is it you need, Director Calder. I've never turned you down before. Is there some reason you feel this time will be different?"

Two and a half years ago the CIA had, after noting her work in the field of restorative facial surgery, approached her. They needed her and she had gladly accepted the challenge. She would not change that course now.

"We are aware of the relationship you maintained with Agent Maddox," Allen broached, answering before Calder could or maybe because he didn't want to bring up the sensitive subject. "I believe the two of you were…intimate for more than a year before his death."

The oxygen in Elizabeth's lungs evacuated without further ado. She swallowed hard, sucked in a necessary breath and told her heart to calm. "That's correct." To say she was surprised by the subject would be a vast understatement. But, within this realm, there was no room for deception or hedging. Those traits were best utilized in the field. And the fact of the matter was Elizabeth had never been very good at lying. She was an open book. Subterfuge and confrontation were two of her least favorite strategies.

Just another reason she had no life. Real life, emotionally speaking, was too difficult. If she kept to herself, she wasn't likely to run into any problems.

But you're about to change that attitude, a little voice reminded. She had made up her mind to dive back into a social life…to take a few risks.

If only she could remember that mantra.

Director Calder picked up the conversation again, "Three months before his death Agent Maddox was involved in a mission that garnered this Agency critical information. He was, fortunately, able to complete the mission with his cover intact."

Elizabeth imagined that maintaining the validity of a cover would be crucial for future use. She nodded her understanding, prompting him to carry on.

"Though the group he infiltrated at the time was effectively eliminated, two members have moved into another arena which has created great concern for this agency."

Outright apprehension reared its ugly head. "I'm not sure I know what you mean." She did fully comprehend that there were certain elements she would not be told due to their classification, but she had to know more than this. Tap dancing around the issue wasn't going to assuage her uneasiness.

"The two subjects involved have relocated their operation here. On our soil," Allen clarified. "They have an agenda that we are not at liberty to disclose, but they must be stopped at all costs."

Elizabeth divided a look between the two men. Both wore poker faces, giving away nothing except determination. She hated to say anything that would make her look utterly stupid but her conclusion was simple. "If you know they're here, why don't you just arrest them or…or eliminate them."

Made sense to her. But then she was only a doctor, not a spy or an assassin. She felt certain they had some legitimate reason for taking a less direct route to accomplish their ultimate goal, though she couldn't begin to fathom what the motivation could possibly be.

"I wish it were that simple," Calder told her thoughtfully. "Stopping the men they've sent won't be enough. We have to know how they're getting their information to ensure the threat is eliminated completely. Otherwise the root cause of the situation will simply continue generating additional obstacles."

Now she got it. "You need these two members of the group David infiltrated to lead you to their source," she suggested. She'd seen a crime drama or two in her life.

"Exactly," Allen confirmed. "If we don't find the source, they'll just keep sending out more assassins."

Assassins. That meant targets.

"How does this involve me?" Her heart rate kicked into overdrive. She moistened her lips as the silence stretched out another ten seconds. This could not be good.

Director Calder turned more fully toward her, fixing her with a solemn gaze that reflected nearly as much desperation as it did determination. "In order to infiltrate this group we need someone with whom they'll feel comfortable. Someone familiar. We have an agent prepared to take the risk and infiltrate the group, but we need to make a few alterations."

Her head moved up and down in acknowledgement.

She was on the same page now. "You want me to give him a different appearance? A new face?" That's what she usually did. No big deal. But why all the beating around the proverbial bush?

"Correct," Calder allowed. "But just any face won't work. We'll be requesting a specific look."

"Someone these assassins know, feel comfortable with," she echoed his earlier words.

"Precisely," Allen agreed enthusiastically. "This part is crucial to the success of the mission. If the targets think for even a second that our man isn't who he says he is they'll kill him without hesitation. There is no margin for error whatsoever, Dr. Cameron. That's why your help is critical."

She looked expectantly from Calder to Allen and back. "What is it you need, *exactly*?" she asked, focusing her attention on Allen since he loved to throw around those extreme adverbs. The requirements sounded simple enough.

"What we need," Allen told her bluntly, "is David Maddox."

Her breath trapped in her throat and shock claimed her expression. She didn't need a mirror, she felt her face pinch in horrified disbelief. Her fingers fisted to fight back the old hurt. "David is dead," she replied with just as much bluntness as he'd issued the requirement. What was this man thinking?

Calder reached across the table and put his hand on hers. Echoes of the anguish she'd felt two months ago reverberated through her. "I know this is difficult, Elizabeth. You must believe that we wouldn't ask if there was any other way."

He was serious.

"Oh my God." She drew away from his comforting touch. Shook her head to clear it. This was too much. "How can you ask me this?"

"Dr. Cameron, there is no other option," Allen said flatly, his tone far cooler than before but his eyes reflected the desperation she'd already seen in Calder's. "We need David Maddox, but as you pointed out, he is dead. So we need a stand-in. We need you to do what you do best and give our agent David Maddox's face."

Tears stung her eyes, emotion clogged her throat, but somehow she managed to say the only thing she could. "I can't do that."

Director Calder leveled a steady gaze on hers. "I'm afraid my colleague is right, there is no other option, Elizabeth."

CHAPTER THREE

JOE HENNESSEY WAITED with Craig Dawson in the corridor outside the conference room. He didn't have to be in the room or even watch the proceedings to know that Elizabeth Cameron would not like the idea. Not that he could blame her if he looked at it from her position but there were things she didn't know...would never know.

"She'll be okay with this," Dawson said quietly as if reading his mind.

Hennessey shrugged one shoulder. "She's your asset, you should know." His indifference might seem cold, but he had serious doubts where this whole operation was concerned. What the hell? He had a reputation for being cold and ruthless.

Dawson cut him a look that left no room for further discussion. He had faith in the woman even if he didn't have any in Hennessey.

Though Hennessey hadn't known David Maddox particularly well, he had met the woman in his life once. And once had been enough. Elizabeth Cameron had cool down to a science. Maybe she was hot between the sheets, but in Hennessey's estimation, a woman that reserved and uptight usually thought too much. Good, hot sex was definitely no thinking matter. It either was or it wasn't.

In his line of work he'd learned to take his pleasure

where he could and not to linger for too long. Dr. Elizabeth Cameron was not the type to go for a thorough roll in the hay and then walk away. She was one of those women with a commitment fetish. She didn't do casual sex. Probably didn't even understand the concept. From what Hennessey had seen, the woman was all work and no play. Completely focused.

If she agreed to do the job, that would be a good thing. He damn sure didn't want a lesser surgeon screwing up his face. Not that he considered himself the Hollywood handsome type but he got his share of second looks. Including one or two from the good doctor. Though he doubted she would admit it in this lifetime. Just like before, she wanted to pretend there was nothing between them. In reality, there wasn't, not really. Just that one night. The night he'd saved her life but she would never own up to it. She would only remember his manhandling and overbearing attitude. But something had sparked between them that night…in the dark.

The chemistry had been there. Strong enough to startle him almost as much as it had her. She'd hated it and her extreme reaction had only made bad matters worse. But then, he loved a challenge. He'd felt the electricity between them again today. But like before, she'd wanted to ignore it. What did all that attraction say about the relationship she'd had with Maddox? Maybe there was a little bit of the devil in all of us, he mused, even the straitlaced doc.

Well, she might prefer to ignore him, but if the director had his way, she might as well get used to having him around. They would be spending the next three weeks in close quarters. Not that it would be a hardship. He thought about those long, satiny legs hidden beneath

that conservative peach-colored skirt. The lady had a
great body. She worked out. He'd watched her. She kept
a hell of a boring routine. Yet there was no denying that
blond hair and those green eyes were attractive even if
she did make it a point to camouflage those long, silky
tresses in a bun and those lovely green eyes behind the
ugliest black rimmed glasses.

Well, attractive or not, hot in bed or not, Elizabeth
Cameron held the key to his future. He hoped by now
she understood that. His survival in the upcoming mission depended upon his ability to fool the enemy.

The idea of sporting another man's face held no real
appeal, but if it got the job done Hennessey could deal
with it. He could even manage to put up with the doc's
company for a couple of weeks and maintain the necessary level of restraint. What he wasn't at all sure he
could handle was her constant analysis.

He recalled quite well the way she'd studied him that
one time. Her lover had apparently related a number of
tales about the legendary Joe Hennessey, none of which
had sat well with Miss Prim and Proper.

Half the stories were exaggerated and the other half
were nobody's business. But that wouldn't keep her
from holding his past, real or imagined, against him.

Hennessey put his life on the line for his country all
the time. The last thing he deserved was some holier-
than-thou broad, however talented, treating him like
he was the scum of the earth. Throw that in the mix
with the undeniable physical attraction and he came up
with distraction.

He'd learned the hard way that if a guy thought with
his privates in this business he ended up dead. He'd had

his share of ladies along the way, but he never let one distract him from the mission.

He didn't intend to start now.

The door swung open and Hennessey came to attention. A leftover habit from his days in Special Forces. Anytime a superior officer was about, he came to attention as was expected.

Directors Calder and Allen moved into the corridor, closing the door behind them. A frown pulled at Hennessey's mouth. Where was the woman? He'd thought the plan was for him to be called in once they'd broken the news to her. Had she outright refused to do the job?

That would be just his luck. Damn. He wanted the best. And she was it.

"Agent Hennessey," Calder announced without preamble, "Dr. Cameron would like to see you now."

Hennessey blinked. "Alone?" He didn't relish the idea of the confrontation with no one else around to temper it.

Calder nodded. "She hasn't committed to the request. She insists on speaking to the operative assigned to the mission first. If she continues to resist, you have my authorization to enlighten her." He qualified his statement with a warning, "Her participation is essential, but she doesn't need to know any more than absolutely necessary."

With a heavy exhale and a nod of understanding, Hennessey stated for the record, "Yes, sir."

As he reached for the door, Dawson stopped him with a hand on his arm. "I know your reputation, Agent Hennessey," he cautioned quietly, "don't do anything you'll regret. Dr. Cameron is a nice lady."

"I think Agent Hennessey is aware of proper protocol," Director Calder suggested, his tone as stern as his expression. He would tolerate no roadblocks now or later. The reprimand was meant for both Dawson and Hennessey.

For the first time since going to the hospital to pick up the good doctor, Hennessey removed his eyewear. He'd worn the dark glasses inside purposely, to remain anonymous until the decision was final. Apparently there was going to be no help for that now. He hoped like hell she wouldn't let that one night influence her decision.

Hennessey leveled an unflinching stare on Dawson. "I have never jeopardized a mission or an asset."

"Just remember," Dawson persisted despite the director's warning, "that she is a very valuable asset."

Hennessey shoved his sunglasses back into place and opened the door. He didn't need Dawson telling him how to do his job. He had no intention of getting tangled up with Dr. Cameron. There might be some sexual energy bouncing back and forth between them, but she definitely was not his type.

Opinionated women were nothing but a pain in the ass.

Like he'd said before, some things don't require thought.

ELIZABETH COULDN'T SHAKE the idea that she knew the other agent. There was definitely something familiar about him. That mouth…the way his presence overwhelmed the atmosphere around him.

It couldn't be *him*.

She would remember if it was him. It wasn't like she could forget that night. That one night. She shivered.

She'd tried not to think about it, but every now and then it poked through the layers of anger and guilt she'd piled on top of the memory. He'd practically held her hostage. He'd made her feel things she hadn't wanted to feel. A hot, searing ache, a yearning deep down inside her. It had been wrong. A betrayal. And with *him* no less. David had told her all about Special Agent Joe Hennessey. His dark, alluring charm that the ladies couldn't resist; his ruthless single-mindedness. An agent like no other.

She wondered if David would have spoken so highly of him if he'd known how close his supposed friend had come to seducing her...how close she'd come to allowing it?

Heat infused her cheeks, rushed over her skin at even the memory of those few hours. He'd cast a spell on her. Made her want to forget everything and everyone else. Thank God she'd come to her senses.

Chafing her arms she banished the disturbing memories. She had to figure this out...had to find a way to make them see that she could not do this. She simply couldn't do that to David's memory.

Only, David would want her to help.

If lives were in danger he would want her to do whatever necessary to help his fellow agents. But she needed more information. Surely they couldn't expect her to do this without further clarification.

And, dear God, could she do it?

Could she recreate David's face on another man?

She stood on the far side of the room, her back to the door. For about three seconds Hennessey hesitated, admiring the view. She might be a pain in the ass, but he could look at hers all day. Nice. All those hours on the stair-stepper clearly made a difference.

He closed the door, allowing it to slam just enough to get her attention. Startled, she whirled to face him.

The frown of utter confusion telegraphed her first thought loud and clear: *What the hell do you want?* She had no doubt expected the directors to return with their man in tow. The last person she'd expected to enter the room was him.

"Dr. Cameron, I'm Special Agent Joe Hennessey." As he moved toward her he reached upward and removed his concealing eyewear. "If you'll recall we met once before."

Her eyes rounded and that cute little mouth dropped open. "You!" The single word was cast like an accusing stone.

He tossed the glasses onto the conference table and propped a hip there. "You remember me," he offered, his smile infused with all the charm in his vast ladies' man repertoire.

She pointed to the door then to him, her confusion morphing into disbelief. "It's you he wants me to prepare for this mission?"

Hennessey flared his hands. "That's right. Is there a problem?"

Her head moved from side to side as all that confusion and disbelief coalesced into outrage. "You're nothing like David," she accused.

Well, she had that right but he saw no point in bursting her bubble where her former lover was concerned. "I'm the same height and build. The hair color is close enough, the eyes will be an easy fix with colored contacts." He shrugged, the control necessary to hold back his own patience slipping just a little. "I don't see the problem."

She blinked rapidly, her head doing that side-to-side thing again as if the very idea was blasphemy. "You're not *like* David," she argued.

He pushed off the table and moved toward her, lowering his voice an octave, slowing the cadence of his words as he recalled the numerous taped conversations he'd listened to. "I can do anything it takes to get the job done, *Elizabeth*." Her head snapped up at his use of her first name. He said it with emphasis, the same way Maddox used to. "You'd be surprised at just how versatile I am."

Her pupils flared. She shivered. But it was the little hitch in her breathing that actually got to him, made his pulse skitter and chinked the armor he wore to protect his emotions. He shook his head and looked away. How the hell had he let that happen?

"You expect me to trust anything you say?"

Well, she had him pegged, didn't she? Apparently she'd accepted every rumor she'd heard as fact. "Bottom line, Doc, I can't do this without you." His gaze moved back to hers and he saw the concern and the hurt there. Dammit, he did not want to hurt her. Maddox had done that well enough himself, but she would never know it. "Will you help me or not?"

She tilted up that determined little chin and glared at him, a new flash of anger chasing away the doubt. "And if I refuse, what then?"

"People will die."

She blinked, but to her credit she didn't back off. "So I've heard. Can you be more specific? I need to know what I'm getting into here." Her compact little body literally strummed with her building tension.

The question kind of pissed him off. Or maybe it was the glaring fact that he couldn't keep his mind off her every reaction, couldn't stay focused. "You know, Doc, according to Director Calder, you generally don't question his requests. I understand this is personal," he growled, "but do you really think Maddox would have a problem with me borrowing his face for a little while?"

Her fists clenched and Hennessey had the distinct feeling that it was all she could do not to slap him. Good. He wanted her responses to be real, wanted to clear the air here and now. He didn't need her hesitation coming back to bite him in the ass down the line.

"David would probably say it's the right thing to do," she said tightly. "It's me who has the problem."

He resisted the urge to roll his eyes at her misplaced loyalty. He couldn't help wondering if, when he died, anyone would think so highly of him. Not very damned likely. He was far too open to lead anyone that far off track. Well, except for his targets and that was his job.

In his personal life he kept things on the up-and-up. He never lied to anyone, most especially a woman.

He liked women. Before he could put the brakes on the urge, his gaze roamed down the length of her toned body, admiring those feminine curves, before sliding back up to that madder-than-hell expression on her pretty face.

He liked women a lot. They knew what they were getting with him. If he and the doc did the deed there would be no questions or doubts between them.

But that wasn't going to happen.

Mainly because it would be stupid.

Not to mention the fact that she looked ready to take off his head and spit down his throat.

Fine. If she wanted to play hardball, he was game. "You want to know specifics?" He leaned closer, so close he could see the tiny flecks of gold in those glittering green eyes. "You've completed makeovers on fourteen operatives in the past thirty months. Two of those operatives are dead." One being the man who taught him everything he knew, but he didn't mention that. He had no intention of giving her any personal ammunition. In addition, holding on to control was far too important for him to let his personal issues with this mission get a grip right now. He kept those feelings tightly compartmentalized for a later time. "If I don't stop these guys the rest of those operatives will end up dead as well."

"That's...that's impossible," she stammered, some of the fight going out of her. "How could they know who and where these people are? Who has access to that information?" Her gaze dropped to his lips but quickly jerked back up to his eyes. She looked startled that she had allowed the weakness.

Hennessey laughed softly, allowing his warm breath to feather across those luscious lips. Damn, he was enjoying this far too much. Maybe he should just cut loose and say what was on his mind. That he would do this with or without her help, but that if she had a couple of hours he would show her what she was missing if she really wanted to know how well he lived up to his infamous reputation.

Dumb, Hennessey. Focus. Apparently she was experiencing almost as much trouble as he was.

In answer to her question, he tossed her a response she was not going to like. "You want to know who has access to those names and faces? Directors Calder and Allen, of course, the president, your former boyfriend, me and *you*." He said the last with just as much accusation as she'd thrown at him earlier.

She shuddered visibly, inhaled sharply, the sound doing strange things to his gut, making him even angrier or something along those lines. "Could someone else have gained access to the files?" she demanded, hysteria climbing in her voice.

He shook his head slowly and prepared to deliver the final blow. "Not a chance. Since Maddox is dead and, well, the president is the president, I'd say that narrows down the suspect list to the two directors outside that door." He hitched his thumb in that direction. "And you and me."

Fury whipped across her face, turning those green eyes to the color of smoldering jade. "If you think this tactic is going to pressure me into a yes, you're sadly mistaken, Agent Hennessey."

"Suit yourself." He straightened, a muscle in his cheek jerking as he clenched his jaw so hard his teeth should have cracked. It took a full minute for him to grab back some semblance of control. "Then consider this, *Dr. Cameron*." He glared down at her, his own fury way beyond reining in now. "If you don't do this most likely my mission will fail, then those operatives will eventually be found and murdered, one by one."

She held her ground, refused to look away though he knew just how lethal his glare could be. "You said two are already dead?" she asked. Her voice quavered just a little.

"That's right," he ground out, ignoring the twinge of regret that pricked him for pushing the jerk routine this far. "And so are their families." He fought the emotion that tightened his throat. He would not let her see the weakness. "You see, Doc, these people aren't happy with just wiping out the list of agents who've gone against what they believe in, they play extra dirty. They kill the family first, making the agent watch, and then they kill the agent, slowly, painfully."

Her eyes grew wider with each word. The pulse fluttered wildly at the base of her throat. She didn't want to hear this, didn't want to know. Too bad. It was the only way.

"So, it's your choice," he went on grimly. "You can either help me stop them or you can try to sleep at night while wondering when the next agent will be located and murdered."

She did turn away this time. Hennessey took a deep breath and cursed himself for being such an idiot. Saying all that hadn't been necessary. But, on some level, he'd wanted to rattle her—to hurt her. He wanted to get to her when the truth was she'd already gotten to him. He'd lost control by steady increments from the moment the director ordered him to start watching her weeks ago.

He had to get back on track here, had to keep those damned personal issues out of this. If the director got even a whiff of how he really felt, he would be replaced. Hennessey couldn't let that happen. He had to do this for a couple of reasons. "I shouldn't have told you," he said, regret slipping into his voice. As much as he'd needed her cooperation, he'd gone too far.

When she turned back to him once more, her face had been wiped clean of emotion, and her analytical side was back. The doctor persona was in place. The woman who could go into an operating room and reconstruct a face damaged so badly that the patient's own family couldn't identify her. No wonder she walked around as cold as ice most of the time. It took nerves of steel and the ability to set her emotions aside to do what she did.

He should respect that.

He did.

It was his other reactions that disturbed him.

"What do you want from me?"

The request unnerved him at a level that startled him all over again.

He focused on the question, denying the uncharacteristic emotions twisting inside him. "I need you to do your magic, Doc." His gaze settled heavily onto hers. "And I need you to work with me. You knew Maddox intimately. Help me become him… just for a little while. Long enough to survive this mission. Long enough to do what has to be done."

For three long beats she said nothing at all. Just when he was certain she would simply walk away, she spoke. "All right." She rubbed at her forehead as if an ache had begun there, then sighed. "On one condition." She looked straight at him.

The intensity…the electricity crackled between them like embers in a building fire. She had to feel it. The lure was very nearly irresistible.

"Name it," he shot back.

"When this is over, I give you back your face. I don't want you being *you* with David's face."

He wanted to pretend the words didn't affect him… but they did. He'd be damned if he'd let her see just how much impact her opinion carried. "I wouldn't have it any other way," he insisted.

"Then we have a deal, Agent Hennessey. When do we start?"

CHAPTER FOUR

ELIZABETH SAT IN her car as the purple and gray hues of dawn stole across the sky, chasing away the darkness, ushering forth the new day.

She'd managed a few hours sleep last night but just barely. Her mind kept playing moments spent with David, fleeting images of a past that had, at the time, felt like the beginning of the rest of her life.

How could she have been so foolish as to take that risk? She had known that a relationship with a man like David was an emotional gamble, but she'd dived in headfirst. The move had been so unlike her. She'd spent her entire life carefully calculating her every step.

She'd known by age twelve that she wanted to be a doctor, she just hadn't known what field. As a teenager, pediatrics had appealed to her, in particular helping children with the kind of diseases that robbed them of their youth and dreams. But at nineteen her college roommate had been in a horrifying automobile accident and the weeks and months that followed had brought Elizabeth's future into keen focus as nothing else could have.

Watching her friend go from a vibrant, happy young woman with a brilliant future ahead of her to a shell of a human being with a face that would never be her own had made Elizabeth yearn to prevent that from ever happening again…to anyone.

She'd worked harder than ever, had thrown herself into her education and eventually into her work. That burning desire to do the impossible, to rebuild the single most individual part of the human body, had driven her like a woman obsessed.

Elizabeth sighed. And maybe she was obsessed. If so, she had no hope of making it right because this was who she was, what she did. She made no excuses.

She dragged the keys from her ignition and dropped them into her purse.

But this was different.

Though she had changed faces for the CIA before, a fact for which she had no regrets, this was so *very* different.

Elizabeth emerged from her Lexus, closed the door and automatically depressed the lock button on the remote. The headlights flashed, signaling the vehicle was now secure.

She inhaled a deep breath of the thick August air. It wasn't entirely daylight yet and already she could almost taste the humidity.

"Might as well get this done," she murmured as she shoved her glasses up the bridge of her nose and then trudged across the parking lot.

The CIA had leased, confiscated or borrowed a private clinic for this Saturday morning's procedure. She noted the other vehicles there and, though she recognized none of them, assumed it was the usual team she worked with on these secret procedures. Of course, she would prefer her own team, but the group provided by the CIA in the past were excellent and, admittedly, a sort of rhythm had developed after more than a dozen surgeries.

A guard waited at the side entrance. His appearance made her think of the Secret Service agents who served as bodyguards for the president.

"Good morning, Dr. Cameron," he said as she neared. Though she didn't know him, he obviously knew her. No surprise.

"Morning."

He opened the door for her and she moved inside. It wasn't necessary to ask where the others would be, that part was always the same. Most clinics were set up on a similar floor plan. This one, an upscale cosmetic surgery outpost for the socially elite, was no different in that respect. The plush carpeting rather than the utilitarian tile and lavishly framed pieces of art that highlighted the warm, sand-colored walls were a definite step up from the norm but the basic layout was the same.

Agent Dawson stepped into the hall from one of the examination rooms lining the elegant corridor. "The team is ready when you are, Dr. Cameron."

"Thank you, Agent Dawson." Elizabeth didn't bother dredging up a perfunctory smile. He knew she didn't like this. She sensed that he didn't either. But they both had a duty to do. An obligation to do their part to keep the world as safe as possible. She had to remember that.

The prep room was quiet and deserted and she was glad. She wanted to do this without exchanging any sort of chitchat with those involved, most especially the patient.

As she unbuttoned and dragged off her blouse in one of the private dressing rooms, glimpses of those no-longer-welcome flickers of memory filtered through her mind once more. The last time she'd undressed for David. The last time they'd kissed or made love.

So long ago. Months. Far more than the two he'd been dead.

Her fingers drifted down to her waist and she unzipped her slacks, stepped out of her flats and tugged them off. The question that had haunted her for months before David had died, nagged at her now.

Had he found someone else?

Was that the reason for the tension she'd felt in him the past few times they were together?

Would she ever know how he'd died? Heart attack? Didn't seem feasible considering his excellent health, but healthy men dropped dead all the time. Or had he been killed in the line of duty?

She shook off the memories, forced them back into that little rarely visited compartment where they belonged. She did not want to think about David anymore, didn't want to deconstruct and analyze over and over those final months they had spent together.

None of it mattered now.

After slipping on sterile scrubs, cap and shoe covers and then washing up, she headed to the O.R. where the team would be waiting.

More of those polite and pleasant good-mornings were tossed her way as she entered the well-lit, shiny operating room. One quick sweep told her that the equipment was cutting edge. Nothing but the best. But then it was always that way. The CIA would choose nothing less for their most important assets.

"He refused to allow us to prepare him for anesthesia until you arrived, Doctor," the anesthesiologist remarked, what she could see of his expression behind the mask reflecting impatience.

"Hey, Doc."

The insolent voice dragged Elizabeth's gaze to the patient. "Good morning, Agent Hennessey." As she spoke, a nurse moved up next to Elizabeth and assisted with sliding her hands into a pair of surgical gloves.

"I think this crew is ready for me to go night-night," Hennessey said in that same flirtatious, roguish tone. "But I wanted to have a final word with you first."

With her mask in place, Elizabeth moved over to the table where Agent Hennessey lay, nude, save for the paper surgical gown and blanket. She frowned as she considered that even now he didn't look vulnerable. This was a moment in a person's life when they generally appeared acutely helpless. But not this man. No, she decided, he possessed far too much ego to feel remotely vulnerable even now as he lay prepared for an elective surgical procedure that could, if any one of a hundred or more things went wrong, kill him.

Those unrepentant blue eyes gleamed as he stared up at her. "Any chance I could have a moment alone with you?" he asked quietly before glancing around at the four other scrub-clad members of her team.

Elizabeth nodded to the anesthesiologist. He, as well as the two physicians and the nurse, stepped to the far side of the room.

"What is it you'd like to say, Agent Hennessey?" she asked, her own impatience making an appearance.

"Look, Doc—" he raised up enough to brace on his elbows "—I know you didn't really want to do this." His eyes searched hers a moment. "But I want you to know how much I appreciate your decision in my favor. I feel a hell of a lot better about this with you here."

She couldn't say just then what possessed her but Elizabeth did something she hadn't done in a very long time, she said exactly what she was thinking rather than the proper thing. "Agent Hennessey, my decision had nothing to do with you. I'm doing this for my country... for those agents who might lose their life otherwise. But I'm definitely not doing this for you."

Looking away, uninterested in his reaction, she motioned for the others to return.

"Let's get this over with," she said crisply.

The team, people whose real names she would likely never know, moved into position, slipped into that instinctive rhythm that would guide them through the process of altering a human face. As the anesthesia did its work Agent Hennessey's eyelids grew heavy, but his gaze never left Elizabeth. He watched her every move.

In that final moment before the blackness sucked him into unconsciousness, his gaze met hers one last time and she saw the faintest glimmer of vulnerability. Elizabeth's heart skipped at the intensity of what was surely no more than a fraction of a second. And then she knew one tiny truth about Agent Joe Hennessey.

He was afraid. Perhaps only a little, but the fear had been there all the same.

Elizabeth steeled herself against the instant regret she experienced at having been so indifferent to his feelings. She doubted he would have wasted the emotion on her, but there it was.

Banishing all other thought she took a deep breath and considered his face. Not Joe Hennessey's face, but the face of her patient. If she allowed herself to think of the patient as an individual just now then she would be more prone to mistakes related to human emotion. This had to be about the work…had to be about planes and angles, sections of flesh and plotting of modifications.

For this procedure she needed no mold, not even a picture. She knew by heart the face she needed to create. The face of the first man she'd ever loved. The only man actually. She'd been far too busy with her education and then her career for a real social life.

"Scalpel," she said as she held out her hand.

With the first incision Elizabeth lost herself in the procedure. No more thoughts of anything past, present or future. Only the work. Only the goal of creating a certain look…a face that was as familiar to her as her own.

ELIZABETH STRIPPED OFF her gloves, quickly scrubbed her hands and then shed the rest of the surgical attire. She cleaned her glasses and shoved them back onto her face.

Exhaustion weighed on her but she ignored it. When she'd donned a fresh, sterile outfit she went in search of coffee. Breakfast had been a while ago and she needed a caffeine jolt.

A cleanup team had already arrived to scrub and sterilize the O.R. Not a trace of the patient would be left behind. It was a CIA thing. Elizabeth knew for a certainty that the clinic would have its own personnel for that very procedure that would be repeated before business hours began on Monday, but the CIA took no chances. Nothing, not a single strand of DNA, that could connect Joe Hennessey to this clinic would be left behind.

For now he was in the recovery room with the nurse and one of the assisting physicians.

Elizabeth sat down in the lounge with a steaming cup of coffee. Thankfully Agent Dawson had a knack with coffee. A box of pastries sat next to the coffeepot. She forced herself to eat a glazed donut when she wasn't particularly hungry, just tired.

Dawson had explained that as soon as Elizabeth considered Hennessey able to move they would relocate via a borrowed ambulance to a safe house. She would oversee his recovery for the next three weeks, ensuring that nothing went wrong. Meanwhile some of the agents whose faces she'd already changed were in hiding, unable to move forward into whatever missions they had been assigned until it was safe for them to return to duty. Some, however, were already deep into missions. Their safety could not be assured without risking the mission entirely.

Her cruise had been cancelled and an additional week of leave had been approved. Director Calder had assured her that the Agency would reimburse her loss which was most of the cost of the cruise. No surprise there. Canceling this close to sail date came with certain drawbacks.

When Elizabeth felt the sugar and caffeine kicking in she pushed up from the table and headed to recovery to check on her patient.

In the corridor Agent Dawson waited for her. "You holding up all right, Dr. Cameron?"

She suppressed the biting retort that came instantly to mind. Dawson didn't deserve the brunt of her irritation. The problem actually lay with her. She'd fallen in love with the wrong man. Had assumed the fairy tale of marriage and family would be hers someday. Two mistakes that were all her own. This particular favor for the CIA had simply driven that point home all over again.

"I'm fine, Agent Dawson."

He nodded. "Agent Hennessey can be a bit brash," he said, his gaze not meeting hers. "But he's the best we have, ma'am. He won't let our people down. He'll get the job done or die trying."

Elizabeth blinked. It was, incredibly, the first time she'd considered that Hennessey might actually lose his life while carrying out this assignment. Clearly, she should have. The business of field operations was hazardous to say the least. David had explained that to her when he'd opted to go back into the field after their relationship had turned personal. She'd tried to talk him out of the change, but he'd been determined and she'd been in love.

End of story.

"I'm glad we can count on him," she said to Dawson, somehow mustering up a smile.

"The transportation for moving to the safe house is ready whenever you are, Doctor Cameron."

She nodded and continued on toward recovery. This was the first time she and Dawson had suffered any tension. The meetings with him were generally brief and superficial. This intensity was uncomfortable. Just something else to dislike about this situation.

As she pushed through the double doors the nurse looked up and smiled. "His vitals are stable, Doctor."

Elizabeth nodded. "Excellent."

She moved to the table and surveyed the sleeping patient and the various readouts providing continual information as to his status.

Heart rate was strong and steady. Respiration deep and regular.

The bandages hiding his incisions wouldn't be coming off for a few days. Even then the redness and swelling would still be prominent. After three weeks the worst would have passed. His age and excellent state of good health helped in the healing.

With some patients, especially older ones, some minor swelling and redness persisted for weeks, even months after extensive surgery. But there was no reason to believe that would be the case with this patient. The work Elizabeth had done was more about rearranging and sculpting, no deep tissue restructuring or skeletal changes. Minor alterations had been made to his nose and chin using plastic implants. Those would later be removed when she returned his face to its natural look. There would be minor scarring that she'd carefully hidden in hollows and angles. Fortunately for him his skin type and coloring generally scarred very little.

Later as Elizabeth sat alone in recovery, her patient started to rouse. The nurse and assisting physician had, at her urging, retired to the lounge. Both had looked haggard and ready for a break. She'd seen no reason, considering the continued stability of the patient's vitals, for all of them to stay with him.

Now she wished she wasn't alone. Her trepidation was unwarranted, she knew, but some part of her worried that she might see more of that vulnerability and she did not want to feel sympathy for this man. Now or ever.

He licked his lips. Made a sound in his throat. The intubation tube left patients with a dry throat. His right hand moved ever so slightly then jerked as some part of him recognized that he was restrained.

His body grew rigid then restless.

Stepping closer Elizabeth lay her hand on his arm and spoke quietly to him. "Agent Hennessey, you're waking up from anesthesia now. The surgery went well. There is no reason to be apprehensive."

His lids struggled to open as he continued to thrash just a little against his restraints.

"Agent Hennessey, can you hear me?"

He moistened his lips again and tried to speak.

Instinctively Elizabeth's hand moved down to his. "You can open your eyes, Agent Hennessey, you're doing fine."

His fingers curled around hers and her breath caught.

Blue eyes stared up at her then, the pupils dilated with the remnants of the drugs his body worked hard to metabolize and flush away.

"Everything is fine, Agent Hennessey."

"I guess I survived the knife, Doc," he said, his voice rusty.

An unexpected smile tilted her lips. "You did, indeed. We'll be moving to the safe house shortly."

"Any chance I could have a drink?" he asked with another swipe of his tongue over his lips.

"Certainly." It wasn't until then that Elizabeth noticed that his fingers were still closed tightly around hers. She wiggled free and poured some cool water into a cup. When she'd inserted a bendable straw she held the tip to his lips so that he could drink. "Not too much," she warned, but, of course, like all other patients he didn't listen. She had to take the straw away before he'd stopped.

She wiped his lips with a damp cloth. "For the first few days we'll keep the pain meds flowing for your comfort," she said, all too aware of the silence.

He mumbled something that might have been *whatever you think, Doc.*

A few hours later, most of which Agent Hennessey had slept through, Elizabeth supervised his movement to the waiting ambulance. She had learned that her determination of when the patient was ready to be moved had less to do with their departure than the arrival of darkness. Made sense when she thought about it. Night provided good cover.

"I'll be riding in the front with the driver," Dawson explained. "The nurse will accompany you to the safe house for the night. Tomorrow his care will be solely in your hands as long as you feel additional help is no longer required."

Elizabeth felt confident that additional medical support wouldn't be necessary, but she couldn't say that she looked forward to spending time alone with Hennessey. What she had done to alter his face was only the beginning of what Director Calder expected of her.

She settled onto the gurney opposite Agent Hennessey and considered the rest of this assignment. It was her job to ensure that this man could walk, talk and display mannerisms matching those of David Maddox.

Elizabeth knew nothing of David's work, but she did know the things he talked about when off duty... when in her bed.

"Feels like we're moving."

Elizabeth stared down at the man strapped to the other gurney. His mouth and eyes were all that was visible but his voice, the cocky tone that screamed of his arrogant attitude, made him easily recognizable.

"We're on our way to the safe house," she explained. He knew the plan, but the lingering effects of anesthesia and the newly introduced pain medication were playing havoc with his ability to concentrate.

"So I get to spend my first night with you, huh?"

A blush heated her cheeks. Though she doubted Agent Hennessey felt any real discomfort just now, she could not believe he had the audacity to flirt with her.

"In a manner of speaking," she said calmly. The man could very well be feeling a bit loose-tongued. He might not mean to flirt.

He made a sound in his chest, a laugh perhaps. "I've been dying to get you all to myself ever since that night," he mumbled.

Taken aback, Elizabeth reminded herself that he probably wouldn't even remember anything he said. Ignoring the remark was likely the best course.

"Sorry," he muttered. "I didn't mean to let that slip out."

She'd suspected as much. Swiping her hands on her thighs she sat back, relaxed her shoulders against the empty shelves behind her. "That's all right, Agent Hennessey," she allowed, "most patients say more than they mean to when on heavy-duty painkillers."

He licked his lips and groaned. The doctor in her went on immediate alert. "Are you feeling pain now, Agent Hennessey?" Surely not. He'd been dosed half an hour prior to their departure.

He inhaled a big breath. "No way, Doc, I'm flying over here." He blinked a few times then turned his head slowly to look at her. "God, you're gorgeous, did you know that?"

Elizabeth sat a little straighter, tugged at the collar of her blouse to occupy her hands. "You might want to get some more sleep, Hennessey, before you say something you'll regret."

"Too late, right?" He made another of those rumbling sounds that were likely an attempt at chuckling. "No big deal." He waved a hand dismissively. "You already know how gorgeous you are."

Maybe his hands should have been restrained. He'd been secured to ensure he didn't roll off the gurney, but his arms had been left free.

"You should lay still, Agent—"

"Yeah, yeah, I know," he interrupted. "Don't move, don't say anything. That's what I do best. But at least I'd never lie to you like he did. Never…" His eyes closed reluctantly as if the drugs had belatedly kicked in and he couldn't keep them open any longer.

Elizabeth let go a breath of relief. She checked his pulse and relaxed a little more when it appeared he'd drifted back to sleep.

Lending any credence to anything he'd said was ridiculous under the circumstances. The drugs had him confused and talking out of his head. She knew that, had seen it numerous times.

But the part about lying wouldn't let her put his ramblings out of her mind. What did he mean by that remark?

Nothing, you fool, she scolded.

She folded her arms over her chest. Then why did it feel familiar? As if he'd said what she'd thought a dozen times over. Because she'd sensed that David had been lying to her for quite some time.

Elizabeth closed her eyes and chastised herself for going down that road. David was dead. Whatever he'd said to her, lies or not, no longer mattered. He wasn't coming back. He was gone forever.

Dead.

She opened her eyes and stared at the bandaged face of the man lying so still less than two feet from her. Nothing he told her would matter. She'd loved David. He was gone. She wouldn't be taking that rocky route again anytime soon.

Nothing that Agent Joe Hennessey said or did would alter her new course.

As soon as this was over she intended to revive her social life as planned. Start dating again.

It was past time.

CHAPTER FIVE

JOE STUDIED HIS reflection for far longer than the bandaged mug warranted. He didn't know what he expected to see or what it mattered. The deed was done.

Twenty-four hours had passed since he'd gone under the knife. He pretty much felt like hell. His whole head could be a puffy melon if it weren't for the pain radiating around his face in ever tightening bands coming to a point at his nose. He'd had his nose broken once, but it hadn't hurt like this.

He glanced at the table next to his bed. There was medication for the pain, except he preferred to put off taking it until the pain became intolerable.

So far this morning, he had avoided spending much time with the doc. He'd been aware of her coming in and out of his room all during the night to check the portable monitors that provided a continuous scorecard on his vitals. He'd felt her looking at him each time but he hadn't opened his eyes, hadn't wanted to talk to her. He had a bad feeling he'd already said too much.

That was part of the reason he had no intention of taking any more drugs than necessary. He vaguely recalled making a few ridiculous remarks in the ambulance on the way here.

Joe exhaled a heavy breath. He was thirty-eight years old. He'd been an undercover operative for the CIA for the past ten. He'd been tortured, subjected to all sorts of training to prepare him for said torture, and not once had he ever spilled his guts like he almost had yesterday.

"Real stupid, Hennessey."

He dragged on his shirt and decided he couldn't hide out in this room any longer. It was 9:00 a.m. and his need for caffeine wouldn't be ignored any longer.

Facing the enemy had never been a problem for him. Hiding out from the doc when she was supposed to be on his side bordered on cowardice.

Joe hesitated at the door. He could admit that. It was the truth after all. Why would he lie to himself? The next three weeks were a part of the mission. He'd simply have to get past his personal feelings. Too many lives hung in the balance for him to indulge his personal interests.

His fingers wrapped around the doorknob and he twisted, drew back the door and exited the room that provided some amount of separation. All he had to do was maintain his boundaries. No slipping into intimate territory in conversation. No touching. If he followed those two simple rules he wouldn't have a problem.

The upstairs hall stretched fifteen yards from the room he'd just exited to the staircase. Three other bedrooms and two bathrooms had been carved out of the space. Downstairs was more or less one large open space that served as living room, kitchen and dining room. A laundry room with rear exit, pantry and half bath were off the kitchen.

The house was located in the fringes of a small Maryland town. There was only one other house on the street and it was currently vacant and for sale. Twenty-four hour surveillance as well as a state-of-the-art security system ensured their safety. A panic room had been installed in the basement. Even if someone got past surveillance and the security system they wouldn't breach the panic room. Though only twelve-by-twelve, the room was impenetrable and stocked for every imaginable scenario.

The smooth hardwood of the stair treads felt cold beneath Joe's bare feet. His left hand slid along the banister as he descended to the first floor, the act taking him back a few decades to his childhood. His parents' home had been a two-story and he and his brother had traveled down the stairs every imaginable way from sliding down the banister to jumping over it. It was a miracle either one of them had survived boyhood.

Joe stopped on the bottom step and hesitated once more before making his presence known.

Doctor Elizabeth Cameron was busy at the sink, filling the carafe to make another pot of coffee Joe presumed. A glutton for punishment he stood there and watched, unable to help himself.

She'd traded her usual businesslike attire for jeans and a casual blouse. He hadn't seen her like this. She wore generic sweats when she worked out, her scrubs or a business suit including a conservative skirt or slacks the rest of the time. He'd begun to wonder as he watched her over the past couple of weeks if she slept in her work clothes. Her cool, reserved exterior just didn't lend itself to the idea of silky lingerie no matter how much she owned.

And yet, when his gaze followed the sweet curves of her body clearly delineated by the form-fitting blue jeans and pale pink top he found himself ready to amend that conclusion.

At about five-four, she would fit neatly into the category of petite without question, but she was strong. He'd watched her work out. She could run like hell. More than once he'd wished she would wear shorts for her workouts rather than sweatpants, but he never got that lucky. He liked it a lot when she took off those unflattering glasses, which was extremely rare.

Just then she turned around, spotted him and jumped. Her hand flew to her chest. "You scared me!"

He took the final step down as she caught her breath. "Sorry." And he was, but not about startling her. He was sorry she'd caught him watching her like that. The last thing he needed was her putting together his loopy comments in the ambulance and his gawking this morning and coming up with the idea that he liked her in ways he shouldn't.

"I was just making a fresh pot of coffee." She gestured with the carafe. "There's eggs, bacon and toast. It was delivered about fifteen minutes ago."

While he was in the shower. Apparently Director Calder didn't want the good doctor to have to concern herself with preparing meals. Joe's reputation for lousy cuisine had apparently preceded him.

"Great." He crossed the room. The closer he got the more her hand shook as she poured the water into the coffeemaker. The idea that he made her nervous intrigued him just a little, though it shouldn't. He imagined she was still annoyed about his manhandling three months ago.

"I hope you like it strong," she commented without looking at him as she shoved the empty carafe under the drip basket. "At the hospital we prefer it with enough kick to keep us going."

He stopped three feet away, leaned against the counter. "That's the only way I drink it."

She glanced up at him and pushed a smile into place with visible effort. "How do you feel this morning?" Her gaze examined the bandages.

"Like hell," he admitted. "You didn't take a baseball bat to my head while I slept last night, did you?"

Worry lined her smooth complexion. "The pain meds should alleviate most of the discomfort."

Lured by the scent of the brewing coffee, he reached for a mug. She stiffened as his arm brushed her shoulder. "I guess if I took two like you ordered, they might," he confessed.

She rolled her eyes and huffed out a breath of frustration. "Men. You're all the same. You think taking pain medication makes you look like a wimp. That is so silly. The more pain you tolerate the more adrenaline your body will produce to help you cope. The more adrenaline pumping the less effective the medication you actually do take."

"Sounds like a vicious cycle, Doc." He set the mug on the counter. His gut rumbled. "Speaking of vicious." He glanced at the foam containers. "I'm starved." He'd had juice and water yesterday. A little soup last night but definitely not enough for a guy accustomed to packing away the groceries.

"You see," she snapped. "That's my point exactly."

He turned back to her. She'd folded her arms over her chest and now glared at him through those too clunky glasses. Somehow he'd pissed her off.

"What?" he asked in the humblest tone he possessed.

"You just ignored what I said." She gestured to his bandaged face. "You've been through extensive surgery and would still be in the hospital if you were one of my *real* patients. Yet you ignore my orders regarding meds. There are reasons the medication is prescribed, Agent Hennessey. What don't you understand about the process?"

Okay, calm down, Elizabeth ordered the side of her that wanted to obsess on the subject. She'd let him get to her already and he'd scarcely entered the room. She took a deep breath, tried to slow her racing heart. How did he do this to her just walking into the room?

"Look, Doc." He leaned against the counter next to her again. "I'm not trying to be cranky. I took the antibiotics. I even took the pain killer, but only one, not two. That dosage dulls my senses. And I need my senses sharp."

Though, arguably, she could see the logic in what he said, he needed to see hers as well. They were going to be here together for three long weeks. Taking a couple of days to get past the worst of the pain from surgery wasn't too much to ask in her opinion.

"Agent Hennessey," she began with as much patience as she could summon, "it wouldn't kill you to take an additional forty-eight hours of complete downtime."

He reached around her for the coffee, taking her breath for a second time with his nearness. She hated that he possessed that kind of power over her. Men like him should come with a warning. Don't get too close. She knew the hazards, had learned them firsthand with David. And David had been a kitty cat compared to this guy. Hennessey's unmarred record for getting the job done wasn't the only thing for which he had a reputation.

He poured himself a cup of coffee then started to put

the carafe away. Elizabeth quickly scooted out of his path to avoid another close encounter.

"Trust me, Doc," he said before taking a sip of his coffee. The groan of satisfaction was another of those things she could have done without. "I'll be the first to admit it if I can't handle the pain without the second pill every four hours. Deal?"

The last time she'd agreed to a deal with him it had landed her here. But then, like him, she had a job to do. People to protect. And maybe that made her an adrenaline junkie, too, although she didn't think so. Sure, her work for the CIA was covert to a degree, but she only saw it as doing her part. It wasn't much but it was something.

Did men like Joe Hennessey look at "their part" the same way? She just didn't know. Figuring out what made him tick wasn't on her agenda. She'd thought she had David all figured out and she'd been wrong and they'd shared thoughts as well as bodily fluids for more than a year. What could she possibly expect to learn about this man in a mere three weeks?

Nothing useful.

Nothing that would add to the quality of her life or give closure to her past.

Considering those two cold hard facts, her best course of action was to steer clear of emotional entanglement in this situation.

"All right, Agent Hennessey," she agreed reluctantly. "You're correct. You are a grown man. The level of pain you can and are willing to tolerate is your call. Just make sure you take the antibiotics as directed." She looked him square in the eyes. "That part is *my* call."

"Yes, ma'am." The wink immediately obliterated any hope of sincerity in his answer.

She had to get her mind off him. Her gaze landed on the breakfast another agent had delivered. Food was as good a distraction as any. Hennessey had said he was hungry.

Each container was laden with oodles of cholesterol and enough calories to fuel an entire soccer team through at least one game. Hennessey didn't hesitate. He dug in as if he hadn't eaten in a month. But his enthusiasm waned when the chewing action elicited a new onslaught of pain.

"Sure you don't want that full dosage?" she asked casually. It wasn't that she enjoyed knowing he was in more pain than he wanted to admit, but being right did carry its own kind of glee.

"I'm fine."

She didn't particularly like the idea that her unnecessary remark only made him more determined to continue without the aid of additional medication. Maybe she shouldn't have said anything at all.

While she picked at the eggs, sausage and biscuits on her plate, he ate steadily, however slowly. Oatmeal or yogurt would have been a much better choice. She wondered if he'd been the one to order the food. There hadn't been any calls in or out. Or perhaps the agent just picked up for them whatever he'd picked up for himself.

Checking on the menu for the next few days might be a good idea.

Elizabeth dropped her fork to her plate. Why had she done this? Why wasn't she on that cruise? She could have said no. That wasn't true.

People will die.

Saying no actually hadn't been an option.

"Agent Hennessey."

He met her gaze. "Yeah?"

As much as he tried to hide it she didn't miss the dull look that accompanied the endurance of significant pain.

She sighed and set her food aside. "Look, let's not play this game. You're obviously in pain. I would really feel a lot better if you took your medication."

"I told you I'm fine."

The words had no more left his lips than he bolted from the table and headed for the short corridor beyond the kitchen that led to the laundry room and downstairs bathroom.

Instinctively, Elizabeth followed. His violent heaves told on him before she caught sight of him kneeling at the toilet.

He'd been pushing the limits ever since he regained his equilibrium after anesthesia. This was bound to happen.

Ignoring the unpleasant sounds she moved to the wash basin next to him and moistened a washcloth. When he'd flushed the toilet and managed to get to his feet, she passed the damp cloth to him.

"I think you should be in bed."

"You know what, Doc? I think you're right."

Unbelievable. What was most incredible was that he didn't try to turn her words into something lewd or suggestive.

She followed him up the stairs and into the room he'd used the night before. He climbed between the sheets without putting up a fuss. To her surprise he even took the other pain pill she offered without argument.

"Thanks," he mumbled, his eyes closed.

When Elizabeth would have moved away from the bed his fingers curled around her wrist and held on. "What's the rush, Doc?" He tugged her down onto the side of the bed next to him.

She tried to relax but couldn't. "You should rest."

"I'm lying flat on my back. I've taken the pills. At least give me this."

If he hadn't looked at her so pleadingly, she might have been able to refuse. But there was that glimmer of vulnerability again and she just couldn't do it.

"What is it that you want, Agent Hennessey?"

"First." He moistened those full lips. Strange, she considered, his lips were awfully full for a man's. There hadn't been a lot she could do about that. The best they could hope for was that no one would notice. "I'd like you to stop calling me Agent Hennessey. Call me Joe."

His fingers still hung around her wrist, more loosely now, but the contact was there. Pulling away would have been a simple matter but he was her patient and she needed him to relax. So she didn't pull away.

"All right, Joe," she complied. "I suppose then that you should call me Elizabeth." Most anything was preferable to Doc. Although she did have to admit that he somehow made it sound sexy.

He licked his lips and said her name, "Elizabeth. It suits you."

She wasn't sure whether that was a compliment or not, but she decided not to ask.

"Talk to me," he urged, the fingers around her wrist somehow slipping down to entwine with hers. "Tell me about your relationship with Maddox. What attracted you to him?"

They were supposed to do this. That's why she was here, beyond the surgery that is. She was supposed to make sure he knew about David's personal life—at least as much as she knew. He needed to get the voice down pat and the mannerisms. Practice would accomplish both. But the details were another matter. She had to give him the details just in case David discussed his private life with someone Hennessey—Joe, she amended—might come in contact with during the course of this undercover operation.

Elizabeth saw no point in putting off the inevitable. Getting on with it was the best way.

"He was nice," she said. And it was true. She hadn't known what to expect out of a CIA handler and his being nice was the first thing she was drawn to. All extraneous assets utilized by the CIA were assigned handlers as a go-between. She didn't say because he certainly knew this already.

"Ouch. Maybe you don't know this, honey, but nice is not a man's favorite adjective."

"Elizabeth," she corrected, feeling even more awkward with his use of the endearment though she felt confident he didn't mean it as an actual endearment.

"Elizabeth," he acknowledged.

Even then, as he acquiesced to her assertion he made one of his own. He drew tiny circles on her palm with the pad of his thumb.

She started to pull her hand away, but decided that would only allow him to see that he'd gotten to her. Pretending his little digs at her composure didn't bother her would carry far more weight. When he saw that he couldn't get to her in that way he would surely let it go.

"I liked his jokes," she went on in hopes of losing

herself in the past. She worked hard not to do that on a regular basis; doing so now was a stab at keeping her mind off how being this close to Joe Hennessey unnerved her. It shouldn't, but it did.

"Yeah, he was a jokester," Joe murmured.

His voice had thickened a little from the action of the painkiller. If she were lucky he'd fall asleep soon. His body needed the rest. Whether he realized it or not his whole system was working hard to heal his new wounds which diverted strength and energy from other aspects of his existence. He didn't need to fight the process.

Something he'd said in the ambulance, about lying, pinged her memory. She'd have to ask him about that later when he was further along in his recovery.

"So he was nice," Joe reiterated, "and he could tell a joke. Is that why you fell for him?"

His lids had drifted shut now. He wouldn't last much longer. Elizabeth was glad. She stared at their joined hands. Hers smooth and pale, his rougher, far darker as if he spent most of his time on a beach somewhere.

As she watched, his fingers slackened, lay loose between hers. His respiration was deep and slow. She doubted he would hear her answer even if she bothered to give one. But he'd asked, why not respond?

"No, Agent Hennessey, those are not the reasons I fell for him." She paused and when he didn't correct her she knew he was down for the count. "I fell for him because he was like you," she confessed, her voice barely a whisper. "He made me feel things that terrified me and, at the same time, made me feel alive." As hard as she'd tried not to look back and see herself as stupid, she couldn't help it. She'd been so damned foolish.

"And look where it got me," she muttered, annoyed with herself for dredging up the memories.

With every intention of leaving the room she started to pull her hand from the big, warm cradle of his and his fingers abruptly closed firmly around hers.

"Don't stop now, Elizabeth," he murmured without opening his eyes. "You're just getting to the good part."

The only thing that kept her from slapping him was the fact that she would likely undo some of her handiwork and have to do it all over again.

Instead, she held her fury in check and went on as if he'd misinterpreted what she'd said. Tomorrow, or even after that, if he questioned her about her comment she would lie through her teeth and swear she hadn't said any such thing. Two could play this game, she decided.

Stating the facts as if they described someone else's life she told Joe Hennessey the story of how Agent David Maddox had come into her life as her handler and proceeded to lure her into temptation with his vast charm.

Hennessey would no doubt recognize the story. He probably practiced the same M.O. all the time. According to what David had told her, Hennessey left a heartbroken woman behind at every assignment. He was the proverbial James Bond. The man who had it all. A new secret life, with all it entailed, every week.

How exciting it must be to live that kind of life with absolutely no accountability to anyone. The broken hearts he left behind would certainly be chalked up to collateral damage just as the occasional dead body surely was.

Elizabeth worked hard at keeping her tone even and her temper out of the mix, but it wasn't easy. The more she talked about the past and considered her relationship with David, the more she realized how she hadn't ever really known him. She only knew what had drawn her to him.

She didn't really know David the man. She only knew David the lover.

She knew what he'd allowed her to see.

That realization was the hardest of all.

Her gaze dropped to Joe Hennessey. This time he was definitely sleeping. She couldn't help wondering if he'd done this on purpose. Made her see.

She tugged her hand free of his and admitted yet another painful truth. No. This was no one's fault but her own. She'd seen what she'd wanted to see.

Nothing more.

And now she knew the whole truth.

Her relationship with David had been based on an illusion that she had created in her mind.

Elizabeth left Hennessey's room.

She progressed down the stairs and walked to the front door. She unlocked and opened it and came face-to-face with the agent assigned to that location.

"I need to see Director Calder," she said, her voice lacking any real emotion.

"Is there a problem, Dr. Cameron?" the agent asked, his dark eyewear no doubt concealing an instant concern for the two principals it was his job to protect.

"Yes, there is," she said bluntly. "I need to go home. I've decided I can't complete this assignment. Please call the director for me."

Elizabeth closed the door. There was nothing else to say.

She'd made up her mind.

Agreeing to this part of his mission had been a mistake. Giving someone David's face was one thing but she could not do the rest. There had to be someone else who knew David's personality well enough to help Hennessey grasp the necessary elements. Surely there were videos the CIA had made, tapes of interviews David had conducted.

However they conducted this portion of the mission from here had nothing to do with her.

She wanted out.

CHAPTER SIX

THREE DAYS ELAPSED before Elizabeth would again speak to him about her relationship with Maddox.

Today was his first "official" Maddox lesson. They were finally getting down to business. 'Bout time.

That first night at the safe house she had left him sleeping and called the director. Not the director of field operations. The frigging director of the CIA himself. She had demanded to be taken home, had insisted that she wanted no further part in this operation.

Somehow Director Calder had changed her mind.

Since Joe had slept through the whole thing he had no idea how the director had accomplished the feat.

At any rate, Joe had awakened the next morning to an edict from the good doctor. She refused to discuss anything about the assignment with Joe until three days had passed. She wanted him to stay on the full dosage of the medication and in bed during said time. He hadn't liked it one damned bit, but what choice did he have? It wasn't like he could disobey a direct order from Calder.

During those three days Elizabeth had attended to his medical needs. She'd changed his bandages. Thankfully at this point the bulkier gauze was gone. The swelling was still pretty ugly as was the redness. He looked like he'd been on the losing end of a pool house brawl.

"Not like that," she said, her impatience showing.

"Show me," Joe countered, his own patience thinning.

It wasn't like he'd been around Maddox that much. Getting his mannerisms down pat wasn't going to be easy without a better understanding of how he moved.

Elizabeth did the thing with her right arm that she was convinced Joe would never get right. A clever little salute of a wave Maddox had tossed her way every time he saw her. It wasn't that big a deal. He doubted Maddox waved at his targets.

Since she waited, glaring at him, Joe assumed she was ready for him to try again. So he did.

She shook her head. "That's still not right." At his annoyed look she threw up her hands. "This is impossible! You're not going to get it. You're not him!"

Enough.

Joe got right in her face. She blinked, but to her credit, she didn't back off.

"You know what, you're right, I'm not him." He grappled to regain some kind of hold on his temper. "What I need is for you to teach me what I need to know, not dog out my every attempt."

She held her ground, her arrogant little chin jutting out even further. "You know what? I think we need a break."

He straightened, shook his head. "Oh yeah. That's what we need. We've just gotten started and already we need a break. At this rate all those agents will be dead and we won't even need to go through with this operation anyway."

Her mouth opened and the harsh intake of breath told him he'd hit his mark way before the hurt glimmering in her eyes told the tale. "Someone else is dead?"

Dammit. He hadn't meant to tell her about that.

Calder had instructed him to keep quiet about the latest hit for fear she would be so shaken she wouldn't be able to continue with their work. Continue, hell, they hadn't even started. Not really.

He booted her words from the other night out of his head. He couldn't keep going over that like a repeating blog. She'd admitted, when she thought he was asleep, that he affected her and her words had affected him. Even half-comatose he'd felt a surge of want deep in his gut.

Maybe it was just the fact that he'd despised Maddox that made him want her. Then again, the truth was, he hadn't known Maddox that well. Maybe he'd despised Maddox because he had the girl Joe wanted.

And he wouldn't have ever known if it hadn't been for that one night.

That night had changed everything.

"Answer me, Hennessey," she demanded. "Who is dead?"

His hope that being on a first-name basis might bring a unity and informality to their work had bombed big time.

"Agent Motley. You may not remember him—"

"I remember him," she interrupted. "He was the first transformation."

She looked ready to crumple but somehow she didn't. Instead she looked at him with hellfire in her eyes. "What about his family?"

Joe hated even worse to tell her this part. "His wife was murdered as well. But his daughter was away with friends so she's okay."

Elizabeth shook her head. "She isn't okay, Hennessey. She won't ever be okay again. Her parents were murdered and she's alone."

Neither of them moved for five seconds that turned into ten. He couldn't help wondering if the person Elizabeth was really talking about was her. She was alone… basically. Her father, retired Colonel Cameron, had died years ago, but her mother was still alive, at least in body. Alzheimer's had made an invalid of her and she no longer recognized her own daughter. She lived in a home especially for Alzheimer's patients. Maddox had been Elizabeth's only viable emotional attachment.

Was that why she had such trouble dealing with this operation?

"She won't be alone, Elizabeth," Joe said softly. He resisted the urge to move closer, to comfort her with his touch. "She has aunts, uncles and cousins. It won't be the same but she won't be alone."

Elizabeth wet her lips. He saw her lower one tremble just a little. "That's good." She nodded. "I'm glad she has a support system."

The way you didn't? he wanted to ask.

"Who are we really talking about here, Elizabeth? You or Agent Motley's daughter?"

Fury flashed across her face. "I don't know what you mean, Agent Hennessey. I'm perfectly fine."

"I think you haven't gotten over losing Maddox."

Judging by the horror in her eyes, completely deflating her anger, he'd royally screwed up by making that comment.

"This isn't a counseling session, Agent Hennessey," she returned coolly, too coolly. "I don't need your conclusions on my relationships."

"Relationship," he corrected, asking for more trouble.

She glowered at him. "What the hell is that supposed to mean?"

He shrugged. Hell, he was in over his head now, might as well say the rest. "*Relationship,*" he repeated. "From what I can tell that's the only long-term commitment you've been involved in. Before or since."

Her hands settled on her hips, drawing his reluctant attention to the way her jeans molded to her soft curves. Damn, he was doomed.

"Who gave you permission to look into my background? Especially my personal life?" she demanded, her tone stone cold now. She was fighting mad.

"I've been watching you for weeks, *Elizabeth,*" he said, purposely saying her name the way he'd heard Maddox say it on the few times they'd met. "It was part of my job. Get to know your routine. Get to know you. Find out who you talked to. Where you went. What you ate. Who you slept with."

She staggered back a couple of steps. "You've been watching me?"

The question came out as if the reality of what he'd been saying had only just penetrated.

"That's right. I've watched every move you've made for weeks," he replied, stoking the flames with pure fuel.

Her eyes rounded. "I haven't slept with anyone since…" Her words trailed off and something achy and damaged flickered in her eyes. Something he couldn't quite name and never wanted to see again.

"Since Maddox," he finished for her. And then he turned away, unable to look at the emotional wreckage he'd caused. It hadn't been necessary for him to push that hard. He could have stopped this before it went anywhere near this far.

"Try again."

What the hell?

He turned back to her and she stood, arms crossed over her chest, glaring at him. "What?"

"I said," she hurled the words at him, "try again. People are dying. You have to get this right."

Something shifted inside him then, made him wish he could turn back time and do those last few minutes over. He hadn't meant to hurt her but he had. But she was too strong, too determined to let him win without a fight.

Dr. Elizabeth Cameron was no coward.

Just something else to admire about her.

ELIZABETH AWAKENED THAT night from a frightful nightmare. David had been calling to her, begging her for help and she couldn't reach him. No matter how she'd tried he just appeared to draw farther and farther away.

She tried to get her bearings now. It was completely dark. Not home. The safe house. Joe Hennessey.

A breath whooshed out of her lungs and she relaxed marginally. The dream must have awakened her.

A soft rap sounded from her door and she bolted upright. A dozen probable reasons, all bad, for her being awakened in the middle of the night crashed one by one through her mind. She felt for her glasses on the bedside table. "Yes?"

"Dr. Cameron, this is Agent Stark. We may have a problem."

Elizabeth was out of the bed before the man finished

his statement. She dragged on her robe and rushed to the door without bothering with a light.

"What's wrong?" The hall was empty save for Agent Stark. A table lamp some ten feet away backlit the tall man and his requisite black suit.

"I'm not sure there's a real problem, but Agent Hennessey has requested that we bring in something for stomach cramps. Agent Dawson insisted I check with you first."

Stomach cramps? Worry washed over her. "I'll need my bag."

Stark nodded. "I'll wait for you at Agent Hennessey's room."

Elizabeth flipped on the overhead light and rushed around the room until she determined where she'd left her bag last. She never had this problem at home. But here, with *him,* she felt perpetually out of sorts.

By the time she was in the hall she could hear Hennessey growling at his fellow agent.

"I don't need the doc, Stark. I need something for—"

"Thank you, Agent Stark," Elizabeth said by way of dismissal when she barged, without knocking, into the room. "I'll let you know if we need anything."

Judging by Hennessey's bedcovers he'd been writhing in discomfort for some time. "Why didn't you let me know you needed me?" she demanded of her insubordinate patient.

"I don't need a doctor," he grumped as he sat up. One hand remained fastened against his gut. "What I need is Maalox or Pepto. Something for a stomachache. Apparently dinner disagreed with me."

Before Elizabeth could fathom his intent he stood, allowing the sheet to fall haphazardly where it would, mostly around his ankles, and leaving him clothed in nothing more than a wrinkled pair of boxers. She looked away but not soon enough. The image of strong, muscled legs and a lean, ribbed waist was already permanently and indelibly imprinted upon at least a dozen brain cells.

"Oh, man." He bent forward slightly in pain.

Elizabeth tried to reconcile the man who refused the proper dose of pain medication with one who couldn't tolerate a few stomach cramps without demanding a remedy.

"Are you sure it was something you ate?" Less than a week had passed since his surgery, there were a number of problems that could crop up. Before he could answer, she added, "Let's have a look."

"Come on, Doc, this isn't necessary," he grumbled.

She held up a hand. "Sit, Agent Hennessey."

With a mighty exhale he collapsed back onto the bed. She didn't really need to see the rest of his face. His eyes said it all. He had no patience for this sort of thing.

When she'd tucked the thermometer into his mouth, she moved to the door and asked Agent Stark to send for an over-the-counter tonic for stomach cramps. He hadn't mentioned any other issues that generally went hand-in-hand with cramps, but she didn't see any reason to take the risk. The medication she requested would cover either or both symptoms.

Hennessey sat on the edge of the bed, the thermometer protruding from his lips, and he looked exactly like a petulant child with an amazingly grown-up body. And a layer of gauze concealing the majority of his face.

She thought of the agent who'd died in the past twenty-four hours and she prayed that her efforts wouldn't be too little too late. She'd taken an oath to save lives. Had her support of the CIA helped or hurt? She had thought her work would save them from this very fate and now it seemed those she had helped were on a list marked for death.

How could that be?

It didn't make sense.

"Normal," she commented aloud after reading the thermometer. She set the old-fashioned instrument on the bedside table next to her bag. "Any other symptoms."

"No." He groaned. "At least not yet."

"Let me have a look at your face." She'd changed his bandages this morning and all had looked well enough. Still some redness and swelling, but that was perfectly normal.

"My face isn't the problem." He pushed her hands away. "It's my gut."

Worry gnawing at her, she reached into her bag and removed her stethoscope and blood pressure cuff. She saw no reason to take chances.

Hennessey swore but she ignored him. BP was only slightly elevated. The thrashing around in the bed and any sort of pain could be responsible for that.

She listened to his heart and lungs. Nothing out of the ordinary. His heart sounded strong and steady.

As she put the cuff and stethoscope away he said, "I told you I was fine."

"Yes, you did," she agreed. "But I would be remiss in my duties if I didn't double-check."

He made a sound that loudly telegraphed his doubt of her motives. "You probably just wanted an excuse to see me in my shorts," he said glibly.

Elizabeth tamped down her first response of annoyance and thought about that remark for a moment. Deciding he wasn't the only one who could throw curves, she sat down beside him. Tension went through him instantly, stiffening his shoulders and making the muscle in his jaw flex.

"Actually, Agent Hennessey, I've already seen most of you the day of surgery." She produced a smile at his narrowed gaze. "Sometimes when they shift a patient from the surgical gurney sheets drop and gowns get shoved up around waists." As true as her statement was, it hadn't happened with him but he didn't have to know that. "But don't worry," she assured him, "the only person who laughed was the nurse, but don't tell her I told you."

Elizabeth would have given anything to see his face just then. If the red rushing up his neck was any indication, his whole face was most likely beet-red.

She couldn't torture him too long. He did have a problem. "I'm kidding, Hennessey."

He moved his head slowly from side to side but didn't look at her. "Very good, Doc, you might get the hang of this after all."

Feeling guilty for her bad joke, she urged him back into bed and tucked the sheet properly around him. Minutes later Stark arrived with the medication. Elizabeth thanked him and gave Hennessey the proper dose.

She settled into the chair near the bedside table and waited to see if the medication would work.

"You should get some sleep, Doc," he said, finally meeting her gaze. "If I need any more I can handle it." He gestured to the bottle she'd left on the table next to her bag.

"That's all right, Hennessey. You're my patient. I think I'd be more comfortable keeping an eye on you for a while."

Resigned to his fate, he heaved a put-upon sigh and closed his eyes.

Elizabeth glanced at the clock—two-thirty. She should go back to bed, but she doubted she would sleep now. Not after that awful dream and not with Hennessey uncomfortable.

She watched him try to lay still, his hand on his stomach and she wished there was a way to make the medicine work faster, but there wasn't. It would take ten to twenty minutes. She thought about what they'd eaten for dinner and wondered why she wasn't sick. Then again maybe she would be before the night was through.

As if the thought had somehow stirred some part of her that had still been sleeping, her stomach clenched painfully then roiled threateningly.

She recognized the warning immediately and reached for the bottle to down a dose.

"You, too?"

Her gaze met Hennessey's as she twisted the cap back onto the bottle. "Guess so." She grimaced, as much from the yucky taste as from another knot of discomfort.

A light knock on the door and Stark stuck his head inside. "Any chance I could get some of that?"

Before the night was finished all three agents on duty had come in for medication.

At dawn Joe lay on his side watching Elizabeth sleep in the chair not three feet from his bed. She looked more beautiful than any woman had a right to. Her long hair lay against the crisp white of her robe. And those lips, well, they were pretty damned sweet, too. He would give anything right now to taste her. He would lay odds that she tasted hot and fiery, just like her spirit.

Oh, she tempered the fiery side with that cool, calm facade, but he could feel the hellion breathing flames beneath that ultracontrolled exterior.

His gaze traveled over her chest and down to her hips and then to the shapely legs curled beneath her. She worked so hard at everything she allowed herself to do. He wondered if she would work half as hard to be happy.

This was one lady who didn't fully understand the meaning of the word. He'd read what was available on her childhood. Nice family. Moved around a lot since her father had been military, but there didn't appear to be any deep, dark secrets. What had made Elizabeth Cameron so hard on herself? So determined not to fail when it came to helping others?

That was the sole reason, in Joe's estimation, that put her out of the suspect pool. No way would she do anything to endanger another human being. She simply wasn't wired that way. No amount of money—if money were even an issue for her—would entice her. He understood that completely.

Maddox was dead and Calder and Allen were directors. Joe had been filled in when he was selected for the assignment. Who else could have accessed those files?

Three months ago when he'd had to step in long enough to save this pretty lady's skin, someone had broken into her clinic. Had that been the beginning? Were the files the target then? Or had the whole exercise been about casting suspicion in a different direction?

There was no way to know. All he'd had was Maddox's urgent request for backup. Maddox claimed he'd stumbled onto a plan to go after the files of Dr. Elizabeth Cameron. Someone had evidently connected her to the CIA. Of course she had no files related to the Agency.

The only thing he did know for a certainty was how terrified she was that night. He'd held her close to him and she'd trembled. She'd had no idea what was happening, nor did she now. He was convinced. In any event, her safety was one of the Agency's top priorities.

The idea that someone might be setting her up had crossed his mind. But there was no proof as of yet. There was no evidence of anything. Only three dead agents. Still, a real player would have known the files wouldn't be in her office.

Every precaution was being taken to keep the rest of those agents safe, but some were in the middle of dicey operations with higher priorities requiring that they remain undercover.

Those were the ones most at risk.

Joe wished like hell there was a way to speed up this process, except there simply wasn't. His fingerprints could be altered with a clear substance that formed to his skin in such a way that no one could tell the difference. But his face, that had been done in the only way possible. Surgically. Until the swelling and redness were gone he had no choice but to stay right here.

Not that it was such a hardship.

He wondered if David Maddox had had the first clue that the chemistry would be so strong between Joe and Elizabeth. Surely he wouldn't have requested Joe to go to her rescue all those months ago if he'd had any idea that might be the case. Then again, he had known Joe's reputation, however exaggerated.

It was true that Joe dated often and rarely the same lady more than twice. But not all those dates resulted in sex. Not that he was complaining about the reputation. He'd always enjoyed the hype.

Until now.

That thought came out of nowhere, but when he analyzed the concept he knew it was true. Something about the way Elizabeth looked at him when she talked about his reputation didn't sit right.

He wanted her to respect him at least to some degree. Funny thing was, he'd never once worried about that before. He studied the woman sleeping so peacefully. Why was it that what she thought about him mattered so much?

His job performance had always been above reproach. He did what he had to do no matter the cost. Not a single doubt had ever crossed his mind on that score. People respected his professional ability, no question. If anyone had ever been suspect of him personally he hadn't noticed.

Maybe that was the issue at hand here. Had the doctor's blatant distaste with his so-called reputation finally made him take a hard look at what someone else thought about him as a man...as a human being?

He closed his eyes and blocked her image from view.

He didn't want to think anymore. His stomach still felt a little queasy and his face hurt.

Why look for more trouble?

CHAPTER SEVEN

JUST OVER TWO weeks after surgery the bandages were gone, but some of the swelling and redness remained. All in all, Elizabeth was quite pleased with Hennessey's progress in that respect.

It was the tension brewing between them that she could have done without.

From the moment the last of the bandages had come off a subtle shift had occurred between them. Quite frankly Elizabeth couldn't say for sure whether it was her or him or if that was actually when it began. But something had changed on a level over which neither of them appeared to have any control.

Or at least she didn't.

Admittedly she couldn't read Hennessey's mind, but she didn't doubt for a second that he suffered some amount of discomfort related to the tension as well.

And to think, she could have been soaking up the sun and drinking martinis the past two weeks.

She blew out a breath and folded the last of her laundry. The Agency had delivered her luggage the day after her arrival, but a number of the outfits she'd packed for her vacation were far from what she would have preferred to wear in Hennessey's presence. The bikinis were definitely off-limits. She'd had no choice but to wear the few, more conservative outfits over and over.

Hennessey stuck with jeans and button-up shirts or T-shirts. He went around barefoot most of the time. For some reason that bothered her considerably more than it should. It wasn't that he had unattractive feet. To the contrary. His feet actually fascinated her. Large and well-formed. Like the rest of him.

She rolled her eyes and pushed aside the stupid, stupid obsession she had with the man.

Watching David's face slowly emerge beyond the swelling and redness only made matters worse. Perhaps that was even the catalyst in all of this. She just couldn't be certain of anything.

The last time she'd gotten too close to Hennessey the yearning to lean into his arms had been almost overwhelming.

Was she losing her mind or what?

Thankfully no other agents had been murdered since Motley and his wife. Elizabeth squeezed her eyes shut to block the image of the face she'd transformed for the very purpose of protecting the man behind it.

Hennessey assured her that the investigation was ongoing but all had surrendered to the idea that whoever was behind these killings couldn't be stopped any way but by infiltrating the group David had once affiliated himself with. Another week at least before that could happen.

The one other agent they had initially tried to send undercover to infiltrate the group several weeks ago had been killed in the first twenty-four hours. Using David's face as safe entry was the only hope of getting anywhere near the truth.

Elizabeth sat down on the edge of the bed. She hadn't let herself think too much about David and the past since that night the whole lot of them—she, Hennessey and their guards—had gotten a mild case of food poisoning. Stomach cramps and a few mad dashes to the bathroom but, thankfully, nothing more disconcerting than that.

For days now she had set her emotions outside the goings-on within these walls. She had separated the bond she had shared with the man, David, from the CIA operative, David. It hadn't been that difficult, to her utter surprise. She'd turned off her personal emotions and looked at this operation as a case.

But would there be repercussions later? She was a trained physician. She understood that the human psyche could only fool itself to a certain point before reality would override fantasy.

She had far too many scheduled patients depending upon her for her to take a chance on suffering a psychotic break of any sort. Not that she felt on the verge of any kind of break, but she recognized that things with her weren't as they should be.

Scarcely a week from now her part in this would be over. Surely she could manage another five or six days. She and Hennessey had learned to be cordial to each other most of the time, had even shared a laugh or two.

But then there was the tension. She'd pretty much determined that the source of the steadily increasing tension was sexual. He was a man, she was a woman; plain, old chemistry saw to the rest.

Though she didn't dare guess how long it had been since Hennessey had had sex, she knew exactly how long it had been for her. Four long months. And that last time with David had felt off somehow. As if they were out of sync, no longer in tune to one another.

Elizabeth pushed the memories aside. Those painful recollections had nothing to do with any of this. She was a woman. She had fundamental needs that had been ignored. End of subject.

When she'd put the rest of her laundry away she went in search of her pupil. Might as well get on with today's lesson. More syntax and inflection. He wasn't that far off. She'd heard him in his room at night practicing with tapes of David's voice. She hadn't asked where the tapes had come from. Interviews from old CIA cases or maybe from surveillance tapes.

As she descended the stairs she wondered if he would let her listen to the tapes. Probably not, since they likely involved cases that she didn't have clearance for. Oh well, why torture herself anyway. David was gone. Listening to old tapes of his voice would be detrimental to her mental health. It didn't take a psychologist to see that one coming around the corner.

At the last step she froze. Hennessey, his back to her, had walked across the room, from the coffeemaker on the counter to the sofa in the middle of the living space. The way he'd moved had stolen her breath. Not like Hennessey at all. Like David.

Exactly like David.

She watched him sit down and take a long swill from his mug. Her hands started to tremble. When had he learned to do that? Their lessons had progressed well but nothing on this level.

Summoning her wits she took the last step down. "Coffee smells great." Somehow she dredged up a smile.

He did the same, but it looked nothing like a David smile.

Thank God.

Wait. The goal was for him to look, act and speak like David.

"You need to work on that smile," she said as she moved toward the kitchen and the coffee. Maybe a strong, hot cup would help clear her head. Obviously she was a little off this morning.

"That smile was for you, not for the mission," he explained.

She poured herself a cup of steaming brew and decided that, as usual, honesty was the best policy. "I saw you walk across the room. It was uncanny." She turned to face him, the hot cup cradled in her hands. "How did you get so good between yesterday and today?"

Strangely, he looked away before answering. "I did a lot of practicing last night. I didn't want you to be disappointed again today."

That felt like a lie even if it sounded sincere.

She padded across the room and took the seat opposite his position on the sofa. Since he never wore shoes she'd decided she wouldn't bother either.

"I'm glad that how I feel matters to you, Agent Hennessey." She sipped her cup as he analyzed her. Her interrogation had roused his suspicions. Just another reason for her to be suspect.

He set his cup on the table that separated them. "How you feel matters a great deal to me, Doc."

Since she had refused to call him Joe he had reverted to calling her Doc. She didn't like it but when one resolved to play dirty, one couldn't complain.

"Let's get started," she suggested, resting her cup alongside his.

"Let's," he agreed.

Well, wasn't he Mr. Agreeable this morning? Very strange indeed.

JOE RAN THROUGH the steps with Elizabeth until noon brought Agent Dawson and lunch. Whenever Dawson was on duty he dined with them, so Joe had the opportunity to study his teacher.

Every aspect of her cooperation in this mission felt genuine. Even after more than two weeks in close quarters, he would swear that she was above reproach. But he had to be absolutely certain. Two days before this aspect of the mission began Director Allen had informed him of another part of his assignment: make sure Dr. Cameron hadn't been a party to Maddox's act of treason.

To say Joe had been stunned would be putting it mildly, but like any other assignment, he did his duty.

Director Calder had told her the truth about why she was needed for his operation…at least to a degree. That part Joe had known. He had also already known how to walk and talk like Maddox. He only needed a little extra help with a few of his more intimate mannerisms. More important he needed to know as many details as possible about the relationship they had shared.

Joe had hoped to go about this in a way that wouldn't cause Elizabeth further hurt, but that might prove impossible for two reasons.

Director Allen, Joe's immediate boss, still wasn't convinced of Elizabeth's innocence—despite Joe's assessment. Joe had learned that Director Calder, Allen's boss and *the* director of the CIA, was the only reason stronger measures hadn't been taken to determine her involvement, if any, with what David Maddox had done.

Maddox had sold out his country in several ways, but there was no absolute proof that he was the one who'd released the names. All indications pointed to him, but there were also a number, Allen had suggested, that pointed to Elizabeth as having been in on it with him.

With Maddox dead there was really no way to be certain.

Unless Joe could fool Maddox's primary contact from his final operation.

The only glitch was the fact that the contact was female.

Joe settled his gaze on Elizabeth Cameron and wondered if she'd had any idea that Maddox had maintained an ongoing relationship with another woman.

If she did, she hid it well.

Nothing about her demeanor over the past two weeks and some days had given him the first hint of deceit.

But she was suspicious.

She'd made no secret of it. Just another indicator that she wasn't one to hide her feelings.

"Aren't you hungry, Agent Hennessey?" she asked, drawing his attention back to the table.

Dawson's scrutiny was now on him as well. He wasn't happy with the situation at all. The more Allen pushed for information on Elizabeth, the more dissatisfied Dawson grew. Joe regarded the other man a moment and would have bet his life that the guy had a little crush on the good doctor. Of course Dawson was married with two kids and as faithful as they came in this business.

Joe pushed his plate aside. "I'm good. Let me know when you're ready to get started again."

It wasn't like he could take a walk, but he could go to his room for a few minutes before the next session of alone time with her.

He closed the door to his room and walked over to the

dresser. He stared at his face, the one that looked nothing like him and more and more like David Maddox.

In a few days the swelling and redness would be all but gone. Then he could move to the next step.

His colored contacts had already been delivered. Probably by tomorrow he would need to start getting accustomed to wearing them. He doubted it would be a problem. He'd done that part before. It was the drastic change in his face that gave him pause.

He'd been mimicking Maddox's speech and movements for weeks before this. But—he reached up and touched his face—this was different.

The counseling hadn't fully prepared him. He'd thought he would be fine with it, but the more Maddox's face emerged the less prepared he felt.

Nothing had ever affected him this way.

That the worst was likely yet to come didn't help.

He had to find a way to prod intimate details from Elizabeth. How Maddox kissed…how he made love to her was essential to Joe's success. He couldn't go into this without being fully prepared on every level.

The only question that remained at this point was how he would get the answers he needed without hurting Elizabeth with the ugly details.

A knock at his door told him his time for soul searching was up.

"Yeah?"

The door opened and Elizabeth strolled into his room. "I need to understand what's going on here, Hennessey," she demanded. "I get the feeling you've been hiding something from me."

Well, here was his opportunity.

Question was, did he have the guts to take advantage of it?

Only one way to find out.

"Here's the thing." He moved toward her, locked his gaze with hers and let her feel the intensity. He needed her off balance. "One of the contacts Maddox had is female. I can't be certain how close they were, considering his relationship with this group preceded the two of you." That part was a flat-out lie but he was improvising here in an attempt to save her the heartache.

A frown furrowed a path across her brow. "How is that possible? He worked as my handler for a year prior to our...relationship. I thought the operation came later, after he'd gone back into field duty."

This is where things got slippery.

"One of the contacts in his last operation was someone he had known for years." He shrugged as if it was no big deal. "An on-again, off-again flame who unknowingly provided him with useful intelligence from time to time. She's my only safe way into this."

Elizabeth wasn't convinced. Far from it.

"Why haven't you mentioned this before?" The frown had given way to something along the lines of outright accusation. "No one has mentioned anything about a woman."

"You know the drill, Doc," he said, careful to keep the regret from his tone, "need to know. The golden rule we live by every day. You had no compelling need to know this part until now."

"If your superiors told you that excuse would make me feel better about this new information, they were wrong," she said in a calm voice but the turmoil of emotions in her eyes belied her unyielding statement.

"We can move back downstairs to have this conversation," he suggested in deference to her comfort. He felt reasonably certain she didn't want to talk about certain details in the room where he slept.

Her expression hardened—the change was painful to watch. "Don't be ridiculous, Hennessey. I'm a doctor. Nothing you say or ask about the human body or the act of procreation will make me uncomfortable in any setting."

With that point driven straight through his chest like a knife she strode over to his bed and plopped down on the end. "What do you want to know?"

The grim line of her mouth and the cool distance in her eyes telegraphed all he needed to know.

Too late not to hurt her. He'd already done just that.

Regret trickled through him, but there was nothing to do but pursue the subject. He needed the information and the damage was done. Holding back now wouldn't accomplish a damned thing.

"We can start with pet names." He shrugged. "Did he usually call you anything other than Elizabeth?"

"What does this have to do with the other woman?"

"Maybe nothing. But I need to be—"

"Yeah, yeah," she cut in. "I get it."

A moment passed as she appeared to collect her thoughts. She stared at some point beyond him. The drapes on the windows were closed, so certainly not at any enticing view.

"Baby," she said abruptly as her eyes met his once more. "He called me *baby* whenever we…" She cleared her throat. "Whenever we were intimate."

"Baby," he murmured, committing the term to memory.

"No." She shook her head. "Not like that. *Baaaby.*
With the emphasis on the first syllable."

"Baaaby," he echoed, drawing out the first syllable
as if it were two.

She nodded once. "Yes. Like that."

He propped against the dresser and let her talk. She
seemed to know what he needed to ask and he appreciated that more than she could possibly comprehend.
She shared the sexual vocabulary Maddox used. His
euphemisms for body parts and the words that he whispered in her ear as they made love. With every word,
every nuance of her voice he felt closer to her…felt the
need to touch her. Tension vibrated through him to the
point that every nerve ending felt taut with anticipation
of what she would say next.

"He liked for me to be on top," she said, careful to
avert her eyes. "When I wasn't on top he was usually…"
She cleared her throat. "He liked to get behind me." She
fisted her fingers and hugged her arms around her middle. "He was very aggressive. Preferred to be in control
other than the being on top thing."

Joe wanted to make her stop, but he couldn't. And
yet with each new detail she revealed, his body grew
harder, he wanted her more.

"Was there a certain…way he touched you?" he ventured, his throat so tight he barely managed to speak.

She blinked, looked away again. "My…ah… breasts.
He always touched me that way a lot. Even when we
were just kissing." She rubbed at her forehead, then
quickly clasped her arm back around her.

He couldn't take any more of this. He'd hurt her and
tortured himself physically. No more.

"Thank you for sharing such intimate—"

"Don't you want to know how he kissed me?" She glared up at him then, the breath rushing in and out of her lungs. All semblance of calm or submissiveness were gone.

Joe straightened away from the dresser. "We can talk about this some more later. There's—"

She rocketed to her feet. "He wasn't that great when it came to kissing."

Her eyes looked huge in her pale face. He couldn't tell if what he saw there was fear or humiliation. Maybe both, and it tore at his guts.

"He used his tongue too much." She paced the length of the room, then turned and moved back in his direction. "But I got used to it eventually." She shrugged her shoulders, the movement stilted. "I was so busy with my work I didn't have time to be too picky about my sex life. Really, what's a busy woman like me supposed to do?"

Her lips trembled with the last and he had to touch her. She was close enough.

"Elizabeth, I'm sorry. I—"

She drew her shoulder away from his seeking hand but didn't back off. "Are you really?" The accusation in her eyes dealt him another gut-wrenching blow. She took a step closer. "If you're so sorry then what prompted your considerable erection, Agent Hennessey?" She reached out and smoothed a hand over the front of his jeans, molded her palm to his aching hard-on.

He moved her hand away but didn't let go of her arm. "Don't do this to yourself, Elizabeth. I explained to you that the female contact was someone he knew before you came into his life."

"And I know a lie when I hear one, *Joe*."

He closed his eyes and exhaled a weary breath. Maybe he should have been up-front with her sooner. He should never have listened to Director Allen. Elizabeth Cameron was far too smart for these kinds of tactics.

"I had known something was wrong for a while," she said, her voice soft, the fierce attitude having surrendered to the hurt. "We hadn't made love in two months when he died. I'd only seen him two or three times. He called, but never talked for long. I guess I knew it was over. I just didn't know why."

It took every ounce of strength Joe possessed not to tell her the truth about David Maddox. He'd used her. He'd cheated on her all along. The latter came with the territory. No man who hoped to keep a clean relationship with a woman stayed in field operations. It simply wasn't feasible.

"You don't know that," he argued, hoping to salvage her feelings to whatever extent possible. "There could have been a lot of things going on that prevented him from coming to you. Your safety for one thing," he offered, grasping at straws. "Remember he sent me in to rescue you that one night when he was too far away to do it himself."

She nodded distractedly as if her heart was working overtime to justify what her brain wanted to reject.

"I would certainly have taken precautions to protect you if I had been in his shoes. Think about it, Doc. He cared about you. You were and still are a valuable asset to the Agency."

Her eyes met his then and something passed between them, a sense of understanding.

"I'm certain you would have, Hennessey." She inhaled a big breath and then let it out slowly. "But you see I've been lying to myself for a while now." She offered a halfhearted shrug. "I guess it made me feel less gullible."

Joe tightened his hold on her forearm, but carefully avoided pulling her closer as he would very much have liked to do. "Sometimes we believe what we want to believe, Doc, even when we know better."

She searched his eyes for so long, he shifted in hopes of breaking the contact. Didn't work.

"Are you really any different from him, Agent Hennessey?"

He wasn't sure how to answer the question.

"I mean," she frowned in concentration, "if having sex with a contact would garner you the information you needed, would you go that far?"

When she put it that way, it sounded like the worst kind of sin. "I wish I could say no, but I'd be lying."

An "I see" look claimed her expression. "Well, at least you're honest."

"I won't lie," he told her in hopes of making the point crystal clear, "unless there is no other way, Doc. Lying is not something I enjoy, but it's part of my job more often than not."

She stared up at him then, puzzled. "Did you know I would give you the information you needed without your having to seduce me?"

"Doc, this situation isn't the same. You came into this knowing the mission."

Her gaze narrowed ever so slightly. "Did I really?"

He had to smile. "To the extent you needed to know, yes."

"But you didn't answer my question," she countered,

refusing to give an inch. "Would you have resorted to seducing me if necessary?"

"I had my orders, Doc, and seducing you wasn't included." When she would have turned to leave, he caught her wrist once more and drew her back. "Had I not been restrained by my orders, I can't say I wouldn't have tried. But the effort wouldn't have been about the mission."

She searched his eyes again…as if looking for answers to questions she couldn't voice. He wanted to lean down and brush his lips across hers. Just for a second, just long enough to feel the softness of hers.

But she walked away before he'd mentally beaten back his deeply ingrained sense of duty and did just that. He closed his eyes and cursed himself for the fool he was. He should have kissed her, should have shown her what a real kiss was like. Not some egotistical bastard's sloppy attempts.

He'd had that moment and he'd let it slip away. Part of him had felt certain for just a fleeting instant that she wanted him to kiss her.

"Oh."

He looked up, discovered her waiting at the door as if she'd only just remembered something of utmost importance and had decided to tell him before she forgot.

"I suppose I should tell you that you might have a bit of a problem with the female contact."

Confusion joined the other tangle of thoughts in his head. "What kind of problem?"

"I believe I would avoid making love to her if at all possible, otherwise I'm certain she will recognize you as an imposter."

His delayed defensive mechanism slammed into

place. What the hell was she trying to say? "You noticed a difference between Maddox and me?" he challenged. He knew where this was headed. She'd gotten a good feel of him fully aroused. He wondered if she would actually have the guts to cut him off at the knees, which was, in her opinion, what he imagined he deserved.

She nodded somberly. "I'm afraid so, Agent Hennessey. David was considerably—"

He held up both hands, cutting her off. "I don't think I want to hear this." And here he'd been feeling sorry as hell for her.

"I was just going to say," she went on as she planted one hand firmly on her hip, "that David was way, way *smaller* than you and I doubt any woman still breathing would fail to notice."

CHAPTER EIGHT

ELIZABETH LAY IN bed that night and considered what Hennessey had told her. Her initial response had been to deny all of it. But she had known he was telling the truth. If she'd had the first reservation, his genuine regret would have allayed any and all.

Joe hadn't lied to her. He'd tried to protect her.

She closed her eyes and remembered the way he'd looked at her as she'd given him the details of her intimacies with David. That the connection had made her restless to the point of becoming moist in places she'd thought on permanent vacation startled her. Just watching him react to her words had set her on the verge of sexual release.

No man had ever managed that…not for her.

All this time she'd considered herself somewhat lacking in the libido department, but Hennessey made her feel alive and on fire. How could that be?

From a purely psychological standpoint she understood that she had been celibate for longer than usual and she was still hurting from those final months before David had died. She'd known something wasn't right. Now she knew what.

There had been another woman.

Maybe his involvement with her had been purely business, but that didn't make her feel any better. Then again, Hennessey could be correct in his suggestion that David had been trying to protect her. But that would be giving him far too much of a benefit of the doubt. Even she wasn't that gullible.

She and David had been over at least two months before his death.

So why had he kept coming back? Why those final calls? Why hadn't he just told her it was over? It wasn't like he had made any sort of major commitment.

Like any other woman, she had considered he might be the one. That the two of them could perhaps move to the next stage. Get married and start a family. But deep down, especially those last few months, she had known it was going to end.

She banged her fist against the mattress. Why on God's green earth would she get involved with another man like David Maddox?

Evidently she was just as gullible as she'd thought. And seriously out of touch with her education level.

For goodness sakes, plain old common sense screamed at the utter stupidity of this move.

And still she couldn't help how she felt.

Yes, Hennessey was CIA just like David had been.

Yes, he was handsome and charming and sexy.

Just like David.

But there was one significant difference.

She thought of the way she'd touched him. Couldn't imagine how she'd ever worked up the nerve to make that bold move. She hadn't actually. She'd acted on instinct. Without thought.

Her heart bumped into a faster rhythm even now at the memory. There was no comparison between the two when it came to matters below the belt. Joe Hennessey was far more well endowed than David. No way would a former lover *not* notice that disparity.

Elizabeth flopped onto her side and pushed away the confusing thoughts. She refused to get involved with another man until she knew all the facts related to her last relationship.

Was it possible that David had used her for more than mere sex?

She chewed her bottom lip and let the concept penetrate fully. Didn't banish it immediately as she did when she was first asked to be a part of this. David knew the identities of the agents she'd transformed the same as she did. At least he had until the last year. They hadn't discussed the last three she'd done because there had been no reason. He was no longer her handler and like any good member of CIA personnel, she hadn't told.

Nor had he asked.

If he'd wanted to know, why didn't he bring up the subject? Never, not once did he ever, ever ask any questions. He hadn't even appeared interested.

But was that a front to keep her fooled?

She sat up, slung off the covers.

The conspiracy theories were rampant now.

She'd never get any sleep at this rate.

Could he, if he were guilty of this heinous betrayal, have listened in on her conversations with Agent Dawson?

Impossible. Dawson always picked her up and took her to a secure location before giving her any details.

They never talked in her car, on her phone, landline or cell, or at her house.

It simply wasn't done.

And David would have known those hard and fast rules far better than her.

A cold, rigid knot of panic fisted in her stomach.

He would also know how to bug her clothing, her purse, her body for that matter, in such a way that no one could tell.

"Oh, God."

Wait. Maybe she'd seen one too many spy movies.

The whole idea was ridiculous.

But people were dead…more might die.

She had to know for sure.

The only way to do that was to go home and look for herself. She would never voice those thoughts about David without some sort of confirmation. It just wouldn't be fair. She had loved him. She couldn't betray him like that simply because Joe Hennessey planted the seed in her mind.

Yes, things had been wrong somehow between her and David those last few months but did that mean he had done anything wrong? She didn't know. One thing was certain, Hennessey had said there were only a handful of people who knew the names of those agents who were being picked off one by one.

David Maddox had been one of them.

Not giving herself time to change her mind, she slipped on her clothes and shoes, grabbed her purse and headed for her door.

Holding her breath she opened it.

The hall was clear.

After taking a moment to gather her courage she eased out into the hall and moved soundlessly to the stairs.

Ten seconds later she was in the laundry room at the rear exit.

Now for the real test.

The house was watched twenty-four/seven.

There was really no way to leave without being caught.

That left only one option.

She dug her cell phone from her purse and called the one person she knew without doubt she could trust.

"HENNESSEY WON'T BE happy about this." Her driver wagged his head side to side resignedly.

"Just get me into my house, Agent Dawson," she urged. "If anyone learns we sneaked out I'll take full responsibility."

Dawson exhaled loudly. "I don't think that'll keep me out of trouble, Dr. Cameron, and it definitely isn't necessary. When it comes to your safety I'm the one who is responsible."

"I'm sorry, Agent Dawson," she relented. He was right. "I don't know what I was thinking. I don't want to get you into any trouble."

He didn't slow to turn around. He just kept driving through the darkness toward Georgetown proper and her brownstone.

"It's all right, Dr. Cameron." He glanced at her, let her see his determination in the dim glow from the dash lights. "If it means this much to you, then I'm more than willing to take the risk."

Why were all the good ones taken?

Elizabeth sank back into her seat.

Just her luck.

The image of Joe Hennessey zoomed through her

thoughts and she immediately exorcised him. Whether or not he was one of the good guys was yet to be seen. Just because he made her pulse leap and her heart stumble didn't mean he was right for her. All it meant was that she needed to recoup some semblance of a healthy sex life. As Hennessey would no doubt say, she needed to get laid. Come to think of it, he would probably be happy to oblige her if she were to suddenly turn stupid again.

And she had zero intention of doing that.

As they neared Elizabeth's home, Agent Dawson said, "We'll park on the street behind your house and enter from the rear if that'll work for you."

She nodded, then remembered he probably wasn't looking at her. "That'll definitely work."

"Once we get out," he went on, "we need to move quickly."

"I understand." Her heart started to beat a little faster at the idea that she might very well be in danger. She'd told herself that being exiled to the safe house was about protecting Hennessey's transformation, but maybe that wasn't all there was to it.

She shivered. Maybe that's what Dawson was worried about more so than getting into trouble.

Surely he would tell her if that was the case.

Something else she didn't need to worry about.

The street was still and dark save for a few streetlamps posted too far apart. Agent Dawson parked his sedan behind another lining the sidewalk and they got out.

"Stay behind me," he instructed.

Elizabeth did as he asked, following right behind him as they moved through the side yard of the house directly behind hers. On this street the homes were small, single bungalows with postage-stamp-sized yards. A tall wooden fence lined the rear boundaries, separating these private yards from the shared space behind the brownstones. She and Agent Dawson stayed outside the fenced area, wading through the damp grass.

Her home, like the ones on either side of it, was dark, but the area around the back door was lit well enough by moonlight that she could unlock the door without the aid of a flashlight.

"Let me check it out first."

She stood just inside her kitchen while he checked out the rest of the house. When he'd returned and given her the go-ahead she took his flashlight, his assertion not to turn on any lights in the house unless absolutely necessary ringing in her ears, and went straight to her room while he guarded the rear entrance.

Though she and Agent Dawson had taken a number of journeys together in the past year, this was her first ever covert adventure with the man. She was quite impressed with his stealth and finesse.

He hadn't dragged her into an alley and held her clamped against his body as Agent Hennessey had, but admittedly, the circumstances were different so there could be no actual comparison.

"Focus, Elizabeth," she ordered, putting aside thoughts of Hennessey and his muscular body.

If David had wanted to learn about her work for the CIA he would have had to "bug" her. She felt confident that the CIA regularly monitored the vehicles they used and, certainly, Agent Dawson would keep himself bug free. But she, on the other hand, had no idea about such things. Hadn't even anticipated the need.

First she checked through every single undergarment she wore to work. Nothing. She ran the beam of light over her room and located the jewelry box. Jewelry really wasn't something she cared to accessorize with but occasionally she did wear a necklace or bracelet.

Nothing unexpected there.

That left only her clothes and her purses.

She did regularly change bags.

And each time Agent Dawson picked her up she had already changed into her street clothes. She wasn't like a lot of the medical professionals who lurked around in public while wearing scrubs. Not that it was such a bad thing, she supposed. She simply wasn't comfortable doing so.

She pulled the door to her walk-in closet almost completely shut, leaving just enough room to reach out with one hand and flip on the switch. Once the door was closed, she set Agent Dawson's flashlight aside and started her search.

Every jacket, skirt and pair of slacks had to be examined from top to bottom, inside and out. She didn't know that much about electronic listening or surveillance devices but, again, plain old common sense told her they could come in virtually any shape or form.

Before diving into her clothes, she went through her bags. There were fewer and they were certainly easier to rummage around in.

Nothing suspicious. A few crumbs from the packs of snack crackers she carried in one. A couple of dollars in another. Wow! A peppermint breath mint from her favorite restaurant in the last one she picked up.

She unwrapped the mint and popped it into her mouth before moving onto her clothes.

This would take forever.

If Hennessey woke up she would be in serious trouble. She wondered if Dawson had told the other agent on duty about their little excursion. He hadn't mentioned it and she hadn't asked.

Hurry! Hurry!

Her hand stilled, backed up and moved over the pocket of her favorite slacks. A tiny bump. Her heart thundering, she reached inside and withdrew a small wad of chewed gum wrapped in tissue.

"Great," she huffed.

The door to her closet suddenly opened and Elizabeth wheeled around to identify her unexpected guest.

Not Dawson.

For several moments she couldn't breathe.

David.

Then the lingering redness and swelling crashed into her brain.

Hennessey.

"We've already done this, Doc," he said calmly but those startling blue eyes gave away the fury brewing behind that laid-back exterior. "Our technicians didn't find anything. You're not likely to either."

"This wasn't Agent Dawson's idea," she said quickly. "I forced him to bring me here." She smoothed her suddenly sweaty palms over her thighs. "I threatened to come alone if he didn't bring me."

"Dawson and I have already spoken."

"Oh." She looked around at the wreck she'd made of her closet. And she'd thought the worst thing she had to worry about was falling prey to Hennessey's charm. Look at what she'd done. She wasn't equipped to play this kind of game. "I guess I'll just clean up this mess."

She manufactured a shaky smile for him. She refused to admit that coming here had been too dumb for words. She'd needed to come. "You don't have to hang around. Dawson will bring me back."

"I sent Dawson back already."

She blinked, tried to hide her surprise. "Okay." She reached for a jacket lying in a twist on the floor. "I'll be quick."

"I'll be waiting."

He exited the closet, closing the door behind him.

Elizabeth stood there for a time, grappling for composure.

David had cheated on her. She didn't need any evidence. She *knew*.

The CIA obviously thought he'd used her as well or they wouldn't have been nosing around in her house. There was no arguing that conclusion. A part of her wanted to be angry, wanted to scream, but what was the point? It was done. David had done this to her.

Elizabeth closed her eyes and fought back the tears. She would not cry for or about him. He was gone. He'd been gone for a long time before he died.

Any other emotional wringers she put herself through related to him were a total waste of energy.

Slowly, piece by piece, she put the contents of her closet back to order, purses and all.

She thought about snagging a few items to take back with her, but she wouldn't be there much longer. There was no need.

As soon as she opened the door she flipped off the closet light. It took several moments for her eyes to adjust to the darkness. She thought about turning on the flashlight but there was really no reason since she knew her way around her own bedroom.

"You finished with what you came here to do?"

She stumbled back, gasped, before her eyes finally made out the image of someone sitting on the bench at the foot of her bed. The voice left no question as to identity.

Hennessey.

"Yes, I guess so."

Since he made no move to get up she sat down next to him.

Joe told himself to get up, to get the hell out of her bedroom, but he couldn't.

He kept torturing himself over and over with the images her words evoked even now. He knew with certainty that Maddox had made love to her in this room. With her on top…with him behind her. His hands on her breasts.

Every breath he drew into his lungs carried the scent of her. Her room, her whole house, smelled of her. Nothing but her. She was a doctor. She was never home long enough to cook. Only to soak in a tub of fragrant water. To shower with her favorite soap and shampoo.

She didn't wear perfume. Only the soap or maybe the subtle essence of the lotion sitting on her bedside table. He hadn't needed to turn on a light since arriving to see any of this. He'd been here with the techs when they'd gone through her things. He'd touched the undergarments she wore next to her skin. Had inhaled the scent of her shampoo.

And then he'd watched her. Twenty-four/seven for weeks. Until he'd thought of nothing but her.

"He used me, didn't he?"

The fragile sound of her voice carried more impact than if she'd screamed at him from the top of her lungs.

"Yes, we believe so."

Silence.

"For how long?"

"That we don't know."

"That's why you said you wouldn't lie—" she swallowed "—like he did."

"Yes."

"So…" She sucked in a ragged breath, tearing the oxygen out of his with the vulnerable noise. "Maybe it was real in the beginning?"

"Maybe."

More silence.

"I loved him, you know."

He squeezed his eyes shut against the tears he heard in her voice. "I know."

"Do you know how he died?"

That information was off-limits to her…but how could he let her wonder. "He died in the line of duty. That's all I can tell you."

"Will you take me back now?"

"Yes."

Joe stood. He reached for her hand and led her from her room, along the short hall and down the narrow staircase. He'd been in her home enough times to know the layout probably as well as she did.

He locked the door for her when they'd exited the rear of the house. Then they walked quietly through the moonlight until they reached his sedan.

Nothing else was said as they made the trip back to the safe house.

Joe took several zigzagging routes to ensure they weren't followed.

Daylight wasn't far off when they finally parked in the garage.

She got out and went inside. He didn't follow immediately.

He needed to walk off some of the tension shaking his insides. He'd alternated between wanting to yell at her and wanting to kiss her. Managing to get by without doing either was a credit to his sheer willpower.

He'd wanted to make her forget that bastard Maddox, but he'd resisted.

She didn't need him taking advantage of her vulnerability.

He might be a lot of things, but that kind of jerk he wasn't.

Inside the house he trudged up the stairs. He dreaded lying down again knowing sleep would not come. Their earlier candid discussion had kept him awake the greater portion of the night as it was.

He'd known when she left the house.

He'd followed but hadn't interfered at first, only when she'd stayed too long he'd had no choice.

The time he'd given her had been enough. She'd come to her own conclusions in her own time which was best. Anything he'd said or asserted would only have been taken with a grain of salt, would have put her on the defensive.

He didn't bother with the light in his room. Just kicked off his shoes and peeled off his shirt, inhaling one last time the smell of her where her arm had brushed against him as they'd sat on the bench in her room.

He stripped off his jeans and climbed into the bed. He was tired. Maybe he'd catch a few winks after all.

The instant his eyes closed her voice whispered

through his head. Every intimate detail she'd relayed today echoed through his weary mind. He fisted his fingers in the sheet, tried his best not to think about how her nipples would feel against the palms of his hands. He licked his lips and yearned for her taste.

He could have gotten up and taken a cold shower. Probably should have. Instead he lay there and allowed the sensuous torture to engulf him. Didn't resist.

He was too far gone for that.

ELIZABETH LAY IN her bed, her knees curled up to her chest. Director Calder had known the truth. Hennessey had known. Maybe even Dawson.

She was the only one who hadn't had any idea that David was using her.

How could she have been so blind?

She clenched her jaw to hold back the fury. How could he do that to her? He'd professed his love for her and all along he'd been using her.

How long had he planned his little coup?

At least one thing was for sure, he hadn't gotten to enjoy the fruits of his evil deeds.

A part of her felt guilty for thinking about his death that way, but the more logical part of her reveled in it. He might have used her, but he'd paid the ultimate price in the end. Along with three of the agents she'd given new faces.

Her stomach roiled with dread.

Who else would die before Hennessey could stop this?

Was there nothing she could do?

Give them new faces?

But if it were that easy the CIA would have suggested it.

No.

It would never be that simple.

Hennessey would have to risk his life to get close enough to the devils behind this to take them out.

One was a woman.

A woman who would undoubtedly expect him to make love to her as David likely had. And then she would know that Hennessey was an imposter.

Heat rushed through Elizabeth in spite of her troubling thoughts. She just couldn't help the reaction. She needed him—wanted him.

But that would be yet another monumental mistake on her part. She didn't need to make any more mistakes far more than she needed to indulge in heart-pounding sex with Hennessey.

But she could dream about him. And how it would feel to have him kiss her and hold her close.

There was no rule against fantasies.

She remembered that night three months ago when he'd held her against him in the darkness. His body had felt strong, powerful. His muscles hard from years of disciplined physical activity and maybe from the feel of her backside rubbing against him.

When she'd touched him tonight…felt the size of him against her palm, she'd wanted to rip off his clothes and look at all of him for a very long time. Just look. Then she wanted to learn all there was to know about him on a physical level.

How he tasted…how his hands would feel gliding over her skin…

She drifted off to sleep with that thought hovering so close she could have sworn it was real.

CHAPTER NINE

Director Calder remained seated at the table but Joe was far too restless to stay in one place. He poured himself a fourth cup of coffee and grimaced at the bitter taste.

"You're absolutely certain you're ready to do this?" Calder asked once more. "Any further delay could be detrimental to our chances, but I'm not willing to run the risk of sending you in too soon."

"Do I look ready?"

Joe faced the man the president himself had chosen to oversee one of the nation's most important security agencies and let him look long and hard. He'd put the colored contacts in this morning. He'd wanted to try them out while Elizabeth was preoccupied going over dates with Dawson.

Calder moved his head slowly from side to side. "You look just like him." He blew out a breath. "It's uncanny, Hennessey."

Joe nodded. "I know." Even he had been shaken this morning. As he'd gone about the morning ritual of going to the john, he'd caught a glimpse of his reflection in the mirror and done a double take. His tousled hair had looked like it always did first thing in the morning, but his face…well, suffice to say it wasn't his.

The swelling and redness was gone entirely—at least

as far as he could tell. It was as if he'd gone to bed last night with a little of both and then this morning *poof.*

He'd gone back to his room and called Dawson. He needed a distraction for Elizabeth until he could get used to the change himself.

She'd mentioned a day or so ago that sometimes this sort of abrupt change happened, but he wasn't prepared. He seriously doubted that she would be either.

Once he'd put the contacts in he'd had to brace himself on the counter to keep from staggering back from the mirror. The transformation had been incredible.

He, for all intents and purposes, was David Maddox.

"We knew Elizabeth was good," Calder went on, "but this is beyond our greatest expectations."

Joe had been watching this new face emerge from the aftermath of surgery and he'd known the transformation would get him by, but this was far more than that. This was almost scary.

He thought about Elizabeth and the way she'd sneaked back to her home the other night. He'd wanted to comfort her. To hold her until she came to terms with the way Maddox had used her. But he'd held back. She hadn't needed any more confusion. She'd needed someone who understood…someone to listen and he'd done both those things.

In the three days since she'd been distant. Not that he could blame her. She'd just learned that the man she'd loved had cheated on her, used her. Had likely never really cared about her. That was a hard pill to swallow, even for a fiercely intelligent woman who was also a skilled surgeon.

Learning the truth had, in a way, facilitated what

had to be done. Elizabeth had focused more intently on their work and so had he. A lot had been accomplished.

He was ready for this mission.

"Where is she now?"

"She's with Dawson. He's going over significant dates with her to see if she recalls anything relevant."

Calder frowned. "Haven't we already done that?"

"I needed her distracted for this meeting." Joe leaned against the counter and forced down more of the coffee.

"You're still convinced she had nothing to do with this," Calder wanted to know.

"Totally convinced." Joe set his cup in the sink. He'd had all of that brew he could stomach. He moved to the table. Though he still felt too restless he needed Calder to see just how convinced he was. "She had no idea what Maddox was up to. I think you know that."

Calder nodded. "I do. It's Allen who's still not on the same page with us. But I'll take care of him."

Joe breathed easy for the first time since this operation started. He knew what Maddox had done. No way would he stand idly by and let Elizabeth take the fall for anything that bastard did.

"Is it essential that we wait the next three days before I go in?" Joe ventured. He knew the plan as well as anyone, but he wasn't sure staying here with Elizabeth for seventy-two more hours was a good idea.

"We have to trust our intelligence, Hennessey," Calder said, telling him what he already knew but didn't want to hear. "Word is that she'll be in-country in just over forty-eight hours. We don't want to rush this thing."

The director was right, no question. But Joe's instincts kept nagging at him to get into position. There was nothing specific he could put his finger on. The best analysts in the world were processing new intelligence every hour of every day. If anything had changed, Joe would know it right after Calder.

The fact that Calder was literally sitting in on this one personally made it the highest priority mission. So far three agents had been ambushed, two while involved in an ongoing mission. Stopping those assassinations was imperative. Additionally, Dr. Elizabeth Cameron had been Calder's brainchild. He had personally brought her into the Agency's family. He and Dawson, discounting Maddox, were the only ones allowed to approach her, until this operation. Joe had a feeling that Calder felt responsible for the woman's safety as well as her actions, good, bad or indifferent.

When Calder had gone, Joe went back to his room to study his reflection in an attempt to grow accustomed to the face staring back at him. It wasn't easy, considering he would have liked to rip Maddox apart himself if someone hadn't beat him to the punch. That the bastard's body hadn't been recovered only infuriated Joe all the more. But three credible eyewitnesses had testified to what they had seen. The shooter had been found but he'd refused to talk and ended up offing himself the first chance he got.

Whoever had sanctioned Maddox's termination was powerful enough that his reputation alone had ensured the shooter wouldn't turn on him.

The remaining questions were about Maddox's associates. Who had wanted the list of agents with new faces? Even if Joe infiltrated the group, could he be sure they would talk? Not even the CIA could stop a nameless entity. A name, a face, they needed anything to go on.

Before more bodies piled up.

"I'm sorry, Agent Dawson," Elizabeth said finally. "That's everything I remember. If there was anything else during that time frame I can't recall."

"That's all right, Dr. Cameron." He closed the document on the computer. "What you remembered will be useful." He stood then. "We should probably get back."

Elizabeth followed him from the borrowed office in the rear of the downtown library. She wasn't sure why he had insisted they review all the newspaper reports from the three months prior to David's death. Maybe to prod her memories. She hadn't remembered anything she hadn't told them already. But she hadn't minded taking another shot at it. She was only human. It was just as likely as not that she could have forgotten something relevant.

But she hadn't.

If she were honest with herself she would admit that getting away from the safe house for a few hours was a good thing. Other than her one excursion back to her brownstone she hadn't left in three weeks. She was thankful for the respite.

The other night when she'd had to face the reality of what she'd denied about David for months she'd almost asked Hennessey to sleep with her. She'd so desperately needed someone to cling to, she'd resisted that crushing need by the slimmest of margins. Thank God he'd had his head about him. All he would have had to have done was touch her, in the most innocent fashion, and she would have surrendered without a fight.

For the past three days she had felt pretty much numb. Empty, really. Everything she'd thought to be true about David was nothing but lies. Learning that truth had hurt, but not so much as it would have had she not suspected that there was someone else months before his death.

But just beneath the numbness she had felt these last few days lay something else that simmered steadily. She told herself it was nothing, but that was a lie. She'd been attracted to Hennessey since that first night three months ago when he'd shown up to play bodyguard. That attraction hadn't abated. Not in the least. But with David's death and the idea that agents she had given new faces were dying, she hadn't been able to think about that for any length of time. Even now, maybe it was the exhaustion or just the plain old emptiness still hanging on, her developing feelings for Hennessey were too far from the surface to analyze with any accuracy.

And why in the world would she even want to go there?

Hennessey was the farthest thing from what she needed as a man could get. He represented everything wrong she'd done in her last relationship.

Why couldn't the irrational part of her that wanted to reach out to him see that?

He was one of those dangerous types. A man who risked everything, every single day of his life. She couldn't count on him any more than she had been able to count on David, excluding his various and sundry betrayals.

What she needed was safe, quiet, bookish.

A man who spent his days behind a desk reviewing

accounts or reports. Not some gun-toting, cocky hotshot who kicked ass at least twice before lunch most days.

She closed her eyes and tried to clear her mind as Dawson took the necessary clandestine route back to the safe house. Thank God no more agents had died.

And although she hadn't seen Hennessey this morning she knew the time was close at hand for his departure. The swelling and redness had been all but gone yesterday. She'd struggled with focusing on the work rather than the end result.

It was far less painful to look at each feature individually rather than to look at his face as a whole. But the one saving grace was his eyes.

Joe Hennessey had the most amazing blue eyes. Even with his face changed, those startling blue eyes made it virtually impossible to notice anything else.

His flirtatious personality emanated from those eyes.

The deep brown of David's still haunted her dreams occasionally, but lately the only man she'd been dreaming about was Hennessey.

Such an enormous mistake.

Why couldn't she get that through her head?

She saw it coming. If she could just hold out a little while longer.

Three more days and she would go back to her life. He would go wherever it was David's associates were suspected of being and most likely they would never again see each other. The end.

She squeezed back the emotion that attempted to rise behind her eyelids. She'd done her job, had prepared Hennessey for the operation. There was nothing else she could do. Nothing else she should do until this was over. Then she would reverse the procedure, assuming he survived.

Getting on with her life was next on her list. She could not wallow in the past or pine after a man who would do nothing but bring her more heartache.

She had to be smart. Making the right decisions about her future had to be next on her agenda. Her career was everything she'd hoped it would be. Now if she could only say the same about her private life.

There was only one way to make that happen.

Put David Maddox and anything affiliated with him out of her head. Move forward and never look back.

It was simple.

But before she could do that she had to be sure she had passed along every tidbit Joe Hennessey would need to survive the coming mission. Even though she fully understood that a relationship between them would be a mistake, she didn't want him hurt. Whatever she could do to facilitate his efforts was not only necessary but nonnegotiable.

By the time she and Dawson had reached the safe house it had started to rain and a cloak of depression had descended upon her despite her internal pep talk. The sky had darkened, much like her mood.

When the garage door had closed, ensuring no one who might be watching had seen her emerge from the vehicle, she got out and went inside. She shook off the nagging weight that wanted to drag her into a pit of regret and dread. This wasn't the end, she assured herself, this was a new beginning.

Hennessey would move on with what he did best and she would refocus some of her energy into her personal life. She'd neglected that area for far too long.

Life was too short to spend so much time worrying about all the things she'd done wrong. All the mistakes she'd made. She had to look ahead, move forward.

How many times did she give her patients that very advice? All the time. The kind of devastation that wrought physical deformities more often than not was accompanied by chronic clinical depression. At times, even after full recovery, a patient would linger in the throes of depression's sadistic clutches. Patients had to make a firm choice, to wallow in the past or move into the future.

She had to do the same.

No more dwelling on yesterday. Time to move forward.

Elizabeth hesitated at the door, pushed her glasses up the bridge of her nose and took a long, deep breath.

"Your future begins now," she whispered.

Without looking back, Elizabeth pushed through the door and into the laundry room of the safe house.

The smell of Chinese cuisine alerted her to the time. Lunch. Stark must be on duty. Whenever he was the agent in charge of bringing in meals, his food of choice was Chinese. Not that she minded, she liked fried rice, a lot.

Agent Stark looked up as she entered the kitchen section of the large living space. "You're just in time, Dr. Cameron."

She inhaled deeply. "I noticed."

"I see you made it back, Doc."

Elizabeth looked up at the sound of Hennessey's voice. Her chest seized and her eyes widened in disbelief. She closed her eyes and reopened them in an effort to clear her vision. It was still him...*David.*

"I started wearing the contacts," he said as he tapped his right temple. "The change in eye color definitely put the finishing touch on the look."

He said the words so nonchalantly. She blinked again, told herself to breathe. She couldn't. Managing a nod was the best she could do.

Hennessey gestured to the counter. "You hungry?"

He moved like Hennessey. He spoke like Hennessey. But no matter that she told herself that what she saw was an illusion she, herself, helped to create, she just couldn't get past it. Pain twisted in her chest, radiated outward, encompassing her entire being.

"I'll..." She swallowed against the lump in her throat. "I'll have something later."

She rushed past him, couldn't bear to look a moment longer. This felt so wrong...so damned wrong.

Taking the stairs as fast as she dared she made it to her room in record time. She closed the door and slumped against it.

A full minute was required for her to catch her breath, to slow her heart rate. To form a coherent thought.

She should have been prepared for this moment. David's face had emerged a little more each day. She'd watched the features move from discolored and distorted to smooth and glowing with the tint of health.

All those things she'd expected...she'd been prepared for. But this...

It was the eyes she hadn't been fully equipped to see...to look into.

David's eyes.

As dark as a moonless night.

She'd gotten lost in them so many times. Not once

had she been able to read his intentions. Whether it was the deep, murky color or just his skill at evasive tactics she couldn't be sure. But the mystery had been part of the attraction. He'd drawn her in so easily.

How in the wide world could she have believed she could do this?

Elizabeth closed her eyes and blocked the tears; forced away the images.

She couldn't do this.

And why should she?

She'd done her part.

There was no reason for her to stay a minute longer.

A light rap on the door behind her made her breath hitch again. She pressed a hand to her chest and reached for some semblance of calm.

She had to get her composure back into place.

All she needed to do was tell Agent Dawson she was ready to go home. Her work here was finished.

No one could argue that infinitely valid point.

Steeling herself against the turmoil of emotions attempting to erupt inside her she straightened away from the door, then turned to answer it.

It would be Hennessey.

It would be tough.

But she was strong.

She smoothed her damp palms over her skirt and pulled in another much needed breath.

Then she opened the door.

David's eyes stared down at her.

Not David, she reminded herself.

Hennessey. Agent Joe Hennessey.

"We should talk about this."

She looked away, let his voice be her buoy. Hennessey's voice. Low, husky, shimmering with mischief just beneath the surface. Not the slow, deep cadence of David. Why was it she'd never realized how very, nearly calculating his voice had been? It wasn't until she'd come here with Hennessey that she'd understood what sexy really was.

David hadn't been sexy...he'd been bawdy.

Elizabeth squared her shoulders and did what she should have done days ago. "Agent Hennessey, clearly I've contributed all to this operation that I have to offer. I'm certain you won't be needing my services any longer. With that in mind, I'm sure you'd understand if I chose not to have this discussion." She braced to close the door. "Please let Agent Dawson know I'll be ready to go in ten minutes."

She had expected him to argue.

She'd even expected him to try to stop her.

But the last thing she'd expected was for him to kiss her.

He took her face in both his hands and pulled her mouth up to meet his.

Just like that.

His lips felt firm but somehow more yielding than she had expected. His mouth was hot...ravenous, as if he was starving and she was dessert. She melted against him, couldn't help herself. The sweet feel of her body conforming to his made her shiver with a need so urgent she moaned with the intensity of it.

Sensations cascaded down from her face, following the path of his hands as he stroked her cheeks with his long fingers then slipped lower to caress her throat.

Her heart beat so hard she couldn't breathe... couldn't think. She just kept kissing him back—kept clinging to his strong body, hoping the moment would never end.

"Elizabeth," he murmured against her lips. "I'm sorry. I…" He kissed her harder….

She tried to pull away…tried to push against his chest. But she couldn't bear the thought of taking her hands away from his chest. Even through the cotton shirt she reveled in the feel of the contours of his chest. She suddenly wanted to touch all of him. To see if the rest of his body was as amazing as his chest and the other part she'd already examined.

His arms went around her and for the first time in months she felt safe in a way that had absolutely nothing to do with professional success or inner strength. She wanted this as a woman…and she didn't want it to end.

But it had to end.

She couldn't do this again.

Her hands flattened against his chest and she pushed away from him, not taking her lips from his until it was impossible to reach him anymore.

He opened his eyes and her heart lurched.

"I have to leave now."

She stumbled back from his reach.

"Elizabeth, I can take out the contacts. We can talk."

She closed her eyes, tried to block the visual stimuli. Told herself to listen to his voice. Joe Hennessey…not David. Not David.

"Please." She forced her eyes open again. "I need to go now. There's nothing more I can do."

He looked away, displaying the profile she'd created. David's profile. The slightly longer and broader nose, the more prominent chin.

She swallowed. Looked away.

"This isn't who I am." He gestured to the face she had sculpted. "You know who I am."

She did. That was true. He was Agent Joe Hennessey of the CIA. A dangerous man...her gaze shifted back to his...with an even more dangerous face.

"I do know who you are." The words were strong but she felt cold and hollow. "And I can't do this with a man like you. Not again. The price is too high."

She turned her back to him in the nick of time. She couldn't let him see the foolish tears.

"I'll let Agent Dawson know you're ready to leave."

She heard him walk away.

Finished.

This was finished. No reason for her to stay...to put herself through this.

All she had to do was go home and forget this assignment...forget the man.

CHAPTER TEN

ELIZABETH REVIEWED THE day's messages, her mind on autopilot. That was the way it had been for most of the day. The only time she'd been able to really think clearly and in the moment was when she'd been with a patient. Thankfully three patients who'd been on standby awaiting appointments had been available to fill her day. So far four work-ins were scheduled for tomorrow and then she'd be back on her regular schedule.

Back to her real life.

Her concentration, such as it was, shattered yet again. Elizabeth tossed the messages onto her desk and leaned back in her chair.

This was her life.

Slowly, her heart sinking just a little more, she surveyed her chic office. Clean lines, no clutter. Diplomas and other accolades matted and framed in exquisite detail draped the smooth linen-colored walls. Short pile carpet in the same pale color padded the floor and served as a backdrop to the sleek wood furnishings. The rest of the clinic's decor was every bit as elegant; the treatment rooms equipped with the same spare-no-expense attitude.

The practice shared by herself and two other specialized physicians dominated the east corner of an upscale Georgetown address. Clientele included patients from all over the country as well as a few from abroad. Business boomed to the point that expansion would surely soon be necessary.

All those years of hard work had paid off for Elizabeth in a big way. Professionally she had everything she desired. Everything she'd dreamed about.

But that was where the dream ended.

She'd deluded herself into believing there could be more. That she could throw herself back into a social life. The chances of that doomed plan seeing fruition were about nil—she recognized that now. The cruise had been a last-ditch effort on her part to wake up her sleeping sex life. Not that she'd had any sort of exciting social life in the past. Admittedly she hadn't. But even dating hadn't crossed her mind since David's death. Absolutely nothing had made her want to venture back into the world of the living and the loving.

Until Joe Hennessey popped back in.

All those forbidden feelings Hennessey had aroused three months ago had suddenly reawakened when he waltzed back into her small world with this assignment.

Elizabeth closed her eyes and let the volatile mixture of heat and desire spread through her. He made her want to embark onto that emotional limb of love again. How could she be so dumb when all those diplomas hanging on the walls proclaimed her intelligence?

A light tap on her closed door dragged her away from the disturbing thoughts and back to the harsh reality that she was once more at square one, alone in her office at the end of the day with no place to go and no one with whom to share her successes or her failures.

She forced her eyes open. "Yes."

The door cracked far enough for Dr. Newman, one

of her partners, to poke his head into her office. "You busy?"

Elizabeth tacked a smile into place. "Not at all. Come in, Dr. Newman." As long as she'd known Robert Newman—they'd worked closely for four years—they had never moved beyond the professional formalities. She suddenly wondered why that was. He was a very nice man. Safe, quiet, bookish, all the traits she should look for in a companion. That she admired and respected him was icing on the cake. Just another prime example of her inability to form proper social relationships.

His lab coat still looking pristine after a full day of seeing patients, he shoved his hands into his pockets and strolled up to her desk. "Do you have dinner plans?"

Now that startled her. Was he asking her out to dinner? They'd attended the same work-related social functions numerous times, but never as a couple. She blinked, tried to reason whether or not she'd misunderstood.

Had she somehow telegraphed her misery through the walls? Was this a pity invitation?

He cleared his throat when she remained speechless beyond a polite pause. "I thought you might not have had time to shop since you've gotten back. Your cupboards are probably bare."

Oh, yes, this was definitely a dinner *date* invitation.

Now she knew for sure just how little attention she'd paid to the men around her. If she'd had any question, the hopeful look in her colleague's eyes set her straight.

How could she have missed this? She'd had absolutely no idea.

"You would probably be right," she confessed, well aware that any continued stalling would be seen as not only a rebuff but rude. She reached deep down inside and retrieved a decent smile. "To be honest, I'm beat. I think I need a vacation to recover from my vacation." It wasn't until that moment that she realized how much her affiliation with the CIA had changed the dynamics of her other professional relationships. How many times had she lied to her colleagues about her whereabouts?

Don't go there. Not tonight.

She pushed up from her chair, glanced around her desk to ensure she hadn't forgotten anything that wouldn't wait before meeting Dr. Newman's gaze once more. Disappointment had replaced the hope. "But I'd love a rain check."

Some of the disappointment disappeared. "Sure."

After a brief exchange of war stories about the day's patients, Dr. Newman said good-night and was on his way.

At that moment Elizabeth realized just how very exhausted she felt. A long, hot bath, a couple glasses of wine and a decent night's sleep, she decided, would be her self-prescribed medicine.

After rounding up her purse she headed for the rear exit. She'd already called Agent Dawson and let him know she was ready to go. When she reached the parking lot he waited only steps from the clinic's rear entrance. He would follow her home and then maintain a vigil outside until around nine o'clock and he would be replaced by Stark.

As she slid behind the wheel of her Lexus she regarded the necessity of this measure once more. She hadn't really felt that the added security was necessary but Director Calder had insisted. She'd finally relented and agreed to one week of surveillance. If he felt that strongly, how could she ignore the possibility that he might be right? After all, ferreting out intelligence and analyzing risks was his business.

The drive to her brownstone was uneventful. Before leaving her car at the curb she couldn't go inside without asking Agent Dawson if he'd prefer to come inside. She'd spent the past three weeks holed up with Joe Hennessey, spending time alone with Dawson would be a breeze.

But Agent Dawson declined her offer.

She'd known he would. Dawson was far too much of a stickler for the rules.

Unlike Hennessey.

Or David.

Wasting her time and energy obsessing over the two men she'd allowed herself to get close to was pointless. Why put herself through the additional grief?

How had it been so easy all these years to move through life without getting her heart snagged? Work had been her focus. Until just over a year ago when David had lured her into a relationship. She'd thought it was time. Why not? Most women her age had already been involved in committed relationships. Why shouldn't she? But it had gone all wrong.

Another thought crept into her mind. Maybe she simply wasn't equipped to deal with failure. Her academic and professional life had succeeded on every level. Perhaps the fear of failure kept her from taking emotional risks.

"No more self-analysis," she muttered.

She unlocked her front door and stepped inside. Left all the questions and uncertainty on the stoop.

Home sweet home.

A long, deep breath filled her lungs with the scents of her private existence. The lingering aroma of the vanilla scented candles she loved…the vague hint of the coffee she'd had this morning.

She dug around in the freezer until she found a microwave dinner that appealed to her. Five minutes and dinner would be served. A bottle of chardonnay she'd bought to celebrate the night before departing on her cruise still sat unopened on her kitchen island. Perfect.

Lapsing back into her usual routine as easily as breathing, she set a place at the table, lit a candle and poured the wine. Just because she ate alone didn't mean she couldn't make it enjoyable.

The chicken breast, steamed vegetables and pasta turned out better than she'd expected. Or maybe she was just hungry. She hadn't realized until then that she'd completely forgotten lunch. She did that quite often. But so did most of her colleagues.

The wine did its work and slowly began to relax her. By the time she'd climbed out of the tub she was definitely ready for bed and well on her way to a serious good night's sleep.

She pulled the nightgown over her head and smiled at the feel of the silk slipping along the length of her body. Practical had always been her middle name, but she did love exquisite lingerie. Panties, bras, gowns. She loved sexy and silky. Vivid colors were her favorites. Her bedtime apparel was way different from her day wear. David had always teased her about it.

Cursing herself, she turned out the light and stamped over to her bed. She had to stop letting him sneak into her thoughts. He was dead. Creating his face on another man had torn open old wounds once more. She needed to allow those wounds to heal. Whatever her future held she needed to get beyond the past.

She pulled the sheet back, but a sound behind her stopped her before she slid onto the cool covers. She wheeled around to peer through the darkness.

"It's just me," a male voice said, the sound of it raking over her skin like a rough caress.

She shivered. "Hennessey?" What was he doing here? Had something happened? She felt her way to the table and reached for the lamp.

"Don't turn on the light."

Elizabeth stilled, her fingers poised on the switch.

"I don't want you to see him. I want you to listen to *me*. Only me."

Her heart started to pound. What on earth was he doing here? Had he relieved Agent Dawson? No, that didn't make sense. This was Dawson's mission….

"I don't understand." She wished her throat wasn't so dry. Every part of her had gone on alert to his presence. Her hands wanted to reach out to him, her fingers yearned to touch him. She would not listen to the rest of the whispers of need strumming through her, urging her to connect with him on the most intimate level.

"I'm leaving tomorrow. I didn't want to go without…"

He didn't have to say the rest. She knew what he wanted. What *she* wanted. She could stand here and pretend that it wasn't real or that she didn't want it, but that would be a lie. Tomorrow he would be gone and if she didn't seize this moment she would regret it for the rest of her life.

Could she do that? Risk the damage to her heart?

She pushed the uncertainty away. Her entire adult

life she had erred on the side of caution when it came to affairs of the heart... but not tonight.

She didn't wait for him to say anything else or even for him to move. She moved. Reached out to him and took him in her arms.

His mouth came down on hers so quickly she didn't have time to catch her breath. She reached up, let her hands find a home on his broad shoulders.

She didn't need to see his face. She could taste Joe Hennessey...recognized the ridges and contours of his muscular chest and arms. She didn't know how she could have done something as foolish as fall for this man...but she had. There was no changing that fact. The best she could hope for was to salvage some part of her heart after he'd gone.

His fingers moved over her, making her sizzle beneath the silky fabric. Wherever his palms brushed her skin heat seared through her. She couldn't get enough of his touch, couldn't stop touching him. Even the thought of taking her lips from his made her experience something like panic.

No matter what the future held for either of them, they could have this night.

His hands slid down her back, molded to her bottom. She gasped, the sound captured by his lips. He urged her hips against his and she cried out. Ached with such longing that she wasn't sure she could bear it.

Joe held her tightly against him, shook with the incredible sensations washing over him.

He shouldn't have come to her like this. He'd known better. For the past forty-eight hours he'd told himself over and over that she'd done the right thing walking away. It was the best move for all concerned.

But he couldn't leave without kissing her one last time. He'd thought of nothing else every minute he hadn't been attempting to talk himself out of this very moment.

He'd thought about that one kiss they had shared. Of the way her body had reacted to his all those months ago when he'd come to her rescue.

He needed to feel her in his arms. He'd walked away the last time without looking back because she had belonged to another man. That had been a mistake. He should have fought for her. They'd had a connection. He'd felt it. So had she, he'd bet his life on it. But he'd walked away and tried to put her out of his mind.

Impossible.

Spending the past three weeks with her had only convinced him further that they had something special. All they had to do was explore it…let it happen naturally.

He had to make her see that.

She trembled when he reached for the hem of her gown and tugged it up and off. God, he wanted to see her body, to learn every hollow and curve. But the light would ruin everything. He needed her to know who was making love to her tonight. He couldn't let Maddox's face interfere. He crouched down long enough to drag her panties down her legs. The subtle rose scent of her freshly bathed skin took his breath.

As he stood her fingers shook when she struggled to release the buttons of his shirt. He helped, tugging the shirttails out of his trousers and meeting her at the middle button. The sound of her breath rushing in and out of her lungs made him feel giddy.

Together they worked his trousers down to his ankles, then stumbled back onto the bed with the efforts of removing his shoes and kicking free of the trousers.

He peeled off his boxers then lay on the bed next to her. He didn't want to rush this. As badly as he wanted to push between her thighs and enter her right now, he needed to make this night special. Take things slow, draw out the pleasure. Like it was their last night on earth.

He slid his fingers over her breasts, pleasured her nipples, relishing her responsive sounds. Unable to resist, he bent down and sucked one hardened peak. She arched off the mattress, cried out his name. He smiled and gave the other nipple the same treatment just to hear her call out his name again. He loved hearing her voice…so soft and sexy.

He kissed his way down her rib cage, tracing each ridge, laving her soft skin with his tongue. He paid special attention to her belly button. Sweat formed on his body with the effort of restraint. He was so hard it hurt to breathe, but he couldn't stop touching her this way, with his hands, his mouth.

He touched the dewy curls between her legs, teased the channel there and she abruptly stiffened. His body shook at the sounds as she moaned with an unexpected release.

When her body had relaxed he immediately went to work building that tension once more. He nuzzled her breasts, nipped her lips, all the while sliding one finger in and out of her. Her heated flesh pulsed around him, squeezed rhythmically. Soon, very soon he needed to be inside her.

Elizabeth couldn't catch her breath. She needed to touch him all over…needed to have him take her completely. She couldn't bear anymore of this exquisite torture. She couldn't think…couldn't breathe.

She encircled his wrist, held his skilled hand still before he brought her to climax yet again. "No more," she pleaded.

He kissed her lips, groaned as she trailed her fingers over his hardened length. She shuddered with delight at the feel of him. So smooth and yet so firm, like rock gilded with pure silk.

Her breath left her all over again as he moved into position over her. She opened her legs, welcomed his weight. His sex nudged hers and she bit down hard on her lower lip to prevent a cry of desperation.

He thrust into her in one forceful motion. For several seconds she couldn't move or speak. He filled her so completely. The urge to arch her hips was very nearly overwhelming but somehow she couldn't move. She could only lay very, very still and savor the wondrous awareness of being physically joined with Joe.

Eventually he began to move, slowly at first, then long, pounding strokes. The rush toward climax wouldn't be slowed, hard as she fought it. She could feel him throbbing inside her. His full sex grew harder as his own climax roared toward a peak.

They came together, cried out with the intensity of it.

As they lay there afterward, neither able to speak with their lungs gasping for air, Elizabeth understood that she had just crossed a line of no return.

She had allowed Joe Hennessey inside her. She, a doctor, had participated in unprotected sex. But worst of all she'd freely given over her already damaged heart.

"Elizabeth, I've wanted to make love to you since the first time I saw you," he murmured, his lips close to her temple. "No matter where I was, I couldn't close my eyes without seeing you."

Her chest felt tight. A part of her wanted to confess to the same weakness, but that would be to admit that three months ago she'd already disengaged emotionally from David. What did that make her?

She squeezed her eyes shut and blocked the thoughts. She didn't want to think right now. She just wanted to lay here and feel Joe next to her. She wanted to let her body become permeated with the scent and taste of him.

Just for tonight.

"When this is over," Joe said softly, "I want to see where these feelings take us. I don't want to let you go."

When this mission was over…then there would be another. Clarity slammed into her with crushing intensity. And another mission after that. Each time Joe would be gone for days or weeks. He could be killed in some strange place and she would never even know what really happened.

Just like before.

She had known this would be a mistake. She couldn't let herself believe in—depend on—a man who risked so much. She'd already gotten too close to him. Letting it go this far was crazy.

"I can't do this." She scooted away from him and to the edge of the bed. "You should go."

He sat up next to her. It was all she could do not to run away. But she had let this happen. She had to face the repercussions of her actions.

He exhaled a heavy breath, turned to her and began, "When I get back—"

She jerked up from the bed, fury and hurt twisting inside her. "If you come back." She hurled the words at him through the darkness, imagined his face—his *real* face.

He didn't respond immediately, just sat there making no move to get dressed. She couldn't see him really, just the vague outline but she could feel his frustration.

"I will be back, Elizabeth. I won't leave you the way he did."

A new rush of tears burned in her eyes. "How can you make a promise like that? You have no idea if you'll survive this mission much less the next one!"

"Elizabeth, don't do this." He stood, moved toward her, but she backed away.

She was too vulnerable right now. If he touched her again she might not be able to stick by her guns. She just couldn't do this to herself again. It hurt too much.

"I know you don't want me to go," he whispered, his voice silky and more tempting than anything she'd ever experienced.

Don't listen!

She had to be strong.

"I want you to go," she reiterated. "I'm not going to fall in love with another man who can't live outside the lure of danger. I won't let that happen."

She had to get out of here. Nothing he said would change how she felt. She felt around for her gown, found it and quickly jerked it on. The sooner she put some distance between them the better off she would be.

"Maybe it's not too late for you," he said causing her to hesitate at the door. She would not let herself look back. "But," he went on, "it's way too late for me. It's already happened."

She walked out.

A numbness settled over her.

What was he saying?

She shook off his words.

Nothing he said mattered.

She had to protect herself.

This was the only way.

Joe dragged on his clothes and pushed his feet into his shoes. A rock had settled in his stomach. He needed to convince her that they could do this, but she didn't want to listen right now.

A part of him wanted to track her down and make her see this his way. But that would get him nowhere fast.

Maddox had hurt her. She was only protecting herself.

Joe was the one who'd made a mistake.

He should have realized she needed more time. Especially under the circumstances. For God's sake, she'd scarcely gotten through giving him the face of her old lover and learning of the full extent of her former lover's betrayal. How could he have expected her to fall into his arms and live happily ever after?

Because he was selfish. Desperate to have her as his own. But he'd screwed up. Succeeded in pushing her farther away. Regaining that tender ground might very well be impossible.

He walked out of her room, surveyed the dimly lit hall but she was gone. If he wanted to, he could find her. She wouldn't be far away. Maybe in the kitchen or behind one of the closed doors right here in this hall. But he couldn't do that. He had to respect her needs.

Coming here had been his first mistake tonight. He wasn't about to make another. Oddly he couldn't bring himself to regret making love with her. Mistake or not, he refused to regret it for a single moment.

Not in this lifetime.

He stole out the rear exit of her brownstone and into the concealing darkness of the night.

Right now he didn't have time to work this out. He had an assignment that couldn't wait another day.

But when he got back one way or another he intended to sway her to his way of thinking. Whatever it took, he wouldn't give up.

They belonged together.

All he had to do was survive this mission.

He had as many of the facts as was possible to glean from the sparse details they had uncovered. He had the face Elizabeth had given him—his ticket into Maddox's seedy world of betrayal.

He would get this done. He would return to Elizabeth and then he would make her see that he was right.

Maybe she didn't feel as strongly about their relationship as he did, though he suspected she did. But that didn't change a damned thing as far as he was concerned.

He was definitely in love with her.

CHAPTER ELEVEN

ELIZABETH STARED AT the tousled sheets on her bed. She'd done it again. Made a huge error in judgment.

She hadn't been able to sleep in here last night. Not with the smell of their lovemaking having permeated every square inch of the room. Even now she could smell the lingering scent of Joe. If she closed her eyes she could recall vividly the way he'd touched her in the dark.

And now he was gone.

She steeled herself against the fear and worry. This was exactly why she hadn't wanted to fall for a man like him again.

Who was she kidding? She'd fallen for him before she'd even known her relationship with David was over. She'd lied to herself, pretended she hadn't felt the things she felt for Joe. Denial was a perfectly human reaction to anything confusing or fearful. Just because she was a trained physician didn't make her any less human.

Or any smarter, it seemed.

Elizabeth quickly dressed, choosing her most comfortable slacks and a pale blue blouse. She needed all the comfort she could get today, including a light hand with makeup. Not that she wore that much anyway, but she just didn't feel up to the extra effort today.

As she exited her bedroom, she refused to think of

Joe and the idea that he'd likely begun efforts to infiltrate the enemy. If she did she would only start to worry about where he was and what was happening to him.

Today was the pivotal test of all her work. His face, his mannerisms and speech. All of it would be scrutinized by the group of assassins he needed to fool.

God, what if these evil people had already heard somehow that David was dead?

She couldn't go there…just couldn't do it.

Work. She needed work to occupy her mind.

When she reached the door she remembered her blazer and she hurried back to her room to grab one.

Again the tangled mass of linens tugged at her senses. She got out of there, took the stairs two at a time.

Determined to put last night completely behind her, she opened her front door and stepped out into the day.

The sun gleamed down, warming her face, giving her hope that this day might turn out all right after all. A new beginning. Another opportunity to do something good and right. Maybe she would never be as smart as she should be in her personal life, but her career could be enough. It had been for a long time now. Why change a game plan that appeared to work?

"Are you ready, Dr. Cameron?"

Elizabeth smiled at Agent Dawson. Nice, safe, quiet Dawson. Like Dr. Newman. The kind of man she should be seeking, but somehow never gravitated toward.

"Yes, I am, Agent Dawson." And it was true. She was ready to move on. And she could as long as she didn't stop long enough to think.

"There's been a change in plans this morning," he commented as they moved toward the vehicles parked at the curb. "I'll need to drive you to the clinic this morning if you don't have any objections."

She shrugged. "No problem." It wasn't like she had plans to go anywhere during the course of the day. If she had lunch she usually ate in her office. Most likely she'd spend what time she had available between patients going over files and finishing up reports.

That was the least glamorous part of her job—paperwork. Not the insurance forms or billing statements prepared by the clinic's accounting staff, but the detailed reports on patient history and recommended procedures as well as results of those performed and updates on follow-up consultations. Lots and lots of reports and analyses.

Elizabeth frowned as she glanced out the car window. Was there some reason he hadn't shared with her that dictated the necessity of an alternate route? This wasn't the way she usually drove to work.

"Agent Dawson." She leaned forward to get a better look at him if he glanced her way in the rearview mirror. "Is there some reason we're going this way rather than my usual route?"

"I can't answer that, ma'am. I have my orders."

Elizabeth leaned back in her seat, but she didn't relax. She had known Agent Craig Dawson for more than a year. Something about his voice didn't mesh with the man she knew. This was wrong somehow.

"Agent Dawson," she ventured hesitantly, "is something wrong?"

He glanced in the rearview mirror for the briefest moment and their eyes met. In that instant she saw his fear, recognized the depth of it.

"I'm sorry, Dr. Cameron," he said, his tone hollow,

listless. "They have my family…they're going to kill them if I don't do what they tell me. Please believe I didn't have any choice."

Terror tugged at Elizabeth's sternum. *They.* He had to mean the people who worked with David…the ones to whom he'd sold out his fellow agents.

Her heart bolted into panic mode.

Was he taking her to them?

Or did he plan to kill her himself…in order to save his family?

She moistened her lips and marshaled her courage. "What're you supposed to do, Agent Dawson?"

His uneasy gaze flicked to the rearview mirror once more. "I have to deliver you to the location they specified. That's all." He looked away. "God, I don't want to do this."

"We should call Agent Stark." She rammed her hand into her purse, fished for her cell phone. Her heart pounded so hard she could scarcely think. "He'll know what to do."

Where was her phone? She turned her purse upside down and emptied the contents. She always put it back in her purse before going to bed after allowing it to charge for a couple of hours.

"We can't do that, ma'am."

The full ramifications of the situation struck her. He'd taken her cell phone. His family was being held hostage.

Agent Dawson was no longer her advocate.

"Stop the car, Agent Dawson." Her order sounded dull and carried little force, but she had to try.

His defeated gaze met hers in the rearview mirror once more. "I'm afraid I can't do that, Dr. Cameron."

Panic knotted in her stomach, tightened around her throat. She steeled herself against it, mentally scrambled to consider the situation rationally.

Her movements slow, mechanical, she picked up her belongings one item at a time and dropped them back into her purse. The lip balm she always carried. Hairbrush. Keys. Her attention shifted back to the keys. They could be useful. She tucked the keys into the pocket of her blazer.

She glanced up to make sure Agent Dawson wasn't watching her, then sifted through the rest. Ink pen. Another possible weapon. She slid it into her pocket as well. With nothing else useful, she scooped up the rest and spilled it into her bag.

Okay. She took a deep breath. Get a clean grip on calm and keep it. No matter what happened she needed to keep her senses about her.

She was a doctor. She'd been trained to maintain her composure during life-and-death situations. This was basically the same thing.

Only it was her life on the line.

Searching for a serene memory to assist her efforts she latched on to the sensations from last night. Smells, tastes, sounds of pleasure.

She clung to the recollection of how Joe's skin had felt beneath her palm. The weight of his muscular body atop hers. She trembled as the moments played in her mind. Their bodies connected in the most intimate manner.

But most of all she held on to the last words he'd said to her…he loved her. He hadn't needed to utter those exact words, the message had been clear.

Whether she lived through this day or not, she could

hold that knowledge close to her heart. She wished she had told him how she felt. Even if it was a mistake, he'd deserved to know. How was it that fear for one's life suddenly made so many things crystal clear?

She did have deep feelings for Joe. If she were totally honest with herself she would have to say that she loved him. She would also have to admit that it was, without question, a huge mistake. But, under the circumstances, that point seemed moot altogether.

Elizabeth turned her attention back to the passing landscape. She needed to pay attention to their destination. That ability was another thing that no doubt spelled doom for her. Didn't they always blindfold hostages in the movies so they wouldn't know where they were taken? Further proof that the outcome for her would not include a dashing hero and a last-minute escape. She would know too many details to risk her survival.

All the more reason to be prepared.

Another thought occurred to her then. "Agent Dawson." Her voice sounded stark in the car after the long minutes of silence. When his gaze collided with hers in the mirror she went on, "How can you be sure they won't harm your family anyway?"

He didn't answer, except the look in his eyes gave her his answer. He couldn't be sure, but he had to try. His work had brought danger to his family. He had to take whatever risks necessary in an attempt to keep them safe. He wasn't a field operative. He was reacting the only way he knew how.

Elizabeth didn't readily recognize the neighborhood. It wasn't the sort of area anyone would willingly frequent. Dilapidated houses and crumbling apartment buildings. Trash lay scattered in parking lots and along the broken sidewalks. Junked cars as well as newer models, some considerably more expensive than the houses they fronted, lined the street. At this hour of the morning no one appeared to be stirring about. But she didn't have to see any of the residents to guess at the community profile. Poverty-stricken. Desperate.

Every city had its forgotten corners. Areas where the government failed to do enough. Where people survived on instinct and sheer determination.

No one here would care what happened down the street or on the next block. Survival depended upon looking the other way and keeping your mouth shut.

Elizabeth had never known this sort of hopelessness. No one should. She hoped this sad part of life wouldn't be the last thing she ever saw.

The car stopped and Elizabeth jerked to attention. Her gaze immediately roved the three-story building that sat on a corner lot. The windows were boarded up and the roof looked to be missing most of its shingles.

Dawson got out of the car and walked around to her side. He opened the car door and waited for her to get out. Vaguely she wondered what he would do if she refused. Would he shoot her? She didn't think so.

The energy would be wasted. She had no choice any more than he did. Making matters more difficult would serve no purpose. Agent Dawson wasn't her enemy. It was the people inside this ramshackle building who represented the true threat.

She got out of the car and he took her by the arm. She didn't resist, didn't see the point.

He led her to the front entrance and ushered her inside where the condition of the structure was no better than the outside had been.

Though it was daylight outside, the interior was barely lit and only by virtue of the sunlight slipping between the boards on the windows. She wondered if there was any electricity supplying power to the building. Not likely.

Up two flights of stairs and at the end of the hall Dawson hesitated. Elizabeth met his gaze, saw the regret and pain churning there.

"I'm sorry, Dr. Cameron."

The door behind him swung open and a man carrying a large, ugly gun stepped into the hall. He quickly patted down Agent Dawson and removed the weapon he carried in his shoulder holster. Then he did the same to Elizabeth. He ignored the keys and pen.

"This way," he growled.

Dawson held on tightly to her elbow as they moved into the room the man had indicated. She wished she had told Dawson that she knew he was sorry and that she understood, but there hadn't been time.

"Well, well."

Elizabeth's attention darted in the direction of the female voice. Blond hair cut in a short, spiky style, analyzing gray eyes. She looked tough dressed in her skin-tight jeans and T-shirt. Her arms were muscular as if she worked out with weights. She wore a shoulder holster which held a handgun while she carried a larger, rifle type weapon similar to that of her comrade.

"I finally get to meet sweet Elizabeth," the woman said hatefully.

Elizabeth felt her muscles stiffen. This was *the* woman. She didn't have to be told. The woman referred to her in a way that David had regularly, sweet Elizabeth.

Unflinching, she lifted her chin and stared at the other woman who seemed to tower over her. "Who are you?"

The witch with the guns laughed, boldly, harshly. "I think you know who I am."

Elizabeth ignored Dawson's fingers squeezing her elbow. His concern for her was needless. She doubted either one of them would make it out of here alive.

"You must be the woman David left every time he came home to me," Elizabeth said succinctly. The transformation on the other woman's face let her know her words had prompted the desired result.

Looking ready to kill, the woman strode up to Elizabeth and shoved the barrel of the rifle she carried into Elizabeth's chest. "You think you know something about me, Miss Goody Two-Shoes?"

Elizabeth held her ground despite the terror sending tremor after tremor through her. "I know David never once mentioned you."

The woman's face contorted with anger. Elizabeth braced herself for the fallout. To her surprise the woman's attention shifted to Dawson.

"Get his wife on the line," she said to her accomplice.

Dawson tensed. "I did everything you asked. You said you'd let them go."

"That's right," Elizabeth interjected, her heart aching for the poor man, "you got what you wanted. Let Agent Dawson and his family go."

Dawson looked at her then, his expression trapped somewhere between thankful that his family appeared to be safe for the moment—since he would soon hear his wife's voice—and downtrodden because of what he'd done to Elizabeth.

The woman said nothing to Elizabeth but tossed a cell phone to Dawson.

"Hello?"

The look of relief on his face told Elizabeth that his wife was on the other end of the line.

"You're all right?" he verified. Horror abruptly claimed his expression. "No!" He stared at the woman who'd given him the phone, then at the phone. "What've you done?"

The oxygen evacuated Elizabeth's lungs and the room suddenly tilted. Had they…? Oh, God.

"Don't worry, Mr. CIA Agent," the woman taunted with a wave of her gun, "you're going to join them… right now."

The horrible woman fired two shots. Dawson jerked with the impact, staggered back then collapsed on his side into a twisted heap on the dusty wood floor. The color of blood spread rapidly in a wide circle on his shirtfront.

Elizabeth dropped onto her knees next to him. She rolled him onto his back and assessed the situation.

Before she could attempt to stop the bleeding, the man with the gun hauled her to her feet.

"He'll die!" Elizabeth screamed at him as if he were deaf or stupid.

"That's the point," he said in that low guttural growl of his.

Elizabeth felt the hysteria clawing at the back of her throat. She felt cold and numb. The urge to scream squirmed in her chest.

She thought of the keys in her pocket and how she might be able to use them. But it was no use. She rec-

ognized from the location of the wound that nothing she
could do in this setting would benefit Agent Dawson.

His family was dead. Maybe he was better off that
way, too. He would never have forgiven himself if he'd
lived.

Elizabeth swiveled toward the woman standing only
a few feet away. "What do you want?" Her voice carried its own kind of malicious intent.

For the first time in her life Elizabeth understood
completely how it felt to want to kill someone. If she
possessed a weapon she would not hesitate to murder
one or both of those holding her hostage.

The woman grinned, an expression straight from
hell. "Everything," she said with sinister glee.

The man grabbed Elizabeth's arm again and pushed
her toward a door on the other side of the room. "Where
are we going?" she demanded, a new kind of fear rushing through her veins.

He cut her a look but said nothing.

The smaller room he shoved her into was empty and
just as unkempt as the other one. Before she could turn
around he slammed the door shut. She rushed to it,
knowing before she twisted the knob that it would be
locked.

A surge of relief made her knees weak. At least he
hadn't followed her in here.

She moved back from the door, took a moment to
gather her wits. Okay, she had to think.

The events of the past few minutes reeled through
her mind like a horror flick. She closed her eyes and
banished the images. She didn't want to see Dawson's
face when he'd heard whatever they did to his wife on

the other end of that phone call. She didn't want to see him fall into a dying heap on the floor over and over.

Things like this didn't happen in her life. She was just a doctor. One who worked at a quiet, upscale clinic. She'd never had to deal with the hysteria and insanity of E.R. work. She'd never been exposed to this sort of horror outside a movie theatre.

Several more deep breaths were required before she could stop her body from quaking so violently.

She reached into her pocket. Keys, ink pen. Not much that would help her in this situation.

Okay…think. First she needed to take stock of her situation. She moved to the boarded-up window on the other side of the room. Peered through the cracks between the boards. Nothing. Not a single pedestrian to call to for help, not that she was sure anyone in this neighborhood would be willing to get involved. But maybe someone would call the police if they heard screaming. She glanced toward the door. Of course if she screamed her captors would come running.

She tugged at one of the boards. The wood creaked and shifted but not enough for her to work it loose.

"Damn."

She walked around the room. Surveyed the floor. Looked inside the one other door that opened up to a tiny closet. This room had probably been a bedroom at one time. She looked up at the ceiling. No removable ceiling tiles or attic access doors. Just stained, cracked drywall.

There was no way out of here. She had to face that fact.

She propped against the wall near the window. She

couldn't get out the window, but it made her feel better
to be near it all the same.

Why hadn't they killed her? There had to be a reason she was still breathing.

The woman with the guns had said she wanted *everything.* What did that mean?

Had David failed to follow through with all the
names of the agents she'd given new faces? That was
the only marketable asset Elizabeth possessed in this
lethal scenario. But why would David betray his country—and her—and then fall down on the job?

Maybe he'd been killed before he could provide the
full list. Why then had it taken these goons three months
to come looking for the rest?

It didn't make sense.

Did criminal activities ever make sense?

She scrubbed her hands over her face and exhaled
loudly. Would Dr. Newman miss her this morning and
call her house to see where she was? When he didn't
get her would he contact the police?

She didn't think so. He could well assume that she'd
had a personal emergency come up. She was an adult
after all, one who had recently rebuffed his advances at
that. He might not care to pursue the question of where
she was this morning.

So what did she do?

Could she just stand here waiting for one of her captors to decide it was time to kill her? Did she dare assume that she was some sort of bargaining chip who
would be kept alive for trading purposes?

She just didn't have any experience in this sort of
situation. But the one thing she did know was that being
a victim, to some extent, was a choice. She could stand

here feeling helpless until they came for her or she could devise a way to fight back.

She'd always struggled to reach her goals, never once giving up. She had to do that now, had to find a way to help herself. She might not escape, but she would die trying.

She had nothing to lose by tackling the boards over the window again. That appeared to be her only viable means of possible escape.

After swiping her damp palms against her pants she grabbed hold of a board and pulled with all her might. It didn't budge much, but it did give a little.

Even that little bit gave her hope.

She worked harder, struggled with all her might.

The first board came loose, sending her staggering backward. She barely managed to stay on her feet.

Her heart pounding with anticipation, she laid the board aside and reached for the next one.

She could do this.

She *had* to do this.

Her life depended upon it.

The door suddenly flew open and Elizabeth pivoted to face what would no doubt be one of her captors.

Her heart surged into her throat.

Joe.

She rushed across the room and into his arms. Tears streamed down her cheeks but she didn't care. She was just so damned glad to see him. How had he found her?

She hadn't heard a scuffle. Had he killed those two awful people holding her here?

"Thank God you found me," she murmured against the welcoming feel of his wide shoulders. "I'm so sorry

I made you leave last night. We should have made love again."

Last night felt like a lifetime ago now, but she had to tell him the truth now, right this second. She wouldn't leave him hanging another moment.

"You were right, Joe, it's too late for me, too. I love you." She drew back and looked into his eyes. "I should have—"

Her stomach bottomed out and every ounce of relief she'd felt drained away as surely as Agent Dawson's blood had.

She knew those eyes...not contacts...recognized those lips... This wasn't Hennessey...this was...

"David." But he was dead...wasn't he?

CHAPTER TWELVE

JOE'S FLIGHT LANDED in Newark, New Jersey, twenty minutes earlier than scheduled. He grabbed his carry-on bag, the only one he'd brought with him and waited for an opportunity to merge into the line of passengers heading for the exit at the front of the plane.

After disembarking he made his way to the terminal exits and hailed a cab. He gave the warehouse address and relaxed into the seat. It was five twenty-two. Thirty minutes from now he would arrive at his rendezvous point and the game would begin.

One call to the man on the ground here in Jersey and his contact had agreed to meet with him at six o'clock.

Ginger was her name.

She'd been expecting to hear from him weeks ago. Lowering his voice and summoning that gravelly tone Maddox used, Joe had explained that his assignment had kept him under deep cover far longer than he'd anticipated, but he was back now. He needed to touch base and get a status on how the operation was proceeding. He'd considered demanding to know why only three agents had been taken out so far but since he didn't know the ultimate reasoning behind that move, he didn't risk it. For all he knew Maddox could have dictated the dates each hit would go down.

As the scenery zoomed past his window Joe's

thoughts found their way back to last night. To the way touching her had shaken his entire world. He'd known it would be that way. From the first time he'd seen her, watched her walk across the parking lot at her clinic, he'd sensed she was special. Maybe too special for him. He wasn't at all sure a guy like him deserved a woman like that.

Making love to her last night had fulfilled every fantasy he'd enjoyed since that night months ago, when he'd first held her in his arms to keep her from walking into a trap at her clinic.

Her body had responded to his as if they'd been made for each other. Every touch had ripped away yet another layer of his defenses. He'd spent his entire adult life avoiding commitment on an emotional level. His work made him unreliable in that department. He understood that. Knew with complete certainty that a permanent relationship would be unfair on far too many levels for any woman to tolerate.

But he just hadn't been able to help himself where Elizabeth was concerned. He'd wanted her more than he'd ever wanted any woman. He couldn't recall once ever being this vulnerable to need.

Elizabeth comprehended the difficulty becoming involved with a man like him entailed. She'd clearly made a promise to herself not to risk her heart to any more men like David Maddox. And as much as Joe wanted to argue that he wasn't anything at all like Maddox, he recognized the career-related similarities. Still he wanted nothing more than to convince her to let this thing between them develop naturally. He wanted to make promises. Promises he might not be able to keep.

It was too much to ask. He would be the first to

admit to that glaring fact. How could he ask her to give that much?

He couldn't.

She had been right to ask him to leave.

He should never have gone to her like that. She'd already been hurt by one man like him. She deserved the chance to find someone more reliable, more available with whom to share her life.

She deserved that and more. And Calder had to find a way to protect her better. He couldn't let anyone like Maddox near her again.

She'd paid far too much for that mistake.

The taste of her lips abruptly filled Joe and it took every ounce of strength he possessed to push the tender memories away.

He had to focus now.

Staying alive had to be top priority.

Maybe he and Elizabeth didn't have a future together but that didn't mean he couldn't hope.

"Stop here," he told the driver.

The cabbie pulled the taxi over to the curb four blocks from Joe's ultimate destination. He paid the fare and got out. The air he sucked into his lungs felt thick with humidity and the smell of diesel fuel from the huge trucks and trailers still rumbling in the distance down Avenue A. At almost six o'clock things were winding down along this particular warehouse-lined street of Newark's Ironbound community. A few trailers were still being loaded. The sounds of rush-hours traffic from the surrounding streets and avenues mixed with the heavier grumbling of the trucks.

He surveyed the deserted warehouses at the far end of the street where encroaching residential developments made the old standing structures ripe for condo-izing. Not exactly a picturesque view for perspective owners.

Dressed in jeans and boots and a T-shirt beneath an open button-down chambray shirt Joe blended well with the warehouse crews headed home for the night. He used that to his benefit and moved easily toward the rendezvous point.

He fell into "Maddox" stride without thought. Focused his energy on giving off a confident vibe. This meeting was his and Ginger's and anyone else planning to be there needed to know that. Maddox never let another human being intimidate him. From watching the videos of a number of his interrogations he liked belittling his assets. Though all agents took that approach to some degree Maddox went further than most. He appeared to get off on degrading those he considered lesser forms of life, which appeared to be most other humans.

The abandoned warehouse where Ginger waited looked in less than habitable condition. He took a final moment to get into character then went inside. He carried the 9 mm Beretta in his waistband at the small of his back and a backup piece in an ankle holster. His preferred weapon of choice was a Glock but for this mission he needed to carry what Maddox would.

"It's about time."

Joe settled his gaze on the woman with blond spiky hair and immediately recognized her as Ginger from the surveillance photos on file at the Agency.

"Patience has never been one of your strong suits." He kept his gaze fastened on hers. No averting his eyes, no letting her read anything that Maddox wouldn't display in this situation.

Ginger sashayed over to him, a high-powered rifle hanging down her back from a shoulder strap. "Did you miss me?" she asked as she slid her arms up and around his neck.

He gifted her with a Maddox smile. "Occasionally."

She kissed him and he kissed her back, using all the insights that Elizabeth had shared with him. Aggressive, invasive. Ginger appeared to like it. Maybe too much.

He set her away. "We have business to attend to," he said in an icy growl that made her eyes widen in surprise. He didn't analyze her reaction in an attempt to prevent any outward response himself.

She inclined her head and studied him. "You're right. We've kept him waiting too long already."

With that ominous announcement she pivoted on her heel, the weapon on her shoulder banging against her hip, and strode toward the freight elevator.

Joe followed. From the intelligence the Agency had gathered there was at least one more scumbag working with this woman. Her known accomplice was male, twenty-seven or -eight, and seriously scruffy-looking. But then, he watched the woman pull down the overhead gate that served as a door and set the lift into motion, that didn't surprise him after meeting the enigmatic Ginger in person. She looked about as unsavory as they came. The third man was the unknown factor, but Joe imagined that he would be every bit as sleazy.

Maddox's taste had definitely altered. Of course a field operative couldn't always be selective when working undercover. However, Maddox had, so far as they had determined, continued his alliance with these three well after the mission ended. If Joe's conclusions were correct, Maddox had used at least two of this group to orchestrate the hits on his fellow agents. The question was, for whom? The why was about money. It didn't take a rocket scientist to figure out that part.

Too bad for Maddox. A guy couldn't take his hefty bank account to hell with him.

The upward crawl came to an abrupt, jarring halt on the third floor and his guide shoved the door up and out of the way. The third level appeared to be nothing but a wide-open vacant space. What could be an additional storage room or office stood at the far end and was separated from the larger space by a single door.

She glanced over her shoulder. "Stay here."

Joe snagged her by the elbow and wheeled her around to face him. "This sounds a lot like insubordination, *baby,*" he offered, his tone at once sensual and accusing.

Again her eyes widened in something like surprise, kindling his instincts once more and sending him to a higher state of alert.

"Just following orders," she said with a shrug before pulling free of his hold and heading toward the door on the other side of the space.

Joe's instincts were humming. Something was off here. A glitch he couldn't quite name. But he understood that the undercurrents he felt were tension filled. The surprise he'd seen in Ginger's eyes. Had she recognized something a little off with her former lover?

There was always the possibility that she and her accomplice had heard that Maddox was dead but Joe doubted that. The info had been kept within Director Calder's realm alone.

Intelligence indicated that the group had been putting out feelers as to Maddox's location.

There was every reason to believe that the two leaders of this little group, Ginger and her male counterpart, Fahey, had orchestrated the three assassinations thus far. Whatever their motivation, the two wanted to hook up with their source, David Maddox, once more. There was nothing on the third party.

Maybe it was the physical relationship between Ginger and Maddox or maybe it was simply a matter of needing the rest of the names.

Joe would be the first one to admit that he'd been surprised by Maddox's duplicity. It wasn't that he hadn't suspected the guy was fully capable of that kind of betrayal. He'd simply believed him to be devoted to his work and his country, if not the people in his personal life, specifically Elizabeth Cameron.

Maybe that sticking point had been the catalyst for Joe's determination to prove that Maddox had betrayed not only Elizabeth but his country.

Almost immediately after he'd started his own investigation, one week after the first assassination, intelligence had started to pick up on activity from this group. Joe had known what that indicated.

That's when Joe had gone to Calder with his suspicions. He'd bypassed his immediate supervisor, Director Allen, and laid all his suspicions on the table for the big dog.

Allen wasn't too damned happy about it. But it had gotten things rolling. Once Calder was hooked, Allen had jumped in with both feet.

Joe hadn't really cared whether Allen got on board or not. All he'd needed was Calder's blessing.

He'd gotten that.

He moved to attention when the door opened and Ginger sauntered back into the main room where he waited.

A figure appeared in the doorway behind her and it took a full five seconds for Joe's brain to assimilate what his eyes saw.

Maddox.

He should have known, Joe thought grimly.

Faking his own death would be the perfect way to get off the hook when he had what he needed.

"It's like looking in a mirror," Maddox said as he came closer.

"Yeah," Ginger agreed.

Fury whipped though Joe. "You betrayed your own people, Maddox."

Maddox shrugged. "Everybody has to retire sometime. I always believed in cashing out when stocks are the highest."

Joe shook his head. "I hate to offer a cliché, Maddox, but the truth is you're not going to get away with it."

The sick smile that Maddox was known for slid across his face. "I already have, Hennessey, or hadn't you noticed?"

Maddox inclined his head and Ginger took a bead on Joe, dead center of his chest.

"You can't do that here!"

Joe's gaze moved beyond Maddox.

Now the puzzle was complete.

Director Kurt Allen.

What do ya know? The third party was an inside man.

He'd known Allen was a bastard but he'd thought that was just his personality.

"We have to stick with the plan," Allen snapped. "No mistakes, Maddox." Allen glanced at Joe but quickly averted his gaze.

Maddox didn't like being chastised in front of a former colleague. "This is my op," he snarled. "These are my people. They follow my commands."

"A whole army of one, huh, Maddox?" Joe couldn't resist the dig. The only player on Maddox's team he'd seen so far was the woman. Allen didn't count as a soldier. Joe hoped the dig would get him what he needed to know where the others were and what they were up to, but asking wouldn't likely work out. He'd have to goad it out of the two traitors.

Maddox's furious gaze landed on Joe. "You don't have any idea who I've got working for me, Hennessey, so don't even try."

"Where's your boy Fahey?"

"He's babysitting your sweetie pie," Ginger sneered.

A rush of fear shook Joe but the rage that followed hot on its heels obliterated any hint of the more vulnerable emotion. He fixed his gaze on Maddox. "If anything happens to her you're going to be in need of a second resurrection."

Allen scoffed. "Why would we let anything happen to her? She's what all of this has been about."

Confusion momentarily gained a little ground over his fury. "What the hell are you talking about? This bastard—" he indicated Maddox "—has been killing off our people."

It was Maddox's turn to laugh now, sending Joe's rage right back to the boiling point. That scumbag was a dead man.

"We have no interest," Allen explained with enormous ego, "in killing off recycled agents. What we want is Dr. Cameron."

"We already have a number of excellent surgeons," Maddox added, "but not one of her caliber. Our wealthier clients deserve only the best. She is the best."

In his line of work Joe had come across the slave trade in most every imaginable walk of life, but this was definitely a first.

"You intend to make her work for you," he restated. "Giving rich criminals new faces."

"And fingerprints," Allen said smugly. "We're even perfecting a way to corrupt DNA, make it unreliable. Amazing, isn't it?"

Joe had heard reports on start-up activities like this. Clinics in obscure places attempting to create the ultimate in escapism. New faces, new fingerprints, even new DNA.

It was a damned shame the Agency's own people were working against them.

"It's amazing all right," Joe allowed. "Too bad neither of you lowlifes is going to see it become a reality."

Ginger took aim once more. "Do you want me to get this over with now?"

Joe's fingers itched to go for his own weapon but that would only get him killed. He needed a distraction.

"You know she'll refuse," Joe tossed out there just to buy some time. But he was right. No way would Elizabeth willingly do this.

Maddox shrugged. "She'll come around, Hennessey. You know the techniques."

The thought of Elizabeth being tortured physically or mentally ripped him apart inside.

"She really thought you loved her," he said to Maddox in hopes of stirring some sentimental feelings.

Ginger laughed. "He doesn't love anybody."

Maddox turned his face toward her, smiled approvingly.

"Then I guess it won't matter to either of you that she's carrying your child."

The lie did the trick.

Ginger's fire-ready stance wavered for a fraction of a second.

Just long enough for Joe to react.

He whipped out his 9 mm and fired twice. Ginger dropped. Maddox and Allen dove for the floor.

Maddox was the first to return fire.

Joe rolled to the left. Pulled off another round, capped Allen in the forehead before he'd gotten a grip on his own weapon.

Maddox started firing. Didn't let up.

Joe rolled, curled and twisted to avoid being hit. With no cover it was the only choice he had.

Maddox disappeared through the door on the far end of the room.

Joe scrambled to his feet and lunged in that direction.

He burst through the door just in time to see Maddox going out the window.

Fire escape.

Damn.

At the window a spray of bullets kept Joe from following the route Maddox had taken.

With the last shot still echoing in the air he risked a look out the window. Maddox was halfway down.

Joe muttered a curse and propelled himself out onto the uppermost landing.

He ducked three shots.

That made sixteen.

In the few seconds it would take Maddox to replace his clip, Joe rushed downward. One flight of rusty metal steps, then another.

Bullets pinged against metal, forcing Joe to zigzag as he plunged down the next flight. He got off two rounds, gaining himself a few seconds' reprieve.

Maddox hit the pavement in the rear alley, landing on his feet and bolting into a dead run.

Joe was three seconds behind him.

His heart pumped madly, sending much needed adrenaline through his veins.

But he had the advantage from this angle.

Problem was if he killed Maddox he might not find Elizabeth until it was too late.

He needed the bastard alive.

Maddox was likely counting on that.

Joe stopped. Spread his legs shoulder width apart and took aim.

The first bullet whizzed right by Maddox's left ear.

The second closer still.

Maddox skidded to a halt. "Okay!" he shouted. "You made your point."

Though he held up both hands in a gesture of surrender, Joe wasn't taking any chances.

"Place your weapon on the ground, Maddox. Now!" Joe eased toward him, keeping a bead on the back of his head.

"All right. All right." He started to lower his weapon, bending at the knees in order to crouch down close enough to lay the Beretta on the ground.

Ten feet, eight. Sweat beaded on Joe's forehead as he moved closer still.

Just as Maddox's weapon reached shoulder level he dropped and rolled.

Joe almost fired, but hesitated.

That split second of hesitation cost him every speck of leverage he'd gained.

"Looks like we have an impasse," Maddox said from his position on the ground. Though he lay on his back he'd leaned upward from the waist just enough to get a perfect bead on Joe's head.

Joe shrugged nonchalantly. "The way I see it, if we both end up dead, then there won't be any report for me to file."

Maddox grinned. "You always were a cocky SOB. But this time you've met your match."

"I don't think so." Joe's trigger finger tightened. "Now put down your weapon before I have to kill you."

"A good agent never gives up his weapon, Hennessey."

The explosion of the bullet bursting from the chamber was deafening in the long, deserted alley.

The hit dead center.

CHAPTER THIRTEEN

ELIZABETH CROUCHED IN the darkest corner of the room. She squeezed the keys in her hand, letting the bite of metal keep her senses sharp.

David was alive.

The son of a bitch.

Fury boiled up inside her, leaving a bitter burn in her throat.

For weeks after his death she had wished she could have spoken to him one last time before he died. If she'd only had the opportunity to apologize for her impatience and frustration with his work. As dedicated as she had always been to her own work, how could she grow disgruntled about his loyalty to the job? And that was exactly what she'd done. She had used a double standard. It was okay for her to work long hours seven days a week, month in, mouth out, but when he failed to show for weeks on end she'd behaved petulantly.

She'd kidded herself and pretended they were two of a kind and his long absences didn't bother her. But they had. To say otherwise was a lie.

So when she heard about his death she'd tortured herself for endless nights. Thinking of all the things she should have said.

All that energy…all that emotion wasted on a man who wasn't worth the time it took to tell him to get lost.

If only she'd known just what a monster he was she might have killed him herself.

Okay, maybe that was an exaggeration.

But she wanted desperately for him to pay for what he had done. He could rot in prison for the rest of his life and she wasn't sure that would be punishment enough. Yet execution was far too quick and merciful.

Elizabeth closed her eyes and cleared her mind. She couldn't be distracted by her hatred and bitterness toward David. She had to focus. Finding a way to escape the man holding her was the only hope she had of saving Joe.

She knew the meeting location.

All she needed was her freedom.

Her fingers tightened around the keys once more.

If she called him in here by crying out in pain as if she were sick, she could…

Well, she wasn't sure what she would do but she could make it up as she went.

God, she prayed, *please don't let him kill Joe.*

If Joe died…there were so many things she wanted to say to him. Too late…just like before.

Determination roared through her. No. She wouldn't let this happen to her again.

She had to do something.

When David had died there had been nothing she could do. Considering what she knew now she was glad. But this was different. Joe was a good guy and she loved him.

Why was it she couldn't do anything personal right? It always seemed as if she went about her relationships backward or sideways or something.

Deep breath.

She could do this.

Pushing to her feet she gathered her courage and prepared to make her move.

As a doctor she knew his most vulnerable spots. His eyes. The base of the throat. Then, of course, there was always the old reliable scrotum.

Another deep breath.

As she exhaled that lungful of air she cried out at the top of her lungs.

She doubled over, moaned and cried, summoning her most painful memories in an effort to make it sound real.

The door burst inward.

"What the hell is wrong with you?"

Elizabeth wailed again, held her stomach as if the pain were so intense she could do nothing else.

He grabbed her by the arm and tried to pull her up. "I said, what's wrong with you, bitch?"

"God, I don't know." She moaned long and low.

He slung the rifle over his shoulder. "Stand up where I can look at you."

"Ohhhhhh!" With that savage cry she came up with her hand, stabbed the key to her Lexus into his right eye.

He screamed.

His grip on her arm tightened.

She tried to get free.

Couldn't.

His fingers wrenched her arm painfully. The keys flew across the floor.

"Don't move!" He held his left hand over his eye. But he kept her close with the other. "I could kill you!" he snarled like a wounded animal.

Her heart thudded so hard she couldn't draw in a breath. She had to get loose.

Then she remembered her one other weapon.

Her free hand went into her pocket. Her fingers curled around the ink pen.

There was only one way to get away from this man.

She reared her arm back and brought it down hard, shoving the ink pen into the soft tissue at the base of his throat.

He released her. Grabbed at his throat as he frantically gasped for air.

She bolted for the door.

He grabbed her by the waist.

She screamed, tried to twist free.

His weight slammed into her back and they went down together.

She landed in a sprawl on the floor with him atop her.

His fingers curled around her throat. She tried to buck him off. Tried to roll. But he was too heavy. Horrible gasping sounds came from his throat as he struggled to get air past the hole she'd made. Blood soaked into the neck of his T-shirt, dripped down his cheek.

The pressure on her throat cut off her airway. She bucked and gasped. Pulled at his arms. No good.

Blackness swam before her eyes.

Desperate, she clawed at his face. At his injured eye and then at his throat.

He howled and fell off her.

She scrambled away from him. Clambered to her feet and raced toward the door.

She didn't slow or look back until she was out of the small house and on the street.

Hysteria slammed into her full throttle. She stood in

the middle of the street and turned all the way around. Where was she?

She'd been blindfolded as she was brought here. The drive had been hours long. She'd dozed off once. She had no idea where she was.

Her gaze landed on a vehicle up the street and she ran in that direction until she could make out the license plate.

New Jersey.

The Garden State.

New Jersey?

The air raging in and out of her lungs, she stood there and tried to think. Avenue A. She'd heard that location mentioned. Warehouse.

A phone. She needed a phone—911. Help. She needed help.

The low drone of an automobile engine sounded behind her. She spun around and her heart leaped. Help!

She ran toward the car. Waved her arms frantically. "Help me! I need the police!"

The car sped forward, hurried past her. The elderly female driver stared wide-eyed at her.

"Help!" Elizabeth cried once more.

It was no use. The woman drove away as fast as she could. Elizabeth looked down at herself then. Blood was smeared on the front of her pale blue blouse. Her hair was likely disheveled. No wonder the woman didn't stop.

Panic slid around her throat like a noose. A crashing sound had her pivoting toward the door of the house she'd escaped.

The sound hadn't come from there.

Thank God.

A phone. She pushed the hair back from her face. Concentrate, Elizabeth. She needed a phone.

She rushed toward the next house. There wasn't a vehicle in the driveway. Please, please let someone be home.

Balling her bloody fist she banged on the door. "Is anyone home?" She banged harder. "Please, I need to use your phone. It's an emergency. Please."

No one was home. If they were, fear kept them from answering the door.

She rushed back out to the street, looked both ways for a driveway with a car in it.

There had to be someone home, car or no car.

Elizabeth rushed from house to house, pounded on door after door.

Finally a door opened. An elderly man stood on the opposite side of the threshold.

"Can't you read?" he groused.

Elizabeth blinked, uncertain what he meant. She tried to calm her respiration. Tried to make herself think rationally.

"See!" He tapped a sigh hanging next to his door.

No solicitation.

"No!" She stepped into the path of the closing door. "I need help. I need the police."

He seemed to really look at her then. Blinked behind the thick lenses of his glasses.

"What happened to you?"

"Please," she pleaded. "I need to call the police."

His gaze narrowed in suspicion and for a moment, she feared he wasn't going to let her inside. Finally he backed up, gestured for her to come in.

He quickly surveyed his porch and yard. "Is somebody after you?"

She shook her head. "No, I don't think so." She looked around the room. "I need to use your phone."

He shuffled toward the kitchen. "It's in here."

Elizabeth rushed past him, almost knocking him over. She didn't take the time to apologize. She had to warn Joe.

Her first instinct was to call 911. But the police might not take her word for what was happening. And she didn't have the exact location. The Agency would surely know Joe's plan for connecting with his contact.

She punched in the number she'd learned by heart long ago. A voice answered on the first ring.

"I need to speak with Director Calder." Elizabeth ID'd herself using the code name and number she'd been given when she first agreed to work with the Agency.

When Director Calder's voice came across the line Elizabeth felt the sting of tears. Thank God.

She explained about David and warned that Joe was walking into a trap somewhere in the vicinity of Avenue A here in New Jersey.

The phone cut out.

"What did you say?" She'd missed whatever Director Calder had said.

He repeated, but again the phone started cutting out and she only got a word here and a word there.

She turned to the owner of the house. "Is there something wrong with your phone?"

In the moments it took him to answer, fear surged into her throat. What if she hadn't completely disabled her captor? What if he was out there attempting to tamper with the phone line? Her heart pounded erratically.

"Damn thing won't hardly hold a charge anymore. Just put her back in the cradle for a minute and she'll be fine."

"Director Calder?" she shouted into the mouthpiece of the receiver but the line was dead.

She depressed the talk button again and again. "You're sure that's all it is?"

The old man nodded. "It's the only one I got. Being cordless lets me use it all around the house but lately it won't hold a charge for long. I guess I left it out of the cradle too long today."

Elizabeth stuck the phone back into its cradle and took two deep, calming breaths. She'd made the call. Even though she didn't know what Calder had said, he'd gotten all she needed to tell him. He would ensure help got to where Joe was supposed to meet his contact.

"You need to wash up or something?" the old man asked. He looked at her face and then her hands. "Your throat's all red and swollen. You sure you're okay, lady?"

She shuddered and considered all the diseases she could catch with that horrible man's blood all over her.

"I'd like to wash up," she managed to get past the lump in her throat. Her body shook so hard she could barely stay vertical. She recognized the symptoms. The receding adrenaline. She'd have to be careful about shock. She'd been through an ordeal.

"Down the hall." He gestured to the hall at her left.

She nodded. "Thank you."

Her legs as weak as a toddler taking her first steps, she staggered to the bathroom.

"Sweet Lord." Her reflection was not a pretty sight. Her hair was a mess. Her face had a few smears of blood but her blouse was the worst. And her throat was red and swollen. Her bloody blouse was even torn.

She shuddered again, wondered if the man who'd been holding her captive was laying in that other house dying. She should call 911.

Being quick about it, she thoroughly washed her hands and face. She ran her fingers through her hair and sighed. That was the best she could do. Before leaving the bathroom she said one more urgent prayer for God to watch over Joe.

Please let him be safe.

When she returned to the living room the old man was still in the kitchen.

"Thought I'd make you some tea," he said as she joined him there.

"Thank you." She nodded to the phone. "May I try your phone again?"

He shrugged. "Probably won't do you any good but you can try."

She picked up the phone and punched in the three digits. The operator answered and she explained about being held captive and injuring her captor to escape. She verified the address with the old man fretting over the tea cups and then hung up.

The police and paramedics would be here soon.

"Thank you," Elizabeth said as she took the tea he offered. "I'm Elizabeth Cameron." She sipped her tea and sighed. The heat felt good drenching her raw throat.

"Rosco Fedder." He sweetened his tea, stirring it thoughtfully. "Sounds like you had yourself a fright, Missy."

She nodded. "More than you can know." That was certainly the truth. She darn sure couldn't tell him that the CIA was involved. He probably wouldn't believe her anyway.

By the time she'd finished her tea she felt a little less shaky. She couldn't stop worrying whether or not Joe was all right. Maybe she should call Director Calder again. The sound of sirens intruded into her thoughts and drew her to the front door.

"They're here." Her voice came out small and shaky in spite of her much calmer state.

Rosco joined her at the door. "You think that fellow survived?"

Dread welled in her belly. "I don't know." But she wasn't worried about the awful man who'd been holding her hostage. She worried about Joe. Had the CIA been able to get help to him in time?

"I'm going over there," she told Rosco. "Thank you for your help."

"That's what neighbors do, lady," he let her know. "They help one another. Most any of the folks in this neighborhood would've done the same if they'd been home. I'm the token old man 'round here. 'Bout the only one retired."

She managed a smile for her Good Samaritan and walked out to the street. Exhaustion made her feet feel as if they weighed a ton each. But she didn't stop until she'd reached the front walk where three police cruisers and an ambulance were parked.

A sedan pulled over to the curb drawing her attention beyond the fray of uniformed personnel rushing about.

The driver's side door opened and a man emerged.

Terror exploded in her chest.

David.

Elizabeth started to run back toward Mr. Fedder's

house. Her heart threatened to burst out of her chest but she didn't slow, just kept running.

"Elizabeth!"

She felt her feet stop beneath her, almost causing her to fall forward.

"Elizabeth! It's me, Joe!"

Her whole body quaking like mad, she slowly turned around in time for him to skid to a stop only a couple of feet away.

"Honey, it's me, Joe."

Hope tugged at her. It was Joe's voice. But the face…

Her gaze settled on his and her heart leaped with joy.

The most beautiful blue eyes stared back at her.

"Joe!" She threw herself against him. His big strong arms closed in around her.

"I told you I'd be back," he murmured close to her ear.

And he hadn't let her down.

She drew back and looked into his eyes again. She wanted to tell him the truth…that she loved him despite her best efforts not to.

But would love ever be enough with a dangerous man like Joe Hennessey?

CHAPTER FOURTEEN

ELIZABETH SLIPPED ON her surgical gown then scrubbed up. As she dried her hands and arms she studied her reflection. Her throat was still bruised but she'd get over it.

Incredibly the man who'd done that damage had survived and the Agency hoped to garner much needed information from him. Elizabeth didn't care how useful he could be to the Agency as long as he spent the rest of his life behind bars…far, far away from her.

She'd been stunned to learn that killing off the agents had been a ploy to lure her into a situation, both as a suspect and as an asset to be protected. David had wanted to steal her away in such a manner that an Agency operative, namely Joe Hennessey, would be blamed for her disappearance and ultimate loss. No one would ever be the wiser that David was alive and he would have Elizabeth to use in his new posh escape clinic. She would have been a prisoner, giving sleazy, however wealthy, criminals new faces in exchange for living another day.

How could she have been so completely fooled by David?

"Dr. Cameron."

Elizabeth hauled her attention back to the here and now, and away from those disturbing thoughts. "Yes."

"The patient refuses to be prepped for anesthesia until after he speaks with you."

Elizabeth sighed. "I'll be right there." She'd been through this routine before.

With the same patient as a matter of fact.

She breezed into the O.R. and strode straight up to the operating table.

"What seems to be the problem, Mr. Hennessey?" She glared down at him, resisting the urge to tap her foot.

He looked around the room at the Agency's specialized team who waited to begin. His gaze lit back on Elizabeth's. "I really need to speak with you alone."

Elizabeth rolled her eyes and huffed her exasperation. "Clear the room please."

When the last of the four had moved into the scrub room, Elizabeth, keeping her hands where they wouldn't get contaminated, glared down at her patient.

"I just wanted you to know that I didn't mean to take advantage of you."

She did not want to talk about that night again. In the past three days they'd scarcely seen each other and when they had he'd wanted to apologize for making love to her. How was that for making a girl feel like she was loved? Not once had he mentioned having treaded into that four-letter territory.

So, of course, neither had she.

It was for the best, she supposed. He would go back to his superspy world and she would return to her work.

No harm. No foul.

They were both alive.

That was the most important thing. Right?

Funny thing was, every time she asked herself that question she got no answer.

"That night—"

She held up a sterile hand. "Stop it, please. I don't ever want to talk about that night again." She hoped she managed to keep the truth out of her eyes but she couldn't be sure. The way he scrutinized her face she doubted she hid much from him.

"I guess I can understand how you feel." He heaved out a big breath.

Elizabeth watched his sculpted chest rise and fall with the action. She wanted to touch him so badly that it literally hurt.

But that would be a mistake.

Whatever crazy connection they had shared during those stressful weeks was best forgotten.

"Just give me back my face, Doc." His gaze connected fully with hers and some unreadable emotion reached out to her, made her ache all the more. "I guess that'll have to be enough."

Elizabeth called in the team and within moments they had lapsed into a synchronized rhythm.

As Joe slipped deep into induced sleep she surveyed the face she'd given him. This was the last time she would see David Maddox's face. And she was glad.

She poised, scalpel in hand, over the patient and took a deep breath. "Let's get this done."

ELIZABETH CLOSED THE door of her office and collapsed into her chair. She was completely exhausted. She just couldn't understand what was wrong with her. No one could claim she didn't get enough sleep. She slept like the dead. Eight to ten hours every night! It was incredible.

And food. She ate like a wrestler bulking up to meet his weight requirements.

As she sat there marveling over her strange new zest for sleep and food, realization hit her right between the eyes.

She was late for her period. Only about ten days and that wasn't completely uncommon. Her cycles never had been reliable. She'd considered birth control pills years ago in order to regulate herself but the risks for a woman her age, though she didn't smoke, were just not worth the bother. Condoms had always worked.

But she and Joe hadn't used a condom.

Mortification dragged at her as if the earth's gravity had suddenly cubed itself.

She was thirty-seven years old. A doctor at that. And she could very well be pregnant by *mistake!*

A kind of giddiness abruptly replaced her mortification.

A baby could be…nice.

Anticipation fizzed inside her. Okay, better than nice. A baby could be amazing!

She had to know.

Elizabeth shot to her feet.

She needed a pregnancy test.

Now.

She rushed out of the clinic without a word to anyone. It was her lunch break anyway. She could do what she wanted. Didn't need anyone's permission.

As she settled behind the wheel of her Lexus she considered the attitude she'd just taken.

Maybe she was changing.

What do you know? She might just like this new feeling of liberation. All work and no play had turned into drudgery.

She drove straight to the nearest pharmacy and bought the test. She couldn't bear to wait until she got back to her office, besides she wanted privacy from her colleagues.

Since she was a doctor the pharmacist gladly allowed her to use the employee restroom in the rear of the store.

Her fingers trembling, Elizabeth opened the box and followed the simple instruction. Then she closed the lid on the toilet and sat down to wait.

Joe popped into her thoughts. If she was pregnant, should she tell him?

She chewed her lip. If she did, he would want to be a part of the child's life. Was that a good thing?

Maybe not.

But how could she not tell him?

Elizabeth groaned. More dilemmas.

Anger lit inside her. As soon as the restoration surgery on his face was complete she'd been ushered away from the borrowed clinic. She hadn't even been allowed to stay to see him through recovery.

Director Calder had refused to give her an update on Joe the two times she'd called.

And in the four weeks that had passed she hadn't heard from him once. Joe, not Calder. He hadn't called, hadn't come by. Nothing.

Obviously when he decided to move on he didn't look back.

It was for the best she knew.

But that didn't make it hurt any less.

She'd shed a few tears, cursing herself every time.

Heck, she'd even forced herself to go on a few dates to try and put him out of her mind entirely. But nothing ever worked.

There was just no denying the truth.

She loved him and her heart would not let her forget.

The minute hand on the wall clock moved to the five. It was time.

Holding her breath she picked up the stick and peered at the results.

Positive.

A thrill went through her.

She was pregnant!

Shoving the box and the telltale test stick into the trash, she struggled for calm. Bubbles of excitement kept bobbing to the surface, making her want to alternately laugh and cry. Don't lose it, she warned. Keep it together. She had patients to see this afternoon. She could completely freak out when she got home tonight.

After washing her hands she made her way back to the front of the drugstore, thanked the pharmacist who studied her suspiciously, then hurried to her car.

She didn't drive straight back to the clinic. She was ravenous. Two drive-thrus later and she had what her heart—stomach actually—desired. Two quarter-pounder cheeseburgers, mega fries and an Asian salad with an extra pack of dressing.

The girls in reception gawked at her as she passed through on the way to her office with her armload of bags. She just smiled and kept going. When she'd gotten into her office and closed the door she dumped her load on her desk and relaxed into her chair. After she ate all this she would surely need a nap. She glanced at her schedule. Not going to happen. Oh well, she'd make up for it tonight.

Still a stickler for neatness, she arranged her lunch on the burger wrapper, with the salad bowl anchoring one corner. The first bite made her groan with pleasure. What was it about being pregnant that made food taste so good?

She would have to get a handle on her diet…just not today.

A tap on her door distracted her from her salad. She frowned. If Dr. Newman asked her to go out with him again she was just going to have to tell him that it would be unethical. Their working relationship prevented her from pursing a personal one with him. That should do the trick without hurting his feelings.

"Yes."

The door opened and the next bite never made it to her mouth.

Joe Hennessey, in all his splendor, from that sexy jawline to that perfect nose, waltzed in.

"They told me that you were having lunch." He glanced at the smorgasbord laid out in front of her. "Looks like there might be enough for me to join you."

Elizabeth snatched up the ever present bottle of water on her desk and washed a wad of fries down.

"What do you want, Hennessey?"

He hadn't contacted her in four weeks. The director of the CIA had refused to give her an update on his condition. How dare he show up here now!

The positive results of the pregnancy test flashed in front of her eyes and another wave of giddiness swept over her. She clamped her mouth shut. Couldn't say a word about that until she knew why he was here. And maybe not even then.

He walked up to her desk but didn't sit down. "I should have called you."

That was a start. "Yes, you should have." She nibbled on a fry. She would die before she'd tell him how lonely she'd been. How badly she'd yearned to have him in her bed.

He bracketed his waist with his hands and took a deep breath. "The truth is I didn't want to see you or even talk to you until I was me again."

Stunned, she dropped the fork back into her salad bowl. "I'm not sure I'm following," she said cautiously but she knew what he meant. He wanted her to see him when they talked...*his* face.

He leaned forward, braced his hands on her desk. She inhaled the clean, slightly citrusy scent that was uniquely Joe Hennessey. Her gaze roved his face. Every detail was just as it was before.

Damn she was good.

Elizabeth blinked. Chastised herself for staring. Since he hadn't answered her question he'd obviously paused to take notice of her staring.

She cleared her throat and squared her shoulders. "You're going to have to explain what you mean, Agent Hennessey."

"Don't play games with me, Elizabeth," he warned, those blue eyes glinting with what some might consider intimidation. But she knew him better now. That was his predatory gleam. And she was his prey...he wanted her.

"Really, Hennessey, you should be more specific."

"I love you, Elizabeth. I can't sleep. I can't eat. I miss you. I need to be with you."

I...I...I, was this all about him? Let him sweat for a bit.

She shrugged indifferently. "I've been sleeping fine." She glanced at the food in front of her. "Eating fine as well."

He straightened, threw up his hands. "What do you want me to do? Beg?"

That could work, she mused wickedly.

"No," she told him to his obvious relief.

He eased one hip onto the edge of her desk and popped a French fry into his mouth. "Then tell me what you want, Elizabeth. I'm desperate here."

His work was her first concern. But she would never ask him to give up his career.

"I don't think we could ever work, Joe," she confessed. She looked directly into those gorgeous blue eyes. "You know the reasons."

He downed a swig of her water and grimaced. "What if I told you I'd gone off field duty?"

She froze, her heart almost stopped stone still. "What did you say?" She prayed she hadn't heard wrong.

"I'm taking a position with a new agency, one that compiles intelligence from all the other agencies and prepares reports for the president. I'd tell you more about it but it's top secret." He grinned. "I'm officially a desk jockey. Is that safe enough for you?"

She shook her head. Afraid to believe. "You can't do that for me. You have to do it for you."

He reached for her hand, engulfed it in his long fingers. "I did it for us, Elizabeth." He peered deeply into her eyes. "And just so you know, even if you kick me out, I'm not going back to field work. I'm done with that. So what's it gonna be?"

Elizabeth jumped to her feet and stretched across her desk to put her arms around his neck. "Yes!" She smiled so wide she was sure it looked more like a goofy grin.

His brows drew together in a frown. "Yes what?"

She knew he was teasing by the sparkle of mischief in his eyes. "Yes, I'll marry you, you big dummy."

A grin widened on his sexy mouth. "Well, now." He reached down and nipped her lips. "I guess that means you're going to make an honest man out of me."

"Actually…"

He kissed her and for a few moments all other thought ceased. There was only the taste and heat of his mouth. God she had missed him. Never wanted to be away from him again.

She drew back just far enough to look into his eyes. "Actually," she reiterated, "I thought I'd make this child I'm carrying legally yours. You okay with that?"

It was Joe's turn to be stunned. "A father? I'm going to be a father?"

Elizabeth nodded.

He kissed her with all the emotion churning inside him. He told her how much he loved her over and over until they were both gasping for breath.

He pressed his forehead to hers. "I'm definitely okay with that, Doc," he finally murmured.

Elizabeth pulled away from him. "You'd better get out of here."

Confusion claimed that handsome face. "You're kidding about that part, right?"

She wagged her head side to side. "I have patients to

see. The sooner I get through my schedule, the sooner I'll be home."

He grinned. "And we can have makeup sex."

Now there was that naughty side peeking out. "But we didn't have a fight," she countered.

"We did have a trial separation," he suggested.

He had her there.

"Go." She motioned toward the door. "We'll have all the makeup sex you want. Tonight."

He backed toward the door. She couldn't help watching the way he moved. So sexy. So chock-full of male confidence.

"I'll be waiting at your place. I'll even have dinner waiting."

Before she could question that promise he turned around and strolled out the door.

Her gaze narrowed. He said he'd have it ready, he didn't say he'd cook it.

Elizabeth pressed her hand to her tummy and smiled at the feeling of complete happiness that rushed through her.

Now she could rightfully say that she really did have it all.

And Joe Hennessey had definitely been worth the wait.

* * * * *

YOU HAVE
JUST READ A
HARLEQUIN®
INTRIGUE®
BOOK

If you were **captivated** by the **gripping, page-turning romantic suspense,** be sure to look for all six Harlequin® Intrigue® books every month.

It all began with a kiss. At least that was the way Chloe
Clementine remembered it. A winter kiss, which is nothing like
a summer one. The cold, icy air around you. Puffs of white
breaths intermingling. Warm lips touching, tingling as they
meet for the very first time.

Chloe thought that kiss would be the last thing she
remembered before she died of old age. It was the kiss—and
the cowboy who'd kissed her—that she'd been dreaming about
when her phone rang. Being in Whitehorse had brought it all
back after all these years.

She groaned, wanting to keep sleeping so she could stay
in that cherished memory longer. Her phone rang again. She
swore that if it was one of her sisters calling this early…

"What?" she demanded into the phone without bothering
to see who was calling. She was so sure that it would be her
youngest sister, Annabelle, the morning person.

"Hello?" The voice was male and familiar. For just a
moment she thought she'd conjured up the cowboy from the
kiss. "It's Justin."

Justin? She sat straight up in bed. Thoughts zipped past at
a hundred miles an hour. How had he gotten her cell phone
number? Why was he calling? Was he in Whitehorse?

"Justin," she said, her voice sounding croaky from sleep. She cleared her throat. "I thought it was Annabelle calling. What's up?" She glanced at the clock. *What's up at seven forty-five in the morning?*

"I know it's early but I got your message."

Now she really was confused. "My message?" She had danced with his best friend at the Christmas dance recently, but she hadn't sent Justin a message.

"That you needed to see me? That it was urgent?"

She had no idea what he was talking about. Had her sister Annabelle done this? She couldn't imagine her sister Tessa Jane doing such a thing. But since her sisters had fallen in love they hadn't been themselves.

"I'm sorry, but I didn't send you a message. You're sure it was from me?"

"The person calling just told me that you were in trouble and needed my help. There was loud music in the background as if whoever it was might have called me from a bar."

He didn't think she'd drunk-dialed him, did he? "Sorry, but it wasn't me." She was more sorry than he knew. "And I can't imagine who would have called you on my behalf." Like the devil, she couldn't. It had to be her sister Annabelle.

"Well, I'm glad to hear that you aren't in trouble and urgently need my help," he said, not sounding like that at all.

She closed her eyes, now wishing she'd made something up. What was she thinking? She didn't need to improvise. She was in trouble, though nothing urgent exactly. At least for the moment.

Don't miss
Rugged Defender *by B.J. Daniels,*
available November 2018 wherever
Harlequin® Intrigue books and ebooks are sold.

www.Harlequin.com

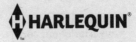

Want to give in to temptation with
steamy tales of irresistible desire?

Check out **Harlequin® Presents®**,
Harlequin® Desire and
Harlequin® Kimani™ Romance books!

New books available every month!

CONNECT WITH US AT:

Facebook.com/groups/HarlequinConnection

Facebook.com/HarlequinBooks

Twitter.com/HarlequinBooks

Instagram.com/HarlequinBooks

Pinterest.com/HarlequinBooks

ReaderService.com

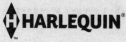

**ROMANCE WHEN
YOU NEED IT**

PGENRE2018

Looking for more satisfying love stories
with community and family at their core?

Check out **Harlequin®** Special Edition
and **Love Inspired®** books!

New books available every month!

CONNECT WITH US AT:

Facebook.com/groups/HarlequinConnection

Facebook.com/HarlequinBooks

Twitter.com/HarlequinBooks

Instagram.com/HarlequinBooks

Pinterest.com/HarlequinBooks

ReaderService.com

HARLEQUIN®

**ROMANCE WHEN
YOU NEED IT**

HFGENRE2018

Love Harlequin romance?

DISCOVER.

Be the first to find out about promotions, news and exclusive content!

Facebook.com/HarlequinBooks

Twitter.com/HarlequinBooks

Instagram.com/HarlequinBooks

Pinterest.com/HarlequinBooks

ReaderService.com

EXPLORE.

Sign up for the Harlequin e-newsletter and download a free book from any series at **TryHarlequin.com.**

CONNECT.

Join our Harlequin community to share your thoughts and connect with other romance readers!
Facebook.com/groups/HarlequinConnection

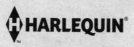

HARLEQUIN®

ROMANCE WHEN YOU NEED IT

HSOCIAL2018

Reward the book lover in you!

Earn points on your purchase of new Harlequin books from participating retailers.

Turn your points into **FREE BOOKS** of your choice!

Join for FREE today at
www.HarlequinMyRewards.com.

Harlequin My Rewards is a free program (no fees) without any commitments or obligations.

MYR18